EXILE BLUES

EXILE BLUES

Douglas Gary Joseph Freeman

Baraka
Books

Montréal

ISBN 978-1-77186-200-4 pbk; 978-1-77186-207-3 epub; 978-1-77186-208-0 pdf

Cover by Maison 1608
Book Design by Folio Infographie
Editing by Elise Moser and Robin Philpot
Proofreading by David Warriner

Legal Deposit, 4th quarter 2019

Bibliothèque et Archives nationales du Québec
Library and Archives Canada

Published by Baraka Books of Montreal
6977, rue Lacroix
Montréal, Québec h4e 2v4
Telephone: 514 808-8504
info@barakabooks.com

Printed and bound in Quebec

Trade Distribution & Returns
Canada and the United States
Independent Publishers Group
1-800-888-4741 (IPG1);
orders@ipgbook.com

We acknowledge the support from the Société de développement des entreprises culturelles (SODEC) and the Government of Quebec tax credit for book publishing administered by SODEC.

Société
de développement
des entreprises
culturelles
Québec

Funded by the Government of Canada
Financé par le gouvernement du Canada

Canadä

"The natural state of mankind is, and I know this is a controversial idea, is freedom. Is freedom. And the proof is the length to which a man, woman or child will go to regain it once taken. He will break loose his chains. He will decimate his enemies. He will try and try and try, against all odds, against all prejudices, to get home."

John Quincy Adams

Montreal, The Plateau, December 1968

"You're beautiful, you know."

She spoke quietly, almost reverently, to the mound of flesh buried under her bedding. His night had been rough and she didn't want to startle him. She wasn't sure if his stirrings meant that he was awake or not. But he was.

He had been peeping out at her and the room for a while waiting for the wooziness to go away. Her white satin bed covers, while shielding him from the chill, magnified the harshness of her stark white room. Light rushed in through her uncovered windows and undulated magically upon the satin surfaces. It made him feel submerged in the Northern Lights. Beyond the windows the outside world came into focus to reveal how it had been utterly transformed during the course of a single night. An enormous snowstorm had buried the city.

It had just begun to snow when he arrived the previous night. He was accustomed to snow falling in big, fluffy, floater flakes that drifted down dream-like from a softly pulsing sky. But the previous night he experienced hostile snow: small, wet pellets of meanness with a mission to blow into every exposed human cavity and prevent normal human functions such as breathing, hearing, and, above all, seeing.

Now his eyes felt sore as he squinted through the brightness. He needed to make sense of things and he needed his vision back. The previous night he squinted through dark billowing smoke in the plane's cabin before tumbling down the emergency chute. A little woman with a thick French accent had yelled at him, "Go, man!" and pushed him out before he was ready. It was the same strangely beautiful little woman who kept staring at him during the flight. He landed not on his feet but on his rump, which forced a large "umph" of air from his lungs. Sirens blared as he found his feet and joined other feet that shuffled, ran, then shuffled some more upon a wet tarmac that threw distorted reflections of colored lights and moving shadows back towards his eyes. A voice through a loudspeaker advised calm. The voices around him were not listening. When he was inside the terminal, he wiped his eyes and could see without squinting. That was when he spotted the tall, goateed, ponytailed guy wearing black combat boots and a green US Army parka, who beckoned to him. The thought materialized that the panic was all smoke but no fire. He had passed Customs without actually passing through Customs.

But that was last night, when he could actually see a city as he was being driven from the airport.

This morning the city lay buried under tons of white that would prevent it from being found for a very long time, he thought. He winced at the thought of his little five-foot, eight-inch self venturing out into that stuff and becoming lost forever. He did not want to die in such a place. The thought of dying and being buried under so much snow that his mother could not find his grave made him shiver.

"Are you alright?" she asked, her voice still quiet, yet now with an edge of concern.

She had seen the bloodstains on his clothes when they brought him to her place. And when they heard the loud thud and rushed into the bathroom to find him collapsed on the floor, sweating with fever, they immediately disrobed him and she had seen the wounds. His back and arms were covered in lacerations and there was a swelling to the back of his head. Their good doctor Freyman said he had the flu and a slight concussion. She left them with instructions; "Watch him for anything resembling convulsions. Don't leave him alone for the next twenty-four hours at least. Get him into a cool bath, but don't let the water get so cold that he shivers. *Bon? À demain.*"

"Yeah, I'm fine." He decided it was time to try sitting up. He stuck his head out from under the bedding. He wasn't fine. There was a sharp pain at the base of his skull. And the rest of his head throbbed. He had all kinds of little stinging pains. His right shoulder was especially sore.

Marianne sat on the radiator wearing a powder blue *khaftan* hoisted high above her freckled crossed legs. Her thick red hair kept the *khaftan*'s hood buoyant. Her hazel eyes studied him through smoke circles she blew after taking long puffs from a cigarette she wiggled between her fingers. She may have been the palest person he had ever seen but she wasn't white. Her room was white. He vowed to himself at that moment to never again use a color to describe a person.

A tiny mound of blown-in snow had formed in the corner of the windowsill behind her. It matched in contour the huge mound in her front yard that was as high as her shoulders. He wondered how could she not be cold sitting on a radiator that surely wasn't working. It emitted no hissing sounds. In Chicago radiators always hissed.

"Aren't you hungry?"

"Yes, I am."

"Will you come out and eat or should I just shove something under there for you?" She thought she heard a muffled giggle that she guessed she wasn't supposed to have heard.

"I'm gonna get up," he said. Realizing he was naked under the sheets, he asked for his clothes.

"Your clothes are still wet. I had to wash them. I couldn't get out to the laundromat to use the dryers because no one can get out this morning until the snowplows come along and clear the streets. But even if we weren't snowed in, I could not have left you alone. Besides, your turtleneck and sweatshirt are too ripped up for you to wear them again. Jamie's coming by to bring you some clothes later on. In the meantime, how do sausage, eggs, porridge, and coffee sound to you?"

"It would all sound very good if I had some clothes to put on," he replied.

"*Mon dieu*, relax," she said, smiling. "You mustn't forget that you were in my tub, so I got to see everything."

He looked at her with what he hoped would be one of his most evil stares ever. She just giggled.

"*Je m'appelle Marianne*," she said. "*Et vous, monsieur, comment vous appelez-vous*?"

They must have told her his name, he thought. Was she testing him?

"Mary Anne," he said. "Mary Anne what?"

He thought he saw a gleam in her eyes. He was mistaken. It was a glint. The kind that signals a sharp blade has been drawn from its sheath.

"Please," she said, "never call me Mary Anne. I am Québécoise. Born here, raised here, and my family can trace our ancestry back to the original French settlers in the 1700s. I've lived all my life in Montreal except for three and a half years at Brown College where those stupid American girls virtually changed my name, anglicized it like they try to do to everything, forever calling me Mary Anne in spite of my constant protestations. In lecture halls, in the dorm, in the cafeteria … as if they were either trying to save me from my Frenchness or stew me in that non-existent melting pot. The disease spread here long ago; Marie-Andrées calling themselves Mary, Robertos calling themselves Robert—or worse, Bob! I am Marianne. It is one word, spelled M-A-R-I-A-N-N-E, with no big accent on the third syllable, *merci beaucoup*. And please, don't punish my name by trying to roll that R."

"Listen, I'm sorry," he said. "I've forgotten a lot of my French. I took it for a couple of years in junior high, and frankly found the whole aura around the language to be quite bourgeois. I wanted to take Spanish, but because I was in the honors class, I had to take French. But I remembered enough to realize that you had told me your name and were asking mine. I'm sorry, okay?"

The French-language bourgeois! Classic American ignorance, she thought, while wondering why she had no urge to fire back with a retort.

"You never answered my question, Marianne," he continued. "What's your last name?"

"Bourgeois."

"What?" he asked incredulously while still squinting through the brightness. "Your last name is Bourgeois?"

❧

Marianne France Bourgeois was born and raised in Montreal. She was raised by a great-aunt, Grande tante Céleste, the youngest of her maternal grandmother's sisters, who had been a nun in the Saint Augustine Convent just outside of Halifax, Nova Scotia. Marianne had been twice orphaned.

Marianne's mother, Céline Bourgeois, was a rebellious, headstrong, intellectual firebrand. She was of an emerging generation of Quebec women who would never again be satisfied with assuming traditional women's places in the staunchly paternalistic and

Catholic society of Quebec, or in the world for that matter. She met Marianne's father, Jack, or Red Jack to his rugby teammates, while both were in post-graduate Anthropology studies at McGill University. They knew immediately that they had so much more in common than red hair and freckles. They fell in love as though it had always been. And they had plans; plans which involved her traveling to France to get at her roots and him traveling to Northern Ireland to get at his. Her becoming pregnant simply made their bond tighter. She delivered their baby girl just as they finished their studies. Céline insisted that she be named Marianne after the feminine icon personifying French liberty that sprang spontaneously from folk culture during the French Revolution of 1789. Not long after they traveled to Northern Ireland, somewhere in those Belfast Hills the Troubles caught up with them and they never returned. Marianne had been left in the care of her grandmother.

Fate was not finished with baby Marianne. Her grandmother and her missionary-pilot husband who were granted custody took little Marianne with them on a fateful trip to bring Christianity to the Shipibo people of the Amazon. A deadly fer-de-lance fell through a hole in the thatched roof of the hut they occupied, and—perhaps as shocked as Marianne's grandmother—landed upon the canopy of the baby cot Marianne was asleep in. Marianne's grandmother swatted at this most venomous of snakes only to have it strike at her so hard that a fang became embedded in one of the bones of her hand. Screaming, and suffering great pain, she ran out and encountered her husband who had heard the commotion and hurried over. When he saw the yellow viper thrashing from his wife's hand, he grabbed at it and had one of his own fingers lacerated. Before the Shipibo could get them upriver to the Missionary Medical Compound they had both succumbed to the venom, leaving little Marianne an orphan again. She was five years old.

A merchant steamer conveyed the bodies and little Marianne back to Canada and took port in Halifax, Nova Scotia. The nuns of the Saint Augustine Convent undertook to see that the two souls received proper ministrations. Sister Céleste Bourgeois resided there. She was Marianne's grandmother's sister and she promptly decided to leave the convent to take custody of and raise Marianne after taking but one look at her grandniece and gasping, "She is the mirror of her mother, a little Céline!"

Marianne blew another circle and looked at him. She snuffed out her cigarette and thought aloud, "that was my last one." She walked over to the closet, took something from a top shelf and gave it to him. "Here. You'll be warm under this furry blanket."

"This feels weird against my skin," he said as he shifted the "furry blanket" about his shoulders. "It looks like a whole bunch of animal skins sewn together."

"In fact," she said, "I bought that beaver-skin bed cover last summer from the Cree up at James Bay."

He sprang to his feet. "Shit! You mean I've got dead animal skins around me? Jeezus!" Without thinking, he dropped that beaver-skin bed cover as fast as he could, exclaiming, "You know, beavers are just big ole water rats! Don't you know that? Jeezus!"

She shrieked out her laughter. He was actually jumping around now, trying to get away from the beaver-skin blanket as if it were alive, which brought Marianne to a near-hysterical laughing fit. He frantically wiped his palms over himself, trying to cleanse himself of whatever "big ole water rat" impurities might still be clinging to his skin. His sudden panic to get away from the skins of big ole dead water rats made him totally oblivious to hunger, the cold, or his nakedness. Marianne bent over laughing.

Preston "Prez" Coleman Downs, now known as Douglas "Doug" Norberg to all but Isabelle, Jamie, and Marianne, had been walking for three blocks from the grocery store.

He lived in a triplex on the west side of De l'Esplanade Avenue in a spacious bright apartment he rented from Marianne "for a third of what the rent really should be," Jamie—Marianne's boyfriend—was fond of reminding one and all. "She wouldn't even rent it to me for twice the legitimate rent even though I begged her on bended knee. She said it was better not to live too close to the person you're involved with. What rubbish!"

"What rubbish!" was Jamie's signature phrase. He came to Canada in 1965 as part of the first wave of American anti-Viet Nam war activists. He professed to be a pacifist and an atheist. He had confided to a not tight-lipped Marianne, however, that his New Jersey family was Jewish and wealthy. He, however, proclaimed himself to be an anti-establishment rebel who shunned materialism. And though he missed his mother and siblings, his father was another story. As early as Jamie's Bar-Mitzvah his father had sought to control his future, going as far as actually trying to arrange his marriage to the daughter of another wealthy Jewish family.

Prez first heard "What rubbish!" that first night he landed in Quebec as he followed Jamie's shadow through the airport chaos. As they approached Jamie's cab parked outside the terminal, two Montreal cops nearly knocked Prez on his face as they rushed to confront Jamie. They argued heatedly in French. Then Jamie exclaimed, "What rubbish!" After arguing back briefly in French, Jamie gave them a card and screamed, "You don't want to make the morning papers, do you?" The cops looked at the card and made no further attempt to stop him. The cops could have mistaken Jamie for a well-known fugitive Quebec nationalist whose organization had been planting bombs in front of the US Embassy. Or maybe they simply took offense at the "Off the Pig" slogan Jamie had painted in a bright white across the front of his Beetle cab's psychedelic trunk lid. But what was certain was that they did not want to tangle with his lawyer, Raymond Bourgeois—"Who is also my girlfriend's uncle," he had screamed at them. Bourgie Ray was the notorious, feared, and celebrated labor, Mafia, and police-union lawyer so corrupt that his contagion was airborne.

Prez wondered if his Jamie flashback was connected to the realization that he was being followed by a black Pontiac. He paused often to shift the grocery bags in his arms as if they were heavy, but they weren't. Even though it stayed almost a whole block behind, it was obvious that the car paused and resumed whenever he did.

When he crossed Villeneuve Avenue, he saw another black Pontiac fuming exhaust vapor parked at the end of the block in front of him. Its roof and windows were cleared of snow on this quiet street where all the other cars sat cold, quiet, and snow covered. The car behind got too close and he was able to see that the car's insignia was Bonneville, not Parisienne, and that it bore New York license plates. As he neared his own building he was shocked to see a crouching figure on the roof aiming a rifle at him.

He dropped his grocery bags and sprinted ahead a few paces before making a sharp turn to his left and toward a laneway. Two bullets kicked up the snow just where he would have been. He emerged onto Saint Urbain Street, where he hailed a cab and asked the driver to take him downtown.

❧

He got out at the intersection of Sainte Catherine Street and Saint Laurent Boulevard and walked in the opposite direction of his destination until the cab was out of sight. Then he went into Le Bijou Bleu, a sleazy blue-movie theater that sat in a fog of smokey blue light. There were rows of ornate wrought iron seating with plush velvet-like Onyx black seats. He marveled anew at the fat round marble columns that led the eye towards the raised stage over which the movie screen was suspended. And then there was that thickly slatted and polished rock-solid wooden flooring that was immune to squeaking. It was troubling that such a majestic place had become a scum collector, he had thought when he was first taken there as part of his emergency contingency plan tour. While the sordid little sex movies played on the screen, guys sat there and masturbated under their coats. Management didn't care as long as the posted warning sign was heeded: DO NOT SOIL THE SEATS.

Prez went to the telephone booth beside the ladies' washroom, a very private area, because no ladies, nor women of any type, came into the Bijou Bleu movie house.

He dialed the number they'd had him memorize, let the phone ring once, and then hung up. He waited five minutes, then dialed again. The phone at the other end was picked up almost before it had a chance to ring.

"*Oui, âllo.* Saint Eustache Home for Girls," said a dusky female voice.

"Oh, I'm sorry," replied Prez, "I thought this was the airport; I'm trying to catch a flight out. Good night."

He hung up the receiver and looked at his watch. He would have to sit in that grimy theater for an hour and a half before "she" would come to pick him up. He went into the men's washroom and opened a little black leather sack that he always carried with him. He shaved his sideburns off and also the little patch of hair he'd let grow under his bottom lip. With pomade and an Afro comb, he packed his hair down as tightly as he could so that it would fit under his camouflage-green army hat.

He suddenly felt very tired and wished that he could just go to sleep. But in that theater, you could watch all the sex movies you wanted, you could masturbate until it fell off; you could even get high. However, if you fell asleep, they'd kick you out.

Prez sat down in the back of the theater hidden from view of the entrance by a big square concrete pillar. He was determined to stay awake. *Keep your eyes open and stay alert*, his mind kept telling him. But he dozed off and was startled awake by a commotion in the front of the theater. Two guys were standing over another administering one hell of a beating. Thud, thud-thud, thud, thud, thud-thud, the licks were raining down on some poor sap. Prez almost thought it funny, noticing how frantically everyone was trying to get away from the beating, until he noticed the glint of flashing steel and realized it was a murder in progress. There was no way anyone could survive such a knife attack.

He scrambled for the side exit and rushed out into the brightness. "You're late!" he heard a voice say. He looked over to the curb to see a dirty-white Saab station wagon with way-too-skinny tires and a long aerial on the roof. Under the dirt and grime, he could tell it was practically a new car. She reached over and swung the door open for him. The car was a mess inside. There were books and papers scattered all over the back seat. He hopped in and looked at his watch; an hour and forty minutes had passed.

"I'm sorry," said Prez. He looked over, and behind the wheel was the little woman from the airplane who had shoved him down the chute. His mouth fell open.

"You know, fella," she said, "I was generous. There's a five-minute leeway on both sides of the appointed time. And you're six-and-a-half minutes late. You would have been on your own. And suspect. None of us would have gone near you again. The network depends on no one making mistakes. And one mistake by a self-appointed, self-righteous 'black nationalist' leader such as yourself could prevent us from helping anyone ever again, and could even send some of us to prison!"

For someone in such a rush to pass judgment, she took her sweet time pulling away from the intersection as the light turned green.

"I'm not a black nationalist," said Prez. "I dozed off. I was exhausted. I got shot at and had to run for my life and you talk as though I just took a stroll in the park."

She double-checked her rear-view mirror.

"You know I'm here totally unarmed and vulnerable," he continued. "I have to depend on you folks for everything, and I'm grateful, but I was almost killed today."

"You folks," he heard her say mockingly under her breath while shaking her head at the pathetic creature beside her. "You're so American ... 'You folks.' Just please, never say 'y'all' when I'm around. I swear I'll shoot you." The smile on her face as she said this was too wicked for him to fathom. "I am Isabelle."

Isabelle had called him "fella," and this was not lost on him. Did she mean "fellah" in the sense that prior to the Algerian Revolution, the Algerian peasants were considered to be passive, submissive, and ignorant victims of colonial oppression who had been conditioned to hate themselves and to do nothing to free themselves from under the yoke of French imperialism? In other words, was she calling him a "nigger"?

Or did she mean "fellah" in the sense of the great mass of Algerians, a lumpen-proletariat, with great revolutionary potential, who when properly ignited and channeled did indeed seize their own destinies and oust the French from their land?

Or, maybe she meant a bit of both.

He was told she wouldn't like him, but was also told not to take it personally. She was a veteran member of the Communist Party of France who believed in the sanctity of the proletarian revolution, reviling nationalism as reactionary, even counter-revolutionary. She apparently reserved her greatest disdain for the FLQ, Pierre Vallières' group. She thought them to be "charlatans" who put bombs in mailboxes instead of focusing their attack on the capitalist class. "They haven't the faintest inkling of what it is to build a popular uprising, much less engineer an authentic revolution in which the dominant relations of production are overthrown and new productive forces arise leading to the qualitative transition from this capitalist epoch to the socialist one."

Isabelle de la Fressange was the most experienced member of the group, with the kind of real experience in clandestine activities one can only get in the cauldron of a revolution. Born in 1939 in Paris, she was a petite woman with a head full of thick disheveled brunette hair that was interwoven with strands of premature silver as if by aesthetic choice. Her prettiness was hidden beneath layers of fierceness. Yet her eyes were a child's, seemingly ever on the verge of a good cry. The effect was exaggerated by her eyelashes, which were so long that everyone wondered how she managed to wear her trademark black-framed sunglasses when she went out on the town to dance, dance, dance. Her finely chiseled features had been permanently bronzed by the North African sun. If no one knew that both her parents were French, no one would guess she was European.

Isabelle's parents, both doctors, had been sympathetic to the Algerians' cause after learning of the abject poverty, social debasement, and torture the Algerians suffered at the hands of the French colonialists. They left their respective practices in Paris and moved to Algiers.

Isabelle was eighteen years old in 1956 when she, against the advice of her parents, joined the French Communist Party in Algiers. The Battle of Algiers had begun and her parents were being secretly investigated.

Her mother had been forewarned of their imminent arrest for aiding and abetting the FLN. They received the warning at, of all places, a cocktail party for the head of the SDECE—the French government's security service. Or, should it be said that it was Madame de la Fressange who received the warning from a young officer in the French Foreign Office with whom she had been intimate all over Algiers. Thus, straight from the party, Monsieur and Madame de la Fressange hopped aboard an oil-bearing vessel headed for Canada with young Isabelle in tow.

She drove like the proverbial bat-out-of-hell once she got out of downtown traffic. Prez marveled at her style, the way she shifted, her timing in overtaking and avoiding traffic, her quick up-shifts and down-shifts. He saw 90 mph on the speedometer with such regularity that it was no longer alarming.

Prez closed his eyes once he had gotten used to the speed and they both were satisfied they were not being followed. A new wave of exhaustion washed over him.

His eyes jerked open with the sickening thought that he was supposed to have been the victim. Washington's not-so-secret war on black America was seeping across the border and he knew the stench when he smelled it.

Montreal, March 1969 – A Friday

Weeks had passed since the attempted shooting of Prez.

That morning the group's electronics whiz kid, after pulling an assortment of devices from an assortment of valet cases, had declared not just Prez's apartment but the entire building clean, no bugs. As a matter of fact, he boasted, there were not even any remote listening posts or devices set up anywhere in a radius of two and a half kilometers. The group's contacts at the phone company and at the courthouse confirmed, no taps had been requested or approved. There had been no snooping around his job. But because there could be no thorough search of the roof until the snow and ice melted, Isabelle's continued hostility toward him fueled skepticism and distrust.

Then Jamie came forward and said that he had been up on the roof and had indeed found something. From his pocket he produced two spent casings. He told the group that they were from a rifle called an AR15 made by a company called Armalite. "The fully automatic version of this weapon, the M16, is the primary infantry weapon of US forces in Viet Nam," Jamie told them.

Marianne was shocked. "Why didn't you tell us this before, Jamie? You knew we were beginning to lose faith in Doug. You should have spoken up sooner."

"Can't speak up if I actually haven't been around too much lately, can I, Marianne?"

Prez was suspicious of Jamie's show of weaponry knowledge and by the fact that the only access to the roof was through *his* apartment.

"*Eh bien*, Doug," said Isabelle as she cast a cutting glance his way. "Time for you to get back to normal." Indeed, he needed to get back to being "Doug." He missed his beloved library job and his community of activists which included French-Canadian nationalists, Canadian Indian activists, and an emerging group of young Afro-Caribbean English-speaking lawyers who were becoming interested in the whole question of Caribbean people's relationship to the African-American Black Power movement. Many of his French-speaking and immigrant friends were community activists opposed to the autocratic style of Montreal's mayor while attaching themselves to the fervency of surging Quebec separatism. He missed those intense "ideological struggles" in Saint Louis Square or on the grass in front of McGill University's Redpath Library. He even missed his coffee breaks with Theresa, his Portuguese co-worker.

～

That evening, after repeatedly pounding on his door to no response, Marianne entered his apartment using her landlady's privilege of having a key.

Two big stereo speakers were pulsing in the corners of his living room. Sitting on the floor between the speakers were two gadgets that both contained glass tubes and a box with a long cord running from it. The glass tubes glowed softly in a haunting way that seemed to orchestrate the moonlight coming in through the windows, the enormous black velvet curtains uncharacteristically left open. The whole room, though bathed in darkness, was not dark.

Suddenly the music didn't seem so loud and incomprehensible as it did when she first heard the throbbing of the bass on her ceiling, the screeching of the horn as she climbed the stairs, and the staccato chords of the piano as she stood outside his door fumbling with her keys after he didn't respond to her knocking. The music created its own light, she concluded. It floated and twisted and made the darkness glow.

She stood mystified; feeling the plucking of the bass strings in her chest, sensing the piano and drums swirling around her head while the saxophone—that tenor saxophone—pulled her somewhere she wasn't prepared to go. That scared her. She needed to remember she had come to scold Prez about the noise.

"Doug, are you here?" she mumbled. Alarmed by the meekness of her own voice, she shouted, "DOUG! YOUR MUSIC'S TOO LOUD!" There was no response so she started walking down the hall following the long cord. Light flickered from his bedroom and she shocked herself by suddenly becoming horrified at the thought of finding him in bed with another woman. She steeled herself and burst right through the love-beads dangling from the top of the door frame.

"Doug! Your ..." He wasn't there. The big brass bed was empty.

The cord went into the bathroom. She followed and there he was standing naked in the tub fiddling with candles on the ledge above. He was oblivious to his surroundings because of headphones.

How suddenly and unexpectedly moments of romantic truth arrive. Nothing can prepare you for it. She couldn't stop looking. She couldn't stop the flushes to her cheeks nor the heat she was feeling in her stomach and below. She couldn't get enough oxygen into her lungs. He was just so beautiful to her.

His tall Afro was glistening and dripping. His skin looked as though he had just been doused by an ocean mist. His lean, hard, and muscular body sparkled.

He sat back down, leaned his head back, and closed his eyes.

She tugged at the cord. At first, he swatted as if a fly was buzzing him. She tugged harder, he looked around.

"What are you doing here, Marianne?"

"Your music is too loud, I think. Or, it was. Now it's perfect. Come and listen with me."

"Is everything okay?"

"Of course." She picked up a towel and went over to him. "Here. Dry yourself. I'll make tea."

He wrapped the towel around his waist and got out of the tub. She just stood there.

"You're making tea, right?"

She placed her palms on his face and placed her lips to his. He put his arms around her, pulled her tight in a deep embrace and surrendered to the kiss. The moist fullness of her lips and the citrusy taste of her mouth bewitched him. Though she was taller than him, it seemed a perfect fit.

He ran his hands all over her luscious back. His fingers traced the circumference of her waist. His palms became full of her buttocks. He looked into her eyes and they were glazed over, moist, and ethereal. He couldn't imagine the kiss ever ending.

"Prez," she whispered, "my clothes are all wet now."

Together, they removed her clothes until she stood, goddess-like, before him. He wanted to look at every inch of her. Marianne was almost five foot ten, and at first glance appeared plump. But she was solidly built and perfectly proportioned, with freckles speckling her body as if comet-dust had sprinkled down upon her one night and, just for her, changed from moonglow yellow to starburst red-orange. Her breasts were full and her nipples orange-red. Prez kissed her shoulders, her neck, and her succulent earlobes. Marianne quivered uncontrollably.

Neither one of them remembered how they got into the bed. They both remembered when he first entered her. She had gasped loudly, "Oh, Prez!" as she tensed and clutched tightly at his arms and back. It was his last moment of mental cohesiveness, because he paused, thinking that he had hurt her.

"*Mon dieu*," she moaned, "*oh, mon dieu.*"

By the time he shouted, "Marianne!" again, they were too spent to do anything but lie in a sweat-drenched, slobbery, mussed heap of intertwined human flesh. They wondered with amazement what the sun was doing coming up.

Neither of them could even manage to phone in sick to their jobs that day. Marianne's office tried to reach her all morning. Prez's supervisor just happened to be Marianne's aunt, the wife of "Bourgie Ray." So, their transgressions against workplace protocol meant nothing to them as they lay cocooned in each other's arms, oblivious to all but sleep. It was late afternoon before they stirred and marveled at the state they were in.

"What was it like for you?" she asked.

"Making love to you?"

"No. Almost being killed, Prez. What was it like?"

Marianne turned her head on the pillow they were sharing so that she could look into his eyes. Forget his body language and his posturing. Forget about the furrow of his brow and the set of his jaw. Forget about his finely crafted monologues on dialectics and praxis; on the failure of the white left, both old and new, to come to grips with the reality of revolutionary black nationalism. Forget about his lecturing on Internationalism. Forget about his cool oft-repeated mantra that one must be ready for jail, exile, or death in the struggle against US fascism. *Mon dieu*, could he talk a lot of *merde*! Forget about it all and look into his eyes.

And she looked as the light went out of them. She saw his eyes cloud over and pain cross his face.

"Marianne, how could you even think about something like that at a time like this? I mean, I was lyin' here just looking at you and feeling all flushed with ..."

"Because," she cut him off, "I love you."

She watched as his eyes lifted and brightened to become two stars blinking with tears he could not keep from cascading down the sides of his face.

And he thought to himself that she was forever making him betray himself.

Marianne kissed at his tears.

He knew he loved her too.

Toward evening as she came in from a walk with her aunt—well, great aunt—and Jamie, Marianne was gleeful as she stooped to pick up the two bunches of lilies of the valley that had been left in front of Tante Céleste's door.

"Oh, I just love the smell of *muguet*," she gushed. "Don't you, Tante Céleste?"

"*Ahh, mais oui*," said Tante Céleste, as she did her very best to keep her eyes from rolling up. Still, she couldn't restrain the sly smile.

"How could he have known?" asked a quite-impressed Marianne.

Tante Céleste so wished that Marianne would say Doug's name instead of referring to him with an omnipresent pronoun. The less obvious it was that they were carrying on the way they were, while Marianne was still supposed to be engaged to Jamie, the better. But perhaps it was only obvious to her, because she was the aunt and she lived downstairs from Marianne. Perhaps Jamie hadn't a clue, or he really couldn't care less. She let slip a giggle at the thought of all the moaning and bed squeaking she had to endure.

"What's so funny, Tante Céleste?" asked Marianne.

"Oh, here it is," said Tante Céleste, digging in her purse. "Sometimes this key is right under my nose and I still don't see it." As she opened her door she asked, "How could who have known, Marianne?"

"Doug, of course."

Tante Céleste giggled again, thinking about the way Jamie had snapped to attention when Marianne said Doug's name. The three of them were returning from a May Day demonstration. The large parade had moved down Sainte Catherine Street like a mass of human lava. There had been a contingent of students who had taken part in the May 1968 demonstrations at the Sorbonne in Paris. Tante Céleste wondered if Prez had managed to converse with them and learn that on May Day in France, bunches of lilies of the valley, or *muguets*, are sold on the streets and given as presents. *Les muguets* represent good luck.

"You mean about the symbolism of *les muguets*?" asked Tante Céleste. As if she didn't know what Marianne was talking about. "He must be having a positive effect on you, dear. I haven't seen you with a cigarette for a while."

After some of Tante Céleste's excellent quiche and café au lait, Jamie left. Marianne was about to depart to her flat with her bunch of *muguets* when Tante Céleste said, "You know Marianne, at the convent orphanage the most beautiful babies were always the mulatto ones." Marianne's steps faltered.

"Oh, what an interesting observation." Marianne felt her face flush and didn't want Tante Céleste to notice. "*Salut*, Tante Céleste," said Marianne as she reached for the doorknob.

"Wait a minute, Marianne. What's the rush? We haven't had a good chat lately."

Marianne let go of the doorknob, dropped her head, and began to sob uncontrollably.

Tante Céleste was greatly alarmed. She didn't even know Marianne had such a cry in her, much less a reason for one.

"Oh my god, child, what's wrong?"

Marianne turned, bent herself way over so that her face was buried in her little Tante Céleste's shoulder, and wept. She wept until she soaked Tante Céleste's blouse. She wept until she had cramps in her stomach that made her clutch at her midsection and double over. She wept until there were no more tears to weep and she just whimpered and gasped for air. And little Tante Céleste feared her bones would collapse under all the sobbing weight. But she held her grandniece up until a voice from somewhere said, "I'm pregnant."

"Oh, my dear, sweet Marianne. Can you ever forgive me? I had no idea. What I said about the orphans ..."

"I know, Tante Céleste. The last thing anyone would think would be that I would get pregnant accidentally. Me, the great control freak." More tears gushed down her face.

Afterward, sitting in Tante Céleste's kitchen, Marianne's eyes were bloodshot from crying and her nostrils inflamed from blowing her nose so much.

"Your baby's father, he will make a good father, no?"

"Dead men don't make good fathers," replied a very weary Marianne. "War resisters like Jamie came here to avoid going to war. Doug was already in a war. He's told me stories. He wants to go back to it. But America will kill him."

Chicago, Summer 1968

"FASTIDIOUS, MOTHERFUCKER! I said FASTIDIOUS. You ever heard that word before, you dumb nigger?" Officer James "Rhodes Scholar" Davies was directing his spittle-laced screaming into the face of a kneeling black boy.

Officer James "Rhodes Scholar" Davies had attained the rank of sergeant on the Chicago police force in a relatively short time. And it wasn't because of his brightness but his malicious self-hate smoldering within. He would just as soon put a bullet in your silly ass for calling him black, or worse, Afro-American. He was a Negro, an American Negro at that, a citizen "of the greatest goddamn country on God's green-assed earth!" And the day you saw him running around with big ole "Zulu" hair sticking up all over his head; the day you saw him wearing loud-colored pseudo-African pajama-like clothes anywhere; the day you heard him refer to some nappy-head, ashy-skinned, lazy-assed, ignorant nigger that he didn't even know from the man-in-the-moon as brother or sister, well that would be the day hell froze over. And it would have frozen over because "Rhodes Scholar" Davis would have gone down there and shot the shit out of the Devil for being so goddamned remiss in leaving all the goddamned niggers running around up here when they should be burning up in Hell. And Rhodes Scholar would have shot the Devil full of holes with his two big-assed, nickel-plated, custom-balanced, Colt 45 caliber semi-automatic pistols.

Civil rights leaders' talk about racist police brutality in Chicago was muted by "Rhodes Scholar" Davis. Police brass and City Hall loved him. He was their equal opportunity show-piece on Chicago's South Side. It was well known, however, that the equal opportunity really at work was that any black male between the ages of puberty and senility was equally at risk of being brutalized, maimed, or even killed by Rhodes Scholar. And he was particularly vicious when there were white cops around.

White police officers would themselves be sometimes ashamed and repulsed at the things Rhodes Scholar did. Once, while wearing his nickel-plated brass knuckles, Rhodes Scholar had hit a kid so hard that one of the kid's eyes came out of its socket and rolled on the dirt. Rhodes Scholar went over to the eye on the ground proclaiming, "Looks like we've got ourselves a little ophthalmologic problem," and pompously stepped on the eyeball, crushing it under foot. Not one of the three white police officers present observed this ghastly incident without vomiting. Yet, none would come forward to corroborate the kid's story when his parents wanted to press charges.

Rhodes Scholar was thus the natural choice to lead the freshly minted Gang Intelligence Unit. He was a tall, muscular, 'high-yel-low' black man with a trimmed mustache, manicured fingernails, and impeccable tastes in all things expensive. His wife was nearly as tall as he, looked more expensive than he, and was certainly as 'high-yellow' as he. They'd been known to brag at parties, "yeah, we're bright, light, almost white!! Ha-Ha-He-He-Ha."

"Let me help you out, a little. I mean you could walk away from this tonight if you just tell us WHAT THE FUCK FASTIDIOUS MEANS!" Rhodes Scholar barked at the youth before him.

The poor kid was sobbing uncontrollably. He was absolutely terrified. And how was he supposed to speak anyway, choking as he was on the gun Rhodes Scholar had shoved in his mouth.

Rhodes Scholar was wearing a pair of fine black leather gloves. "I can pick up a dime with these things, man," he once bragged to his partner.

His nickel-plated forty-fives were harnessed in their custom shoulder holsters. In his hand was a little Czech-made 25-caliber automatic pistol with a rival gang member's name etched on it, the type of which Rhodes Scholar and the GIU kept a nice cache.

"F-A-S-T-I-D-I-O-U-S!! What do you think it means? You think it has something to do with speed, nigger? I mean, all of you black-assed studs think you're so fast, don't you? Motherfucker, I'M TALKING TO YOU!! The word fastidious begins with f-a-s-t. Do you think the word had anything to do with speed?! LOOK AT ME, WHEN I'M TALKING TO YOU!!"

The kid looked up, drenched in tears, mucus flowing from his nostrils, and nodded.

"No, you stupid son-of-a-bitch; the word means being obsessive about cleaning up the garbage off the streets."

BANG, BANG!!

Rhodes Scholar fired a quick two-shot burst into the kid's mouth, jerking his head violently back, causing the top rear portion of his skull to crack open, and leaving him sprawled on his back right in the park that served as a truce gathering and communal party site for the rival gangs. The crimson flow of a young life spilling out would forever stain that hallowed soil. Rhodes Scholar threw the pistol on the ground beside the murdered youth and as the unmarked car screeched away, he yelled, "Killer Knights! Killer Knights thang!"

There was a truce established between K-Knights and King Kobras that had been holding. The truce zones had increased, and the killing had stopped. Oh, sure, there would always be punch-outs. There was even a knifing that resulted in the attacker being expelled from his gang for breaking the truce. But the truce had held and was still holding solid.

But all that was before the King Kobras had found Baby D in the park with the top of his head blown off. And a gun with Prince Earl of the Knight's name on it lying next to the body.

Prez had gone to Prince Earl, who swore he didn't do it.

"Aw, c'mon. Prez!! You KNOW me, man! Me with a little fuckin' 25 cal. A fuckin' pea shooter. AWW MAANNN!! Every livin' ass and swingin' dick know that Prince Earl don't fuck wid no small shit, man. Everybody knows I don't handle nothin' smaller 'n a three fifty-seven Magnum. A fuckin' 25?! With my name on it, even!! What? I'm stupid now, too?! AAWWW!! C'Mon. 'N besides, nigga, I GAVE MY FUCKIN' WORD!!"

Prez believed him. But that wasn't going to bring Baby D back to life.

And matters weren't helped at all when Prince Earl's mother's Buick Electra 225 was hit with a Molotov cocktail. Whenever you want to stir up trouble big time in the ghetto, mess with someone's mother.

~

"Hey, Prez?" It was Prince Earl on the phone. "You know I gave you my word that I wouldn't do no roll-down without tellin' you 'bout it first. Well, homes, they fuckin' wid my Momma. They burned up her car man, 'spose she was in it, man. We rollin', man. AND DON'T TRY TO TALK YO' SHiT EITHER, MAN! 'Cause we packin' heavy and we rollin' hard. They ain't gettin' away wid dat shit, man."

"'They,' who, Prince Earl?" Prez asked, very calm yet very firm. "'THEY,' WHO, Prince Earl?" It was 9:30 on a Friday night.

"Da fuckin' Kobras, man. What?! YOU DAFFY OR SOMETHiN', PREZ?!

"DA FUCKIN' KOBRAS!!" screamed Prince Earl into the telephone.

"You mean just like you shot Baby D?" Prez knew he was playing with fire here because he really didn't know if the Kobras were involved or not, but he had a hunch. And he needed Prince Earl to pause, if only for that proverbial second. "Prince Earl, give me an hour to check it out, man?"

There was the tensest silence on the other end that Prez had ever heard. Finally, a "fuck you, man. Hell no!"

"But, Prince Earl, you know you gettin' played, man. You know it. Give me a half-hour, then. The pig is playin' you, big time!"

It would take Prez maybe twenty minutes to get to Prince Earl's home. If he had no other hand to play, he was certain he could get Sharon, Prince Earl's sister, to get their mother to talk to Prince Earl just long enough so that Prez could assemble his group and start some door-to-door peace-keeping. Sharon would do it, he thought, for old time's sake.

"Prince Earl. Have I been wrong yet?"

"O.K. motherfucker, you got your half-hour. Better make good use of it, Prez. Better make damned good use of it."

"Wait for me to call, Prince Earl. Wait for my call, man. O.K.?" pleaded Prez to the sound of the dial tone.

Seventeen minutes and thirty seconds. That was how long it took for Prez to get to Sharon's. Once he hit the Eisenhower expressway, he never lifted the accelerator from the floor. That was faster than the eighteen minutes flat he had done when Sharon phoned him on that sweet summer's night not that many moons prior to tell him that nobody was going to be home for a while and she thought she was ready for it, but that he should hurry up before she changed her mind.

Prez was replaying that first night he made love to Sharon, when he saw the burned-out rubble of Mama Bell's car. *Jeezus!* he thought as he pulled his car up behind. The air was contaminated with a too-familiar molten-metal stench. He could tell the fire trucks never even showed up. There was not a sign of water having been used anywhere. He thought about how hot it must have gotten around the burning car and how dangerous it must have been for the children in the neighborhood. He wondered if anyone had suffered from smoke inhalation. Then, he thought that if no fire trucks came, then no ambulances came either. And, of course, no cops. That is, good cops who do a good job of looking out for the neighborhood.

Prez went around to the driver's side of the car, which was where the Molotov would have hit, and looked around for bits and pieces of broken glass. He found larger chunks than he anticipated, took one look at them, and rushed right up to Sharon's door and rang. Mrs. Bell came to the door.

"Hello, Mrs. Bell."

"Well, hello Preston. It's been a while, hasn't it? But I should have known you'd be comin' around. You militants seem to go hand-in-hand with burnin' and shootin'. Oh, but I forgot, you're no militant. You're a political party member."

Prez regretted telling Sharon anything about himself. When she began to really get serious about Prez, she began to worry that something would happen to him and pestered him to disassociate himself from the Black People's Party. Little did he know that Sharon's very best friend was her mother, in whom she confided everything. And soon he was getting badgered by Mrs. Bell about going back to college, becoming a lawyer, and fighting the system that way instead of through dangerous militant confrontations. One night, Sharon had given him an ultimatum after seeing a TV news flash blare that two "ex-members" of the BPP were involved in a shoot-out with the police. Two police officers and one ex-BPP member were killed. One ex-BPP member was captured. And the cops were looking for a third assailant.

A third "assailant," thought Prez at the time; assailants are instigators. He knew those boys didn't initiate anything. They were trained not to. Later he learned the three of them had been ambushed due to the work of an informant. They had to return fire in self-defense. "It was the BPP or me!" she had said. So Prez gave her an intense embrace, and then just walked out the door. Sharon didn't even bother to call after him.

"I'd really like to just use your phone, if I may, Mrs. Bell." Prez never asked after Sharon, especially to Mrs. Bell.

"Well, you certainly know where the phone is in this house, don't you, Preston," she replied, still speaking to Prez from behind the screen door and not inviting him in.

"Yes ma'am, I do. Is it alright if I come in and use it?"

"Ain't no lock on that screen door, boy. You know that. You know where the phone is."

Still not inviting him in, and not opening the screen door either, Mrs. Bell turned around and went back down the hall.

Prez rushed straight into the living room to the blue phone beside the blue sofa upon which he had spent many hours with Sharon.

"Prince Earl?!"

"Yeah, man. What you got to say, Prez?"

"Brother-man, you and the Knights gotta cool it. You dig?! You gonna have to ice that roll-down 'cause it wasn't the Kobras, man. Do you trust me, Prince Earl?"

All Prez could hear on the other end was Prince Earl's measured breathing. "You cool wid me Prez," Prince Earl finally said.

"Then dig, brother. It wasn't the Kobras, man. This shit jumpin' off is way deeper than that. I got the proof, man. Do you trust me, Prince Earl?!"

"I said, YOU COOL, dude!"

"I'm asking you if you trust me. You gotta say yes, or you gotta say no. Which is it, brother-man?"

"Yeah, Prez. I trust you. The K-Knights, we all trust you, man."

"Then I'm gonna ask you to do something, my brother. And you have to do it my way, O.K.?"

"O.K., Prez, your way."

"I'm at your Mama's right now, and—"

"You where, you silly-assed nigga?"

"At your Mama's, man. I'm just using the phone, that's all."

"Does Sharon know you're there, stupid?"

"Listen, Prince Earl, I came over to check the damage to Mama Bell's ride. I came over here as fast as I could 'cause I suspected this whole thing stank, and I was right. I haven't seen Sharon and wouldn't want her to see me. I just have to make one other phone call, then I'm leaving."

"Who else you got to call, Prez?"

"Big Diesel," said Prez, and waited for the inevitable.

"Goddammit, Prez. You know I don't want that nigga nowhere near my Mama's crib. That's all part of the truce. He stay away from the crib and he stay away from Sharon. What the fuck's wrong wid you, Prez? I'm still thinkin' about bustin' caps in that big nigga's ass 'cause 'o my Mama's ride and now you want us all to PARLAY! FOR FUCKIN' WHAT, MAN?!"

"You both need to see what I found and hear me out," began Prez. "If you don't want to get played, you're going to have to bury your animosity towards each other. You already said you trusted me. You already agreed to do it my way. Are you going to go back on your word now, Prince Earl?"

After a long sigh, Prince Earl said, "I guess you want Truce Rules?"

"That's right." said Prez.

"Well, you either a genius … or a fuckin' fool, Prez."

Truce Rules meant that the two warring parties' representatives would show up for the meeting alone and unarmed. And when they reached the white flag zone, so designated by Prez, they all must strip down to their underwear to show that neither weapons nor wires were present. Thus, only three people would actually be there talking: Prez and the two gang leaders, Prince Earl and Big D.

The legacy of slavery is manifold in the black community. The destruction of African ethno-cultural lineages amongst Afro-Americans has resulted in some strange manifestations. One such being black folks walking around with names like Herman Wilfred Dieseling the Third.

Objections to and protestations against such a state of affairs have taken on many forms. Some subtle, some not so much. As when eleven-year-old Herman Wilfred Dieseling III up-ended the desk of his sixth-grade teacher, who had the lack of wisdom to snicker as he performed the first roll call of the new school year and said, "My god, boy. Where'd you get a name like Dieseling?"

The eleven-year-old toffee-complexioned boy in question already stood six feet tall and weighed two hundred and twenty-five pounds. He hated his name, but he hated people who made fun of him or his name even more. So, it was with grievous error that Herman Wilfred Dieseling III was suspended from school for a week for assaulting a white teacher. He would have overturned the desk of any complexioned teacher under those circumstances.

Now Big Diesel was six foot three, three hundred and twenty-five pounds. Oh, he was big and round and jolly-looking. But there was not a soft patch of flesh anywhere on his body. And things could be the farthest from jolly if Big Diesel was not happy. Once his anger propelled him, it was like a big ole diesel locomotive had rolled through, flattening everything in its path. The only thing that could stop Big D cold was his mother. She wasn't even five feet tall. And she called him Hermie!

The same with Prince Earl's mother; she could stop him cold; which is why he rarely went around to his mama's anymore. He didn't like his tough-guy image being blown.

Prince Earl was truly tough; his dark-chocolate body had the scar tissue over stab wounds and bullet holes to prove it. He was a lean six-footer with finely chiseled features, a genuinely handsome man who was a supreme athlete. He would show off on the basketball court by standing under the rim and with a tremendous vertical leap, propel the tip of his head straight through the underside of the hoop.

With Prince Earl, one could appeal to his sense of honor. With Big D—and it wasn't that he didn't have a sense of honor— one must appeal to his sense of logic.

Prez rolled an empty keg over into the middle of the shed to use as a table. They found milk crates to sit on, but there were only two. It worked out well, because with Prez standing, he could tower over them for a change. And tonight, he needed every little psychological advantage he could muster.

So Prez stood in the shed behind Mama Bell's house still feeling dwarfed by these two big dudes and wondering where Chi-Chi and Goon had set up their lookout posts. They were the other two members of Prez's unit and he knew they would have already been there and in place at least by the time the three of them went into the shed.

From his pocket he pulled a folded-up paper bag, from which he dumped onto the upturned keg chunks and bits of charred broken glass. With his right hand he made a "voila" gesture.

"What do you see?" asked Prez.

Both Prince Earl and Big D, with heads leaning forward almost touching, stared down at the broken glass. Then, with incredulous looks on their faces that questioned whether or not Prez had lost it, they looked at each other. Prez knew he had to start talking fast.

"What do the guys like to drink?" Prez asked. "Now I know neither of you drink, but I'm talkin' about the blood on the street, in the hood. Think about it."

"Mostly, they drink rot-gut, Prez. You know that, man. Cheap wine," said Big D.

"What about champagne ... or vodka?"

"Nigga, what?!" interjected Prince Earl. "Where a mother-fucker gonna even find that kinda shit around here, man? You gotta go downtown. That shit's too damned expensive anyway. But you know all that shit, Prez."

Then Prince Earl's mood quieted. And he looked at Big Diesel. Then they both looked down at the glass again just as Prez was turning over a few of the larger chunks.

On one large chunk they could the letters S, M, and maybe part of an I. On another chunk, they could clearly see the letters F, F. Another piece had what appeared to be a V but was really a broken N. Then there was an O. Big D said "Smirnoff."

"A vodka bottle," said Prince Earl. "Who the fuck even drinks that nasty shit around here?"

"That shit's from Russia, anyway, homes," said Big D.

Whoever threw that Molotov cocktail, had a taste for Russian vodka, and could afford it. Big D got up from his double milk-crate seat and went to look out the window of the shed.

"So, you Knights didn't shoot Baby D, did you?"

"No, man," said Prince Earl. "I already told Prez. I gave my word about the truce. And you might not like me Big D, but you know I always honor my word."

"What's going down, Prez?" asked Big D, still looking out the window, but at nothing in particular.

"It's the GIU," said Prez. "They trying to get you brothers to start killing each other all over again. So, they kill Baby D, and plant a pipe at the scene with Prince Earl's name scratched on it. Then, they torch Mama Bell's car to make Prince Earl think that the King Kobras are comin' after his Mama. Then, the next thing that's suppose to happen is the Knights and the Kobras kill each other off; and the Pig would have been laughin'. Laughin' like they've been laughin' at us since slavery. Laughin' all the way to fuckin' eternity, my brothers, at dumb blacks, not smart enough to unite and fight the power."

Then Big Diesel turned from the window and walked over to where Prince Earl was sitting. Prince Earl got up and they grasped each other's hands in a Black Power hand-shake before each gave the other the salute of their respective gang; finishing it all off with each giving the peace sign.

"You a fuckin' genius, Prez," said Prince Earl.

"No, he ain't," said Big Diesel. "He just reads a lot."

6

Montreal, Summer Solstice, 1969 – Pre-dawn

"Why is she here?"

"Who?"

"Oh Prez, don't you dare."

"Shh, Marianne," he said, holding his forefinger up to his lips while easing the door shut behind him. "What's wrong with you? Hey, that's my old robe. I was looking for that."

"What's wrong? Oh, there's nothing wrong. You're perhaps just being yourself." In her best rendition of a Southern drawl— "find 'em and fuck 'em. Is that it, Doug?"

"Goddammit, Marianne! You're the one who broke it off. You needed your goddamned *espace*. You wanted your goddamned *ouverture* so you could keep it up with Jamie and have a pseudo-philosophical justification for it."

"Such large ideas so early in the morning, and I haven't even had my coffee."

"Well, why did you come here knocking on my door before coffee? You never do anything before coffee. Especially at five-thirty in the morning."

"Oil your fucking bed springs, you stupid jerk!"

"Marianne! You never talk like that."

"Prez, are you coming back to bed?" Tala opened the door and stood with just a towel wrapped around her.

"Prez? You know him as Prez?" asked a shocked Marianne.

"Of course, strange question," answered Tala. "His mother calls him Preston Jr. His uncles still call him Little Preston. I've called him a few things I won't mention here now, but to the world that knows him and loves him he's Prez." Tala gave her big sunshine smile. She walked over and offered her hand. "Hi! I'm Tala from his home town."

Marianne bristled, then glared. She gave Tala's hand a hard once-up and once-down shake. At that moment Tala realized there was something between Prez and Marianne which made her bristle and glare back.

Prez intervened. "Tala, meet Marianne. She lives downstairs. How about coming in for coffee, Marianne? Is that OK with you, Tala?"

He held the door as each deliberately rammed his chest with their shoulder as they walked in.

"I'll serve in the living room," he said. "Make yourselves comfortable." They ignored him and began talking.

"I saw you getting out of the cab last night," Marianne said to Tala. "I was quite surprised to see *Prez* coming in with you, because he never brings anyone home."

Oh really, thought Prez. *What about that* find 'em and fuck 'em *bit you threw at me? And, you spy on me? Aha!*

"Why didn't you come out and say hello, then?"

Oh yeah, thought Prez, *and then give me a boatload of shit afterward.*

"It was just a coincidence that I happened to be looking out the window. I had company over."

Coincidence my ass, thought Prez. Company? *That would have been punk-assed Jamie. You and your goddamned ouverture, which seemingly ... obviously ... only* you *are allowed to practice.*

They were talking like old school chums when he returned with the coffee.

"When I first saw him," said Marianne, "he looked like he had been through a little war. He was injured, bleeding. He passed out."

"He had been. He's not supposed to be alive, the way they came at him. He's never told you about any of that?"

Prez heard a car door slam. He went to his window and looked down.

"You have company," Prez announced to Marianne. "Don't rush out wearing my robe. Jamie will think the wrong thing."

Tala's eyes squinted, one eyebrow raised and her lips pursed.

"Oh, *mon dieu*, who cares? Give me that towel, Tala. Here." She tossed the robe to Tala. "And, don't forget, dinner at my place. Don't be late."

Tala looked at Prez. "It's not what you're thinking," said Prez.

"Cut the bullshit, Prez," said Marianne as she closed the door behind her.

This was not the 1969 summer solstice morning Prez had envisioned when he learned Tala was coming to visit. She would only stay until Sunday morning so there was a lot to try to cram into one day. He had wanted the whole time with her alone. There was just so much to sort out. But his Saturday morning was still quite young, so young that the sky was still lighting itself. There was so much about the city he had fallen in love with and he wanted to share as much as he could with Tala.

It seemed as if their relationship—the one she had always said they didn't have—had been so complicated right from the time she kicked him in Lincoln Park all those years ago. She thought then that he was just a kid who thought he was a man because he could beat up grown men. He believed love to be

45

boundless fusion of two souls. But they would always be out of synch, he thought.

So she caught him off guard again when she arrived, put her little bag on the floor, kissed him deeply, and said she'd missed him. He didn't understand. *Tala*, he thought, *is this really you?* She had promptly undressed and walked into the bathroom while he was peeing and started to draw bathwater. He was shocked. Then she insisted he get in the tub with her. She lay back against him and took his arms and wrapped them around her. They sat in the hot water until it became tepid and she was so still and quiet that he knew she had fallen asleep. He gently woke her and told her it was time for bed. She got out drowsily and Prez toweled her dry. He wrapped a giant cuddly towel around her and led her to his bed. He pulled the covers back and asked if she had brought any nightclothes. No, she slept nude. Prez could feel his heart thump-thumping in his chest. He could feel himself becoming aroused.

"Okay then, hop into bed and sleep peacefully. I'll be in the living room. Good night, Tala."

She got into bed and as soon as her head touched the pillow her eyes were shut. He tucked the bedding up around her and turned to go. Just as he was about to turn out the light she whispered his name. He looked around and she held out her arm motioning for him to come to her.

"Turn out the light," she whispered.

She lifted the bedding and he slid in beside her. She turned over on her side and tried to pull him close. But he was too aroused, embarrassed about it, confused, knew not what was happening. He wasn't about to get close to her down there.

"Come on," she said, "put your arm around me."

He resisted and she tugged harder.

"C'mon, Prez."

"I can't, Tala."

"What—put your arm around me?"

"No, get too close."

"C'mon Prez. Cuddle up to me. We'll make everything cozy so we can get a good night's sleep together."

She reached down and took his hardness and snuggled it in between her butt cheeks, squeezed his arm around her, and fell asleep. Prez lay there throbbing and thinking that if he did not go crazy within the next few minutes it would be a miracle.

The next thing he knew he was being awakened by Tala nibbling on his earlobe. "Please, Tala, what is going on?"

"Make love to me."

"Are you sure?"

"Oh yeah," she giggled.

He rolled over on top of her and the touch of her body against his, the smell of her, the taste of her mouth and tongue were enough to make him wonder about the existence of God and heaven—two things he did not believe in.

"Don't come in me, okay? Please."

"Alright."

Soon she dug her knees into his side, buried her face into his neck and let out such a deep, guttural, growling moan that all he could do was hold on and not let her go.

Her body then relaxed and she seemed to melt into the sheets.

"Thank you," she whispered. For what, he wanted to know? "For keeping your promise."

7

Montreal, Summer Solstice, 1969 – Sunrise

It was becoming a perfect morning.

"Hurry! Get dressed. We have to catch the sunrise."

"Where?"

"At the lookout."

Prez grabbed a bunch of keys and took Tala out the back door.

"Are you trying to keep Marianne from spying on you?"

"No. My car is out in the back," scowled Prez.

"You have a car?"

"Well, sort of. It was sort of given to me. Anyway, I'm now its exclusive driver."

"That's a lot of sort-ofs." She stopped and stared. "What … is that?"

"A 1965 Citroën 2CV roll-back top. It's my getaway car! Get in! We have to get to the lookout before the sun comes up!"

He closed the passenger-side door after Tala. She was well into the rhythm of her own sweet protestations: "I'm not riding in this thing. It's yellow! It's the ugliest car I've ever seen!"

Prez hopped in.

Tala was looking all over the little car as they started rolling along. "Hey, it rides kind of smooth," she said. Prez rotated a little knob that Tala hadn't even noticed and a radio came to life. Prez rotated another knob and as the little yellow Citroën made its way down the alley and onto the street the voices of Robert

Charlebois and Diane Dufresne trailed along. As they sat at the stoplight on the corner of Mount Royal and Park Avenue, Prez pointed up and to his left. "It's up there—the lookout. We're right in the heart of the city, don't forget!"

As they drove up the zig-zag road Tala exclaimed, "Wow. It feels like we're in the country."

"That's exactly how I felt when I first came up here. It's an entirely different world up here."

Tala leaned her head back and closed her eyes. "I love the smell of the air."

They passed a couple of people jogging up and a group of bicyclists flying down in tuck positions. After a series of curves they passed through a stretch of road nestled in what looked like a miniature mountain pass.

Prez slowed a little and said, "I read that this used to be part of a volcano. Those rocks are millions of years old."

He stopped, turned the car around, and headed back down, pulling off the road into a parking area to the right. Prez stood on his seat and grabbed Tala's elbow to help her stand on her seat. They put their heads up through the little Citroën's roof-top opening and leaned on the roof of the car.

"It's beautiful up here," said Tala.

They could see so much of the city. It stretched before them like a storybook rendering.

"It's my special place, my open-air haven, my place of solace. I come here in daylight and the night-time. I've been up here in all four of the seasons. Look over there towards that bridge. That's the Jacques-Cartier Bridge. The sun will come up over there."

Sure enough, the sky began projecting its most radiant hues of mauve and magenta with wisps of yellows mixed in. The bridge stood with its feet awash in the sparkling waters. Vehicles with far less presence than ants could be seen moving across the bridge's surface.

Prez got down and came around to open the passenger-side door. He took Tala by the hand and pulled her over toward the railing. He pointed down the mountainside; there were cars just visible through breaks in the thick foliage. "That's Park Avenue." He looked at Tala's face and her eyes were still fixed upon the bridge. He could see the lights of the sky shimmering on her skin, which slowly began to brighten. He turned and there it was—the sun was just emerging from its slumber. Slowly but surely it rose behind the mountains that could be seen far off behind the bridge. It rose with an indescribable, breathtaking majesty that provided the first and last words on the powerful beauty of nature, the relative insignificance of people, and the ephemeral nature of existence. He moved behind Tala and, with both his arms around her, gave her a squeeze.

"This is so beautiful," she said. "You know, I've never seen a sunrise before."

How strange, thought Prez, *he had never been atop the royal mountain at sunrise with anyone.*

Prez pointed to his left and let his finger trail upwards. "That's Mount Royal Avenue, where we started from. It runs towards the East End. The river over there, that's the Saint Lawrence. It's a major shipping route. I've worked down at the docks loading and unloading ships."

"Really? You did that kind of stuff?"

"It's beautiful down there too, the Old Port, Old Montreal. Old Montreal has cobblestone streets like Georgetown." He pointed towards the right, about where the sun was coming up. "That's downtown Montreal."

"Okay, we crossed Park Avenue, it's just down there, right?" asked Tala.

"Yep."

"Which way does it run?"

"Huh?"

"You said Mount Royal runs east-west. Park Avenue must run north-south."

"Yep."

"Oh? The sun rises in the south up here?"

"Huh? Tala!" He started laughing. "You are too smart for your own good!" Prez had never thought about that.

"Well, what's so funny?" She became annoyed and tried to twist out of his embrace.

He squeezed her tighter and wouldn't let her go. He sucked on her neck.

"You stop it! Either let me go or answer the question."

"I think they might have messed up a little bit."

"Who?"

"The people who laid out the city. I think you're right. The sun rises in the east. The streets are maybe a little bit twisted, but you have to admit that takes nothing away from the beauty, does it? You are really something, Tala! What a firecracker. You can get ticked off at me so quickly. How come?"

"I'm not quite sure …"

"Beautiful up here, though, isn't it?"

"It surely is the most beautiful city I have ever seen and I haven't really seen any of it yet from the ground."

"There's more up here to see. C'mon."

He grabbed her hand and ran up some stone steps. They were getting higher and deeper into the forest. They walked through the trees, observing the morning light penetrating through the shadows. The light fell to the ground in strips and at one point they spent minutes hopping and skipping to a just-made-up game, "don't touch the light."

Soon they were at a clearing and they walked down a dirt path for a bit before Prez stopped and pointed down to a man-made lake and chalet on the shore.

"That's Beaver Lake."

Sunlight had not yet breached the wall of trees, so an intriguing luminance imbued a thin layer of mist that floated upon the surface of the water and whiffed around the stone façade of the chalet. As they walked down the hill toward it through wet grass the air smelled musty-sweet. At the lower level of the chalet they found an unlocked door. A sign pointed toward washrooms.

"Hallelujah!" exclaimed Tala. They both laughed as she ran off.

❧

Back in the car, the moments of silence between them were becoming tense. They hadn't had the real conversation.

"You came to see me to give me some news, huh? How's your father, by the way?"

"Oh, you know my father, you can never really tell. He would probably make the best poker player if he was a gambler."

"Yeah, like back in the Old West, sitting across from gunslingers in ten-gallon hats.

"I also wanted to see you. Not just bring you news."

"Like a little vacation. I can dig it. This is a wonderful city for that."

"You're ignoring what I said. I wanted to see *you*."

"You must be starving."

"Oh, yes."

"I know just the place in Old Montreal." He drove down the mountain and turned right on Park Avenue. "You see the park area on your right? One of the men who helped design Central Park in New York City helped lay this out."

"Really?"

"Yeah."

The cobblestone streets of Old Montreal seemed too narrow for regular-sized cars but the little yellow Citroën was right at home. Prez parked and came around to escort Tala onto the cobblestones.

Rose-tinted light hovered in the sky above drab-looking gray stone buildings as they walked by not-yet-opened storefronts with leaded glass and heavily lacquered wooden doorsills.

At Place Jacques-Cartier, near the intersection with Saint Paul Street, Prez found a restaurant open for breakfast. They walked in and were engulfed by dimness. The wide, dark-stained wooden floor planks creaked rhythmically. The walls were exposed stone overlaid with intricate wooden latticework. The ceiling was vaulted and trimmed in oak molding. The burgundy curtains were thick, and had been pulled back to allow a clear view. The heavy-legged wooden tables seemed almost too massive for an intimate breakfast. But they found some cozy little round tables beside a window.

"*Ahhh … Bonjour, monsieur! Bonjour, madame! Pour deux*?"

Both Tala and Prez jumped. Where did he come from?

Prez laughed. "*Oui monsieur, bonjour, pour deux, s'il vous plaît.*"

As they were led to a table Tala turned and gave Prez the most quizzical look he had ever seen from her. "You speak French?"

"No, no."

After they were seated, "Well, what was that I heard back there?"

"I just know a few French words. Believe me. That's all. I try. It breaks the ice if you at least try. Now for the really funny part, me pretending to read the menu and order in French. But have no fear, because I already know what we're having."

They talked up a storm while waiting for the fellow to return with the menus. "Hi, Dougie!" a cheery female voice interrupted. "That will be two orders of *crêpes suzette*, a tall glass of milk for the gentleman, and what will the lady have—"

Prez looked up. "Theresa! What are you doing here? It's so good to see you. How are things in your new job? Oh, Tala, this is my only black friend in Montreal. Meet Theresa. Theresa, this is my dear friend from back home, Tala."

"Preta! That's me. Hi Tala."

Tala blinked and looked again. *That's a white girl*, she thought. But Tala couldn't pin down ethnicity. Theresa was quite dark-complexioned, but that could just have been due to taking a lot of sun. She could have been Chicana, Puerto Rican, Brazilian. Tala couldn't tell. But she knew Theresa wasn't black. "So nice to meet a colleague of Doug's."

The ladies shook hands.

"Don't tell me you're working here on weekends," said Prez. "Of all places—I mean the coincidence."

"Yep. Gotta work my tail off this summer to make sure we have enough for a house down payment. Getting married next year, you know."

"Now, Theresa, you know it worries me to hear you talking about working your sweet tush off. It is still sweet, isn't it?"

"Oh yeah," she said as she turned around and wiggled it.

They both laughed out loud.

"And yours, is it still sweet?"

"Most definitely," he said as he got up, turned around, and shook his.

They laughed out loud again.

"And your fiancé, is he working his off too this summer? Let me take that back. We don't want him losing any of that already too-skinny ass. He already looks like a zipper when he turns sideways and sticks out his tongue."

They laughed really loudly.

"You leave my honey alone, Dougie. It's so nice to meet you, Tala. I'll be right back with your first glass of milk. And you're both having crepes, I know. "

"Dougie?" Tala teased. "It's a bit weird to hear you talking like that with her. Like you two are great buddies or something."

"You know, I think we are. We talk to each other about anything and everything. She was really the first person, sometimes the only person, who I could just talk to and be myself with here. She would listen to what I had to say at union meetings and stick up for me. She tells me everything … sometimes way too much." He laughed a bit nervously. "We talk all the time, or rather we used to, before she transferred to a new department. Now we meet for lunch or a break from time to time. She cracks me up with her sick Portuguese sense of humor."

"What's Preta?"

"It's what her father calls her. It means 'blackie' in Portuguese. She gets very dark in the summer."

"Does she know about you?"

"You heard her call me 'Dougie'."

Well that doesn't answer my question, Tala thought.

After breakfast, Prez drove east.

"That's the Jacques-Cartier Bridge again in the distance."

As they drove across Tala said she could see for miles. There were big ships on the water and she thought about Prez loading and unloading them. She wondered how hard that type of work was. She wondered about the loneliness.

Prez tapped his fingers atop the steering wheel to Pauline Julien on the radio.

He pointed towards a Ferris wheel below. "That's La Ronde amusement park. Bring back any memories?"

They had participated in sit-ins to desegregate Glen Echo Amusement Park back in Washington and had bitter memories of that struggle.

After crossing the bridge Prez swung onto a street called De Lorimier Avenue. After a few blocks he pulled over and parked. He came around, opened the door for Tala and took her by the hand. They walked up towards the corner and there Prez stopped and looked over a big ragged field strewn with bricks, bottles, and beer cans.

"You won't believe this, but there used to be a famous baseball stadium here. It's where Jackie Robinson broke the color barrier in white baseball."

Tala's was astonished. She looked at the site. She looked around at the neighborhood.

"It's nothing like I pictured it. I'm shocked."

"You are also, I think, insulted."

"That's a good word for what I'm feeling right now. This doesn't look like a place where history was made."

"What neighborhood does, before or after the fact?"

"But this looks so barren and desolate. It's an eyesore. Playing for the Montreal Royals must have seemed like an exile."

"Well, this is the spot where it all happened. The stadium was called the Delorimier. And Tala, he was born in exile—just like we were."

He drove westward. "Remember all those church steeples we could see from the mountain?" He stopped at the corner of Rachel Street and Henri-Julien Avenue. "That is the Saint-Jean-Baptiste Church. It's the third largest church in Montreal. Who would guess this neighborhood could host such grand historical structures when the row houses are so tiny? And, up the street on the corner, a *dépanneur*—a corner store with a twist: they sell booze. It's like back home."

"You're losing me. How is this similar to back home?"

"Dépanneurs sell booze. Churches sell an equivalent. Back home you see neighborhood landscapes dominated by churches and liquor stores. But in both places, you only see that dominating juxtaposition in poor or working-class neighborhoods. So, what's the ultimate purpose? These are some similarities that help me understand a book I'm reading."

"What book?"

"*White Niggers of America*. Basically, it says that the French Canadians live under a sort of neo-colonial domination perpetrated by the Anglo financial and political classes. Quebeckers have been systematically held back by legalized and institutionalized prejudice which has relegated them to the lowest rungs of society. Moreover, and this plays to the book's title, they have been treated as less than human by the white Anglo power structure."

"Really? Is that true?"

"It appears to be. But the fellow who wrote the book, Pierre Vallières, is a member of an organization called the *Front de libération du Québec*—or FLQ. They believe in planting bombs and urban guerrilla warfare to achieve French-Canadian freedom. So that's where I have strong disagreement. Their violence is a turnoff. And another thing, the name of the church, Saint-Jean-Baptiste ..."

"That's Saint John the Baptist," Tala said.

"Yeah. Well, Saint-Jean-Baptiste Day is a big holiday here; it's in a couple of days, actually. I read that some countries in Europe celebrate Saint-Jean-Baptiste Day, but it's a religious or cultural festival for them. Here, it's very political. Saint John the Baptist is Quebec's patron saint, according to the Catholic Church. Quebeckers have succeeded in transforming religious symbolism into a political tool.

"Things here are complicated, just like back home. The same big question lurks in the shadows: is it about class or is it about race and ethnicity? And do you work from outside or from inside the system for change? For us the idea of a black president of the United States is so remote, so outlandish that it's beyond being funny—it's just too absurd. But what if there was a black president? Tala, I'm asking you: what if there was a black president? Do you think that's what it would take for things to go in a positive direction for Afro-Americans?"

"That's just such a strange question. It'll never happen, so why bother trying to answer it?"

"Well, as of June last year the prime minister of Canada is a French Canadian."

"Really?"

"Yep. And guess what? At last year's Saint-Jean-Baptiste celebration there was a big riot and some French-Canadian nationalists threw beer bottles at him. You would think they would be happy to have a prime minister who was one of them. But no, instead they had a big riot. The debate that should have been a reasoned and respectable one became unreasonable, disrespectful, and violent—and nothing positive was achieved. People just got angrier."

"What debate?"

"Whether Quebec should be an independent country or whether it should be a part of Canada."

❧

They walked down Saint Laurent Boulevard.

At Prince Arthur Street they turned left and walked toward Saint Louis Square.

"I think this is my second favorite place in Montreal. Let's go sit by the fountain. The way the park sits surrounded by classic architecture reminds me of Lincoln Park."

"Really?" said Tala as she looked around. "It's way smaller."

"Yeah, but the houses ..."

Then someone called out.

"Doug! Hey, Doug! Over here!"

A bunch of Prez's work colleagues were in the park sitting on a patch of grass.

"So, who's the chick, Doug? Is she why none of us can get you into bed?" said the attractive big-boned, dark-haired girl.

"Oh, I thought Marianne was the problem," said the barely-five-foot-tall girl whose attitude clearly punched way above her weight.

A tall, handsome Italian fellow who was Prez's best friend at work stood to introduce himself and the others. "I am Roberto and I am so pleased to meet you. The big broad with the big mouth is Lora. The little one with the big mouth is Marie-Claire. We have another Marie here, Marie-Josée. My lady Toffee. And now the gentlemen ... oh, I guess I'll sit back down." Everybody laughed.

Prez took over. "This is Alain and over there is Max." Prez held his hands to mimic a megaphone, "short for Maximilian!"

There was a round of handshakes as Prez said, "And this is my dear friend Tala from back home."

A joint got passed around while various conversations continued. A big beach ball bounced over followed by a little girl in hot pursuit who tripped over Tala and was righted to her feet by a laughing Prez.

"Show of hands," said Toffee, "has anyone ever seen Doug laugh before?" Looking at Tala she said. "So, you show up and suddenly we have a laugh factory in our midst."

"Toffee! That's such a gross exaggeration," said Prez.

"Well, dude," piped in Roberto, "that's a pretty true assessment."

"Tala, don't listen to any of them. It's the summer solstice and they're smoking weed too early in the day to be sane. By the way, Tala and I saw the sunrise this morning."

"Good god, man, you're the only person I know who would get out of bed for a stupid sunrise. Now that's insanity," said Roberto.

For Prez it was time to go.

"Okay, we're off. There's a few more things I'd like to show my friend before she leaves."

There was a round of, "It was so nice to meet you." Then Lora said, "Why not come over to my place tomorrow evening? That would be fabulous!"

"Can't," said Prez. "She's leaving in the morning."

"How long have you been here?" Toffee asked Tala.

"Since last evening," said Tala.

"One day?" said Marie-Claire. "You're only here with Doug for one day?"

Roberto had become painfully pensive. He had for some time taken note of Doug and his co-worker Theresa during breaks or lunch bent over laughing on the grass in front of the library.

As they drove westward on Sherbrooke Street Tala remarked so quietly that Prez knew she was really thinking out loud: "it was so carefree back there."

He motored quickly through the intersection at University Avenue and said, "Montreal's Golden Square Mile starts here. This is where all the wealthy Anglos lived about a century ago, so this area is considered a very symbolic reminder of their domination. Something like seventy percent or more of all the wealth in all of Canada was concentrated right here."

"Whoa there!" she exclaimed.

"Yeah, I know. The opulence of some of these buildings is really something."

"I'm talking about your driving, man. I had forgotten you think you're in a race whenever you get behind the wheel. That last yellow light was really just about red."

"Relax. You know not to worry. I taught your little Beetle a few tricks, didn't I? That's McGill University, where I work."

"Where?"

"Back there. Oh, you should have looked quicker. You missed it."

"Is that where they had the computer riot?"

"No. That was at Sir George Williams University. I'll show you."

He took a left at Guy Street and parked close to the intersection of De Maisonneuve Boulevard. They got out and Tala gave him a look when he closed the roof. "Pigeons," he said. They walked east on De Maisonneuve until Prez stopped in front of a big building that took up the whole block.

"This is the Hall Building. The computer department is up there." He pointed to the upper floors of the building. "Last

February a bunch of mostly Afro-Caribbean students took over the computer center to protest inaction on the part of the university in addressing their complaints of racial discrimination. Max, Toffee, and Roberto were outside on the street in a supporting demonstration. The protesters and university officials were talking and it seemed they had worked things out and then the police showed up. Some protesters started throwing punch cards out the window, then the computer center caught fire and they started throwing equipment out the window."

"Who started the fire?"

"Don't really know. The police say it was the protesters. The protesters say it was the police. But it was the big turning point in the whole affair.

"I showed up late. Thick smoke poured from the windows. People were yelling for the fire department to rescue the protesters before they all perished in the fire.

"But then I started to hear other voices that seemed louder, chanting something very disturbing. They looked meaner and angrier than the students supporting the protesters."

"What were they saying?"

"Let the niggers burn!"

Washington, D.C., Spring 1953

New leaves were sprouting on the big oak trees that lined both sides of Sherman Avenue. The leaves would grow big like the greens his grandma put in her terrible big gray pot on the stove. And the trees were so tall that when they were full and lush in summer, they touched at the top, forming an extended archway under which Sherman Avenue ran for as far as the eye could see.

Five-year-old Preston Coleman Downs, Junior, sat on his front porch with his father. Everyone had a front porch, and a nice lawn in front that sloped down toward the sidewalk; perfect for rolling things down, such as marbles, balls, and little bodies like his own.

Little Preston would listen as his father told him the name of every car that went by. His daddy not only knew their names, but their year of manufacture and all kinds of strange things like cylinders and transmissions.

Preston Sr. was especially proud of his own car, a brand-new powder-blue-and-white 1953 Chevrolet Bel Air that had wide whitewall tires and a three-speed stick shift on the column. It was in that car that Preston Sr. would later sit Little Preston on his lap at the old family place in Spotsylvania County, Virginia and let him steer the car down a country road. Little Preston loved being with his father, whether it was lying on the grass with his daddy at Hains Point beside the Potomac River and watching the faces in the clouds go by, or watching his daddy laugh his head off when he was with his brothers. Or simply, like now, just sitting on the front porch under the lush, green, peaceful canopy of big oak trees and listening to his father speak with such authority.

It was one such spring afternoon when his daddy abruptly stopped talking and disappeared into the house. Up his front steps and right onto his front porch came two white men. Now, it wasn't as if Little Preston had never seen white people before. He watched the Mickey Mouse Club on TV and had a crush on Annette. Some of the people in his neighborhood—even in his own family—were so light as to be practically white. But these were real white men like Joe Friday and Frank Smith on *Dragnet*.

"Hey s-s-sonny b-boy, was th-that your d-daddy we j-j-just saw ru-r-run into the house?" began the shorter of the two men.

He never looked down at Little Preston, probably because he couldn't keep still long enough. He sure looked everywhere else, though; through the windows, through the door, around the side of the house, over his shoulder, up and down the street, and all over again.

"You go t-t-tell your d-daddy th-th-that Mr. St-St-Stein would l-like to see him."

Little Preston laughed. He had no idea a person could talk like a cartoon character.

"You sound like Porky Pig!" he blurted.

Next thing he knew he was choking and his throat felt like it was being crushed. His eyes felt like they would pop out of their sockets. And beneath his feet there was only air.

64

"I'll f-f-fuckin' k-kill you, y-y-you l-little sk-sk-skinny-assed ni-ni-nigger!!" screamed the stutterer as he held Little Preston up against the wall by his throat. Something in Little Preston's head kept flashing white behind his eyes, as he simultaneously kicked, punched, and tried to scream for his daddy. But no words would come, and no daddy would come, and he was getting so tired and sleepy he just wanted to close his eyes for good and go to sleep for a long time when—

"Ow!" Little Preston felt his butt hit the porch and the back of his head bounce off the brick wall.

He was crying now, but he wished he could stop; just long enough so that he could go and punch the man who had hurt him so. He tried to get up but felt too weak and landed back on his butt. He rubbed his head where it had hit the wall, and cried and screamed through his tears, "I'll get you; you just wait!" He tried getting up again, and again his legs gave out. So, he got on his hands and knees and tried crawling. It was at this point that Little Preston sensed an eerie stillness all around him. It was as if the whole world had stopped moving except him. There was a heavy silence. All he could hear were the tires buzzing over the pavement as they drove by. The stillness was absolute, entrapping Little Preston, leaving him motionless in mid-crawl.

Little Preston first noticed her stacked-heel, lace-up, black Oxford shoes with very shiny tips. Next, his eyes went higher to the lace around the bottom of her petticoat-like dress, over which was her ever-present white apron.   She had on her gold-rimmed glasses, which she once told Little Preston she only wore when she needed to "see real good." And his Grandma Denie needed to see real good at this moment because in her hand she held a little silver-plated, two-shot Derringer pistol which she had pointed at the two men. She grabbed Little Preston and shoved him behind her.

65

"Git inside, boy." She fixed her stare into the eyes of the shorter man. "Now back away and stand beside your friend over there and don't neither one of you move."

Both the white men knew now that all they had to do to stay alive was to comply with her commands. But what was she waiting for? The cops? What a joke that would be. Mr. Stein, who controlled the numbers racket in this part of D.C., and owned every gas station for miles, had the police in his pocket. But Mr. Stein knew Denie Williams when both were young hustlers during the twenties. She was the toughest broad he knew. But he needed it to be known that if her son Preston's gambling debt was not paid off by the end of the week, he would not live to see the next.

"They hurt me, Grandma!" screamed a tearful Little Preston through the front window.

"I know, baby. But they won't hurt you no mo'," Grandma Denie said.

No sooner had his grandma uttered those words did Little Preston hear the screeching of tires coming to an abrupt halt. His uncles were rushing out of his Uncle Cadgie's big white convertible Mercury. They were up on the porch so quickly that the two white men didn't have time to react to being put in headlocks, frisked, and dragged to the car. They were shoved into the back seat. The car pulled away from the curb at a relaxed pace that belied the pummeling the brothers were administering to Mr. Stein's goons.

❧

Later that evening, and much later than Little Preston and Gussie were accustomed, they sat on the front porch with their father, his brothers, Grandma Denie, their mother Mattie, and an ever-changing assortment of family members, close friends, and neighbors who came to sit and talk in hurried whispers or just stare quietly into the night. All the family members and a few of the close friends brought money. The neighbors, they just came to fraternize with the Williams boys.

The only thing he loved about as much as being with his daddy was when his daddy and his daddy's brothers were there. What a fun time that was. They were always happy, and joking, and laughing, and telling Little Preston and his baby brother Gussie all sorts of things they didn't understand and Preston guessed, by the look on his mama's face, they weren't supposed to know. His mama would look at his father, and then at all the uncles, and try to ask very quietly, "Now, do you really think Little Preston and little Augustus should be listening to you all talk about what you do with your lady friends and how you make your money?"

"Sorry, Mattie," they'd say in near unison, snickering under their breath, before bursting into raucous laughter.

There was Uncle Troy, at six feet, three and a half inches, the tallest of the four brothers, slender of build, and sharply featured like his mother Denie. He was just as light-complexioned as she. He was also the eldest of the four. From there on down the brothers got darker, reaching the milk-chocolate skin of his own father, Preston Sr. Next in line was Uncle Rolando, who could pass for his daddy's twin except that he was, at five eleven, three inches taller than his daddy. But they both had the same smooth skin, wavy hair, and thick eyebrows that formed perfectly above their light-brown, long-lashed eyes. Both of them had the same moustaches above the same mouths, and the same teeth that were perfectly straight and gleamed so white when they laughed, both from the same places in their stomachs. In between his uncle Rolando and his daddy was his Uncle Cadgie, the wild one of the bunch. At five ten, he was all muscle, possessing thick thighs, a massive torso, thick neck, big fists. And according to what little Prez heard when all the brothers were together, his lady friends thought he was built like a tree trunk everywhere.

"That's because they ain't seen mine," one of them would always quip. Oh, how the brothers would howl, bark and crow. Little Preston always marveled at the spectacle of the brothers together.

It would be years before he understood that his daddy and his uncles had different fathers—which explained why his grandma and his uncles were Williams, but his daddy, his mother, his baby brother, and himself were Downs.

The Williams boys weren't braggarts and they really didn't like to be seen to be too much different than their peers. But they were. No one else in the neighborhood would dare stand up to the white man like that. The Williams boys' reputations were the stuff of legend. They refused to suffer abuse or fools—no matter who it was, or what their station in life. As infrequently as they went to church, they very much lived by the golden rule. And they also had a reputation for taking no prisoners. Thus, no one ever expected those two white men to ever be heard from again ... by anyone. Including Mr. Stein, who would have gotten his money if he had simply rung Denie up on the phone and told her the situation instead of trying to strong-arm his way around the neighborhood. That wasn't necessary.

Negroes knew the score; had known it for generations. White folks ruled. And Negroes would just as soon stay out of their way, because being around white folks only left one open to humiliation, degradation, abuse, and violence. What white folks wanted they got. And most Negroes would just as soon give in to white demands as try to fight the power.

There was, however, a new, militant, fearless crop of post-World War II black men coming of age. Some were brilliantly defiant, like that Black Muslim minister up in Harlem. Imagine—calling the white man a "devil." Some were not so brilliant, like the Williams boys, who could not expound upon the similarities between the United States' efforts to keep the black man oppressed in Africa and efforts to keep the black man oppressed at home, in America. But one thing they did know: the white man would never again be allowed to come into the neighborhood and put his hands on Negro women and children. That's where the Williams boys drew the line, especially when it came to their beloved Little Preston and Gussie. Cross that line and you might meet your maker.

"Preston! You'd better git this little black thing you married outta my face in a hurry befo' I do something the lord will have me regret!"

"He's in the bathroom. But, so what? I'm not afraid of you, Denie Williams!"

"Well, you should be, with your little, black, ugly self!"

"Denie, you're the ugly one. No matter how light your skin is, it can't hide the fact that you're ugly inside. Ugly, hateful, mean ... and thoughtless. Your own grandsons are within earshot of you screaming at their mother and calling her black! What do you think that's going to do to their little minds, their little souls?"

"Well, Miss Mattie Adams, don't think you're so much better 'n the rest of us, with your college degree 'n all. This is my house and you will not tell me how to run my house."

"Mrs. Mattie Downs, Denie. I am legally married to your son. Respect that. I'm not trying to tell you how to run your house. I simply came back here to tell you that I was taking the boys across the street to my friend Lois's house while you cook those chitterlings. They don't like the smell. Whenever you start to cook those things Gussie starts sucking his thumb and Little Preston starts crying."

"Gussie is a thumbsucker. That's got nothing to do with my chitterlings. And as for Little Preston, hmmphh, that boy cries when I cook anything in the big pot. That's Cadgie's fault; a damned fool of a son if I ever had one."

"What do you mean it's Cadgie's fault, Denie?"

Denie turned her back to Mattie and began looking into her spice cupboard, muttering to herself that people should just stay out of her kitchen because things were never where they were supposed to be.

Mattie was not taking that bait. She would not allow herself to be sidetracked into defending herself against a shaded accusation that she was the one responsible for Denie not being able to find the spices she was looking for. It was all a ruse anyway, because though Denie loved being coy, she really let that slip. She really didn't want to tell Mattie what Cadgie had said to Little Preston.

"What did Cadgie tell him, Denie?" Mattie queried again, this time with that North Carolina temper seething just below the surface.

Denie, still with her back to Mattie, mumbled, "Cadgie said that we cook dead people in the pot . . ."

Mattie, momentarily stunned, as she always was when confronted by abject stupidity, blurted out, "He said *what*? Denie!"

"Cadgie said that chit'lins stink because dead people smell real bad when we cook 'em in the pot."

"Oh, my lord," said Mattie. Denie glanced over and saw a truly dumbfounded young woman seemingly unable—for once—to muster any words. So Denie decided to rub it in some more.

She got down from the stool she was standing on and closed the cupboard door. She walked over to Mattie and put her arm around Mattie's shoulder. "You must promise not to say anything."

Mattie remained stone silent and unmoved by her mother-in-law's opportunistic use of physical interaction. And besides, Mattie never made promises she wouldn't keep.

"You know Cadgie, he was jes' playin' with Little Preston, he didn't mean no harm tellin' the boy that nobody messes with a Williams, 'cause they'd be killed, cut up, and cooked in the pot! Cadgie sure is a fool sometimes sayin' stuff like 'lots of people try to mess with the Williams family, that's why every weekend, we be cookin' somebody in the pot.'"

"My lord!" began Mattie. "Oh, my lord. Cadgie has lost his mind! Saying something like that to my child. No wonder Little Preston is so afraid of that pot. Where's Preston? He must tell his brother to stop saying things like that to my boys!"

"They Preston's boys, too," cut in Denie. "I think you forget that sometimes. Don't you be naggin' Preston about this mess. You jes' let Preston be a man and a father the way he sees fit, not the way you think he s'posed to be. Little Gussie's a thumb-sucker because you're always nagging at his father about this 'n that. Not because I cook up some chit'lins."

"Denie, Preston is never going to be the man he can be as long as he's living in your house. Preston! Preston!" screamed Mattie, as she walked out of the kitchen and down the hall.

But Preston had left the house as soon as his mother started cooking her chitterlings because he couldn't stand the smell either. Oh, he loved eating them, smothered in hot sauce and liberally sprinkled with salt and pepper. He also knew that when chitterlings cooked there was going to be a fight between his mother and his wife. And he never knew how to handle those fights. They would always contain references to his wife's complexion, and his family's ignorance. He would therefore get blamed for having a wife too dark and a family too dumb, and for not having the backbone to do anything about either one.

Looking out her kitchen window, Denie saw Mattie rushing across the street to her friend Lois's house. Gussie was in her arms, sucking his thumb and pulling at his ear with his other hand. Little Preston was being pulled along while screaming for his daddy. That was how he began his sixth year.

Soon Little Preston reveled in his first summer of running freely out of doors. Well, except for his mother's line-of-sight rule. He was allowed to cross Girard Street by himself but if she stuck her head out the side window she needed to see him.

Almost immediately he was breaking the rules. He was running with James and Butch and his cousin Anthony. He wasn't supposed to be off Girard Street, in the first place. He wasn't supposed to be playing with Butch, who was practically twelve years old, in the second place. And he certainly wasn't supposed to be standing on an upturned garbage can trying to peer into the bathroom window of sixteen-year-old Paula Pervis who, according to Butch, would appear naked in the bathroom to wash herself as she always did after her dance class. Little Preston was already very nervous. Perhaps scared would be the better word. He had never seen a naked girl before, and if his grandmother was right, a sin of such magnitude would surely bring the ultimate in God's wrath in the shape of a lightning bolt from on high. And he really didn't want to look. But Butch kept calling him a "sissy" and a "mama's boy" if he didn't look. Both his grandmother and mother had slapped him silly for asking what a dick was even though, as he knew now, it was something that he had and that rightfully belonged to him. He feared that if he were caught looking at a naked girl, and all the things he had heard a naked girl had, such as "titties," "booty," and "fuzzy muff," there was no telling how bad the pain he would suffer would be. Not forgetting, of course, the lightning bolt from God.

He huddled beneath the open bathroom window with James, Anthony, and Butch, waiting to hear Paula come into the bathroom. James and Anthony developed a severe giggling fit that brought a sharp whispered reprimand from Butch: "Are you young punks stupid or somethin'? What'cha tryin' ta do, blow it, suckers? Get us busted? Shut up!" At that, it took all Preston's willpower to keep still, because his feet wanted to start running.

They heard someone come into the bathroom. First, Butch got up on top of the garbage can and peered over the window ledge. The big grin that bloomed on his face from ear to ear told them it was naked Paula Pervis. Anthony started pulling at Butch's pants legs so hard, Butch almost toppled from the garbage can. Butch glared down at Anthony, biting at his lower lip and shaking a fist at Anthony. Butch got down so that Anthony could have his turn. Anthony's eyes got so big, Little Preston thought they would pop out of their sockets. When he got down, his eyes were still big and Little Preston knew for sure that if his eyes stayed like that, Anthony's mother and his mother would find out what they had been doing. "They big," said a mesmerized Anthony. "They real big."

James, the shortest of the four, had to stand on his tiptoes to see into Paula's bathroom window. His little head kept bobbing up and down as he peered in, straining to remain high up enough to see.

"Your turn, Preston," whispered James as he got down from the garbage can.

"No. I don't want to look," whispered Little Preston.

"What you mean you ain't gonna look?" demanded Butch in a threatening whisper. "You better git your little squirrel-ass up dere before I kick it up dere!"

"Yeah," whispered James excitedly, "we all looked. You hafta look!"

Anthony, his eyes still wide, whispered to his cousin, "Ya gotta see. They big."

"They big" rolled around in Little Preston's head and finally settled in the pit of his stomach, making him feel weak-kneed. What was big? Everything Paula Pervis had or just some of those things? Oh, how he didn't want to know.

"Don't be a sissy," whispered Butch, this time with even more menace in his voice.

With much hesitation, and a bunch of regrets all lined up before the fact, Little Preston climbed atop the garbage can. He steadied himself, and began to rise from his crouched position, very slowly, very deliberately, and very, very quietly.

He could hear Paula Pervis humming as water ran. The toilet flushed, startling him, and he stooped back down into his crouched position.

He looked down at the three pairs of big brown eyes looking up at him, one pair still very big. Butch shook his fist.

Finally, he resolved to do it. He swallowed hard and began raising himself up from his crouched position. He was holding on so hard to the window ledge that his fingernails had dug into the wood. He could hear that Paula Pervis was still humming and moving around in the bathroom. Something dropped on the floor and she exclaimed, "Oh, darn it," causing his knees to go weak. But nothing could stop him now. Then more water ran, louder than before, almost drowning out Paula Pervis's humming. Perfect, he thought. He wouldn't get caught with all that noise to protect him. Slowly he rose, first seeing the rose-colored ceiling and walls. Next, a tilted-open window above the bathroom door came into view. Then he could see that there was a huge mirror on the wall that reached as high as the ceiling, and he was beginning to see the top of Paula Pervis' hair. His heart raced with anticipation as "They big" careened around in his head and churned around in his stomach. He could feel his own eyes getting bigger as Paula Pervis's face and neck came into view. Then—

"Preston Junior! Preston Junior, where are you?"

Little Preston jerked his head around, expecting to see his mother standing right there under him. His entire body jerked with such force that the garbage can bobbled and began to topple over. Butch and James grabbed for the garbage can to keep it from falling but Little Preston's feet were now kicking it as he clutched the windowsill.

First Butch, then James and Anthony took off running down the laneway, allowing the garbage can to crash over onto the ground and leaving Little Preston dangling from Paula Pervis's bathroom windowsill. Inside, the water abruptly stopped.

"Who's there? Who's out there?" demanded Paula Pervis's voice. Then, "Ma, Ma! Come quick!"

Little Preston let go of the windowsill and hit the ground running. He caught up to James, then Anthony and Butch before they reached Girard Street. The laneway came out halfway up the block from Little Preston's house but as soon as he looked down the street, he could see his mother's head sticking out the window. He ran down the street as fast as his little legs could carry him.

"Here I am, Mama!"

"Is everything alright, Preston Junior? You look like you've just seen a ghost."

"Oh, I was just having a race, Mama."

Mattie looked back up the street and saw Butch.

"You know I told you I don't want you playing with that boy. He's much too old for you to be playing with, Preston Junior."

"Yes, ma'am."

"Don't you just yes-ma'am me. You mind me and don't play with that boy anymore. Now get in here and eat your lunch."

76

"Yes, ma'am."

As Little Preston walked around to the front of the house to come inside, Mattie looked up the street again and this time saw all three boys. They were all out of breath and clearly had been up to no good. She wondered what could they possibly have gotten into on a summer's afternoon on the block where they lived. *Probably nothing serious,* she thought. And she really didn't have anything against Butch. He was a good kid at heart, struggling to find his way in the world while being raised by his single parent, an alcoholic father. In her gut, though, she had a bad feeling about Butch. And even without her instincts screaming conflicting sentiments at her, she knew a twelve-year-old, who looked much older, shouldn't be playing with six-year-olds. And that was that.

10

Washington, D.C., June 1953

Little Preston heard his parents talking about the monthly checks from the US Army that Butch's father received. But he also knew that Butch had a job in the kitchen of a fancy Georgetown restaurant so he didn't think things were that good in Butch's house. He also took notice of an extremely glamorous lady who occasionally stayed there. He wondered who she was and why for those few fleeting days Butch's father was stone sober, shaven, and handsome. And Butch seemed happy.

Then the lady would go away and Butch's father would start drinking again. Like the night Prez was awakened by the sound of crashing glass. His parents were already at the window looking out. Butch's father, clad only in undershorts, had heaved a garbage crate full of fruit peelings right through the big plate-glass window of Mr. Stein's corner grocery store. Bedroom lights began switching on in the neighborhood.

"Goddammit, Stein! You bring yo' fuckin' ass over here from Poland and you won't give us nuthin'. Not even r'speck. Where are you with your bad breath? The kids all say you got bad breath when you scream at 'em ta git outta yo' sto'." Hic. Hic. "Oh, sheeit!"

The cancer in his gut transformed each hiccup into a searing pain.

"Hic. Oh, that hurts. You better come on outta there, Stein, 'n talk to me. You got some explaining ta do. I know you're in there hidin' behind something all scared 'n shit like when we found yo' asses in that concentration camp. Yeah, I was driving one of those tanks, I was in the 761st. I saved your ass! Fuckin' Langston, where are you when I need you? Do you know *From* ~~Beaumont to Detroit~~ *Stein? 'You Jim Crowed me/Before Hitler* ~~...~~ *wing me/Right now this*

...ather fell right on top of
...sat up, looking into the
...re bedroom lights were
...uld be heard in the dis-

...ide his father.
...d come inside before the
...ops. Please get up. Don't
... here. Please get up."
...a and I'll take the other."

...om up the street.
... It was Mr. Dixon from

...k to his apartment, bed-
...ae time the cops arrived,
... And when Lieutenant
...ed storefront and lighted
...chstick he dropped to the

...ae neighborhood was try-
ing to sleep, the howling of an ambulance broke the silence.

It had come to take Butch's father away. No one ever thought they'd ever see Butch cry, but there he stood, barefoot and in his pajamas, with tears rolling down his face, as his father was loaded into the back of the ambulance. Butch's father was never seen again and Butch, rarely. He needed two jobs to take care of himself and his father's medical bills, and he was nowhere near sixteen years old.

Then the mailman began delivering two mysterious envelopes to Butch's mailbox every month. One was postmarked from Los Angeles, California. The other was local, from Washington, D.C. Soon after, the neighborhood's first example of graffiti appeared on the wall in the empty lot where the kids played baseball, marbles, and tag. It was brushed onto the wall in lavender paint. It simply said, "THANK YOU ALL," and was signed with a capital B that had wings.

The wings on the B became the subject of great conversation and debate amongst people in the neighborhood. Did the wings mean that Butch had big dreams and aspirations and would one day fly away from there? He was certainly smart enough. And if he could harness his energy productively, well, just maybe.

Others thought the wings meant Butch wanted to be a track athlete like his father had been, but not Little Preston who was already faster than Butch.

A small but vocal group of neighborhood mothers, including Mattie, put forward another interpretation of what the wings meant. Those wings, they said, were the wings of angels. Butch was not destined to be of this world much longer.

11

Washington, D.C., July 1953

The week leading up to the Fourth of July weekend was always rife with fireworks and firearms going off. But at the storied intersection of Fourteenth and U Streets, on a fateful Wednesday, one knew the difference.

Butch, heading home from work, had just gotten off a U Street streetcar and had run across Fourteenth Street on a red light trying to catch the northbound streetcar. A motorcycle cop had been riding southbound when he saw Butch jaywalk. He swung a U-turn, hastily jumped off his motorcycle, ran up behind Butch, and, without a word, jerked Butch around by the shoulder. Butch, reacting, let go a punch that clipped the cop on the chin. The cop backed up a step, drew his revolver, dropped to one knee, and *boom!* The cop was over six feet tall. Butch, barely five feet nine. This was as cold-blooded as it could get.

❬

Butch's funeral was held at Reverend Clark's All Souls U Street Gospel Church on the following Monday, July 6, 1953. The collective rage of Washington's Negro community had reached a level that was dangerously close to the boiling point. The funeral was an opportunity to cool things down and give people the perspective to heal.

"You all know how precious a life is. It is so precious that God gave the life of his only son that the rest of us could live in peace, love, and harmony. That one life was so precious to God that he gave it as the ultimate sacrifice so eternal life would be a reality for mankind. Yes, he did," began Reverend Clark to an overflow audience of mourners who were steadily echoing "Amen" all around the church.

"Yes, one single life so precious that its sacrifice marked a turning point in the history of the world. This life that we mourn today, this precious young *black* life, that's right, people, don't be afraid of your *blackness*, don't be ashamed of your *blackness*!"

Fans stopped swishing. The Amens stopped. The restless rustling of butts in pews and feet on the church floor stopped. There was a hush in Reverend Josephus Clark's All Souls U Street Gospel Church such as those divine walls and stained-glass windows had not witnessed before. Mouths were agape, and looks of disbelief were on many faces. But all eyes were now on the Reverend Josephus Clark. He had just crossed a bridge, and they all knew it. They all also knew there was to be no turning back.

"That baby was shot down in cold blood, like a dog, because of the color of his skin. Look at him lying there asleep for all eternity now. I ask you to look at his smooth brown skin, that head full of black bushy hair, those full lips, that little pug nose. You are looking at something you cannot escape, who you are and where you came from. There are only two choices you can make now. Either you continue to scorn yourselves and continue to be victimized by a system that despises you. Or you begin to love yourselves and stand up for your rights as black people and as human beings."

From amongst the chorus of "Amens" there sprang a "Teach it, brother!"

Butch's father was in a wheelchair in the front of the church beside his son's coffin.

"I said, teach it, brother! You tell it like it is! You tell the truth! For once you all gotta hear the truth! Else your own boys be layin' here like my Butch is right now. He was the best boy anybody could ask for."

Butch's father lifted himself from his wheelchair. Even full of morphine as he was, the pain in his stomach made him grimace as he stepped toward his son's coffin.

"And you know what? I haven't hugged my boy since he was six or seven. Don't you all let another day pass without hugging yours."

Butch's father began to weep. He bent over and caressed Butch's face as he wailed and wailed. Parents could be seen all over the church holding their children close to them. The whole place was filled with the sounds of sobbing, sniffling, and nose-blowing.

Little Preston sat upright between his mother and grand-mother. He needed to understand exactly the difference between his little brother asleep on his mother's lap and Butch asleep in that box they called a coffin. If Butch was just sleeping, why was everyone crying and why were the men so angry? And why, after helping carry the coffin, had his daddy come over and knelt before him and Gussie and promised that what had happened to Butch would never happen to them?

Just then, the church doors swung open and in walked a very tall, elegantly dressed, glamorously made-up woman that some of them recognized right away as Thelma Theron, the Negro opera star who was more popular in Europe than she was in the United States. It was the woman who was sometimes in Butch's house. She held a wreath fringed with African violets and she walked right down and knelt in front of Butch's father.

"I'm very sorry I'm so late, Clifton," she said as he wept on her shoulder. She went over and laid the wreath in front of Butch's coffin. As she looked down at him she weakened and wobbled. A couple of deaconesses got up, but she motioned them away. Then she raised her eyes upwards, closed them and started singing: *"Whoa, there was a woman in the Bible days, she had been sick, sick so very long, but she heard 'bout Jesus was passin' by ..."* Little Preston knew that song. His grandma had the Sam Cooke record. *"If I could just touch the hem of His garment I know I'll be made whole."*

12

Washington, D.C., late July 1953

After Butch was gone, the neighborhood just wasn't the same anymore for Little Preston, James, and Anthony. They still ran all over the place, racing and playing tag. They still played ball and marbles in the lot where Butch's "Thank you all" graffiti remained on the wall. And whenever they would venture down the laneway under Paula Pervis's bathroom window they'd stand still for a moment, look up, and salute. Then they'd immediately go and sit on the front steps of Butch's empty apartment.

But they stopped whatever they were doing when police cars drove by. The eyes of the cops seemed to be aimed at them like those ray-guns they saw on TV shows.

And then there was that afternoon when the police came to their lot and chased them away. The police whitewashed over Butch's "Thank you all."

"My lord," exclaimed Lois to Mattie and to James's mother, Mrs. Moorehouse, "why on earth would the police come out here just to paint over what Butch wrote?"

"I'll tell you why, honey," said Mrs. Moorehouse, "guilt! They know they killed Butch in cold blood so they want us to forget all about him. They want us to go on as if that boy never lived!"

By nightfall practically everyone in the neighborhood had seen the whitewashed wall. The next morning, when daylight broke, someone had drawn a pair of lavender wings on the walls and written between the wings, "Butch Lives."

It took a few days for the police to show up and whitewash over that. But the very next morning, the "Butch Lives" graffiti reappeared. This clash captured the imagination of the whole neighborhood. No one seemed to know the identity of the graffiti writer, or writers; or, if they did, no one was talking. Eventually, the graffiti evolved into a simple capital B with wings—the Flyin' B.

In the blocks surrounding Girard Street, bigger, older, boys lived. It had long been practically impossible for them to peacefully experience those tranquil summer hours when twilight shepherds in the night. For simply standing around on street corners, sitting on steps, or leaning against the trees talking, laughing, and singing they would be beaten, bloodied, and even locked up at the station. But Butch's murder had shaken them and they took the Flyin' B as their emblem. They painted it all over the place, even on the walls of Precinct Number Thirteen.

The boys believed they and their neighborhood were under siege. They devised a scheme to fight back and called it "cop-running." A decoy group of boys would be stationed on a given corner. When the cops gave chase, this group of boys would lead the cops into an alley ambush of stones, rocks, and bottles. Soon, the police hesitated before giving chase and instead would simply stop the police car on the other side of the street and use a bullhorn to order them to move on. If ever there was a hate-filled relation borne of the very nature of the origins of the United States of America, this was it: white cops against black youth.

The boys considered their new treatment at the hands of the police a victory. They weren't being chased any longer, and were not fearful of the police, though they still realized who had the guns. And no one would ever forget Butch. Some of them had Flyin' B tattoos applied to their arms. Every kid wanted to be a B-Boy.

13

Washington, D.C., August 1953

August came along and blew its hot, funky breath on a black populace already suffering under severe psycho-emotional discord brought on by Butch's shooting. While the neighborhood struggled to right itself, plans were afoot to upend their lives in a devastating manner.

Little Preston first saw the calamity that would traumatize and haunt him for the rest of his life while looking out the back window of his daddy's car on a Sunday drive downtown.

He and Gussie always rode looking out the back window. They loved watching the people, the yards, and the trees whiz by as their father drove down Sherman Avenue. Though their neighborhood contained poor and working-class black families, it was a tree-filled neighborhood of low-rises and row houses; it was far from being just another ghetto or "concrete jungle."

Some blocks, like Little Preston's, had trees so lush that the branches seemed to sweep the ground. The houses had long front lawns, were pushed further away from the street, and never went higher than two stories.

Other blocks had trees with whole sections of branches lopped off facing traffic. This was done so that the branches would not interfere with streetcar cables. Preston Sr. hated driving along these streets because he didn't want the streetcar tracks to "mess up my whitewalls." Little Preston hated these streets because the lopped-off branches made the trees look ugly and deformed.

Then there were the blocks that had three- and four-story buildings closer to the sidewalk and to each other. Here the trees were bare more than halfway up their trunks. But at the top, above the roofs, they were thicker and greener than any trees Little Preston had ever seen. At the tops of the trees, flocks of wrens, sparrows, robins, cardinals, blue jays and little birds with yellow breasts whose names Little Preston never did learn would flutter from one treetop to the next, causing a commotion as the top of one tree, gushing out birds, bent toward another.

But on this particular otherwise balmy, lazy, playful Sunday afternoon, with children playing hopscotch, tag, hide-and-seek, rope-skipping, and baseball-in-the-middle-of-the-street; with folks washing their cars, cutting their grass, or just sitting in the shade under a tree, or on their porches … On this particular otherwise calm and peaceful Sunday afternoon with the drive not marred by too much traffic, nor too many streetcars, nor even the intrusion of a single police cruiser interloping with police eyes ever leering … On this particular Sunday afternoon …

Screeech! Little Preston and Gussie had to hold on tight to the top of the back seat to keep from falling backward. Their father's powder-blue-and-white 1953 Chevrolet Bel Air came to an abrupt stop at the corner of Barrie Place and Sherman Avenue.

"Look at what they're doing, Mattie! Remember those big oak trees that used to be in the lot over there?" Preston pointed to the southeast corner. "I used to play down here with Rolando and Cadge in the fall when there would be so many leaves on the ground you could hide all day and not be found. And over there used to be Ole Man Gaye's yard. What a garden he had there." Preston reached across Mattie to point through the passenger-side window to the destruction on the southwest corner.

"People used to come from all over just to see his sunflowers, and watermelon patch. Look at it, Mattie! That man's yard is all gone. For Christ's sake, Mattie. Those white folks downtown are the dumbest-assed people alive."

Little Preston's eyes got wide and he quickly turned himself around to look out the back window. His daddy had just used angry language that he was not accustomed to hearing his daddy use. Usually when his daddy—or anybody else for that matter— used that kind of language around him and Gussie, his mama was quick to get after them. But not this time.

"I know, Preston, it's a shame. But what can you do?"

There was a deep sadness in his mother's voice that Little Preston hadn't heard before. She took his father's arm that had been pointing out the window and put it around her shoulder. Then she slid over until she was resting her head on Preston's chest. His father bent over and kissed her forehead.

"What can you do?" she asked again to no one in particular, while looking over at Ole Man Gaye's yard, or what was left of it.

Little Preston scrambled up to his knees so that he could peer out the side window to see what had brought on this strange interlude between his parents. He knew Ole Man Gaye's yard. He had seen the big sunflowers, watermelons, and assorted other plant life. They had actually walked up to the edge of the garden one Sunday afternoon, and Little Preston remembered all the sounds of things buzzing and chirping about there. But he was not ready for what he saw. His eyes widened and his jaw dropped. He rubbed his eyes in disbelief.

Except for a patch of grass between Ole Man Gaye's house and his neighbor's to the south, all of Ole Man Gaye's big corner lot was gone. Even part of his front porch. There was just a big hole and dirt all over the place. There was a big yellow machine with a huge scooper on it sitting in front of the house. Little

Preston looked around and saw more yellow machines of different sizes, some with scoopers, and some not. And it wasn't just Ole Man Gaye's yard that had been destroyed. It was his neighbors' yards, too. It was the whole block.

"Gussie, move!" Little Preston scrambled to the other window and looked out to see the same destruction on the other side of the street. Then he turned to look behind them again, to the north of Barry Place, and it was his world: still trees and yards, with no big ugly yellow machines about. He continued to go from window to window—"Gussie, move!"—trying to absorb the contrast between the ugliness on the south side of Barry Place and the beauty on the north side. He did not understand what was happening. But he knew that what was happening to Ole Man Gaye and his neighborhood to the south of Barry Place was not good.

"Daddy, where'd all the flowers and the watermelons go?"

"It's those white folks downtown, son. They want to destroy anything nice we have just to make things better for themselves."

Mattie interjected. "Preston Junior, the city wants more cars to be able to drive up and down Sherman Avenue, so they're widening the street. It's going to be four lanes instead of two. But for them to make it wider they have to make more space, so that's why they're cutting people's yards and porches away. And cutting down all the trees."

Little Preston thought for a moment. "Does that mean we'll be able to see more cars when we sit on the porch, Daddy?"

"Son, that means we won't have a front porch to sit on." Preston was angry. It was a deep, seething anger. It was in his belly. And his head didn't know what to do with it. "Goddammit, Mattie, they're gonna destroy the neighborhood!"

That Saturday afternoon, Old Mr. Mack next door turned on the sprinklers in his front yard as he had done so many times before. With an up-and-down pumping of his crutch held high above his head, he beckoned all the neighborhood kids to put on their swimsuits and come play in his yard. He had done that every summer since he returned from the Great War as a member of the Black Rattlers, the storied 369th Infantry of the Ninety-third Division, US Army. If his little black angels couldn't swim in the public pool on Georgia Avenue just because they were Negro children, they could run freely in his yard. And he still had his bolo knife with traces of German blood caked on it to protect those children. He would sit rocking his huge shadow back and forth with his cane across his lap as if he were on guard duty. His little doll-sized French wife would sit on the steps with her face cupped in her palms and her elbows on her knees, always smiling, especially her eyes. This was a farewell, thought Little Preston. This would obviously be the last time he and his friends could romp under Mr. Mack's sprinklers because the big machines were going to destroy his yard on Monday, just as his own yard would be destroyed.

Sure enough, Monday came and so did the destruction. Little Preston watched from his living room window. Big ugly yellow machines belched dirty, sooty exhaust smoke while ripping up the ground. Hordes of grimy white men blowing cigarette smoke and speaking in strange tongues dug up their yards and demolished their front porches. He was not allowed to go out of the house. Summer was brought to an abrupt and premature end. In many ways, so was his childhood.

As he looked out at all the commotion and destruction, he wondered if this was what war looked like. He resolved to ask old Mr. Mack next door. But well after he and Gussie had been put to bed, sirens and flashing red emergency lights continued well into the night. Little Preston got up and rushed down the hall. His front door was wide open. His parents and grandmother were standing outside. He rushed over to the window and saw two big white men putting a big stretcher into the ambulance. Little Preston knew it was Old Mr. Mack. He watched Mr. Mack's little French wife get into the ambulance, her head high, her body smiling. His father walked back inside, very sad, holding an old dented army helmet with a rattlesnake emblem on the front. "She gave it to me," was all his father could manage to say.

14

Washington, D.C., September 1953

"He must'a been a light-skinned Negro."

Any hopes that Preston had of a quiet Sunday dinner with his wife and mother at the same table went up in a mushroom cloud of smoke with that remark from his mother. They had all been sitting amiably enough around the tiny table set up in what should have been a dining room, but which had served as Denie's bedroom since she had moved with her three boys (Preston came along later) into that flat, almost thirty years prior. This was after her Dominican husband ran off with a mestiza and started another family.

They had been discussing pleasantries such as the weather:

"Oooowhee! It's been a hot one this year. Can you remember a hotter one, Mumma?"

"I surely can't, son. What about you, Mattie?"

"Oh, I tell you, it can get awfully hot and muggy down home, but it's different than this. The air doesn't get as heavy."

And family:

"I saw Matilda while I was waiting for Preston to pick me up from work the other day. That girl looks good for eight months. She is carrying a little low. She sends her love, Denie."

"Oh, what a sweet girl. She just can't sit still long enough to carry any other way. That Rolando's so lazy lately? Seen your brother lately, Preston?"

"No, Mumma, I haven't."

And the neighborhood:

"Hey Mama, me and Mattie ran into Bale Turner the other day when we went to register Little Preston for elementary school. He and Gail were there signing up Brenda. They got themselves a new car, a white Caddy!"

"Well, ain't that nice. That's practical for him."

"What do you mean *practical*, Denie?" asked a bait-biting Mattie. "When can buying a Cadillac ever be practical?"

"When you got a butt as big as he got, honey!" Denie laughed.

And, yes, Little Preston entering first grade:

"Don't they grow fast!" exclaimed Denie. "You must be excited about starting school, boy."

"Yeah, Grandma."

"Principal Carruthers told us that this year Monroe was going to teach the children Negro history starting right from first grade. I think it's about time."

"Yeah, Mama. Did you know that Banneker Junior High, where Little Preston did kindergarten last year, is named after a Negro man? He helped build Washington."

Denie scowled. "I'm sure a lot of colored people helped build Washington, Preston. After all, the city was full of slaves."

"No, Mama, I mean he helped draw the city. And Mr. Carruthers said he was a free black."

"He was a mathematician and draftsman, Denie," said Mattie. "He actually drew up the blueprints for Washington. Where the streets were going to be, where the buildings were going to be, which way they should face; that sort of thing."

"Well, do tell!" said a duly impressed Denie who had actually stopped chewing to listen to this amazing piece of information. "He must'a been a light-skinned Negro."

Little Preston felt how heavy the weight of a dead silence could be. He felt it pushing against his face as he looked at his father with a forkful of food suspended just in front of his mouth and at his mother and grandmother who stared hostilely at each other.

"Denie, I'm so sick and tired of hearing you put down dark-skinned Negroes. You are a sick, hate-filled woman. You're even worse than racist white people. No matter how light your skin is, you're still a Negro. Just like me. Just like every dark-skinned Negro you see. No better! I've had it! Preston, I swear, I've had enough."

Mattie got up from the table. Her rapid footsteps down the hall were followed by the slamming of the front door. No one had to look out the window to know that she was headed across the street to Lois's place.

Preston Sr. was not known for letting anything stand between him and a meal. But his appetite was gone. He helped his sons finish eating, then cleaned them and put them in front of the television. He cleared the table and washed dishes. Then he went to sit out on the concrete slab that had replaced their front porch. He looked up and down Sherman Avenue. It was now a treeless, four-lane thoroughfare, not the boulevard that anchored his sense of home. His life was at a critical juncture, because he knew that the time had come for him to choose between a future with Mattie or a life without her.

While their father sat on the porch pondering the deep complexity of his family problems, Little Preston and Gussie sat in front of the television. *Amos 'n' Andy* was on and Gussie laughed hysterically at "Kingfish" Stevens and the other characters, especially when Kingfish, with his exaggerated, wide-eyed, thick pouty-lipped look would address his TV wife. "Sapphire, Sapphire! Ooh, Sapphire!"

Little Preston thought they were all stupid, especially Kingfish. He didn't know anyone who acted like those Negroes on that show. And if there were such people, he was sure his family would have nothing to do with them.

After *Amos 'n' Andy* an animated story came on: *John Henry*.

John Henry was not like the other cartoons he was accustomed to seeing. The animated characters in *John Henry* looked as if they had been made from Play-Doh. And John Henry was dark brown. Little Preston had never seen a Negro cartoon character before. He was transfixed.

"John Henry was a steel-driving man," the cartoon began.

A big strong Negro man who could outwork a machine. Imagine. That cartoon gave little Preston a lot to think about. After watching the John Henry cartoon, it was hard for him to sit through other cartoons. They all seemed so dumb to him.

15

Washington, D.C., Beginning of Summer 1955

What a glorious June day it was. Little Preston stood beaming at the front entrance of Monroe Elementary School clutching his straight-A report card. His teacher told him that he was skipping third grade and going straight to fourth the next school year. He was hoping that Lucinda Davis would come by. Today, for sure, he would say more than just hello. He would even show her his straight-A report card.

Little Preston thought back to how his first-grade year had started. On the very first day, he got punched in the face by Brian "Brickhead" Brown. "You got a baby face," Brickhead had yelled at Little Preston before hitting him. "And yo' mama gotta hold yo' hand 'n bring you ta school 'cause you a sissy!" Little Preston had just stood there. He didn't even blink. He looked at Brickhead, who bullied boys the previous year in kindergarten, too, and didn't even blink. "Wha's a matter, sissy, you don't know how ta fight?" Frankly, Little Preston didn't.

Weeks later, during a lunch period on the school yard, he was watching Lucinda skip double-dutch with her friends when Brickhead came up to him and pushed him.

"Hey, punk! Ya lookin' at my girlfriend o' sumthin', wid yo' sissy, baby face?"

Little Preston froze. Not because he was scared, but because he felt an anger welling up in his stomach that he'd never felt before.

"I said, ya lookin' at my girl, ya punk?"

The next thing he knew, Mr. Gray and Miss Beverly were pulling him off of Brickhead, who was under him on the ground, crying and bloody around the nose. The girls who had been skipping rope were screaming. As he was led away to the office, he noticed the initial look of horror on Lucinda's face change into a sly grin.

It was his Uncle Cadgie who came over that night after school and talked to his parents and grandma and seemed to make them not so mad at Little Preston. It was also the night he learned a lot about his father.

"Hey, Little Press, how ya doin', kid? You alright, little man?"

Cadgie was Little Preston's favorite uncle. In some ways that he didn't understand, his Uncle Cadgie was his favorite person in the whole wide world.

"Mama and Daddy are real mad at me, Uncle Cadgie. I didn't start it. I was just there in the yard looking at the leaves and the girls jumpin' rope. Then Brian, he just come up and start pickin' on me like he's always pickin' on everybody. I didn't start it!"

Little Preston started to cry. His uncle put his arms around him and hugged him.

"It's okay, kid. It's okay. But I hear you busted the boy up pretty good. He'll probably think twice before he bullies anybody else. That's if you didn't scramble his brains up so bad he can't think no more."

Cadgie laughed hard. It made little Preston start to laugh through his tears.

"Where'd you learn to punch like that? You have any idea?"

"Uh-uh," replied little Preston.

"Well, kid, all us Williams boys got good hands. We're all fighters, especially your daddy. Out of all of us, your daddy is really the best fighter. Did you know he was a real boxer in the ring? A prizefighter?"

Little Preston pushed his head away from his uncle's chest and looked up at Cadgie, totally incredulous.

"My daddy? You talkin' about my daddy, Uncle Cadgie?" Little Preston couldn't imagine his daddy hurting a fly.

"That's right, Little Press. Your daddy was the best at his weight class."

"What?"

"Okay. Forget that part."

"But, what did you mean, Uncle Cadgie?"

"Okay. Listen. You look at your daddy, and me, and your Uncle Troy. You see that we're all different sizes. Well, in prize-fighting, the rules say that only men who are about the same size can fight each other. That's to make sure someone who's too big don't fight somebody who's way too small. Do you understand?"

"I think so."

"Well, your daddy was the best of any man his size. He was an amateur champion, then he—"

"But, what's an amateur champion, Uncle Cadgie?"

"What? Boy, you ask too many questions. Listen, your daddy was the best fighter. Your daddy was a champion. But he hurt somebody real bad one time. He knocked a guy down and the guy never got up again. Your daddy wouldn't fight no more after that, little man. Your daddy is afraid that he's going to hurt somebody else like that and he doesn't want to. And he don't want you and Gussie fightin', because he don't want you and Gussie to get hurt, or hurt nobody. But, let me tell you, and your daddy is going to tell you this one day, too. You can't just stand by and let somebody pick on you or hurt you. You have to defend yourself. This is the Williams brothers' code of honor, and your daddy, you and Gussie, me, all your uncles, we're all Williams boys. We don't go lookin' for trouble, but if it come lookin' for us, we deal with it, we take care of it. But, remember, son. Never go lookin' for trouble. You don't have to. In this world, little Press, trouble will find you."

Little Preston heard a car horn toot-toot. He looked up to see his mother waving at him across the roof of their car from the passenger side. He wondered why his father was home so early. His little brother was in the back seat. There was a trailer attached to the back of the car. It was full of furniture. Behind his daddy's car was his Uncle Troy in a pickup truck with more stuff, and behind him his Uncle Rolando in his taxicab with even more stuff. Bringing up the rear of this rather awkward-looking grand parade was his Uncle Cadgie. He had the top down on his convertible Mercury, which was loaded down as well.

"Hi, Daddy! Hi Mama! Wow! Do we have a house? Are we moving?" He waved at his uncles. "Where is it? Do we have our own bedroom? Do we have a real kitchen to eat in? Do we have a yard again? Are we gonna get a puppy? Daddy, you promised!" Little Preston had talked himself into near-hyperventilation.

"Shut up and get in," said his mother. "Here ..." She gave him a book with a ribbon tied around it. "This is from me and your father." Little Preston and Gussie excitedly looked out the rear window. As they pulled away from the curb, little Preston looked over to the school and remembered something.

"Mama, does this mean I won't come back to Monroe next year?"

Just as he said that he saw Lucinda coming down the school steps with Brickhead, whose arm was hooked around her neck as he was talking up a storm. She looked over and saw little Preston in the back of his father's car. Then she looked at all the stuff in the trailer and the other cars following. She looked back at little Preston, and with a sad smile on her face, gave a little wave with the fingers of her hand that clutched her school books in front of her chest. Brickhead was so busy being Mr. Boyfriend that he didn't notice a thing. She turned to look again as she and Brickhead walked down the street.

Little Preston turned around and sat down on the back seat. He decided that he was now too big to be looking out the back window of his family's car like his little brother. Besides, he wanted to start reading his new book, *John Henry, The Steel-Driving Man*.

16

Southeast Washington, D.C., 1957

Even though it was little Preston's second summer in Southeast, he still had not adjusted to the absence of a proper front lawn. There was just a small square of grass in front of their new row house. It wasn't large enough to do anything on. But everyone on his Fourth Street block and throughout this new housing project seemed to have the same idea. They planted colorful flowers around the edges of their little squares of green.

The rest of the area in front of the townhouses was all sidewalk, from the front door to the curb. Thus, it was on the sidewalk that all neighborhood activity took place, such as the men in their fold-up chairs sitting in front of their fold-up tables playing games and drinking, anything from a tall glass of lemonade to other stuff that remained hidden in brown paper bags. Or, the girls playing hopscotch or skipping double-dutch in pairs. The women were often together talking, whether standing in front of someone's home or walking casually about the neighborhood. The casualness in their gait belied their maternal vigilance. One eye was always on the kids.

This was a new neighborhood made possible in post-Brown-versus-Board of Education Washington, D.C. when the congressional committee that oversaw all financial expenditures for the city suddenly found some extra money. Little Preston's ears perked up whenever the grownups discussed such things like, "it's an election year, they want us to vote for them." And "to continue to pay taxes without Congressional representation." And "to serve in the military which was 'still de facto segregated'." Like Sergeant White next door, who left his young wife at home alone with the children for months on end.

"Hi, Daddy. Hi, Ma. Can we have some water?" Little Preston burst through the back door with Gussie, his cousin Anthony who was spending the weekend with them, and his newfound crew in tow. "They're building a sports field one block over where Putt-Putt lives. We'll be able to play real baseball and football, then. It's gonna be ready maybe in two weeks, huh, Putt-Putt?"

"Well, how're you boys doin'?"

In unison, "Fine, Mr. Downs."

"And you're all staying out of trouble, I hope?"

In unison, again, "Yes, Mrs. Downs."

"Well, you tell your parents I said hello."

In unison, "Yes, ma'am."

"So, Putney, is that true? Will there be a park behind your house soon?"

"Oh, yes, ma'am. They're almost finished."

Putney "Putt-Putt" Cleveland was the shortest of Little Preston's new crew. He was almost as short as Gussie. But he was older than Little Preston by almost a whole year. His skin was so dark that his eyes looked yellow. And his short bow legs were already rippling with muscles. He was a roller-skating wizard who carried his skates with him everywhere. He could skate almost as fast as the streetcars could run, and keep going for blocks without getting tired. It was as if he had a motor in his butt that would make him "putt-putt" along.

Then there was Stephen "Shaggie" Ferguson, from one of the neighborhood's few white families. He spoke with a lisp, had a shock of thick light-brown hair that almost covered his eyes, giving him a shaggy-dog look, and pants that always looked as if they were going to fall down.

And Fat Head. Jeremy "Fat Head" Jenkins was a tall, handsome, well-proportioned, brown-skinned boy who was born with a rare scalp disorder that prevented him from growing any hair. He was a large baby at birth, and as babies sometimes do, he looked as though he was all head when he was born. It was his father, a very large man, who took one look at him and said, "Just look at that fat-head baby boy. The boy comes out weighing ten pounds, eleven ounces, and ten pounds of it is all his fat head! Ha!" Then he scooped up his son with one huge hand and gave him such a long hug that the nurses were afraid the baby would be smothered. "Hey, that's my fat-head baby boy." The "Fat Head" tag stuck, even though now his head was quite slender and perfectly shaped. All the older girls had a thing for Fat Head, to the great consternation of Putt-Putt, who at the tender age of almost ten, knew something about what was under a girl's dress, and wanted all the attention himself.

"Okay, y'all stand in line if you want some water. Everybody has to wait their turn. We'll do it by how tall you are. The shortest go first. Don't y'all be messing up my mama's new kitchen, now. Anthony, you go after Shaggie. Okay, I'll pour. C'mon Gussie, you the shortest."

"Okay, when you finish, rinse the glass and put it upside down on this towel here."

"Press, I'm gonna need more water after all this work, man," bristled Putt-Putt.

"I know, man," offered Fat Head, giggling while he tried to drink and spilling water on the floor.

"Look what you did, Fat Head!" yelled Little Preston.

"You in trouble, now," chided Shaggie. "The president just may put you in jail for that."

Fat Head giggled more, and of course spilled more water on the floor.

"Look! What you doing, Fat Head?"

"Don't presidents get voted on?" inquired a quite serious Putt-Putt. This made Fat Head giggle even more. By this time Preston Sr. had to leave the kitchen because he was finding it hard not to burst out laughing himself and he wasn't sure if that would get him in trouble with Mattie.

"I'd vote for Press any day," said Shaggie.

"Me, too," said Anthony. "What about you, Gussie?" Gussie nodded.

"Not me," said Putt-Putt. "He's too bossy."

Fat Head was now spilling water all over his T-shirt. Once Fat Head started laughing about something, he couldn't stop.

"Fat Head!" said Little Preston, rushing over towards him.

Mattie got in the way. "It's only water, Preston Junior. I'll clean it up. If you all are finished drinking, go on out and play. But don't go far, Preston Junior, we'll be having dinner soon. Make sure you keep an eye on Gussie."

They all raced out the door and when they got around the corner, they stopped to catch their breath. They had stopped right in front of the house of a very pretty little mocha-colored girl, with long wavy hair, doe eyes, and a perpetual sad smile on her lips. Her name was Romaine. Romaine Farrow.

"Why you still laughing, Fat Head?" asked a sneering Putt-Putt, thinking that the same thing couldn't be funny that long.

"Can't say," came the reply from Fat Head, now leaning up against one of the little trees and holding his belly.

"What you mean, you can't say?" asked a bewildered Putt-Putt.

"I mean, the president might really put me in jail if I say."

Fat Head looked so funny leaning up against the tree laughing that both Gussie and Anthony started giggling.

"What's so funny, Fat Head?" asked Anthony.

"Didn't you hear, back in the kitchen?" said Fat Head before changing his voice over to a whiny-sounding falsetto voice, "Preston Junior, Preston Junior—what a sissy-sounding name."

"You makin' fun 'o my mama, Fat Head!" Whack-whack. Thump-thump!

"Hey, Press. I'm just playin', man. Stop it! That hurts, man! Ow!"

Both Putt-Putt and Anthony tried to pull him off Fat Head. Gussie started crying. Shaggie ran to get Little Preston's father. By the time Preston arrived Fat Head had managed to crawl under a parked pickup truck, and Little Preston was on his hands and knees trying to punch at him. His father hoisted him up by the seat of his pants. Little Preston thrashed about in mid-air.

"Preston Junior! Stop it! Stop it now!"

His father had never called him just "Preston" before. There was also an edge in his father's voice that he hadn't heard before.

"Okay, boys," said Preston. "This is not good." He put Little Preston down. "Preston, Gussie, Anthony, let's go. You too, Jeremy, Stephen, Putney. Follow me." Off they all marched, Preston taking long, forceful, angry steps, Little Preston hopping as he tried to match him stride for stride, Gussie not even trying to walk but trotting along, and Anthony, Jeremy, Stephen and Putney all trotting and wishing they could disappear for a while, at least until Little Preston's dad cooled off. They had never seen him so angry.

Coming through the front door, Preston said, "You boys sit down in the living room. Not you, Preston Junior. Come into the kitchen. Mattie," said Preston as he went over by the stove where his wife was busy cooking dinner, "it seems our first-born has problems controlling his temper. He was beating up on his friend Jeremy. It was not nice to see."

Mattie turned to give her son a look that confirmed the awful seriousness of the moment. Then she turned back to her work at the stove without saying a word. Little Preston could swear, though, that her ears actually perked up and turned backward a little.

"I just wanted you to know what was happening," Preston continued, still speaking to Mattie, "in case Preston Junior doesn't have a good explanation for his behavior, which will mean he'll be going to bed without his dinner tonight, and you won't have to cook so much."

Little Preston was panicking inside now, not so much for the fried chicken, mashed potatoes, and collard greens, which were always delicious, but for the lemon meringue pie and ice cream that they were going to have for dessert. He swallowed hard, sitting there waiting for his father to continue.

"That was a pretty little girl sitting on the porch around the corner, son. What's her name, anyway?"

Little Preston was truly perplexed at this line of questioning and the cheerful, almost playful tone in his father's voice.

"Huh … ahh," said Little Preston.

"What'd you say, son? Her name's what?"

"Romaine, Daddy."

"You like her, son?"

"What?"

"Do you like her, Preston Junior?"

Little Preston looked over at his mother for help, but her back remained turned to the conversation.

"Ma …" pleaded Little Preston.

"I believe your father is speaking to you now, Preston Junior. So, don't call me until he's finished."

"Son, I asked you if you liked her."

"I guess."

"So you think she's pretty and you like her, is that it?"

"I guess."

"You think she'd make a nice little girlfriend, son?"

Little Preston was really squirming in his seat, now. "Mama..."

"Don't call on your mother for help, son. Only you can answer these questions. So, please answer."

"I don't know, Daddy."

"What do you mean you don't know, son? Is this not something you've thought about before?"

"I guess."

"So, is that why you were trying to beat up on your friend Jeremy like that?"

Even Mattie stopped what she was doing to absorb the weight of the question.

"Preston Junior, I'm talking to you. Is that why you were hitting your friend Jeremy?"

"Wha... I don't know what you mean, Daddy."

"Do you think by beating up on your friend Jeremy, you're gonna make Romaine think that you're something special?"

"Huh? No. No, Daddy."

"Are you sure, son?"

"Yes. Yes, I'm sure."

"Okay, let's go into the living room."

Once in the living room, he motioned for Little Preston to remain standing, and began speaking.

"Boys, friends are special people. Now that you are friends, you will always be friends. And you have to always treat one another like special people. That means that you never try to hurt one another. And if one of you makes the other mad, you don't fight each other. If you can't talk it over, because maybe you're still too mad, you should just walk away until you're not mad any more. Do you understand?"

In unison, "Yes, sir."

"Are you sure you heard that, Preston Junior?"

Fat Head almost giggled, and Little Preston gave him a quick, mean stare. "Yes, Daddy."

"Okay, we're getting ready to eat now, so Stephen, Jeremy, the boys'll see you after dinner, okay?"

17

Washington, D.C., late Summer 1957

The summer went on almost like a fairy tale for the Downs family. Mattie and Preston Sr. became frequent hosts in an invigorating social scene. And though his parents didn't drink or smoke, Little Preston could tell they really enjoyed their new friends, who all seemed to drink and smoke. And talk about a young Southern preacher named Martin Luther King, Jr. They were glad that a Negro leader was finally standing up and telling the truth about American racism and not getting ruined like Paul Robeson who had once sung on stage with Butch's mother. "It's like they'll always want us to be riding in the back of the street-car," Prez heard one of the adults remark.

For his part, Little Preston and his friends had a completely different relationship with streetcars. It had to do with the streetcar tracks.

The craze that summer was roller skating and all the kids had skates. It was a common sight to see a father gingerly guiding his wobbly child along the pavement until there was a little momentum built up. "Alright, there you go. Don't be afraid. Just be steady, nothing fancy. Keep your feet pointing straight. Straight! Not all cockeyed. Keep your feet pointing straight, will you? Steady now. That's right. Nice and steady. See. There you go. Alright, are you ready? I'm gonna let go. Just be steady. You ready?"

And then there were Little Preston and his skating buddies, led by Putt-Putt. They were a galloping herd that ripped all around the neighborhood at breakneck speed. They never skated on the sidewalk. And because their neighborhood did not contain any big thoroughfares, all the traffic was local and the parents knew what to look out for when they were driving. Their skating had a certain aura of derring-do, like they had no concern in the world for their own safety, like they were invincible.

From right after breakfast to just before dinner they'd skate all around the neighborhood. But jumping the streetcar separated the leaders from the pack by racing parallel to the tracks, jumping in and out between them while doing forward and backward scissors. There were only two other skaters besides Putt-Putt who could lead the pack: Little Preston and Shaggie. But Putt-Putt was the true leader, because he could do something no one else they knew could do—rolling backflips.

It was mid-August and the weathermen on TV were alternating between "sweltering" and "suffocating" to describe the humidity-drenched heat that had descended upon the capital city. Prez was alternating between trying to sleep on his right side and his left, having a sore back from a failed rolling backflip.

In the middle of the night he and Gussie were awakened by their mother's gut-wrenching wailing. Little Preston ran over to Gussie's bed to put his arms around him because Mattie's crying made Gussie cry. Their Uncle Cadgie was the first to enter their bedroom. He was crying. Then came Rolando and Troy. They were all crying. All three uncles came over to the boys and hugged them. Cadgie and Rolando kept looking at their faces and smoothing back the boys' hair with their tear-soaked palms.

Troy couldn't look at them without saying, "They're just like him. Those boys are full o' their daddy."

Cadgie picked Little Preston up and Rolando picked Gussie up. They went downstairs and beheld a strange sight. Their mother and grandmother were sitting on the sofa together, holding each other and crying on each other's shoulders. Their grandmother had not been over to their new house since they moved out of her place. And they had never observed the two women show any form of affection toward one another. Even Gussie noticed, looking quizzically at Little Preston before saying, "Look, Press, Mommy and Grandma love each other." Little Preston looked at them with amazement.

"Put me down," said Little Preston to his Uncle Cadgie after he surveyed the living room and saw no sign of his father. "C'mon, Uncle Cadge, put me down." His uncle didn't want to because the adults had not figured out what to say. But Little Preston squirmed and kicked his feet so much that his uncle put him down. Little Preston ran into the kitchen. No daddy. He looked out in front, and didn't see his father's car. "Where's Daddy?"

His mother and grandmother began to cry even harder then.

His uncles started sobbing more. "Where's Daddy?" he demanded. He looked at all the adults in the room again, looked at Gussie crying in his Uncle Rolando's arms, and ran into the kitchen, took a long-handled scrub brush from under the kitchen sink and began beating the floor with it.

"Where's my father? Where's my father?"

Cadgie rushed into the kitchen, snatched the scrub brush from Little Preston, swung him around by his shoulders, and knelt down in front of him.

"Your daddy is dead, Preston Junior. He's dead ..."

112

Tears streamed down Little Preston's face. They gushed. But he made no sound. His body became rigid, his eyes were squeezed shut. His fists were clenched.

"Those white men killed him, didn't they, Uncle Cadgie?"

Cadgie marched him back into the living room where for a brief moment everyone's weeping had stopped long enough to look at Little Preston to make sure he was alright. "Those white men killed my father, didn't they?" he asked of the adults in the room. Something was happening inside of him as he realized that at this time in his life when he needed them to give him answers they were failing him. He steeled himself, wiped his face and went over to his mother.

"It's okay, Mama, I'll be big one day and I'll take care of you and Gussie. And I'm going to kill the men who killed my father."

Just as he was about to take off running back into the kitchen to grab that brush again to do some more smashing, his Uncle Cadgie grabbed him.

"Listen, boy, nobody said anybody killed your father. What are you talking about killing someone? Your father would not like you talking like that. Not at all. You don't really mean that anyway. You're just mad and confused."

"Can you tell me that those white men didn't kill my father? Can you tell me?"

The truth was that his father had been found in a hotel room, seated in a chair with a bullet hole through his head. The hotel was owned by one of Stein's associates who owned a string of sleazy hotels, all of which had special rooms set aside expressly for gambling. And the hot game had become Russian roulette. Slip a single bullet into the cylinder of a gun, spin the cylinder, place the barrel of the gun to your head, and pull the trigger. Each trigger pull was worth $500. The final pull, number five, was worth a thousand dollars. If you were lucky, you could walk away from a game $3,000 richer. If you weren't, you'd end up like the popular young Negro singer Johnnie Ace, who shot himself backstage at the Howard Theater.

At the funeral Mattie and Denie could not stay away from the coffin. They kept getting up to go look at Preston, stroke his face, smooth his hair, and kiss him. Gussie kept falling asleep. Little Preston sat perfectly erect throughout and never looked at the coffin, never acknowledged the presence of a single living soul.

The sermon, preached by the ever-militating Reverend Josephus Clark, spoke of the gallantry with which Preston had represented dark Washington during his forays into the world of amateur and professional boxing. "But Preston Downs carried the heavy burden of regret. When the unfortunate accident occurred in his bout with Heathie Nettles and that boy died, Preston came to me with tears in his eyes asking me to help him beg God for forgiveness, because he never intended to take that boy's life. His heart was so heavy. And you know why, because he was angry in that fight. By the time he finally got Nettles pinned into that corner in the ninth round, Preston couldn't make himself stop punching. He said it was the screams of Heathie's wife at ringside that finally snapped him out of it. Let us not carry anger in our hearts because it will cloud our minds, blur our vision, and lead us down the path to unrighteousness. You may recall, Preston laid the championship belt he won from Heathie Nettles across his coffin; 'laying a champion to rest.'

"I know many of you are angry. None of us believe Preston would gamble with his life. But there is no one we can point a finger at anyone and say, without hesitation or doubt, 'you are responsible for the death of our beloved Preston Coleman

Downs.' We're about to lay a champion to rest. It is not the boxing champion I refer to here, but the champion husband, the champion father, the champion son, the champion brother, the champion friend, and we're going to honor his memory by championing life as he did by putting anger to rest."

Little Preston had listened and had heard no mention of his father being asleep. And he had listened hard through the wheezing noise of his own breath, through the merciless throbbing of that bass drum in his chest and through the electric pulses continuously stabbing at his fingertips and toes. His whole body felt like it might explode. He watched as two deacons began to close the lid on the coffin, and the brothers, along with two cousins and two very close friends of Preston's from his boxing days rose as pallbearers, and he bolted towards the coffin and screamed, "Don't close it, my daddy's in there. Leave him alone!" He started kicking and punching the two deacons. His uncle Cadgie grabbed him, lifted him off his feet, and began to carry him out. He let out such a piercing wail that some covered their ears. He heard his mother scream, "Oh, my lord, Preston Junior! Preston Junior! Stop it! You hear! Stop it!" He looked over at his grandmother and she looked away from him in disgust.

❧

Almost immediately after the funeral, his mother moved them into a new apartment in another part of town on A Street, Northeast, near the intersection of East Capitol Street, which was the boundary line separating Northeast from Southeast Washington, and Seventeenth Street. Down the street from their front door was Eastern High School and down the back alley was Mount Moriah Baptist Church.

115

The new neighborhood may have been more populous with larger residences, but their apartment was a tiny one-bedroom unit. There was a long narrow hall with entrance ways to a front room crammed with a sofa, coffee table, and end table; next, the one bedroom stuffed with two double beds; a bathroom looking like it had been installed in a closet; and at the end of the hall a kitchen littered with a fuse box, hot-water tank, a small stove, refrigerator, and rust-laden sink. They ate and did homework at a very small square table pushed up against a wall.

On Sundays he could hear the rollicking choir and band. He often saw youth activities taking place in the church yard. One day he overheard his mother talking to his aunt and telling her that for the first time since before she left home to go to college, she felt the need to belong to a church. Practically the next day they were churchgoers.

They didn't have a lot, but what they had was clean and neat. Little Preston and Gussie would often hear "cleanliness is next to godliness" from their mother. Every Saturday morning was clean-the-house day. After that it was off to the laundromat. And while the clothes were in the machines, off to the grocery store. Their sole vehicle, a red wagon, was a beloved addition to the family and Preston felt it was his responsibility to pull it no matter how heavy. He had to take care of his mother and little brother.

18

Washington, D.C, Spring 1958

Whack! Thump-thump-thump! "Oh shit, man!" Thump. Whack-whack-whack! Crash!

"Oh shit, man. C'mon! I'm down. I'm down, man. Oh shit. What the fuck! I can't breathe outta my nose."

The leader of the Anacostia Destroyers lay in a heap amongst a pile of garbage cans in the back alley behind Mount Moriah Baptist Church. This invasion by the Anacostia Destroyers was literally in Prez's own backyard.

"I told you Anacostia punks not to be coming around here starting trouble."

Prez had filled out over two years. He was a regular at the YMCA on Seventeenth Street. He went there to box and lift weights. His self-discipline effectively checked his temper most of the time, but he had no tolerance for the bullying of gangs. He was fighting more on the street than in the gym.

"And you tell your brother, that punk-assed Catfish, that I'll kick his ass, too, a lot worse than this."

Prez figured it must have taken him about ten whole seconds to kick Kingfish's butt. It all happened so fast that Kingfish's boys didn't have a chance to get there and gang up on Prez; nor did the customary circle of Eliot Junior High chanters, taunters, and screamers that formed around street fights and crawled up and down streets and alleys like some kind of huge amoeba with the fight in the middle. By the time the first of the crowd showed up Prez was helping Kingfish to his feet.

"Hey, man, what's going down?" the crowd shouted. "What happened, Prez? Kick his ass, man!" "It's over? What da ya mean, it's over?" "Fight, fight, fight, fight!" The crowd could be insatiable. But Prez would have none of it.

"It's over, I said. Me and Kingfish have decided to be friends, you know. No more fighting. No more us being worried about the Destroyers coming around for anything but a good time. Ain't that right, Kingfish?"

Of course, Kingfish had agreed to no such thing, but if he wanted to get out of that back alley with his brains not scrambled up, and walking under his own power, he knew he had to agree. Some members of his gang were there now, but the crowd would never allow them to gang up on Prez. There was one thing that still mattered among them: honor. All fights must be fair. No weapons, and no ganging up on anyone. And a word given was a word not broken. Prez was in top form, giving his opponent an honorable way out. Now Kingfish understood why they called him Prez. He acted like he was some kind of president, going to war on your butt one minute, then holding out a hand of friendship the next. Prez wondered where he got the name "Kingfish." He hated it but would not hold that against him.

What wasn't known was that this was only part of the story as to how Preston Coleman Downs, Jr. came to be known as Prez. All anyone had to do was to look under Prez's bed at the stack of old 78 rpm records Prez had inherited from his father via his Uncle Cadgie. These were some of the same records his daddy used to play when they would sit out on the front porch during those wonderful summer nights on Sherman Avenue. They'd be sitting there with the music coming through the window and drifting up into the air all around them. The tenor saxophone had such a big, round, full sound without being overpowering. One minute it would float, the next it would hop, skip, and jump, while the next, it would sprint a little; all the while dripping honey.

"I like that, Daddy," Little Preston would say as his father would sing the words, "I just can't get started with you ..."

"Oh, do you now, son? You didn't know I could sing, did you?"

Little Preston would go into a giggling fit.

"No, Daddy, I meant the horn. I really like it."

"Oh," a slightly dejected Preston would reply, with Grandma Denie saying under her breath, "Hmph, that baby boy ain't nobody's fool," and Mattie giggling into her hands.

"That's Prez playing his tenor saxophone, son. He's the best. That's why they call him 'Prez.' He's the president of all the saxophone players."

19

Washington, D.C., Fall 1958

Preston Coleman Downs Jr. entered seventh grade at Eliot Junior High School that September as a transferee. It was the first time that he and his little brother went to schools in different parts of town. Though it felt odd, it was only proper. Gussie was still a kid. But Prez felt he was now a grown man, practically, and he had a reputation to look after.

He was surrounded by a new group of friends, his own crew; tall, skinny Sticks; big, armadillo-like Tons; big, doughy Dee Cee, and his virtual twin Brennie-Man.

On the first day of school, Prez strolled up Eliot's big, wide concrete steps accompanied by his buddies. They had established a reputation as the tough bunch over the summer, so being with them carried a certain panache. As a bunch of girls approached, it was reasonable to think they just wanted to hang. But Lorraine Lorton jumped in front of Prez and let fly the meanest left hook he'd ever seen. Prez responded by ducking under Lorraine's left, spinning her around and pinning her in a bear hug from behind.

"Ow, man! Get that booty, Prez!"

"Shit, man! Your first day here and you humpin' up on some prime bootay!"

"Oh, man. Nobody, but nobody, has ever gotten next to that, Prez!"

"Yeah, yeah! Get that booty, man!"

It wasn't just the guys in his crew who were egging him on. And it wasn't just guys, either.

"You get your damned hands off me, you lowlife son of a bitch! You let me go right now or I'll kick your ass! You think you so bad! You ain't shit! Git your goddamn hands off me! You hear? Lemme go!"

Lorraine was screaming at the top of her lungs as she squirmed, and wiggled, and kicked backward with the heels of her shoes.

"Calm down! I'll let you go. Just calm down. You swung at me, remember. You started this. What's this all about anyway? Stop it, girl! Stop it and I'll let you go."

Only Prez and Lorraine saw absolutely nothing sexual in what was taking place between them.

"Okay. Okay, I'm going to let you go now. But don't try to hit me again, okay?"

"Just take your fucking hands offa me, you shitface!"

Jesus, thought Prez, *where did a girl get a mouth like that?*

Prez quickly loosened his grip and pushed her away, shoving her into the arms of the group of girls with whom she had been standing. They caught her, and held onto her, because she spun her tightly coiled body around and, like a cobra, was ready to strike again.

"If she's your friend," Prez said, speaking to the group of girls, "you better hold her there. She don't need to be jumping up in my face anymore. You understand?"

From the group of girls came:

"Oh, man, you ain't so bad!"

"Who the hell you think you are?"

"Maybe we should let her go so she can kick your ass!"

121

"Maybe we should all just kick your little black ass!"

From somewhere else in the larger crowd sounded the alarm, "Hey, Moses comin'!"

Principal J. J. Moses came bounding through the door of the office and plowed his way down the hall. An ex-defensive lineman with the fabled Green Bay Packers football team, he always looked as though he was ready to get down into a low crouch and lay a massive hit on anything moving. Prez, of course, had never seen him before, didn't know who he was, but was not averse to giving his undivided attention to any man who was that big.

"Son, I've never seen you here at my school before. And the first time I lay eyes on you, you're causing trouble! Worse than that, you're pushing a girl around! I don't know who you are. I don't know where you've come from. But I can tell you one thing, you won't be attending class here!"

A massive, meaty, mighty, hand came down in a flash and before Prez knew it, he was being dragged down the corridor by the back of his shirt collar. The front of his shirt collar was choking him, and two buttons popped off as he was hauled down the hall. His shoes dragged and scuffed along trying to regain his footing.

"Principal Moses! Principal Moses! Excuse me, Principal Moses. What happened is not his fault. He didn't start anything. He was just minding his own business."

Principal Moses stopped in his tracks just as he was about to push open the door to the office. Surprised that anyone would dare address him at the very height of his anger, he let go of Prez and turned to see who was calling after him. A most mesmerizing girl had come to Prez's defense.

"Oh, it's you, Miss Wilbanks. Ready to stand up for another lost cause, I see."

"But, Mr. Moses, it really wasn't his fault. Someone else started it. All he was doing was trying to keep somebody from hitting him. That's all. Honest, Principal Moses."

"Well. Is that so?" Principal Moses placed his fists on his hips as he looked around to scan the faces of all the students who were gathered around watching these events unfold. A few of them tried to duck away before Principal Moses had a chance to see them. Or, so they thought.

"Not so fast, Mr. White," said Principal Moses, shaking his head and giggling to himself that William "Reeves" White, all six feet three of him, would think he could hide behind his schoolmates and escape being questioned.

"Mr. White, did you see what took place between this young man—whose name I don't know—" Principal Moses cast an evil leer back at Prez "—and the young lady?"

"My name's Preston Coleman Downs, Junior, sir."

Principal Moses' eyebrows raised for an instant. He had not expected to be addressed in such a respectful manner by someone he initially thought to be a common street thug. And he certainly did not expect the boy to be Preston Downs's son.

"Well, well, Mr. Preston Coleman Down..."

"Junior, sir."

Amid muffled giggling from the crowd of students, Principal Moses cut Prez another evil stare, then continued speaking to all six feet, three inches of William Reeves White, who was still trying to maneuver himself into a position well behind his much shorter schoolmates. "Mr. White, what went on here?"

"Well, ah, Principal Moses..."

"Speak up, son! I can hardly hear you!"

This made Reeves flinch. Now there was more giggling, not so muffled.

"Alright, that's enough!" cautioned Mr. Moses. "I said speak up, Mr. White."

"Ahem, ahem. Well, ahem, Principal Moses, Prez was just walking up the steps and had to duck this wild swing from one of the Mo-Girls."

"Prez?" Principal Moses leaned in close to Prez's face. "Is that your *nom de guerre*?"

"Excuse me, sir. I don't know what that is."

Principal Moses' eyebrows really shot up now. "What have we here? A young street tough who isn't afraid to admit when he doesn't know something? Well, well, well."

"I'm not a street tough, sir," replied Prez.

"Oh? With a name like Prez? And with a reputation that obviously precedes you into my corridors of learning?"

"What do you mean, sir?" asked Prez, now trying to be half-coy.

"Do you know this tall gentleman?" asked Principal Moses.

"No sir," replied Prez.

"Well, he certainly seems to know you, Mr. Prez. And what about you, Miss Wilbanks, do you know Mr. Prez here?"

"Well, no, Principal Moses. Not exactly."

"What do you mean 'not exactly?' Either you know him or you don't. Or is it that you know of him?"

"Yes, Principal Moses."

"Yes, you know him, or yes, you know of him?" Principal Moses was getting impatient. "Answer me, Debra Wilbanks."

"Of him," said Debra.

"I see," said Principal Moses, sensing in Debra a much more than casual interest in Prez. "I'll tell you what else you know, Miss Wilbanks, especially since your cousin Lorraine is the leader of the Mo-Girls; you know that it was your cousin who took that—how did you characterize it, Mr. White? 'Wild swing?' —don't you?"

Debra was silent.

"Miss Wilbanks!" demanded Principal Moses, "it was your cousin, wasn't it?"

Debra remained silent.

"Well, Mr. White, was it Miss Lorraine Lorton, leader of … oh, forgive me, how could I forget, 'president' of the Mo-Girls who threw that 'wild swing'?"

Principal Moses knew he would not get an answer. Nobody ratted on anybody in that school. Not even big chicken Reevie-Boy, who was only fearless on the basketball court. But Principal Moses knew these kids better than they knew themselves, as he liked to boast.

"Miss Wilbanks, for the last time, it was your cousin, wasn't it? You come into my office. Now!"

"Wait!" exclaimed Lorraine. "It was me." Even though she was so angry at Debra for coming to Prez's defense, she would not stand by and see her cousin get into trouble for something she had done.

A sly smile made its way across Principal Moses' lips.

"No, this isn't right!" interjected Prez, stunning Principal Moses and the student crowd.

"Excuse me, Mr. Downs. What did you say?"

"I started it, sir." Principal Moses didn't know these kids as well as he thought.

"And how did you do that, Mr. Downs?"

"I called her ugly."

"You what?"

"No he didn't," said Lorraine.

"Yes, I did, sir. You can let her go now."

"Okay, okay. I've heard enough. Both of you in my office, now! The rest of you, off to your homerooms, and you'd all better have an A-plus year!"

20

Washington, D.C., Spring 1959

"Wanna dance?"

It was the girl who had spoken up for him his first day at school last year. Prez had asked around about her. Debra was a grade ahead of him, already thirteen, and was going to high school next year.

Smokey Robinson and the Miracles were spinning on the platter. Practically everyone in Wellington's basement was singing, "My mama told me, you better shop around." Everyone was dancing, and clapping, and laughing and sweating. Wow, Prez thought to himself, a real party. He had heard about these things, but had never been to one. He was the youngest of the crowd, just twelve, but had been accepted into this in-crowd because of his street-fighting and athletic prowess at school.

"And don't tell me you don't know how, either. I've seen you at school cuttin' up with your boys 'n all with that little portable radio of yours. All the girls talk about it. We wonder why we've never seen you at any of our parties. Well, here you are now, and I want you to dance with me. C'mon!"

Just as she pulled him out into the middle of the dance floor, another song began, *Anyone Who Had a Heart*, by Dionne Warwick.

Dionne Warwick's voice was the sweetest he had ever heard. And Debra Wilbanks, the sweetest girl he had ever seen. Perfect.

He had never slow-danced with a girl. Her cheek snuggled up against his neck and her free hand roaming across his shoulders and around the back of his head made his senses spin.

"Prez," said Debra, "It's nice slow-dancing with you." James Brown was now singing, "Please, please, please, please ..." This was the third slow record in a row. The party was falling into a kind of slow-dance groove. Prez peeped around him on the dance floor and saw couples kissing, feeling each other up, and grinding their bodies together.

Prez's right arm was around Debra's waist. He had her hand in his. He made sure his body did not press against hers. His neck was erect to accommodate her bewildering need to keep her face buried there. He realized he was nervous. He wanted to be a cool, calm, and collected gentleman. And certainly not to be stupid and misinterpret Debra's actions. So, when she kissed him on the neck the first time, he wasn't sure. But the second time, she actually sucked his neck right up to behind his ear, causing him to have the largest, most painful erection he had ever experienced.

Debra shifted herself so that she could rub up against him. He was now really nervous. Perspiration dripped from his armpits. After a tug-of-war of sorts, Debra finally pried his hand from her waist and pushed it down to her buttocks. Prez just let his hand lie limp there for a moment then put it back around her waist. Debra stuck her butt out a bit and pulled his hand onto her right buttock and pushed. "Now, leave it there, Prez. Okay?" she whispered. Then she went back to rubbing herself up against him with an abandon that proved illuminating to Prez. He thought that there must be something wonderful and joyful about the way she was feeling. And he was sure, they were now girlfriend and boyfriend.

Next thing he knew "Louie Louie" was spinning and the basement was again a pounding, writhing, sweating, mass of bodies. Debra was now in the middle of the dance floor dancing with a group of girls. She looked over and blew him a kiss as she wiggled and dipped to the music, which put a yard-wide smile on Prez's face.

Prez walked over to his buddies standing around the record player arguing about the song's lyrics.

"C'mon, man. Hey, Tons, he's not sayin' that, man. C'mon."

"Yeah, he is, man," replied Wellington, "He's sayin' 'fuck,' man. What else do you do with a girl across the bed?"

"Don't be stupid, Tons," someone else said. "They wouldn't make no record like that, man."

"I'm tellin' you," said Wellington, "he sayin' 'fuck the girls all across the bed.'"

They all broke out in raucous laughter to the evil stares of girls within earshot of their conversation.

Then Wellington started singing at the top of his lungs, "Ah, Louie, Louay … y'all check it out now. Here it comes, here comes the good part. Listen up y'all. Fuck the girls all 'cross the bed! Yeah, y'all hear that. I told ya, fuck the girls all 'cross the bed."

Wellington hadn't noticed that the dancing had stopped. He hadn't noticed that he was practically alone on the dance floor as his party-goers respectfully made their way up the stairs. And how he managed to not notice the enormous shadow of his father standing right behind him would be talked about for weeks after.

As they solemnly filed out the front door, all Prez and the guys could do was to shake their heads as they listened to the squeals of big Wellington, their beloved "Tons," getting thrashed by his father.

21

Washington, D.C., Summer of "fiddy-nine"

Prez began hanging out with boys much older than him at a corner on the southeast side of Lincoln Park. School was out. Gussie was with his aunt and his mother was teaching summer school.

"Lookit! Lookit, I tell you. Dem stupid white men ober at Chevrolet want us to buy their bran' new shiny nineteen hundred and fiddy-nine Impala cause it's da—lookit what it says here, heck, I can read." It was now high noon on what was a sweltering June day and old Preach Chambers was holding court at his usual spot, sitting on the mailbox just in front of Richardson's Drugstore. "It says right here, 'Da last and de best of de big Chevies of da decade!' Now ain't dat what it says? Lookit! Dey so stupid."

Lincoln Park separated the white haves from the Negro have-nots. The US capitol just eleven blocks west could just as well be on the moon. But the corner was a gathering point and a vantage point. People like Prez were not welcome west of the park. And their treatment by the police indicated there was a de facto rule that the park itself was off-limits to the black populace of the Lincoln Park area.

"But I tells you one thing," continued Preach, "even tho' dey can't count, they sho'nuf ain't stupid to cut the top off'n dat car. 'Cause it gonna be a hot one dis year. Dis summa 'o fiddy-nine gonna be a hot one!"

Under his soiled, sweat-stained fedora, Preach's face dripped sweat that gathered at the bottom of his scraggy beard.

"Hey you! You wid da funny hat on. How old ye be?"

Under the floppy white canvas hat peered the eyes of nineteen-year-old Alvin Proctor. Everyone was in awe of Alvin. Al was a multi-sport phenomenon who had fielded offers of a football scholarship from Caltech, a basketball scholarship from North Carolina State, and a track scholarship from Bowling Green. But he decided to stay in Washington to be near his mother and younger siblings after his father, a noted and decorated Washington police detective, was found dead with a bullet through his head.

"Hey, boy! I says, when you born, son? How old is ye?" Preach sat up real tall on the mailbox now, his back straight, neck erect, jawline flexing. "Ain't you got no manners, boy? Didn't yo' daddy teach you to be r'specful o' yo' elders? Well, den, boy, what is it? Yo' age. When you born?"

"I was born in 1940. I'm nineteen years old."

"Whhaaa! ... Is you really, son?" Preach was dumbfounded that on his very first try, he picked on the right one. He just couldn't believe it. From his back pocket he pulled his ever-present brown paper bag, uncapped the bottle and threw his head back for a long pull of rotgut wine. "C'mon! You was really born in fordy? Naawww! Ha!"

Still holding his brown paper bag in one hand and his *Washington Star Post* newspaper in the other, Preach continued, "Okay, you dere whose daddy taught him real good manners, heh, heh ... you say you be nineteen now? Okay, now listen bery careful." Old Preach took another long pull on his wine, wiped his mouth with his hairy old forearm, recapped his bottle, and let out a big "Aahhh" that exposed all of his toothless gums. He put the bag back into his back pocket and squinted down real hard from his perch on top of the mailbox at Al. "When you gonna start yo' third decade on this earth, sonny-boy? Ha!"

"When I turn twenty-one."

"Well, I'll be … Hot damn!" Preach slapped his hand on his thigh. "Hot damn, boy! Hot damn! Ha!" Preach began unfurling the newspaper page that had gotten crumpled during the time he had begun his inquiry, and through the multiple pulls on the wine bottle. He said, "Dat boy's smart!" The other kids looked on and smiled. Any of them could have answered that easy question.

Some of the older boys and girls had paired off and were engaged in various forms of communication, verbal and other-wise. A couple of the bigger guys had begun a non-contact spar-ring session that Prez thought had the promise of escalating into a serious full-contact contest. That petered out quickly under the scorching weight of the day. A quartet of boys with a trio of girls began harmonizing under the shade of one of the big oak trees. Against this backdrop, Mr. Richardson came out of his drugstore with a bag full of garbage in one hand and a sandwich and soft drink for Preach in the other.

"I've told you, Mr. Chambers, that you should be putting real food in your stomach, and not that stuff you keep hidden in your brown paper bag. That stuff will eat a hole right through your stomach and destroy your liver if you're not careful."

"Why, thankee Mistah Rich'son. You's always so nice to me." Preach hastily and messily refolded his newspaper and sat on it again.

Preach munched on his sandwich and slurped down his soft drink. The vocal septet was singing an a cappella compil-ation of Platters songs. Everyone else seemed to be just lazing around laughing and talking, when *screech!* Car doors slammed shut.

"Why don't you niggers move along, now?"

The cop who got out on the driver's side was a huge, red-faced, cigar-chomping, beer-bellied man who wore his police cap cocked to one side.

"I said fa you niggers to move along, now! Git!"

The cop who alighted from the passenger side was practically a twin of his partner, only smaller. His police cap, however, was cocked in the opposite direction. He was also more intimidating than his bigger partner. His billy club, which he continuously slapped into the palm of his hand, seemed larger. And so did his gun. It had a barrel so long, it stuck out the end of his holster.

"Are you niggers deaf? Did y'all hear me say git?"

The stillness was defeating and strangling.

"Whew. It be a hot one today, don't it, Mr. Officer?" said Preach, once again unfurling his newspaper to the page containing the advertisement for the 1959 Chevrolet Impala.

"Yo' car!" he continued, squinting down at the car from his perch, "It's yo' car in the paper, see!" The big cop came over to the mailbox and snatched the paper away from Preach.

"Lookit!" exclaimed Preach pointing to the Chevrolet advertisement in the paper, "Ain't that yo' car? How come you gotta top on yours?"

"Look here, Teddy, he's right. The old nigger ain't so dumb after all. It's not every day someone can identify the model of a car under all the black and white paint, big letters, and lights."

As the other cop came to look at the paper, Preach continued. "Well, thankee kindly, sir, fa sayin' I ain't so dumb."

All the kids remained stone quiet, stone still, and stone staring at the cops. Preach continued, "Hm. Too bad they got the ad wrong."

"Whaddaya mean wrong? We got a '59 Impala, and that's what's in the paper, here," replied the big cop.

"No, No! I means da part 'bout da decade being ober."

Preach looked down at the kids and winked.

"Listen, old nigger, maybe you ain't so smart after all. Of course, it's the end of the decade. It's the end of the fifties. It's 1959!"

"Do tell," said Preach. "You 'gree wid dat, sir?" speaking to the other cop who remained silent except for the sound of his billy club slapping his palm. "A decade be ten, right. Mr. Officer?"

"That's right . . ."

"Ha! Gotcha!" exclaimed old Preach as he slapped his palm on top of his thigh. "Gotcha!"

The smaller cop took out his billy club and started beating Preach from behind, then the big cop joined in. Preach fell off the mailbox. The wine bottle in his pocket broke and gouged a deep wound in his leg. The cops kept hitting him.

"Ow! Ow! Ooh. Oh, Jesus, you killin' me!" Blood flowed from his head and mouth.

The girls began screaming, "They're killing him, they're gonna beat him to death. Make them stop. Do something!"

First Alvin Proctor, then some of the other older boys rushed the cops and grabbed their sticks from them. They threw the sticks to the other side of the street and backed away. Mr. Richardson came rushing from his drugstore and exclaimed, "My god! Have you killed him? Call an ambulance! Aren't you going to call an ambulance?"

Just as he turned to go back into his drugstore to call for an ambulance, they heard a gunshot.

The kids reflexively jumped, ducked, and raised their arms to shield themselves.

"Who's shot?" "They shot somebody!" "Who's hurt?" "Is anybody hurt?"

Alvin Proctor was lying on the ground beside a tree.

"Oh my god!" said Mr. Richardson. "You can't just go around shooting people."

He and some of the kids rushed over to Alvin, who was unconscious, but breathing. He had been shot in the shoulder. The impact had sent him reeling backward, causing him to hit his head against the tree and knocking him unconscious.

The girls were screaming and crying, the boys were shouting at the cops. Three additional squad cars arrived before the ambulance. The cops, guns drawn, shoved the kids away from Alvin and made them face a wall with their hands behind their heads.

"If any of you move, we'll shoot!"

The ambulance put the old man on the stretcher, Alvin on the floor, and careened away with sirens blaring.

"Who are you?" asked a sergeant of Mr. Richardson.

"I own this drugstore," came the reply.

"I see," replied the sergeant, looking up at the sign. "Did you see what happened, Mr. Richardson? It is Mr. Richardson, isn't it? Well, good. Did you see anything?"

"Well, of course I did. Your police officers were beating that old man, then they shot that boy!"

"Which officers do you mean?"

"Those two right over there."

"You mean they both discharged their sidearms? It appears the Negro boy was only shot once. Is that right? Once? Well, how can both of my officers shoot him if he was only shot once, Mr. Richardson?"

Mr. Richardson fell into a silence. A thick silence heavier than the heat and humidity on that Washington summer's day. A silence that made them all sweat more profusely than before. From the wall upon which the kids were lined up came a voice. It was a voice that broke through other voices around it advising it to be quiet and reminding it of the virtues of silence at a time like this.

"I said I saw who did it. And I saw how he did it."

"Who said that?" asked the sergeant.

"Oh my," said Mr. Richardson when he realized it was Prez. "He's just a child. I don't even think that boy is thirteen yet. Certainly not fourteen. He's just a child."

"I'm no child. I saw what happened. And I saw who did it. And I saw how he did it. And I'm not afraid to say it."

"Be quiet, Prez!"

"Are you stupid, man?"

"You wanna go into the paddy wagon, man?"

"You're gonna end up in a lot of trouble."

"No, he's gonna end up dead."

"Listen, Prez. I know what you're thinking," whispered one of the older guys. "But, man, this ain't about being brave. This is about being smart. Just don't say anything else."

Prez listened, and understood. This was something he had to do, though. He had to stand.

There was a large crowd of kids gathering across the street. They were starting to shout at and heckle the cops. Saying things like, "Get off our block." "Leave 'em alone." "This is Block-boy territory. You'd better get in your cars and get outta here!" "B-Boys forever."

Prez was shaken. He hadn't heard anything about B-Boys for a long time. Ever since he was a kid and his daddy was still alive. He wanted to turn around and look to see who was saying those things. But he was scared and hated to admit it to himself. Even though he was able to make his mouth move and say what he had so far, he was afraid to move his body because he didn't want to get shot. The more he felt his inner self shake from the fear of the awful violence the police could unleash, the angrier he became, until he heard his voice say, quite loudly, "I said I saw who shot Alvin and I saw how he did it and I'm not afraid to say it!"

He was suddenly more afraid of being afraid than he was actually afraid.

"The short cop from car fifty-four. He shot Alvin! I saw him."

Prez was still facing the wall. Sweat was dripping from every pore he possessed. He could feel his body shaking and hoped that no one else could see how scared he was. His head hung and his eyes were squeezed shut; he was waiting to be shot. He thought it best to get shot in the back. That way, you couldn't see it coming.

"What did you say, boy?" growled the sergeant.

Prez could hear footsteps rapidly coming in his direction. He hung his head even lower and squeezed his eyes shut even tighter. The rapidly approaching footsteps brought a solemn, fearful hush over the whole group along the wall.

From across the street Prez could still hear the crowd: "Butch lives!" "Get off our block!" "B-Boys forever!"

Prez still couldn't believe what he was hearing. His legs were getting stronger. He stopped shaking. He wasn't going to be shot in the back, he decided. He wasn't going to be shot without fighting back, even if he couldn't win. He was going to fight the bullet. As the footsteps were practically upon him, he spun, ready to fight, ready to let his fists go with the fastest and mightiest barrage of punches anyone had ever seen. For old Preach-Mouth. For Alvin. For Butch. And somehow, for his daddy.

"Preston. Come with me, son."

It was his mother's boyfriend Ellis. Detective Ellis Perkins of the Washington, D.C. police department. His rank was lieutenant, so he outranked all the other cops at the scene. He grabbed Prez by the arm and yanked him along toward his unmarked police car.

The kids along the wall turned and began shouting.

"Hey, who are you?" "Where you takin' him?" "You some kinda cop or somethin'?" Only Tons and Lightblood knew that Ellis was Prez's mother's boyfriend.

Ellis turned around, still yanking Prez along, and went back to the group lined up along the wall.

"I am Detective Perkins of the D.C. Police Department." Ellis met the looks of astonishment on some of their faces with, "Yes, there are some Negro detectives on the force. The boy has to come down to the police station and tell what he said he saw."

"But I saw the policeman with the hole in his holster shoot Alvin, too," one of the older kids said. "So did I," said another. "Me, too," said a third, who added, "he didn't even take his gun from the holster. He just kind of lifted the whole holster. Or spun it, or something, and just shot right through the hole."

"What are you kids talking about a hole in a holster?" asked Ellis. He knew that the standard-issue police sidearm was a revolver with a four-inch barrel and the standard-issue holster was one that completely enclosed the barrel. He went over to the sergeant with whom he had a heated exchange. The sergeant then went over to the two cops from car fifty-four and they got in their car and sped off.

"That's not what I ordered you to do!" screamed Ellis in the face of the sergeant. With his nose practically touching the sergeant's, Ellis spat his Army Master Sergeant venom. "I gave you specific orders, Sergeant!"

"You git right outta mah face, you hear? I don't give a shit about your war decorations, or your college education. You still a nigga! Detective or no. You still a nigga! Git the hell outta mah face! You Nazi nigger!"

Ellis turned from the sergeant, grabbed Tons from the group of kids and put him into the back seat of his car with Prez. Then he came back over to where the other kids were being held by other cops. He placed himself between the kids and the cops, then said, "The rest of you, I want you all to leave, now. I want you to get out of here. Go across the street where your friends are and then go home."

Some of the cops began moving towards the kids and Ellis turned to confront them, brandishing two ebony-handled Walther P38 semi-automatic pistols. He had taken them from a dead German officer. His reputation as a master marksman was well known on the force. As was the fact that having served under the current chief of police in the war—the same man who had planted many of those decorations on Ellis's chest—had gotten Ellis the special permission to pack those sidearms. But the white cops on the force hated seeing that German-made weapon. They'd say, "That's a goddamn Nazi gun you got there! You a Nazi? You must be. You like their guns. You a Nazi nigger!" What Ellis liked was the accuracy of the weapon, and the quick reloading. Once at the police range he had put two cliploads of bullets, fourteen rounds, into a six-inch area of a target quicker than anyone else could fire six and reload their revolver.

"Hey, Sarge, he can't do that, can he?"

"What about it, Sarge, do we let 'em go?"

"Can't we just arrest all of 'em?"

"Shut up, Patrolman," said Ellis. "You boys all get back in your cars and head back to the station, now. You too, Sergeant." The sergeant hesitated. "Sergeant," barked Ellis, "I am giving you a direct order. If you want to keep your badge, you will obey my direct order and get the hell out of here and proceed directly to the station where I will meet you in the captain's office." As the sergeant got into his squad car and drove off, Ellis turned to the other cops and said, "We'll have to file reports and take this up with the captain now, won't we?" This made the white cops wince. Their captain was the kid brother of the chief of police.

As Ellis drove away with Prez and Tons, Prez turned to look out the back window and was astonished at how large the crowd of kids had grown on the other side of the street. They were shouting and gesturing at the cops. The cops, abandoned by their sergeant, made a hasty retreat from the scene.

❧

Later that evening, Mattie, Ellis, and some other neighbours gathered over at Tons Murray's parents' place to discuss the events that had occurred in front of Richardson's Drugstore. While the adults conversed upstairs, Prez, Debra, Sticks, Dee Cee and some other young people from the neighborhood were downstairs with Tons in the Murrays' basement, playing music and talking about what had happened. "I saw what the cop did, man," said Prez. "He didn't even take his gun out of his holster. He just kinda twisted the whole thing up and pointed it at Alvin, man. I'm telling you. It all happened so fast. Then *bang!* He shot Alvin, man. For no reason. He just shot him for nothing. That's why that cop has that hole in the bottom of his holster, so he can shoot people without even taking his gun out, you know, like some kinda quick draw without drawing, you know what I mean? He just shot Alvin, man. For nothing!"

Upstairs, the parallel conversation continued. "What do you think's gonna happen, Ellis? Is that cop gonna get away with shooting that boy?" Mattie asked.

"We put on American military uniforms and went overseas to shed all that blood fighting the Nazis and Tojo just to come back home and get treated like pure … pure …" Mr. Murray's strict religious beliefs prevented him from uttering profanity. "Is anything gonna happen to that cracker? Or is it just too bad for another dead Negro boy?"

"Alvin's not dead. He's a tough kid, you know? They extracted the bullet from his shoulder and what I heard was that he's going to recover alright. His mother is a wreck, though. You know, losing her husband and all. She said the strangest thing at the hospital. She said something about the cops trying to kill her son like they killed her husband. You remember Detective Proctor, don't you? You remember he was found shot through the head in what was called a suicide. Well, Alvin is his son. Even the chief came to look in on him."

"I didn't know that, Ellis," said Mattie. "But are they going to do anything to that cracker cop who shot that boy?"

Ellis paused to take a deep breath and looked down at the floor before continuing. "They're saying it was an accident. That it was his 'faulty' holster. All they're doing is issuing Officer Briggs a regulation sidearm and holster."

Downstairs, Prez started up again.

"All those cops coming with all their guns out. I wonder how bad they'd be if they didn't have any guns. They'd have to treat us with more respect if they didn't have any guns, you know. Because they're just white punks with guns, you know. I'll bet they can't fight a lick."

"Prez, you have to stop talking like that," said Debra. "All you can think about is fighting. Do you think that really decides who is a better person? Well, do you? Don't you all remember Reverend Williams' sermon last Sunday?" Debra asked. "He was telling us all about the preacher down south who's starting to get us organized so that we can fight for our rights. That preacher, Reverend King, that's what he says, too. 'Turn the other cheek.'"

"Okay, Debra," said Prez. "Yeah, Jesus did say that. And so did that preacher. I saw him on TV. They both say that violence is not right."

"Prez! Are you punkin' out on us, man?"

"What you sayin', man? You ain't gonna fight no mo'?"

"Damn, Prez. Did that shit up on the corner get in your head, man?"

Prez had no ready answer for any of those questions from his crowd. All he knew was that what Debra was saying about that preacher in the South was making him feel different than he had ever felt before.

"My daddy," continued Debra, "says that it takes a braver person to be non-violent than violent." For once Debra was catching a glimpse of a different person under the tough-guy face that everyone knew as Prez the street-fighter. For once she felt as though she was reaching a place inside of him that neither she nor anyone else had ever reached before. She felt a sense of power. But she was also scared of where this whole new thing would lead.

"Hey, is this a party? Ain't nobody cut up on the dance floor in the last fifteen minutes. Let's dance, y'all!" Tons was ever ready to dance and act the fool. "Where's that Clyde McPhatter?"

Just then Tons's father came downstairs.

"Ellis just heard; old man Chambers died."

The floor of Tons's basement became the subject of intense scrutiny again. Only Prez's eyes locked onto Mr. Murray's.

"Who's gonna tell his family?"

"I don't know, son."

Mr. Murray turned to go back up the stairs.

"But somebody's got to tell his family that the cops killed him!"

"Preston Junior!" Mattie had wisely thought to come downstairs behind Mr. Murray. "I'm sure someone will notify that poor man's family. It's a shame what happened to him."

"Mama, they killed him like he was nothing. And then they shot Al down like he was a dog or something."

"Preston Junior, I'm telling you that there's nothing we can do about any of that. We just have to let things run their course."

"What course is that, Mama? The same one you told me and Gussie was gonna tell us who killed my daddy?"

Mattie hit Prez so hard everybody felt it but Prez. "Mama, you should stop hitting me. You only hurt yourself, 'cause it don't hurt me."

"Listen, son, you shouldn't talk to your mother like that." Ellis had made his way downstairs with the rest of the adults. He went right up to Prez, got in between Mattie and Prez and pointed his finger at Prez, mashing his finger into the frontal knob of Prez's nose.

Quicker than lightning, Prez swatted Ellis's finger away and pushed Ellis back.

"Oh my god, Prez!" exclaimed Debra in a state of shock, "Have you gone crazy?"

"Get outta my face!" said Prez to Ellis. "You're not my father!"

Prez lunged at Ellis. Mr. Murray grabbed him by the arm.

"Ellis, that boy is hurting."

"I know, Wellington. I know." He walked over to Prez with his arms outstretched.

Prez was frozen. He seemed to neither blink nor breathe. "I know you're feeling bad, son. It's not something that is easy to get over. Seeing someone you know, a friend, get hurt like that. Get shot. We've seen our share, haven't we, Joe?"

"Sure have," said Mr. Murray.

Mr. Murray placed his forefinger to his lips. Then he pointed over to where Ellis and Prez were standing. Ellis had his arms around Prez. Prez's head was tilted back as if his body was wracked with pain. His fists were clenched. His mouth was wide open, but no sound emerged. Tears were streaming down his face.

Gussie went over to his big brother and hugged him from behind. "Don't be sad, Prez. Okay?"

It was only then that Prez's fists unclenched, his body relaxed, and he returned Ellis's embrace.

"I'm sorry, Mr. Perkins. I'm sorry I pushed you."

Then he turned around, bent down and said to his little brother, "Gussie, I'm never going to let those cops hurt you, ever. Okay?" Gussie gave him a big smile. Gussie could smile like the sun. It was impossible for Gussie to smile and it not become contagious. Prez smiled back at him and hugged him.

At the home opener basketball game Prez had Debra's dancing on his mind as he watched her swish her booty and kick up her heels as captain of Eliot Junior High School's basketball cheerleaders.

It was halftime and a perfect moment for his boys to get on him about his feelings for Debra.

"Hey, Prez. What's happenin', man? What you doing in that art class with the rest o' them sop-assed sissies? What you tryin' ta prove, my man? You tryin' to show Miss Deb how sophisticated you can be o' somethin'?"

"Yeah, man. You s'pose to be some bad-assed thumper and you already pussy-whipped by that sweet little Debra. Wid her phat self. Now, ain't cha, Prez? C'mon, man. You can square wid us, man. We yo' boys."

"Ah, man. She sure can shake that booty, though, Prez. Check it out, man. Look at that action. That's the only reason you come to the games. Huh, Prez?"

There were eleven other girls on the cheerleading squad and they were all fine, phat, and funky with their stylish, sensual athleticism. But, to Prez, none of them even came close to Debra.

"Y'all should be cool, you know. Stop buggin' me about Debra. And leave my art class alone. You know? Just shut up about all that stuff, man!"

"Look out, y'all. Git ready ta run. Prez is gettin' a little peed off, now."

"Hey, man. I got my hat. I'm ready to fly, man."

"Hey, Prez. You wouldn't whup on your own boys, now would ya … jus' 'cause you all hung up on sweet Miss Deb, now?"

As the game clock wound down, Eliot Junior High was leading Peabody Junior High by just a few points.

Someone on the Peabody side obviously thought they could rattle the Eliot team with catcalling, booing, and threats. Prez looked across the floor at the loudest mouths and took note. Some of them he recognized as being members of the Anacostia Serpents and well into their high school years. This bothered him because he knew there was going to be trouble after the game and he couldn't enjoy being there, not even with sweet Debra in front of him.

"Y'all check out those Serpents over there?" queried one of Prez's crew in a rather excited voice.

"You're just seeing them, now Dee Cee?" said Prez. "Man, they've been there the whole game."

"What 'cha think, Prez? Why all them Serpents here, man?" inquired "Sticks" Wheeler, who would have been playing if it were not for deep animosity between himself and the coach.

A few of the Serpents took out rubber bands and used them to shoot broken paper clips all the way across the gym floor and up into the bleachers. One of the Eliot players had been struck and was bent over holding his face. Prez and his crew stood and glared at the Serpents on the other side of the gymnasium.

His attention was drawn to a seated figure whose face was buried beneath the brim of a cap. He sat slumped in the front row with his hands jammed down into his pants pockets. He only sprang to life when, by customary show of friendship, the two cheerleading squads swapped sides and the Eliot Junior

145

High School Strutters went over to the Peabody side of the gym to perform. Just as Debra was making her way past the bleachers where the Serpents were sitting, this fellow stood up right in Debra's path and took off his baseball cap. She stopped and looked into his face with surprise. It was obvious that they knew each other. This fellow, with his moderate height, light honey-brown skin, heavily lashed and browed eyes, and a head full of wavy hair, was "super fine" by the standards black girls imposed upon the Negro male populace. He swayed and swooned all around Debra as he spoke to her with a big toothy smile. There was an instant where a frown appeared when Debra turned and pointed over towards where Prez and his boys were standing and this fellow looked up. Just before she turned to join her cheerleading squad, this fellow planted a big kiss on her cheek. She laughed and trotted off. He stood for just another moment and scowled at Prez. He then made two fists, held them waist-high and bowed ever so slightly at Prez as if a karate match were about to begin. Prez stood, made a fist with his right hand and extended his arm so that his fist pointed at this fellow. It was Prez's signature gesture of challenge.

"Sticks. Hey, Sticks, man."

"Yeah, Prez?"

"I want you to cut out, man."

"What! What are you talkin' about, man?"

"There's gonna be some shit after the game, man, and I don't want you involved."

"Prez, man, what you talking about, man? If anything goes down I'm right here with you and the boys."

"Yeah, man. I know. You one of us, always, but I don't want you involved in this kind of thing, man. Basketball is your gift and getting into trouble isn't what you're supposed to do!"

"Prez, goddammit. I'm with y'all all the way, man."

146

"Sticks! I said split, man. We'll catch you later over at Tons's place, okay? Now, cut out, man. Go on!" Sticks left, just as Prez knew he would.

One of the advantages of being the basketball coach and the vice-principal was that Mr. Schnapple could switch hats any time he needed to. Coach Schnapple, forewarned by an incredibly intuitive Debra, became Vice-Principal Schnapple, and followed the students out of the gymnasium and onto the schoolyard where Prez and "Super Fine" were going to fight.

There had already been some pushing, jostling, and missed punches thrown by members of both sides, but the showcase fight featuring Prez and the super-fine leader of the Serpents was about to get under way.

"You ready, shorty? You ready to get your ass whipped?" swaggered the Serpent.

Prez was in his trance-like state. He just stared at Super Fine. He noticed a prominent scar over his opponent's left eyebrow and guessed that his opponent was susceptible to a right hand and would overreact to a feint to that side.

They squared off and Prez twitched his right shoulder, faking a right-hand lead, and came right behind it with a left hook. *Bam!*

Super Fine went down. Hard.

"Damn, Prez sure flattened that fool, man!"

"Oh shit, man, did you see that fake he put on the sucker, man? Oh, shit!"

"One punch, man. Prez just threw one shot, man!"

"I think Prez broke something on that sucker, man. Did you hear that crack, man?"

Super Fine had rolled over onto his knees. The leader of the Serpents mumbled as he shook his head, trying to clear the cobwebs. "Don't worry, punk, I'm gonna git up and whip your little, short, black ass." He kept rubbing his jaw line, and then mumbled, "Oh shit, my jaw, man. You did something to my jaw! I'm really gonna kick your black ass, now."

"Stay down, stupid, and I'll just walk away and we'll consider this over. But if you keep talking shit, you won't leave here on your feet," said Prez.

"I'm getting up, you punk." His speech was even more of a mumble, and slurry now. "I'm gonna kick your ass! I know karate. You caught me when I wasn't ready."

"Well, alright then, get on up. Your karate ass is mine!"

"Frederick! Frederick! You stop that fighting right now!"

Just when the Serpent leader had righted himself upon two wobbly legs, Prez had simply walked up to him and let go with a thunderous uppercut.

"I said stop that fighting, Frederick!"

Mr. Schnapple turned to Prez with hateful scorn in his eyes and blurted out, "You're just a common thug, a common street tough who needs to be put away!"

"Mr. Schnapple," said a voice from the crowd, "the other guy started it."

"Yeah," said another, "he doesn't even go to this school and he's here causing trouble."

"Frederick!" asked another. "Who the fuck is Frederick?"

"What's with you, Mr. Schnapple? The other guy is wrong. Prez goes to our school, not the other dude!"

When he looked deeply into the face of white Mr. Schnapple, he realized that the Serpent he had just knocked senseless was Mr. Schnapple's son. He looked around and saw the look of absolute horror on Debra's face, and instantly knew that she knew the whole story, too. Prez sensed that his fists had just handed him a Pyrrhic victory.

"You're fighting on school property, Mr. Downs. Your hoodlum ways are going to land you in big trouble this time. I'm calling the police!" Mr. Schnapple was livid.

"Preston! How could you?" blurted Debra. She had never called him Preston before.

"Preston? Who the fuck is Preston?" came a query from the crowd.

All the teachers called him Downs or Mr. Downs, and all the kids called him Prez. It was always that way. No one called him Preston except his mother. His grandmother and uncles all still called him Little Preston, or Preston Junior. But no one else called him Preston.

He walked over to Debra and looked at her with pleading eyes. "What's wrong with you, Debra?"

"All you know how to do is beat people up. God, Preston. You could have killed him!"

The crowd was behind Prez all the way.

"Aw, what's wrong with you, Mr. Schnapple, the other guy is wrong, not Prez."

"Nobody supposed to come around our school from outside causing trouble."

"The other guy is bigger and older than Prez, Mr. Schnapple! C'mon, man, it's the other guy's fault."

Debra would not stop. "You didn't have to hit him again, Preston. You could have just walked away."

"He could've too, Debra. Stop calling me Preston, will you?"

"I'll call you whatever I want. What are you going to do, beat me up, too?"

"Debra, what is wrong with you?

149

All of a sudden, Prez felt as if the crowd were spinning in an ever-tightening swirling mass around his head. Voices faded in and out of his consciousness. He started feeling dizzy and closed his eyes to regain his balance. Just then a big, heavy hand landed on his shoulder.

"Come into my office, will you, Mr. Downs?"

It was Principal Moses. In a strange way, Prez was relieved to see him. Prez followed him through the crowd, up the big, wide steps and down the "corridors of learning."

Hot on their heels, like a man possessed, was Mr. Schnapple.

"John, I'm calling the police on that little hoodlum!"

"Wait a minute, Fred. Can we go into my office and talk about this? I do have the situation under control."

"Well, you didn't out there in the school yard. You weren't even out there."

"But you were, Fred. You were out there even before any punches were thrown and could have stepped in long before you did. Why didn't you?"

This made Prez sit straight up and pay attention.

"Maybe we should come into my office and talk this whole thing over. That's now a formal request, Vice-Principal Schnapple. Fred. Let's go."

Prez could hear a lot of shouting. Something banged on something. Then more shouting. Then a prolonged period of quieter conversation. After what seemed like a very long time, Prez heard a door open and looked towards Principal Moses's office, expecting to see them both emerging, only to realize it was the sound of the main office door behind him opening from the corridor.

"How you doing, Little Man?"

Prez leapt to his feet.

"Uncle Cadge, man, oh, man! What're you doing here? Oh, man. I'm so glad to see you. I haven't seen you in such a long time."

It had been about three years since Prez had seen his grand-mother or his uncles. It had been about three years since his daddy died.

"Your mother called. She asked me if I wouldn't mind coming over here to your school to pick you up today. She thought it would be a good idea if the two of us spent some time talking about things, you know?"

"Ahh, so you're Preston's older brother. I'm J.J. Moses, the principal here at Eliot Junior High School."

"Nice to meet you, I'm Cadgie Williams. Yeah, you got that right, his older brother, but not his oldest brother. That'd be Detroit. I understand he played ball over at Dunbar with your older brother way back when indoor gyms still had dirt floors."

"Oh, man. You got that right," chuckled Principal Moses. "Those guys are about that old, now aren't they?" He chuckled some more. "Please come with me so that we can talk about your nephew."

"Sure, Principal Moses." He looked at Prez and gave him a wink.

Prez sat in the office waiting for the adults to finish their talking. At the base of his skull he felt the dull throbbing of an oncoming headache. He hadn't had one since they'd moved from Sherman Avenue. He tried and failed to think of something pleasant. He realized that his pleasant thoughts seemed to revolve around Debra and today she had let him down. Now his thoughts of Debra only caused him pain. He resolved never again to have a girl as a pleasant thought.

"Let's go, Little Man."

Prez hadn't even heard them come out of the office. He had been leaning his head back against a metal file cabinet. It was cold, and cold on his head always made it feel better.

"But before we leave," said Cadgie, "You have something to say, don't you? And it's more than just, 'I'm sorry.' We need to know this won't happen again."

Vice-Principal Schnapple stared at him, stone-faced and rigid-jawed. Principal Moses seemed very calm.

"I'm sorry about what happened. Even though I didn't start the trouble by myself, I'm sorry it happened."

Prez turned to walk out the door, but his uncle blocked his path.

Prez grimaced at his uncle, then turned around and said, "And I won't fight on school property any more …" Prez let that sentence trail off and felt like a punk for not saying everything he meant to say. Then he continued, "But I won't stand around and let somebody beat up on me or any of my friends."

Cadgie's eyes rolled up into his head. Principal Moses closed his eyes, pursed his lips, and brought his hands up to his lips as if he were in prayer. Vice-Principal Schnapple just continued to stare at Prez as though Prez represented everything he despised in Negro youth.

"Besides," continued Prez, "where's the other guy? How come I'm the only one in trouble? Just because he wasn't good enough to beat me doesn't mean he's not just as much to blame as me for what happened."

Prez looked Vice-Principal Schnapple right in the eyes. To his surprise, Mr. Schnapple broke their eye contact. He lowered his head, crossed his arms in front of him as if he had gotten a sudden chill and said, "Well, you know, Mr. Downs, you have a point there. We cannot reasonably ask any of you to simply take a beating, now can we? However, if a teacher is around, you should approach that teacher and make the teacher aware of the threat you perceive. And I can assure you that Mr. Frederick Schnapple will also be getting his reprimand, especially for committing the offense of causing trouble at another school amongst students not even his age. However, Mr. Frederick Schnapple cannot be here right now because he is with his mother at the hospital getting his broken jaw wired up."

Principal Moses flinched. Cadgie was ready to break Mr. Schnapple's jaw. And Prez just continued looking at Mr. Schnapple. Sensing the tension in his uncle, he asked, "Is it alright if I go now, Principal Moses? It won't happen again, sir. I'm sorry about your son, Mr. Schnapple."

"Yes. Yes, you may leave now. See you bright and early Monday morning. And no more of this kind of behavior from you, Mr. Downs. Is that understood?"

"Yes, sir."

Saturday, June 18th 1960

"What are you doing in the dictionary so early on a Saturday morning, Preston Junior?"

"Just looking up a word, Ma." He loved the fat Webster's dictionary his mother had given him for his thirteenth birthday

"Gussie, we're late and your aunt is waiting. Come along now. What are you doing in the bathroom?"

"Maybe he fell in, Mama."

Mattie gave Prez that "Don't-you-dare-mess-with-me-this-morning" look.

"Well, what's the word? Maybe I can help."

Of course, Prez knew that his mother probably knew the definition of the word he was looking for, and therefore, the correct spelling, which was really throwing him off. But he needed to do these things for himself. And besides, maybe she was just being nosy.

"It's alright, Ma. I can find it."

"Gussie," Mattie pounded on the bathroom door, "open this door this minute."

The door opened and Gussie stood there with his pants still around his ankles, tears coming down his face.

"What's wrong?" asked a now-concerned Mattie. Gussie knew how to play the tears card.

"There's no toilet paper."

"Well, why didn't you just say so?"

"I thought you'd be mad at me."

"Oh, Gussie, why would I be mad at you because we ran out of toilet paper? Preston Junior, go next door to see if the Hendersons have any."

"Yes, Ma'am."

Prez cut Gussie an evil stare. He had to get up from the dictionary and his writing pad. As he went out the door, he was still going over in his mind what he had just read: "A showy trinket or ornament such as would please a child, a piece of finery of little worth, a pretty trifle; a gewgaw (!)" He had to make some sense of it all before he and his boys made their way over to Lincoln Park.

With Gussie's butt duly wiped, Mattie rushed out the door, pulling Gussie along. Prez watched them from the front window until he was sure they were around the corner, then waited a few more minutes to be sure his mother wouldn't double back on him as she had done many times before, claiming to have forgotten this or that. Then he'd be out the door to meet up with his friends at Lincoln Park.

Washington, D.C. is in the South. Make no mistake about that. It's below both Mason-Dixon lines: the real one surveyed in the 1760s that delineated the boundary between Maryland and Pennsylvania, and the metaphorical one of the 1860s that separated the slave states of the South from those of the "free" North. Washington gets hot and muggy like any good southern city, but Lincoln Park was an oasis.

❧

The locals, of course, did not do their hopping, darting, and flitting at high noon when the bountiful sun had a habit of punishing such infidels by transforming its oozing heat into a hot mallet. So, it was with a sense of bewilderment that Prez and his crew had first encountered Prince Eduardo Flowers that previous Friday.

"What the fuck's he wearin', man?"

"I dunno. Looks like pajamas!"

"I've never seen pajamas with a hood."

"You got that right. Whatever he's wearin' looks real stupid to me. What's he doin' Prez, some kinda karate?"

Prez was agape. He had never seen such a fluid display of speed, power, and control, lightning-fast hand movements and powerful kicks, performed with ballet-like spins and leaps. The hooded figure crouched, ducked, parried, and kicked from ground level while doing what appeared to be push-ups on one arm. And that's when Prez noticed.

"You know, y'all ought to shut up. That dude is bad."

His boys fell into an instant silence. None of them had ever heard Prez refer to anybody as "bad."

"Yeah, y'all. Just shut up and check the cat out. Y'all so busy bein' stupid that you haven't noticed he's crippled."

There, under the shade of a magnolia tree, the punching, lunging, spinning, crouching, leaping, kicking figure came to an abrupt halt. He was perfectly motionless, standing perfectly balanced on that one good leg. The other leg, along with his arm on the same side, were slightly shriveled. His eyes were closed. His breathing, imperceptible.

Prez and his friends moved in closer to get a better look. This guy looked strange to them. He had Negro skin alright, but his eyes looked almost Chinese. And his hair was long, straight, and glossy black.

"Prez, what the fuck's he doin'?"

"Shut up, Tons. It's his religion. We have to be quiet until he's finished."

"Finished what?" said Dee Cee. "He looks kind of stupid if you ask me."

Prez noticed the dude's eyes open and his head lift to see who had just uttered such a remark.

"Dee Cee. I said shut up, man." But it was too late.

"You there," came the voice from beneath the hood. "You must learn that the gift of silence must be treasured whether it is being given or received. Do you know the crane? Ahh ... you don't. It's a bird, a tall bird that wades in water to fish and fight. It is always silent while on one leg out of respect for the mission nature has allotted to it. You, my big friend, would see the bird and think it fragile and vulnerable on one leg. Just like you think I am in the crane stance. But you cannot push me over. Would you care to try?"

Dee Cee went over and gave him a push. Sure enough, the hooded figure didn't budge.

"I didn't push you too hard that time."

"Well, you may push harder."

Dee Cee gave him a harder shove. Again, the cat in the pajamas was rock solid.

"Aww. What are you afraid of, Dee Cee?" said Tons. "I'll push the chump."

Tons rushed at the motionless figure with both of his arms outstretched and his big beefy hands in front like a battering ram. Just when he should have made contact, he was spun and flipped to the ground.

Prez and the rest of the gang doubled over with laughter.

"You weren't supposed to do that," said Tons, looking up from the ground.

"No, sir. You weren't supposed to do what you did," replied the strange-looking Negro with the Chinese eyes.

This was how they came to meet Eduardo Flowers. The boys immediately began calling him the Flower. For the rest of that

157

day they sat under a magnolia tree while the Flower told them tales of how kung fu had opened up worlds of opportunity to a poor kid who had been hobbled by polio.

"I come to this park all the time, since I was a boy. My Filipino mother would bring me. My Negro father wouldn't come here. Well, he did once, and the police came and beat him and arrested him. For me, this park has always been a haven. It connects me with my childhood. No one has ever bothered me. They do not know that I am an American Negro. The police see a funny-looking foreigner limping along who could not possibly present a threat to their authority, so they shun me. The other whites see a cripple from another land, so they pity me. No one sees a man. Except you boys. That is why I love the way you call me the Flower. What a lovely expression of affection and respect. Where I teach, the whites bow very low and call me Master Flowers. They are afraid of me because they know I could kill them with a single blow. They also want to take from me that which cannot be theirs to possess, my skills and my knowledge. They really don't respect me. And you," he said, turning to Prez, "I've watched you for a long time, coming over to your corner to try to prove your manhood. I must say you have some prodigious talents."

"I don't know what that word means."

"Ah-ha! You are indeed a smart one."

"No. I don't know what the word means."

"It means you have enormous potential to learn and to grow as a man because your natural openness and honesty pushes you to seek the truth. And, therefore, you would make an excellent student. You have great fighting instincts and lightning reflexes. And yes, you can hit pretty hard, for a boxer on the corner, I suppose, even though you do not understand the way of the fist, nor your inner power. You also do not understand the nature of conflict. The first task of a great fighter is to avoid conflict by seeking resolutions to disagreements. Otherwise, you will be doomed to be defeated one day, by the only one who can truly defeat you: yourself. Ah. I see my car is here. The Secret Service have come to take me to my dojo where I give them instruction."

A shiny black Chevrolet Impala pulled up to the curb with its chrome reflecting a blinding array of the spectrum of sunlight, as if it were a prism.

"Wow!" said Brennie-Man, "check that out."

"Please," said the Flower Man, "do not be impressed by baubles."

As he hobbled away towards the car, Prez yelled after him, "What's a bauble?"

"It's what the whites used to trick the Indians into giving away Manhattan Island."

"What?" said Prez.

"You will tell me next time, won't you, Mr. Prez?"

"You see the Flower anywhere, Dee Cee?"

"Naw, Prez."

They were standing under the magnolia tree where they had met the Flower.

"Hey, Prez. You should hear the cats singin' over by the park house. They blowin', man. They doin' all the Platters' stuff, man. C'mon."

"Maybe later. I want to wait a bit longer." Prez sat down on the grass. "You know, sometimes I can still smell it."

"Smell what, Prez?"

"All the stuff in the air the night Mr. Richardson's place burned. Like smoke and fire, and soot, and a rotten smell, man. Like, I smelled this funny smell in the air when the cop shot Alvin. It's all rolled into one smell, man. It gets all up in my nostrils and it bothers me."

"Yeah, man. Well, his store is right across the street. I mean it used to be. And it didn't happen all that long ago. So, you gonna smell something for a while."

"But it's not that, it's not just that kind of a smell after a fire. I told you. It's something else, something worse than just a fire smell."

"Prez, man, what can be a worse smell than a burning building?"

"Skin, man."

"What?"

"The smell of skin burning."

Tons left Prez lying in the grass under the magnolia tree looking up through the branches watching puffy clouds drift by. Prez thought about his father and the times they used to spend looking up at the faces in the clouds. He wondered why, as he got older, he could no longer see faces in the clouds. Thinking about his father made him hurt inside so he squeezed his eyes tight to keep from crying. When he opened them again, there was a face staring down at him. Her brown eyes, alive in a perpetual smile, gleamed at him from behind heavy eyelashes. Her wide mouth was so full it seemed in a perpetual pout. She had golden freckles on her nose and cheeks. Her hair was swept up in braided space buns.

"You are Prez, aren't you? Your friends told me you were over here lying in the grass. Hm. You don't look so tough. But I guess you are. At least, that's what people say."

"Who are you?"

"My father thinks you're special, too. But he thinks before you reach the destination that life has set for you, you will have a great detour, or something like that. He talks funny sometimes."

"Your father is the Flower?"

"Who?"

"Mr. Flowers. He's your father?"

"Yes, he is. I'm Tala." She offered Prez her hand.

"Oh, I'm Preston. Preston Coleman Downs, Junior," he said as he took her hand and realized that he didn't quite know what to do with it. If he shook it too firmly, he could come off looking like a dude trying to be tough. If he shook it too loosely, she could think he was weak. So, he raised her hand to his lips and kissed it. For a split second he felt her hand flinch as if she would jerk

161

it away. But when he looked up at her face, she seemed just as bewildered as him.

"Do you always do that when you meet a girl?"

"I've never done that before."

"You've never kissed a girl's hand before."

"No. Never."

"You ever kiss a girl before?"

"Not really."

"What does that mean, 'not really'?"

"It means I've been close, but I've never really kissed a girl before."

"Well, Mr. Preston Coleman Downs, Junior, I guess that means you're a virgin."

Prez's eyes widened, his face flushed. "No, I mean a kiss that I started."

"Oh, I get it," smirked Tala, "you're just so fine you don't have to start a kiss because all the girls can't wait to get their lips on you. Is that it?"

"Yeah, well I s'pose you could say that. But, it's 'cause I don't want to, you dig. I mean, I could have, you know, lots of times. You know, started a kiss. But I figured I should wait until the right girl came along; you know. Why rush it?"

"Do you always sweat on your nose and upper lip when you're nervous?"

"Who says I'm nervous? What's there to be nervous about? I don't see no shit to be nervous about."

"So, you do always sweat in those funny places when you're nervous, huh?"

"Yeah," said Prez and he burst out laughing.

Tala laughed, too, which made Prez laugh harder. Tala laughed more then blurted out, "You make me nervous, too."

"But I'm doing the sweating!" laughed Prez.

"Oh. My stomach is hurting. I've got to stop this laughing."

"Me too," said Prez. "Okay, let's stop."

Wiping their eyes and trying to right themselves, they both turned and saw Prez's gang standing there looking at both of them like they were nuts. This made them start laughing again.

"What the heck's so funny, Prez?" said Dee Cee.

"We were just talkin' 'bout yo' mama," blurted Tala, still laughing.

"Oh, shit!" said Prez, "You can joan, too?"

"Yo' mama so ugly, the blacksmith put horseshoes on her by mistake!"

Prez abruptly stopped laughing. "Wait a minute, girl! Whose mama you talkin' about?"

"It's okay, Prez," cut in Tons, "yo' mama so ugly, they don't even use no horseshoes when she's around, they just use her instead!"

"Wait a minute, whose mama you talkin' 'bout, sucker!" Prez was getting mad.

"Naw, naw, naw," said Sticks, who had just showed up in time to wade into the dozens, unaware that Prez was starting to think all the joanin' was directed at him, "yo' mama so ugly the horses refuse to step on her! Yeah! They throw the rider off first and get the hell outta there!"

"That's your ass, Sticks," said Prez as he made to go after him.

"What, man! I ain't talkin' 'bout yo' mama."

"Well, whose mama you talkin' 'bout then, punk?"

"Whose mama did you think we were talkin' 'bout, Mr. Prez?" interjected Tala, who was now no longer laughing.

"I thought Dee Cee's," said Prez, irritated at himself for sounding whiny and for even answering the question. He could get mad if he wanted to and didn't need to explain anything to this girl, no matter how beautiful she happened to be, no matter how much he was drawn to her.

163

"Well, so it's okay for us to talk about Dee Cee's mama but not yours?"

Prez turned and faced her directly. He put his hands on his hips, cocked his head to one side and said through lips drawn taut with smugness, "That's right."

"No. It's not right. Besides, joanin' is just having fun. It doesn't mean anything about anybody's mother, really. It's just one of us trying to out-clever everybody else. That's all. My father's right, you are going to be your own worst enemy."

"What's this, girl? Makin' up words now? 'Out-clever,' huh? What dictionary am I goin' to find that in?"

Quick as a flash, Tala's fingernails struck out at Prez's face. Quicker than a flash, Prez caught her by her wrist. She was stunned, but only momentarily. She kicked out, catching Prez hard on his shin, breaking the skin and causing a spot of blood to appear. It hurt so bad, Prez couldn't keep his eyes from watering. But he wouldn't let her go, nor allow his face or body to show any of the pain that was bursting around his shin like an electric shock.

"Don't do that again, Tala."

"Let me go. And don't ever call me 'girl' again."

"Or else what? You gonna 'out-clever' me, I suppose?"

Prez released her and she snatched her arm away, spun on her heel, and quickly walked away, rubbing her wrist as she went. Prez realized he had held her wrist too tightly and that she would probably have a bruise. He looked down at his shin; blood was beginning to trickle down his leg. He watched her walking away, her buttocks swishing hypnotically with her every step. Her hair, a mass of shaggy tufts that stood out everywhere, reflected many different shades of dark auburn and brown as it bobbed and bounced around on top of her head. As she passed the statue of Lincoln and the freed slave, she turned to look back at Prez. Was that a smile he saw? He wanted to run after her and hold her body tight to his, to tell her that he wanted to lie with her.

"Hey, Prez," said one of his boys, "don't bleed all over the grass, now."

"Yeah, man," said another, "she's gone now, so it's alright for you to cry, man."

"I know, man," said someone else, "that shit musta hurt like hell."

"Huh, Prez? Getting kicked in the shins? That shit hurts, man. Don't it?"

"Hey, Prez. Man, what the fuck? Oh-oh, y'all. Somebody better run across town and tell that sweet little Miss Deb that some way-out girlie done come over here and kicked Prez in the shins and it went straight to his heart. Lookit that dude just watching her. Prez, what the fuck, man?"

Prez strolled over to the water fountain, took the bandana he had tied around his neck, wet it, and dabbed at the blood trickling down his leg.

"I'm just concerned that this red shit gonna git all over my sneakers, ya know." Prez said it too loudly. He rinsed out his bandana, folded it and tied it around his forehead. He adjusted the waistband to his gym shorts. He reached down and pulled up his socks, reached down further to touch the ground as if he were stretching. Then gave a big yawn accompanied by a big wide arm stretch and said, "Hey y'all, let's head over to the ball court and shoot some."

The guys looked at each other, looked down at Prez's shin, down which another little trickle of blood was starting, looked at each other again, and burst out laughing.

As they walked from the park, Sticks came running up from the back of the pack.

"Hey Prez, man, why you figure the same cop car's been checking us out the whole time we been in this park?"

"Cool out, Sticks. They're just driving around the park. We gonna have to send you back home to your mama for another ass-whipping if you don't be cool."

"No Prez, something's not cool, man. That same cop car's been circling around the park ever since we got here. Y'all just ain't been payin' attention."

"And you're sure it's the same car, huh?"

"Yeah, Prez," said Sticks. "I smell those cop cars even before I see 'em. They bother me, man."

"Damn, Dee Cee," said Prez, "don't get too worked up about no car cruisin' around the block. I mean, if they was really after your ass, they'd have come into the park by now to get you."

"I don't think that car is cruising, Prez," said Tons. "I think they looking at us, man."

"Okay," said Prez. "Y'all cool out for a minute, now. Maybe it's nothing. Maybe it's something. Hold up right here. Let's just stop for a minute and sit in the grass. Don't anybody even look over there at 'em. Brennie-Man! I said don't look! C'mon, we gonna sit right here for a bit. They'll see that we ain't doin' nothing and they'll go away."

But the cops didn't go away.

25

D.C. General Hosptial, Later that evening

"How bad is Brennie-Man, Mama?" Prez spoke through gritted teeth as he fought against the excruciating pain in his leg. "Ma, is he going to be alright?" This was far worse than getting kicked in the shin by Tala. He could feel his face wet and hot and taste the salty tears. His leg felt as though it was weighed down with a huge, throbbing ball of pain so heavy Prez couldn't imagine ever walking on it again.

"Where is Brennie-Man? Somebody tell me how he is!" He noticed his mother had left the hospital room, although he couldn't remember her leaving. Nor could he remember the arrival of his grandmother and his uncles. "Where's Gussie?" he asked.

"He's with your aunt," offered Uncle Cadgie.

"My baby," sniffled a red-eyed Denie. "They almost killed you, too."

Prez forgot his leg for a split second as he looked in awe at his grandma. He hadn't thought the woman had a tear in her, much less the great gushing that covered her face. Did she know something he didn't know? Was he hurt much worse than he thought? And what did she mean by "they almost killed him too"?

"Uncle Cadge, it's only my leg, right?"

"Yeah, just your leg."

Prez panicked and realized he had not actually seen his leg. He was under hospital bedsheets. Did he still have his leg, or had the cops shot it off? In a flurry of motion, he leapt off the bed, causing the IV needle to dislodge from his arm, and knocked the whole IV contraption over onto the floor. He was patting frantically for his leg. When he realized it was still there, the strength ebbed out of him and he began toppling over. His Uncle Troy caught him. As his Uncles Roland and Cadgie tried to clean up and right what Prez had knocked over, his Uncle Troy placed him back upon the bed. The door opened ever so gently and a familiar face peeped in.

"Hi, folks, it's just me." It was Doctor Cardoza. "The nurse will get everything back in order here; I see we've had a little accident. Is everything alright, Preston?" Before Prez could answer, the doctor said, "Well, splendid. May I have a word with your family? Thank you. May we speak outside, if you don't mind? Actually, I'd like you to come down the hall to my office. We should have a bit of privacy away from the rather large ears of our friendly police. And don't you worry, Preston, Nurse Agnes will stay right here with you until we get back."

As the doctor was leaving the room with Prez's family, Prez noticed the uniformed white cops stationed on either side of his door. The part of him that would have normally submitted to fear and panic was quickly flushed away by the mighty cosmic infusion of centuries of slave insurrectionists whose blood Prez could feel heating up his veins, swelling his head, and fomenting a righteous contempt in place of fear and dread. As the door closed, he caught the eye of Nurse Agnes. Surely, she lived out in the white suburbs, probably where the two cops came from, Prez thought. Prez looked hard at her, wondering, if she were a man, whether she would also be a cop. She noticed his intense gaze, and with sad eyes smiled ever so slightly at Prez.

"They wanted to come in here and take you out, take you down to the police station, but Doctor Cardoza wouldn't let them. He said that if you died in their custody, they could be charged for denying you medical treatment. That was a pretty smart move on the doctor's part, don't you think?" She got close to Preston and whispered in his ear, "Especially since you've only got what's known as a flesh wound." Prez looked at her quizzically. "You either got hit with a bullet fragment that ricocheted, or some pavement or rocks the bullets kicked up. Shhh!"

"What about my friend?" asked Prez. "Is he in another room?"

Her eyes became much sadder. "Someone else will tell you about your friend. Here, sit up." After reattaching the IV, she placed a pillow under his leg. Then she took the chair beside Prez's bed, turned it, and sat nervously watching the door.

The painkiller in the IV made Prez drowsy. He didn't notice Nurse Agnes jump in reaction to the door opening. Nor had he heard his family re-enter with the doctor. All he remembered was speaking to his mother with a voice that didn't seem to come from him.

"The ceiling is spinning, Mama. Or maybe I dreamed it. And my ears are ringing and humming. And I feel very hot. But maybe I'm dreaming it all up. Maybe I'm really not awake."

Mattie looked at the doctor, who looked at the nurse, who shook her head and shrugged her shoulders. Denie came over and whispered something to Mattie who said in reply, "Yes, I thought about that, too. But how could he remember that? He was only three years old."

"It's the painkillers making him quite drowsy and perhaps a bit delusional, but please check his temperature again, will you?" asked Doctor Cardoza of the nurse. "Do you know what he's talking about, Mrs. Downs?"

"Well, yes. But this is so strange. When he was a baby he had a bad ear infection that resulted in his having a very high temperature for a couple of days. I'd come into the bedroom sometimes and he'd be lying there in the crib with his eyes wide open looking up at the ceiling and making circular motions with his little arms. We thought it was so cute at the time. Then we realized, for him the ceiling was spinning. He was so feverish he was delirious."

"He probably suffered some sort of auditory damage as a result. Are you aware of that? Has he ever had a hearing test?" asked Doctor Cardoza.

They all stood around the hospital bed as Prez pointed to the ceiling, making circular motions.

"It's going around and round. Just like when I was a baby. I can see it going around, even though I know it's really not. Even if I close my eyes, it'll still be spinning, even though it's not. It will stop when it stops. Just like my leg. It'll stop hurting when it stops. Please, don't give me any more painkillers."

The nurse looked at the doctor, who looked at Mattie, who looked at her mother-in-law and her brothers-in-law. Then Mattie looked back at the doctor and nodded. Doctor Cardoza nodded at the nurse and she removed the IV from Prez's arm.

"Well, Preston," said Doctor Cardoza, "if the pain gets to be too much, you just let us know. A chunk of your flesh was torn away. It could get quite painful as it starts to heal. You just let us know if you need anything."

"How long will I have to stay here? I want to go home."

Suddenly there were a lot of other voices outside in the corridor. There was shouting and some obvious scuffling with bodies being pushed against the door of Prez's hospital room. As Prez's family began to nervously take up positions in front of him, the door burst open, giving everyone a start. Prez sat bolt upright in his hospital bed upon hearing a voice he knew well.

"You're not a doctor. You're not family. You can't go in that room," said the slenderer of the two police officers stationed outside.

"I am his lawyer, sir, attorney Eddie Flowers, senior partner and lead civil rights attorney for Flowers Fellows & Fischi. You certainly know my firm. Be advised that your presence in front of the hospital room of young Mr. Downs may be in serious violation of his civil rights, since he has been neither charged with, nor arrested for anything.

"Sir, you look confused. Is there a superior of yours around with whom you can consult to help you through this? Sir, do you wish to arrest either myself or young Mr. Downs? We shall take your silence for a negative response, then. Please step aside."

As attorney Eddie Flowers led his entourage into Prez's hospital room, he turned to an assistant and asked that the two officers be given his business cards. One card said: Flowers Fellows & Fischl Law Firm. And in fine print: Civil rights, criminal, constitutional law. The other card, which the two officers gazed at longest, said: MASTER FLOWERS, Instructor. In fine print: Aikido, Shaolin Kung fu. The address was on Massachusetts Avenue, right in the heart of Embassy Row.

26

D.C. General Hospital

Attorney Eddie Flowers watched as the two police officers disappeared through the big swinging doors at the end of the hospital corridor, then turned and asked of Doctor Cardoza, "Can young Mr. Downs go home, or must he remain in hospital?"

"There isn't any medical reason to keep him here. His injuries are well dressed and his mother can apply a new dressing as needed. I can explain it all to her. Certainly, his wound will make any attempt at walking very painful for a couple of weeks, which is why I'm going to request that he be confined to bed for a couple of days. But certainly, he can go home."

"Please, forgive me, Doctor Cardoza, but you have alternately referred to young Mr. Downs as having sustained an injury, and a wound. As a lawyer who will be representing the family, should the need arise, of course, I need to know whether in your professional opinion, Mr. Downs sustained an injury, which may be characterized as unintentional, or whether he has sustained a wound, which, due to the circumstances of this case, is the result of an intentional act?"

"Mr. Downs was wounded. Bullet and concrete fragments were removed from his leg."

"Where are they?"

"I don't know." Turning to a nurse, Doctor Cardoza issued an instruction that sent her scurrying off.

"Can we count on you to testify to these facts in a court of law if such becomes necessary?"

"Why yes, of course. Without hesitation."

"Thank you, kind sir. Shall we take young Mr. Downs home now?"

"Mama, Uncle Cadgie, come here." Prez himself was somehow forgotten in all the activity and his voice startled everyone.

"What is it, little man?" asked his Uncle Cadgie. His mother simply looked down at the floor. She knew what it was. And as the others studied the expression on her face, they knew as well.

"Where is Brennie-Man?" Prez studied the faces of the adults. Only his Uncle Cadgie and Master Flowers would not look away from his stare. Their eyes were angry and sad at the same time. "Where are my clothes?" Prez had gotten up from the pillow, swung his throbbing leg over the side of the bed and sat up so abruptly that he nearly knocked the IV stand over again. "Can I please have my clothes? I want to get up."

"Alright, Preston, just a minute," said his mother. "We'll take you home in a minute."

"I don't want to go home. I mean I do, but first there's something I have to do. Can I please have my clothes? Uncle Cadgie . . ."

Prez motioned for his uncle to come near. His uncle listened then turned and said, "Mattie, please, let the boy have his clothes. Where are they? Can he get dressed now?" At that he went over to the door and held it as he motioned for everyone to leave so that Prez could have some privacy. Cadgie then pulled Doctor Cardoza aside and made a request that caused the doctor's eyebrows to rise in alarm. But the more Cadgie spoke to him, the more relaxed the doctor became. Finally, he nodded okay and left the room.

Denie put her arm around Mattie's shoulder as they exited. They both had tears flowing down their faces; tears of sadness, and tears of fear. They were scared for their Little Preston. He was in the midst of a very difficult rite of passage. They knew that the remnants of his childhood had been yanked viciously from him and that he would never be the same again. Moreover, they knew that black children's stymied childhoods migrated directly to an all-too-often-tragic adulthood. There could be no greater fear for a mother and grandmother than that their man-child would be hurled straight into premature manhood in the belly of the American beast. Whichever turned out to be worse—the violent physical threats of an oppressive American system, or the interwoven racism which was just as brutal—chances were that the man-child in rebellion would not survive to adulthood. He'd be lucky to live long enough to get a driver's license, much less attain voting age. And it was always the brightest and strongest who met such a fate: bright enough to see through the veils of subterfuge that hid the reality of American apartheid, and strong enough to try and stand up for the truth.

"What do you think is taking that boy so long to get dressed?" Denie inquired of Mattie.

"I don't know. Maybe his leg hurts him too much. Maybe I should go in and see."

Just as she was about to go in the doctor came out followed by Cadgie who held the door for Prez. Prez took a deep breath and limped down the corridor to the elevator door. The doctor pushed the button marked M. When the door opened Prez whispered something to his uncle. He quickly turned and quietly told Mattie and Denie that Prez wanted them to wait there. In the morgue he stood beside the doctor who pulled the white sheet from his friend's face.

"He looks peaceful like he's sleeping," said Prez. "Where did they shoot him?"

The doctor looked to Prez's uncle for assistance.

"Can't you just tell us, doc?" asked Cadgie.

"Alright. Your friend sustained two posterior entrance wounds from—"

"No, doc, not medical mumbo-jumbo, please."

"That's alright," said Prez. "I already know he was shot in the back. I want to see."

"But why, Preston Junior?"

"I need to see what they did to my friend. I need to know what they did to him so I'll never forget. I need to see."

"No, Preston Junior. You're about to make a big mistake. You don't need to see the work of evil to remember it. Once you look the devil in the face your own soul is damaged for the rest of your life. Brendon is dead and you can't bring him back. You said he looks peaceful. Don't you think that is what he would want for you?"

"You're right, Uncle Cadgie."

In the elevator going back up Prez told his uncle what happened.

"We had been in the park. We crossed Thirteenth Street and the cops turned on their sirens and lights and started chasing us for no reason. We were trying to get to the laneway behind where Mr. Richardson's drugstore used to be. Then they started shooting. I was way out in front; then I remembered Brennie-Man wasn't too fast. He was always last, you know, bringing up the rear. So I cut back to go get him. I figured if I ran with him, I could make him go faster. But just when I turned around towards him his eyes got real wide and he stumbled and fell flat on his face. I didn't realize he had been shot. So, I started shouting, 'C'mon, Brennie-Man! Get up! Get up and run, man!' But he didn't get up. And just as I was about to go over and get him, two cops ran over. One kicked Brennie-Man real hard in his ribs. The other cop, with the shotgun, leaned over Brennie-Man and shot him in the back! He shot him while he was already down on his face. I mean, where the hell was Brennie-Man gonna go? So, I started yelling at them to stop shooting Brennie-Man. That's when they realized I was there and they started shooting at me. I took off and was halfway down the laneway when I fell flat on my face. My leg just came out from under me. I looked down and my leg was bloody. I got up, though, and ran to Tons' house. His mother brought me to the hospital. They murdered Brennie-Man for no reason. We weren't doing anything. Nothing at all, Uncle Cadgie, I swear!"

Prez could feel tears pushing behind his eyes. His chest heaved with anger, and blood throbbed at his temples.

"I'll never forget Brennie-Man and what they did to him."

The headline of Washington's prominent, supposedly liberal newspaper, the *Washington Chronicle,* told one story: "Negro Males Shot While Looting White Lincoln Park Establishment, Charges are Pending."

The Afro-American Times headline told a very different one: "Negro Youth Murdered, Another Injured by D.C. Police in Unprovoked Lincoln Park Shooting, Charges are Pending."

27

Montreal, Summer Solstice, 1969 – Supper

"Grande tante Céleste! It's been a while since I've seen you. How are you?" Prez gave her a big hug. "This is Tala, a dear friend of mine from back home. Tala, this is Marianne's great-aunt Céleste."

"You're so pretty," Céleste said to Tala. "You are of mixed parentage, no?"

"Afro-American and Filipino."

Tala and Céleste shook hands warmly.

"Jamie and Marianne are in the kitchen?" inquired Prez.

"Doug! Doug! What's happening, brother man?" Jamie rushed down the hall doing his best rendition of what he thought was a classic "soul brother" greeting.

Before he could clasp Prez's hand, Prez turned and put his arms around Tala and said, "Jamie, meet my dear friend from back home, Tala. And please, none of your pitiful theatrics—taking her hand while looking at it as if it's the most delicate thing you have ever touched. And don't try to kiss it. It is not yours to kiss." Jamie looked caught out. Céleste snickered.

"Hi," said Tala. "Pleasure."

"Oh no, the pleasure is all mine. Marianne's in the back."

"Lead the way," said Prez. "After you, Tante Céleste."

"No. I can't stay. I've something in the oven. I'll be back."

Tala and Marianne greeted and hugged like two long-lost sisters.

"Jamie! Smoke that thing outside, please," demanded Marianne.

"But, Marianne," said Prez, "you smoke."

"Not lately," said Jamie. "I have no idea what that's about except Marianne just being her usual flakey self."

"I'm serious, Jamie." Marianne stood in front of him and pointed towards the kitchen door. "Go smoke on the back balcony. Prez will tell you how he solved the Citroën's carburetor problem."

"Oh, alright," he whined.

Prez stepped out onto the back steps with Jamie to tell him.

"Can I help you with anything?" asked Tala.

"Well, please recommend a good waste disposal service," said Marianne as she cut a quick glance over in Jamie's direction.

"Oh no! Really? Can't help with that. Why not try the Yellow Pages?"

"And what about you, Tala?"

"Oh. I really have nothing to dispose of. Nothing at all."

Céleste had just come back in and overheard the exchange and giggled with them.

Dinner was roasted chicken, scalloped potatoes, and lightly breaded asparagus served under the most delicate white-wine sauce. They broke French baguettes and washed it all down with a good red wine, except Prez didn't drink the wine. He had apple cider instead. And poor Jamie?

"Here are your raw sesame green beans and bloody beef strips just as you like them. Ugh! Jamie thinks he's eating Japanese. Enjoy," said Marianne with a wink at Tala.

The conversation was loose and lively. Céleste, however, was somber.

"I have a new TV. It's nice but the shows aren't. The characters on *Lurch for Tomorrow* are so devious and vain. They lie so much!"

"The old art-imitating-life-imitating-art phenomenon," said Jamie. He shifted his attention to Tala. "How long have you known each other? How did you meet? Was it love at first sight, or did you hate each other's guts?"

Prez cut in, "I don't think she liked me at all. I was with my boys in the park. I thought she was the most beautiful girl I had ever seen. Until she kicked me."

"She *what*?" asked Marianne.

"Prez, shut up," said Tala, cutting in. She glared at Prez. "Who says we're in love, Jamie?

"We met at Lincoln Park, a park in our neighborhood in Washington, D.C. Actually, it was my father who wanted to invite Prez to join his kung fu class, and he asked if I wouldn't mind speaking to him about it. But I won't digress there right now. I'm picking up your bad habits." She glanced at Prez. "It was a beautiful day in the park. At least it started that way."

"That was in 1959—in the fall." said Prez.

"You've known each other for ten years?" asked Jamie.

"No, it was the summer of 1960 when *we* met," said Tala. "I was sixteen and in my freshman year in college. I had a twenty-one-year-old boyfriend so Prez was just a kid in the park." She laughed. "But seriously, he was impressively mature for his age." She looked at Prez. "You know, Prez, you really grew up that summer."

28

Washington, D.C., August 1960

Prez had a court appearance the morning of Brennie-Man's funeral. The judge reminded Prez of his grandfather, except the judge was a white man.

"The court notes that the grand jury has chosen not to indict. As the defendant's attorney has pointed out, it is probably certain that the grand jury was exclusively composed of whites based upon the research data he presented that tallied past grand juries. If the good white citizens on the 'People's Panel' won't indict it indicates they saw no merit in your evidence and arguments before them.

"Clearly, I see none. You have presented conflicting physical evidence, your police officers have given contradictory statements and your presentation has been so convoluted you may as well be a pretzel. Indeed, when this court sniffs, the skunk of vendetta rears it ugly head. The integrity of this court will never be compromised by attempts to further political agendas and careers.

"The court notes the facts of this case. Mr. Downs and his friends were in Lincoln Park along with a host of other individuals of both sexes and races. It was a summer afternoon. There had been no trouble in the park or in the vicinity of the park. There were no All Points Bulletins or other alerts issued for the park, the general vicinity, for Mr. Downs or any of his friends. Yet, and for reasons which the district attorney still cannot enunciate, there was a police car continuously driving around the outer perimeter of the park and two more parked on side streets adjacent to the park. As Mr. Downs and his friends emerged from the park, the police car that had been circling the park began driving in their direction. Mr. Downs and his friends began running. The other two police cars became involved in what has been described by the DA as an effort to apprehend them—again for reasons undisclosed and unknown. An officer— still unidentified—drew his service revolver and fired a number of shots in the direction of the running youths, striking one of them in the back and killing him. Mr. Downs was struck and seriously wounded in the leg.

"I note that the district attorney has made it a point to use the term 'fleeing' when speaking of the youths running from the park. If he seeks to invoke an image of youths fleeing from police due to criminality or to imply the police were exercising their lawful duties, he has failed to show how such a character- ization is warranted, and the evidence before this court does not establish it. That is why I have chosen to use the word 'running' and not 'fleeing.' I am being as careful and precise here as I can possibly be.

"Absent probable cause, a person cannot be apprehended or arrested for running, which is not a crime under our criminal code.

"The district attorney advances the conclusion that young Mr. Downs poses a threat to his neighborhood and society at large and thus must be placed under the authority of juvenile officers in the interest of public safety. Yet all he has presented is the following: That Mr. Downs does not have any criminal rec- ord, is an honors student and a first-class athlete who happened to have been running from a park when he was shot by police for reasons which have yet to be put before this court. None of this supports the conclusion that Mr. Downs poses any sort of threat whatsoever. That leaves me to wonder if the district attorney is thus indirectly putting forward the argument that getting shot by the police is in itself and of itself proof of one's being a danger to society and/or having engaged in criminality.

"Preston Coleman Downs, Junior, you are being entrusted to the care of your mother. The district attorney's reasons to have you removed from your home and placed into the custody of juvenile court officers are completely without merit. The court shall not be used to further political agendas or careers." He looked sternly towards the prosecutor's table.

"Please, Mrs. Downs, do take your child home. Court is adjourned."

29

Washington, D.C., late August 1960

In the days and weeks following the burial of Brennie-Man—Brendon Fraser Whitaker, Jr.—there was a marked difference in the neighborhood's mood and behavior. The adults were constantly ill at ease. Negro parents forbade their children to set foot in Lincoln Park. To compensate, there were more house parties. The streets in front of their homes became their playgrounds. But those same streets became ominous trails of evil when police cruisers drove down them. The cops would stop mid-block and glare. They wanted the hate in their eyes to be seen. They wanted you to know they knew where you lived.

And they knew exactly where Prez and his family lived. Sometimes they would spend what seemed like a whole shift parked in front of their apartment building. At other times they would roll right down the back alley behind the church and park facing his building. One Friday night there were even two cars, one in the front and one in the back alley. Mattie was scared out of her wits and called Ellis, who, mercifully, was at the precinct. She was able to give Ellis the numbers of the two squad cars. He was furious. He and his partner hopped in an unmarked car and rolled down the back alley, parking right behind the patrol car. Ellis flashed his headlights. The officers in the squad car didn't move. He flashed again then put his car in gear and nudged the patrol car with his front bumper. Still there was no acknowledgment from the officers in the squad car. Ellis backed away, put it in gear again and rolled hard into the rear bumper of the squad car, knocking its occupants forward with a jolt. Now their doors flew open and they emerged quite angry, their hands reaching for their holsters. But Ellis's partner was already standing beside the passenger door of his unmarked car holding a Tommy gun. This froze the two white officers. One of the officers looked at the other and motioned to get back into the car.

"Just a minute. I haven't dismissed you." Ellis emerged with deliberate slowness from behind the wheel. He placed his hands on his hips in a sweeping gesture that exposed his Walthers in a double shoulder holster under his jacket.

"I had a look at the roster and the schedule before I left the station house, and you boys are supposed to be off. You know what else? I could find nothing that authorizes you boys to be parked in this back alley. Now you need to tell me what you are doing here and under whose authority."

"We were having a lunch break, Lieutenant."

"Well, I tell you what, the two of you will be having a very extended lunch break as soon as I write my report. You're going to be suspended without pay for insubordination and disrespect to a supervising officer while in uniform and while on duty."

"But you already said you checked and saw that we are off duty."

Ellis walked up to the big mouthy one. "Yes, but I am on duty—very much so."

He didn't bother to check the car out front. He knew it would be long gone.

Mattie had already been considering moving. That incident made it a certainty. She had spoken with Ellis, with her neighbors, and with her best friend Lois about it. She was hesitant to take her son Preston out of another school before he could finish it. And both her sons had fared so well in that neighborhood. They had lots of friends and the adults were truly neighborhood parents; they looked after everyone's children. But the horrifying Lincoln Park events and the constant police harassment left her no choice. She had to get her sons, especially her oldest, away from there.

With the rental section of the classified ads under her arm and her best walking shoes on her feet she set out that Monday morning on a mission to find a new home for her sons and herself. Prez also had something to attend to that day.

❧

The August sun was baking the day. Prez wetted his bandana under the cold faucet in his kitchen before venturing out. As he rounded the corner onto East Capitol Street from Fourteenth with his crew in tow, neighborhood youth noticed. When they saw Prez in the lead, they wondered what was going on, so the little procession became two swarms that moved down both sides of the street. When they reached the corner in front of Mr. Richardson's burned-out pharmacy and looked down East Capitol, they could see another group of youths approaching. Kids from around the park took notice and everyone converged on the corner expecting a rumble. Tala was somehow among them. When the crowd recognized Freddie Snaps and the Serpents, the dead-dry heat of the August air became electrically charged. But something was different. Prez was not standing ramrod straight with a fist pointed at his adversary.

A circle formed with Prez and Freddie Snaps in the middle. Freddie Snaps stepped forward. Then Prez stepped closer. As people wondered who would throw the first punch, Prez untied the green bandana from around his neck and held it out. Freddie Snaps did the same with his black bandana. They exchanged them. They grasped each other's hands and shook. They hugged. Then they turned to face the crowd, holding each other's hands high with their green and black bandanas. Debra started to cry. She may have had a clue but she was still shaken. Everyone else was shocked; everyone, that is, except Tala, who recognized Prez's potential to be extraordinary from the day they first met. She couldn't wait to tell her father.

"It is time," said Prez, "for us to stop fighting each other. My friend Brennie-Man is dead and it wasn't the Serpents who did it. Al got all shot up right here on this corner and it wasn't the Serpents who did it. Old Preach Mouth is dead. The cops killed him too, right here on this corner. We know who did those things. And we know none of us burned down Mr. Richardson's Drugstore. So it's time for us to stop fighting each other because I don't think we are enemies. I think we are really brothers and sisters. I think we need to start acting like it."

"A new day. A new hope for us to succeed. That's what this is," began Freddie Snaps. "Prez is correct to analyze things the way he has and we have got to get right because so far we haven't been. There are too many more important things for us to think about than fighting each other. We cannot do anything about freedom unless we do it together. Hey, everybody. This is a really good thing happening here. Snap out of it."

He started to clap his hands rhythmically.

"I've been going down south with my mother and Deb's mom. There's a lot of stuff happening to try to desegregate the South and win equality for the Negro. Sometimes we forget that we too are in the South. I've been to sit-ins and I've been to marches. Here's a song we sing sometimes:

"Oh freedom, oh freedom, oh freedom over me
And before I'd be a slave, I'd be buried in my grave"

When Freddie Snaps got to the end of the song, he invited everyone to join in. "C'mon, y'all." Soon the whole street corner reverberated with the words, "And before I'd be a slave, I'd be buried in my grave."

Later that evening after the boys were in bed and Mattie and Celia were sitting on the front stoop catching the night breeze and listening to the neighborhood's ambient noises, Celia said, "I saw one of Preston's little friends today. Cute little child. Quite mature looking for her age, though."

"You're talking about Miss Debra Wilbanks. Hmph! That girl cannot keep her lips off my Preston Junior!"

"Oh my," Celia giggled. "You know about that?"

"Girl, the whole neighborhood knows about it. I'm surprised you saw her. They meet around the corner and then they kiss like they're slurping licorice sticks or something! Oh yes, I've been told. Who do they think they're fooling anyway? And Preston Junior always gives it away." She mimicked her son, "'Hey Mama, I'm just going out to meet some friends.' Some friends, he says. Lordy, I tell you, Celia. But I'm not worried because that boy has a good head on his shoulders. And Miss Deb, as the boys call her, so does she. I believe she has a good heart too. I just wish these children would stop behaving like they invented their little sly maneuvers. We did!"

"Sure did, Mattie. If they only knew!"

"I try to give my son credit for being smart and mature. He's known all along that his school principal is more than a former pro football star, that he's Debra's father and that Debra's mother is the famous lawyer Wilhelmina Wilbanks of the NAACP? He's carried himself well, I think. But he thinks people have honor and they don't. I don't want the moment he realizes that to be the moment of his death. He's all torn up inside. He needs healing. Away from these streets. I really do feel badly about taking Preston out of his school, especially since he only has one year before he's in high school, but I know what he's into around here. We're moving."

Washington, D.C., September 1960

Their new Langdon Park neighborhood was very different from the flat Lincoln Park/Capitol Hill neighborhood they had moved from. It wasn't dominated by the architecture of Washington's ubiquitous brick row houses. City blocks were not neatly demarcated. There weren't any back alleyways. Nor was there the airborne pungency of car exhaust from the Seventeenth and East Capitol Street intersection, which spilled traffic eastward towards the Anacostia River or westward towards the Capitol.

Here was the realm of neat, mostly small and modest single-family homes sided with aluminum or vinyl in an almost rural setting. The houses were laid out upon lots comprising more earth than one would be accustomed to seeing in a city. The air was quieter and more aromatic. The lush park from which the neighborhood took its name was a mere half a block away.

Lincoln Park was essentially a flat greenspace in the midst of a traffic roundabout. Langdon Park was more a little forest full of big trees. There was a ball court, a football field, a baseball diamond and barbeque pits. Thank you! One could weekend-party in Langdon Park with gusto. Then go to the little church across the street at Mills Avenue and Franklin Street on Sunday and ask Jesus to forgive your whole smorgasbord of sins, both committed and desired.

That Sunday after they moved into their new home, the little white church on the corner was buzzing. The streets around the church were impassable due to the overflow crowd. For blocks you could hear the piano chords backing the choir and congregation singing rocking praises to God and his son Jesus Christ. This was surely due in large part to the fact that all the doors and windows were open in hopes that the Lord would send through many breezes of cool air. At the end of the service those inside spilled out, led by the black-robed pastor of the church walking arm-in-arm with a white man also in black robes. The congregation itself was liberally salted. Prez wondered if what he saw was actually what the dream of integration looked like.

He asked his mother if he could go to that church's service the following Sunday instead of their home church in the old neighborhood of Lincoln Park. His mother agreed, almost immediately thinking it would be good for him if he could start to break his ties with his old crowd.

It was with great surprise that he walked into the New Bethel High Congregation for Everlasting Worship on that next Sunday to find a rather sparsely attended service with not a white face in sight. The church was much smaller than he expected. It looked a bit like his church in miniature. The chancel section was the most packed part of the church, as it seemed practically the whole of the congregation in attendance sang in the choir. In front of them was the requisite pulpit with five empty seats, including the pastor's Mercy Seat. The pastor, the Very Reverend Farnsworth Pennington, stood up the whole time, though he hardly ever stood behind the lectern except when he needed to wipe his sweat with a large white towel or take a swig from a flask he kept behind it. Prez could tell that the pulpit was sturdily constructed because Pastor Pennington jumped, swayed, danced, bounced, and stomped upon it throughout the service and the pulpit never so much as squeaked.

Prez stood to light applause when the pastor asked for visitors to please stand.

"There we have a fine young man, no doubt desirous of living the pure life of a sheep in Jesus' flock. Come here today all by hisself when the average young man his age would rather be out tending to the bizness of the devil. But here he is come into the house of the Lord as his first order of bizness as a new family come to us here in Langdon neighborhood from—where you come from, son?"

"The Lincoln Park area, sir."

"Praise the Lord, son. Alright, sit down."

Prez couldn't believe how poorly the man spoke. He really had to pay attention because the pastor's grammar was so bad, he sounded as if he was speaking another dialect. And when he did open the Bible it seemed he wasn't reading but reciting from memory—his eyes would squeeze tight, his head sway back, he'd rock on his feet and recite some words Prez just knew could not have been written down that way in the Bible. When Prez glanced around everyone else had their Bibles open and were nodding away in affirmation, most of them with their eyes closed, too. But no one was actually looking at the Bible. So Prez tried not to feel too badly that he was unable to find the passage the pastor said he was reading from even though he was sure he had turned to the right book, chapter, page and verse. Prez just shut his eyes, threw his head back, and said "Amen" when the pastor said to say amen.

At one point he reached for a hymnal and instead his hand found a slim little booklet tucked into the book tray behind the pew in front of him. He looked about and noticed that they were in abundance. He looked at the front cover: *God Loves All His*

Children Equally but Separately. There was an illustration of an old white man's white-bearded face formed by clouds in a blue sky. Beneath his puffy smiling face and beaming blue eyes an African-American child sat cross-legged under his puffy-cloud left hand, and a white child sat the same way under his right. Between the children floated a puffy-cloud white angel holding a harp.

Prez turned the booklet over and at the bottom of the back page was a square emblem featuring two crossed flags, one American, the other Confederate, on a white background. In a circle around the flags was written the words: Bladensburg Citizens' Council, States' Rights-Racial Integrity.

After the service was over a group of young people came back to talk to him. There were six of them. They were all the pastor's children and they all had biblical names: Mary, Magdalene, James, Joanna, Salome and Josephus. Twin sisters Joanna and Salome were two years older than Prez, and baby brother Josephus one year ahead. The other siblings were much older.

"So nice of you to come. What's your name?"

"Preston Coleman Downs, Junior."

"You all just moved in a couple of weeks ago, huh? Where'd you go to school before?"

"Eliot Junior High near Eastern High."

"Oh, it's rough over there, we hear." Will you go to Taft? Where are your mother and little brother?"

They ask a lot of questions, thought Prez with a giggle.

"What's so funny?"

"Oh, nothing. It's just that before I can answer one question somebody is asking me another."

They all laughed out loud. They liked each other. But it was the oldest brother James that Prez felt an automatic bond with.

"Okay, so what do they call you for short?" asked Joanna.

"They call him Prez," said James. Prez looked at James and wondered how he knew that. "Al Proctor is our cousin. That's how I know about you."

They walked out and stood on the church steps and continued talking. Eventually, Prez had to ask, "What's this?" as he held up a copy of the little booklet.

"That's from my daddy's best friend's church," gushed Mary, the oldest.

"His name is Pastor Jacob Jeremy Jasper," said Magdalene.

"And his church is over in Bladensburg, Maryland, not that far from here," said Mary.

"It's called the Holy Ghost Fellowship Evangelical Cathedral," said Magdalene.

"How close are we to Maryland?" asked Prez.

"Hop in a car and you're there in ten minutes," said Josephus.

"That man is a white man who thinks he is better than we are." That raw fact was spoken with authority and not a trace of emotion. What an old soul Salome was. No one uttered a word in disagreement. Prez was taken aback a bit.

"Well, he's Daddy's best friend, Salome. You're too militant sometimes." said Mary.

"They grew up together in Bladensburg. They've known each other all their lives," said Magdalene.

"They would die for each other," said Mary.

"They almost did in the war. They were in the army together," said Magdalene.

"Then they went to seminary school together on the GI Bill," said Mary.

"Daddy said he would not have made it through seminary school if it weren't for Pastor Jasper," said Magdalene.

"Every alternating first Sunday the two churches come together," said Mary.

"We go there or they come here," said Magdelene.

"But what is this?" Prez asked again, holding out the little booklet. The two oldest girls appeared a bit embarrassed. The twins both rolled their eyes.

"It's racist propaganda," said Salome. "I've spent the whole summer, me and my best friend Tala, protesting at Glen Echo Amusement Park. They won't let Negroes in. You know about that, don't you?"

Prez was really taken aback. "No, I don't. I've never even heard of Glen Echo." Lincoln Park was following him. "You don't mean the Tala whose father is Master Flowers?"

"That's exactly who she means. You know her?" asked Josephus.

"That's two people from my old neighborhood that your family is close to."

"Some call that 'destiny'," said Salome.

"I have different thoughts on that," said Prez. "Destiny is the destination; fate is the trip."

"Brilliant," said Salome.

"How's Al?" asked Prez.

"Man, he's been back at Finley's for a while now. But his competition days are over. "He's got bullet fragments in his shoulder so he mostly training younger guys, trying to help them as much as he can. You should come in, man. You have what it takes. You could be ready for the '64 Olympic trials if you start now. Al would be really glad to see you.

"News, my man. First, the cat that owns your place was a middleweight contender. His name is Garland Edwards and he fought Holly Mims. That's top-ten action. He's a friend of Mr. Finley's so between Al and Garland you're in at Finley's easy. Number two, the family that lives under you, they're away on vacation now but should be back any day now."

194

"Well, what about 'em?"

"That brings up number three and there are two of 'em. It's the daughters, man. Don't worry, they are way too old for you. They're the same age as Mary and Magdalene. But they are so fine, dudes come from miles around just to hang out on the porch with them. It might get a little crowded when you try to get into your front door. That can be the real problem."

"Okay. Be cool," said Prez.

Back home, Prez undressed, folded and hung up his good clothes, put on his track sweats, and plopped down on his bed. He read through the little booklet:

God's Word Says to Segregate. The word of God says do not mix the races.

In Exodus God says, "So shall we be separated, from all the people that are upon the face of the earth."

In Leviticus 20:24 God says, "I am the Lord thy God, which have separated you from other people."

In Deuteronomy 7:3 God says, "Neither shalt thou make marriages with them."

In Jude 7 God tells us exactly what will happen because of integration and intermarriage: "Even as Sodom and Gomorrah, and the cities about them in like manner, giving themselves over to fornication, and going after strange flesh, are set forth for an example, suffering the vengeance of eternal fire."

But perhaps worse is that if we allow integration and intermarriage, we will cause our innocent babies to suffer for an eternal time. In Deuteronomy 23:2 God says, "A bastard shall not enter into the congregation of the Lord; even to his tenth generation shall he not enter into the congregation of the Lord."

Our Southern way of life and our way of thinking is ordained by God himself as he gave it to Moses in the Ten Commandments. The laws of God are more powerful than the laws of man. The decision of the US Supreme Court that says we must integrate is not more powerful than the Commandment of God to Moses: "Thou shalt not covet thy neighbor's house, nor his manservant, nor his maidservant."

Prez went and got his mother's big black King James Bible and double-checked the scripture passages quoted. He couldn't find any discrepancies. He closed the pamphlet and shoved it in a drawer. He needed to get out and shoot some ball or maybe take a jog. It was too bright and sunny for him to be feeling so dark and dreary. Sitting on the toilet, he thought if there were justifications for segregation in the Bible, there had to be even more for integration. He had been brought up believing that all God's children were equal in everything, not just in being loved by Jesus. He had always interpreted that to mean skin color didn't really matter—"red and yellow, black and white, they are precious in his sight, Jesus loves the little children of the world," the hymn went. If people were all essentially the same, then how could there be words in the Bible that justified segregation without more words to repudiate it? The answer, he thought, must lie in the New Testament, which is supposed to be the word of Jesus Christ whom God sent to correct the wrongs of the Old Testament world. That was such a good thought. It made Prez feel almost brilliant. But he was actually more than a little worried. Suppose there were no words in the New Testament to justify integration? All he could think of was that Jesus said love thy neighbor, which he heard on a regular basis in church. There had to be others. He decided not to go out. He grabbed the big black Bible, went back to his room, and settled in to find those passages that said segregation was a sin.

Given the size of the Bible, Prez figured he'd be finished in about a year, so he dove in.

"Preston Junior!"

He jumped up, looked at his watch—4:30 p.m. It was too early for Sunday dinner and Gussie was sound asleep. Prez wondered how his brother could nap in the middle of the day.

"Yes, ma'am."

"You and Gussie come out here for a minute, will you? I want you to meet some people."

"Yes, ma'am." He kicked at Gussie. "Wake up, man."

"This is Miss Connie Mae Stevens. She's a friend of ours from back home."

"Well, what fine-looking boys, Mattie!" said Miss Stevens, "I'm actually a year ahead of your mother but we all grew up around Daniel's Chapel Baptist Church in Enfield. And this is my fiancé, Mr. Ronald Lawson."

The guy was huge, like Deb's dad. Prez shook their hands. Next it was his aunt's turn, "and this is my new friend Reverend Lon Dorsey. He gave the guest sermon this morning at Mount Moriah."

"And what a rousing sermon it was," said Mr. Lawson with a booming voice that seemed to make stuff shake.

Prez thought he heard someone else coming up the stairs and turned around to see the most muscle-bound man he had ever seen. "And this," said his mother, "is our new landlord, Mr. Garland Edwards." Prez wondered if he could even lift his arm to shake hands without destroying his suit jacket.

"I'm not sure I like the landlord label. But I do own the house. And that is my name."

He grabbed Prez's hand and rolled and squished it around. It happened so fast that Prez wasn't ready to position his hand to avoid the squish-shake, a typical bullying tactic. So Prez just let him have his fun, never flinching nor uttering a word of protest. This defeated Mr. Edwards' purpose and he gave Prez a hearty slap on the back. "Nice to meet you. Heard a little bit about you."

Mattie looked surprised. But before she could figure out what to ask, Mr. Lawson continued speaking to Reverend Dorsey.

"Your sermon hit home in a number of ways. We just can't go on allowing the white man to think he is God's chosen one. The Bible is for us too. And we have just as much right as he does to all the freedoms of the Constitution. We fought for it. We died for it."

"We're still dying for it," said Mr. Edwards. "Only now we're dying here at home and it's them wearing different uniforms doing the killing."

Mattie got a worried look on her face. She kept cutting her eyes over to see how her son was taking it all in. Miss Stevens was giving her fiancé a prolonged dirty stare because she had told him what had happened to Preston Junior and yet he initiated such a conversation. He ignored her.

"Men must be men. We have to stand up and fight for what we believe in, especially now." And he looked hard at Prez.

"And you know," said Mr. Edwards, "it's like being in the ring. You can't show fear. That's half the battle lost if you do."

"But just this morning in Sunday school we were talking to the children about loving thy neighbor and turning the other cheek," said Celia.

"Those are most assuredly the ideals that we'd like to instill in our children," said Reverend Dorsey. "But we can't be fools either. God doesn't want any of his children to be fools. The word of God is a very powerful thing."

"But is God always right?" The adults' heads snapped around to look at Prez.

"Son, never question the word of God!"

"Preston Junior is always asking questions," Aunt Celia laughed nervously. *Please don't say another word, Preston Junior,* she thought.

His mother wrung her hands and pursed her lips. *He's still traumatized,* she thought. Just like after his father died and he screamed out loud that he didn't believe there was a God because if there was, his father would still be alive. She wished his Uncle Cadgie were there.

"I don't think he meant that he didn't believe in the word of God," said Mattie.

Prez said, "It's just that I've been reading some of the words of God and I don't believe in them."

The preacher gasped; the other men seemed to eagerly await whatever was coming. Prez got up, went to his room, and came back with the Bible and his notepad. He began to read.

When he finished, the adults' faces were ashen and angry.

"Where did you get that stuff from, son?" asked Reverend Dorsey.

"From right here, in the Bible."

"No, no, I mean how did you know those words were in the Bible?"

Prez got up, went to his room, came back and showed them the booklet: *God Loves All His Children Equally but Separately.* His mother took it first. It got passed around with the adults flipping through the pages.

"Celia, ahem, I mean, Miss Adams, where did you put my briefcase?"

"Right there in the kitchen."

"May I get myself a glass?"

"Right in the cupboard," said Mattie.

"Would you gentlemen care to join me?"

All the men went into the kitchen. There was the sound of glasses clinking, liquid pouring, the ice tray being pried from the refrigerator, and more glass-clinking. Miss Stevens got up to use the bathroom. Aunt Celia closed the Bible, confiscated Prez's notepad, and placed them both out of sight. Mattie sat and continued to wring her hands and purse her lips.

After some time, the men came out of the kitchen and Prez could hear what they were saying.

"They're just another White Citizens' Council—the Klan, pure and simple."

"Bladensburg is right down the road from here. Not ten minutes."

"Bring the bottle with you."

Reverend Dorsey was holding the booklet in his hands. He walked over to where Prez was seated and bent over close to Prez's face. His breath reeked of alcohol, which Prez hated. But he just sat and said nothing.

"Never ever again doubt the Word. Am I clear, son?"

Prez did not respond.

Raising his voice, he said, "I said never doubt God's word again, boy!"

Prez, surprised at his own composure, remained still and quiet. He knew to try and ignore male drunkenness.

"Easy now," said Mr. Edwards—to whom, Prez wasn't sure.

"THiS!" the reverend's voice screamed, as he held the booklet aloft before continuing in a quieter, controlled voice, "has nothing to do with the word of God and our Lord and Savior Jesus Christ. These words are the thoughts of madness and hate. The organization responsible lives in hell with the devil. Their church is really Satan's palace. Oh, I know the little inno-cent-looking pamphlet sounds good and reads righteously because it quotes passages from the Bible."

As he spoke, the reverend began tearing pages from the booklet.

"And when you go to the Bible," continued the reverend, "there they are in black and white, the same words. But it's how the white man uses language to trick us, to make us believe something is there which really isn't." He tore pages in half and half again. "The truth is that this is all a lie!" The halves and quarters were torn into even smaller bits. "The truth is that this is all … it's all … bullshit!"

He rushed over to the living room door and out onto the balcony and threw the "devil's confetti" into the air.

"Bullshit!" the reverend yelled again as he leaned over the side of the balcony, cursing the drifting bits of paper.

Of course, it would be Prez with a broom and dustpan who would have to sweep that "bullshit" from the driveway.

Tala and Salome had been chiding Prez since he turned sixteen that May.

"It's time for you to get your license, man. We're tired of driving you everywhere."

"I'll use your car for the test, Tala."

"Oh, no you won't!" She laughed. "Use Salome's. She's right down the street from you."

"Sweet sixteen, huh, Prez. At last."

"Don't start, Salome. That was over a month ago."

"What? I just wanna say that even though you don't have a license, we know you can pop a clutch. Yeah, you just can't pop a cherry."

"Howard University will not accept you in that condition," said Tala. "But, seriously," she stopped laughing, "we'd like for you to come with us this morning."

Prez agreed to do something as unnatural for him as not breathing; training for non-violent protest.

"We don't serve no nigras in heeyah, boy. So why don't y'all just git up and git on outta heeyah. I said git!"

Prez sat bolt upright, rigid as a board, and not because he was scared. He was mad as hell. Just before being addressed as a "nigra" he had to sit idle while Lorraine Lorton got a pile of flour poured all over her head. She gasped for air so hard she seemed to choke.

Then big Leroy Dunnigan was actually pushed backward while sitting in a chair, almost smashing his head on the floor. And Prez had to just sit there and do nothing.

So Prez steeled himself for what was coming next, because he was told not to move from that chair and not to strike out in self-defense or, especially, in anger.

"You little rat-faced nigra, you ain't movin'!" Prez felt something on top of his head. It started moving and getting wider. It was warm.

"Lookit that! Never seen no cornbread that burnt befo'."

The molasses began slowly moving down his forehead towards his eyebrows. He took an extremely deep breath and wiped the molasses away from his eyes with the towel he had been given.

This horrendous abuse continued down the line of seated young Negroes. Prez's little brother Gus was there too. Not so little anymore, he was a strapping handsome boy almost six feet tall. He had agreed to come along with Prez just to see what it was like. He didn't like the idea of not defending himself against a physical attack, and was shocked that Prez would take part in anything like that. Prez, ever aware, realized that his little brother was a bit afraid.

"Lookit what we got heeyah! A dandy-lookin' nigger if eva there was one. Nigger got himself some penny loafers, a powder-blue cardigan. I tell you! Nigger even got a goddamn process on his stupid head. Nigger, you ain't white, you just a goddamned nigger! Sitting here lookin' stupid and … hey, buddy, come over heeyah, this one is scared to death. Well, what the hell you doing here if you scared?"

Prez looked over. He was ready to intervene.

"You over there, the burnt-cornbread nigra! Whatchew lookin' at? Better keep lookin' straight ahead and pay no attention to what's goin' on over heeyah!"

Prez looked away.

"I said you just a nigger. That process o' yours don't make you white. Well, since you still sittin' heeyah after I told ya ta leave, guess I'll have ta give that process a spit-shine." He spat on Gus's head.

Prez jumped up and punched him.

"Prez!" screamed Salome.

"Goddammit, Downs. Goddammit! You just knocked Raymond out. What in heaven's name is wrong with you? Get some ice," pleaded Chauncey.

"I'm not sure you're supposed to use ice cubes. Just pour some ice water down his underwear," offered Leroy.

"That's so goddamn 'street,' Leroy."

Chauncey began to curse everything and everybody that was "street." Prez turned Raymond over and lifted him to a sitting position. He applied the bag of ice to the back of his neck.

Tala was too angry at him to even look at him. She wanted to scratch his eyes out. She felt betrayed. She had convinced the committee that Prez was really ninety percent intellect and ten percent "street" even though it appeared the inverse of that was true.

"Wha' ... what happened?" a very groggy Raymond said, straining to open his eyes. "That's cold. My neck is freezing. Man, my head hurts. What happened?"

"Prez hit you," said Salome.

"You spit on my brother," Prez said, still holding the ice pack to Raymond's neck.

"I told you exactly what the training would entail," said Tala.

"I guess I didn't really think anyone would actually spit. Shouting '*nigger*,' pouring stuff over our heads, that's one thing. But to actually spit on another person is too violent."

Salome said, "Didn't we agree that for Prez it was going to be one strike and he's out?"

As Prez and Chauncey lifted Raymond up and sat him on a chair Chauncey asked Prez if he had anything to say.

"Yes. Can we sit?" The seven of them pulled chairs around Raymond. "When I was a little boy I was fascinated by the tale of John Henry—a big strong black man who on one single day beat a machine at laying railroad tracks. The effort killed him. He was so obsessed with his tools and his way of working that he forgot that the tracks were being laid to carry people to a destination. It is the destination that is sacred, not the tools you may be accustomed to using. Non-violent tactics are a tool. But freedom is our destination. And just like a dead John Henry never riding that freedom, those of us who die in this struggle will never be free because freedom is for the living."

"Mr. Ninety Percent! Didn't I tell you?" exclaimed Tala.

Prez wondered what the heck she was talking about. He took a little paperback book from his pocket. "This is *Negroes with Guns*. It was written by a man who lived in North Carolina and who started his local branch of the NAACP. His name is Robert F. Williams. He was in the Army. In fact, some of the fathers from my old Lincoln Park neighborhood knew him, they were in the Army with him. You know that, Tala.

"Robert F. Williams and his whole community were being brutalized and murdered by the Ku Klux Klan and nobody would protect them. The Klan even tried to lynch him and the only reason he is still alive is because he defended himself."

Opening the book, Prez started reading: "'It has always been an accepted right of Americans, as the history of our Western states proves, that where the law is unable, or unwilling, to enforce order, the citizens can, and must act in self-defense against lawless violence.' I am not saying that I disagree with the tactic of non-violence. And I am not saying that I like weapons, because I don't and you know that. I am strengthening my point that non-violence is not the only valid tactic to achieve our freedom, so don't pretend that it is. And don't claim that any other tactic is illegitimate. And don't dare say that if we witness acts of violence against our people, which will cause them to be brutalized or murdered, that we are to do nothing about it. That's a form of suicide."

The others looked a bit dumbfounded. Or was it awestruck? No one said anything until Leroy joked, "Anybody got a joint?"

"You know you can't smoke in here, Leroy."

"Hey, Chauncey, man, can't you take a joke?"

"This is not a time for joking. We have a very serious matter before us. Well, I suppose, two. The first is settled. As Mr. Downs has admitted that he is not suited to do non-violent actions. because he cannot remain non-violent. That also must apply to you, Mr. Gus Downs, and you too, Leroy. You all come from the streets. You have that street way about you. You are unsuited to be in this organization."

"Don't stop there. Include me, said Lorraine. Heck, I've had my own girl-crew since I was eleven.

"This is bull, Chauncey," said Salome, "You all don't know this but my family's first home was in Columbia Heights. My first boyfriend was a B-Boy. Does that make me unsuitable? Are you going to kick me out?"

"Well, kick me out too." said Tala, "because I'm a Lincoln Parker and I still flash my green. Do you know anything about Lincoln Park, what that neighborhood has been through, or exactly what Prez's contributions have been to bringing peace there?

"I'm afraid Chauncey has no idea what you're talking about," said Raymond. "I'm not sure he needs to. His business is to make sure the rules and regulations of the D.C. chapter of this organization are adhered to."

"You talk all that turn-the-other-cheek talk," said Gus, "and you want to train us to take all kinds of abuse from racist white people. You want us to be passive and forgiving while we are being hurt, maimed, and maybe even murdered. You claim to want to achieve freedom. Well, I think you're both full of shit. My brother cracks one of you in the jaw and you can't find forgiveness in your hearts so that we can achieve some unity. Rules and regulations? I think you're just making stuff up as you go along here to cover up that you are prejudiced. You are bourgie snobs."

"That is the most ridiculous thing I've ever heard," said Chauncey.

"Gus is right," said Leroy. "I've heard the talk—that saying you older cats have. You say there's the race struggle, the class struggle, and the ass struggle. This is the class struggle going down right now. And you are bringing it on."

"No, it's not about class," said Tala, "it's about caste. It's about the social stratification of sub-classes to further entrench structures of privilege and entitlement. When we say that somebody is 'street,' we are placing them in a sub-class, even below someone who is working class. 'Street' really means somebody who doesn't have a regular job, is on welfare, or hustles for a living. We help maintain stereotypes that end up victimizing us all.

"Thanks for listening," said Prez. "I'll leave. No hard feelings here." He got up and walked out. Gus, Leroy, Lorraine and Salome followed him out the door. Tala got up and followed them to the door. She stood outside and watched them turn on U Street and guessed they would stop at Ben's Chili Bowl. Damn, she thought, as she shielded her eyes while looking up at the sky, a half-smoke sausage and a beer would do the trick right now.

She heard the phone ringing behind her but ignored it. Someone else could get it. She turned around just as Chauncey had put the phone down. He sat down and dropped his forehead into his upturned palms.

"Medgar Evers is dead. They shot him in the back."

32

Washington, D.C., June 19, 1963

The streetcar stopped a few blocks from where he wanted to get off. "Everyone off here," the driver shouted. "Can't go any further." There were four streetcars in front of them not moving. The traffic was also at a standstill. Cab drivers made it worse by attempting impossible U-turns only to become stuck in weird diagonal positions.

Prez jogged down the street. Even before he reached the intersection where Garfinckle's Department Store stood he could hear the terse words and threats being exchanged between the white police and the largely African-American crowd. The police, alerted that there would be a protest, had arrived before sunrise and cordoned off the sidewalk. They blocked the entrance to the store. A white man in a suit stood outside the door and appeared to decide who would be let in. Those allowed in were all white since the store only employed whites. Worse than that, African-American customers were not allowed to try on shoes and clothes.

At 10:00 a.m. when the store was supposed to open to the public, a pudgy white police sergeant standing beside the suited man yelled into his bullhorn: "You must move away from the door and clear the sidewalk. If you don't move, we will move you!"

Horns kept honking, profanities spewed like fireworks, and racist taunts flew at the protestors like projectiles.

"We have the right to be on the sidewalk," a protester yelled.

"You won't move me," exclaimed another voice. "You won't move any of us!"

"Whoever said that," screamed the sergeant into his bullhorn, "you can take your coon ass back to Africa. Now git your black asses off the goddamned sidewalk and out of the street!"

"Ain't nobody movin', filthy cracker!" someone yelled.

The sergeant gave his bullhorn to a patrolman and grabbed the patrolman's nightstick. The patrolman seemed just as shocked as the protestors when the sergeant rushed towards the protestors with the nightstick and raised it to strike. But no sooner did he raise it than it was snatched from his hand and held high above his head. The crowd roared in approval. Prez was close enough to see that it was Wellington who had the nightstick. Reevie-Boy and Dee Cee stood on either side of him. Prez squeezed through the crowd to reach them.

"You late, Prez."

"Like old times now, ain't it, Prez?"

"Great to see you, man."

"We all here like we promised."

Prez looked around at them and almost got soggy-eyed.

"I missed you cats, ya know. But here we are now, in the present, living for the future."

Prez walked up to the sergeant and said, "I'm here to negotiate."

"Y'all hear that? This little nigger wants to 'negotiate.'" The sergeant guffawed and looked around at his officers who obliged with nods and smirks. Still, their fidgeting body language betrayed their trepidation. They knew they were not in control of the situation.

"Sergeant whatever-your-name-is, I could be just as rude and disrespectful as you. I could call you an ignorant Neanderthal who was still living in caves when my African ancestors were inventing math, calculating the distance between the earth and the stars, and building the Pyramids. I could call you a redneck humanoid that lacks enough melanin to acquire any skin tone so you take your big fat gut and flat butt to a beach and lie in some sun to try to get a tan. But I would rather address you respectfully as sir, and ask you, sir, if you would like your nightstick back."

"Just knock that little nigger's head off, Sarge," said a tall officer standing behind the sergeant.

Prez looked at the tall officer who made that remark, smiled really wide and said, "No, you do it. If you're so tough, you do it! If you're man enough, you do it! Take off your gun and your badge and I challenge you to a fair fight right here, right now."

Just then a firm hand was planted upon his shoulder. He turned. It was Reverend Josephus Clark, who had presided over Butch's funeral all those years ago. "Calm down, Preston Junior."

Another hand was placed on his other shoulder. "It's alright, Prez. We're all here. But this is not the way." It was Chauncey.

An arm went around his waist and squeezed him. "Preston, peace, not violence, will win the day, especially in the face of ignorance." It was Tala.

"Good morning, Sergeant." Prez was awfully glad to hear the voice of Master Flowers. "I am Attorney Flowers. I represent a number of prominent and respected civil rights clients, some of whom have sponsored this demonstration against the hateful, racist practices of the Garfinckle's chain of retail establishments. Of course, that should be of great interest to you and the Washington, D.C. police department. Are you here to serve Garfinckle's or the citizens of this city? Whatever brings you here, be advised to be careful not to violate the Constitutional rights of these people."

The sergeant was momentarily dumbfounded before regaining his composure. "You look here, Attorney; or so you say ..." Flowers handed him a business card. "Oh, you're *that* Flowers, the karate expert. Well, well. You listen to me, karate or no, lawyer or no, I am the police and I am the law. And when I say move, you move, and pronto. So, git! You tell these people they have to leave or they will be forcefully removed and anyone who resists will be locked up!"

"No, sir, you are not the law. You are entrusted with the duty to protect the public and property by enforcing the law. City Ordinance 14.0811b prohibits the closure of any pedestrian or vehicular thoroughfare without a notification of such closure being posted at least twenty-four hours before such closure is to take place. The exception, of course, is an emergency situation. But you arrived here before dawn this morning and well prior to the arrival of any of these citizens, so your presence here is not in response to an emergency. May I ask, Sergeant, why are you here? Who called you? And when?"

The sergeant was now flummoxed into silence. Prez turned and looked around. Behind the Reverend Clark was a phalanx of older guys from his and Butch's old Columbia Heights neighborhood, the original B-Boys. Around Chauncey was a contingent of people from his organization.

"I say we just bash their nigger skulls in and throw 'em in the fuckin' jailhouse, Sarge. What are we waiting for?" A group of officers rushed towards Master Flowers and Prez, knocking the sergeant to the ground as they did. Suddenly there was a melee of nightsticks, fists, and feet. Instinctively, Prez covered the sergeant, who was prone on the ground and struggling to get up. As Prez helped him up, he felt a sharp stinging blow to the back of his head that made him wince. He touched the point of contact and his hand came away bloody. The sergeant saw and looked around.

"Petersen! Petersen! Stop it! Put that nightstick down! All of you stop it now and fall back into your positions! Now! You okay, son?"

"Yeah," said Prez.

"You sure? Anybody else would have dropped from a knock like that. You need medical attention?"

"Sergeant! Will your Officer Petersen be reprimanded, or must we sue the force and the city?" said Flowers.

"Look. I'm alright," said Prez. "We just want to be treated like people. So here we are. You want us to move but we are not going to. We want Garfinckle's to treat us like people and will not stop the protest until it happens. How would you like it if you and your family couldn't go somewhere because of the color of your skin?"

Prez looked over and saw Brennie-Man's brother, angry, shouting profanities at the cops, and thought nothing had changed since the cops murdered Brennie-Man. He turned to face the crowd, took his green bandana from his pocket, and hoisted it high above his head. The surging began to subside. He made eye contact with as many of the guys as he could and the surging ceased. He turned to face the sergeant. He held his hand, palm open, over his head and Wellington gave him the nightstick. He gave it to the sergeant.

He noticed Freddie Snaps and the Serpents were there. They came to the front with him. Debra was there with her cousin Lorraine and the Mo-Girls. They all stood there stoically, not moving, until many hours later when Garfinckle's doors opened to let those employees who had come to work go home for the evening. They let them by.

He turned to Tala and said, "What a complicated day."

"What do you mean?"

"They're burying Medgar Evers today and here we've been trying to keep the freedom train on the track. It's also Juneteenth."

"I forgot about that."

"Mourning and celebrating simultaneously is what we seem to be really good at. It's so late. I gotta get home. It's my mother's birthday."

33

Washington, D.C., Saturday, July 6, 1963

Prez was invited to the annual Greek Letter Fourth of July bar-beque held at Rock Creek Park. It was so rare that an incoming freshman was invited that even Tala was impressed. At first, he balked at going, telling her, "they're just a bunch of square cats running around looking silly and doing silly-ass things." She convinced him that the experience would be good for him and that he risked offending a lot of guys given that he had received personal invitations.

Chauncey saw Prez enter the grounds and trotted over with another guy.

"Prez! How ya doin', my man?"

"Hey, Chauncey. How ya doing? Thanks for the invitation."

"Just doing my part, ya know. This is my older brother, Darnell." They all exchanged handshakes and shoulder bumps. "He's big but he's smarter than he is big. He has to be, he's Tala's boyfriend." Chauncey laughed out loud as Prez pondered leaving. Especially after Darnell quipped, "Yeah, I'd rather sue somebody than punch them."

Chauncey nudged Prez and pointed at carloads of girls driving by.

"You see right through that clearing?" Chauncey pointed. Prez squinted. "C'mon, Prez, you see the space between those two big trees that lean toward each other? The creek runs between them. Look just past there. See that bridge? Well, on the other side of the bridge is all the bush you'd ever want to see." He noticed the quizzical look on Prez's face. "You're such a kid sometimes, man. You don't know what I'm talking about. Even Darnell knows and he's still a virgin! Ha!"

Prez looked at Darnell who said with a stilted voice, "He's crudely talking about girls."

"No, no, no," said Chauncey. "Tell him right. Tell him exactly what bush is."

"He's talking about their privates, sir."

"Oh shit, stop being Shakespeare so we can have a beer."

"Alright then. Bush, my good fellow, is pussy." Chauncey and Darnell bent over laughing.

"And we are Bushmen," said Chauncey. "We like to get all into the bush. And there's a whole bunch'a bush over there. Sororities are having their picnics too. We all usually end up having one big picnic."

"Is that all you cats think about?" said Prez.

"What? Pussy? You better believe it. Class struggle, caste struggle ..." said Chauncey.

"And ass struggle," said Darnell, as he slapped five with Chauncey.

"Hey, look. Ooowee!" said one of the guys in the group. Girls were walking toward them. "Have you ever seen so much stuff in one place before? Look at 'em."

A procession of shorts, skimpy tops, and sheer billowing summer dresses moved toward them. There was a round of greetings. "Hey, how y'all doing?" "Great to see you all." "Wonderful day for our annual get-together, huh?" "When do y'all start pledging?" "We already started. Early bird catches the worm, you know." "You all parked way over there, huh. How come?" "We like our privacy." "We like your privates!" "Don't be nasty."

"Seems to be more sororities here than fraternities." "That's 'cause in the world there are more of us than you."

They danced to Martha and the Vandellas' *Heat Wave*, *The Harlem Shuffle* by Bob and Earl, *Two Lovers* by Mary Wells, *Baby Work Out* by Jackie Wilson, and *Our Day Will Come* by Ruby and the Romantics.

The hours passed and both the day and Darnell exhausted themselves. Tala looked at him snoring and seemed a bit put off.

Prez noticed and went over to her. "May I sit?"

She got up and walked to another tree and sat on the grass. Prez followed, and sat down beside her.

There was something that he couldn't quite pin down, a bouquet about her. Maybe it was her sweat from her dancing. Perhaps the heat had melded the beer and barbeque with her femaleness and the heady blend was seeping out through her pores. She seemed so preternaturally fresh to him, as if he were meeting her anew. Barbara Lewis's song on the radio—*Hello Stranger*—was perfect.

She finished her beer and got up to fetch another. She stood with a group passing around a joint before returning. She sat cross-legged swigging beer and swaying to the music. Her little dress was hiked up way over her knees. "It's too damn hot." She lifted the fabric away from her chest and flapped it as she blew air down onto her cleavage. Prez was delighted that she had those golden freckles on her chest. The moist outlines of her nipples invited him to imagine the taste. "Man, aren't you hot?" she said while flapping the front edge of her dress over her thighs. Prez could see her panties. He was getting woozy imagining being inside her. Then he glanced just above her. There was a tiny spider dangling.

"Don't move!"

"What? A bug?"

"Yeah," said Prez as he got up. "Let me get it. Be still." She let out a little "eek!" and stiffened her body while squeezing her eyes shut. Prez swished it away. "There," he said. "it's gone." She quickly stood.

"Where is it?" she said as she looked all around her feet.

"It's gone. Don't worry. Here, sit on this." He took off his shirt.

Damn, she thought as she sat down, he has a better body than my boyfriend. She wondered why she still thought of him as a kid when he was a full-grown man. Yes, she was older and people would always be judgmental. Salome had already warned her not to "rob the cradle." And he was her father's protégé, almost a surrogate son. Her father wouldn't approve.

Prez was wearing shorts and was aroused. She stared at his crotch, then closed her eyes and put her head back. Prez pulled a few sheets of folded paper from his pocket.

"What is that?"

"A speech by Frederick Douglass called *The Meaning of July Fourth for the Negro*."

"Shut up, Prez." She got up and pressed her forefinger lightly against his lips. "Just shut up. It's too hot here. Let's take a walk by the creek. Maybe that will cool things down."

Just as he bent down to pick up his shirt—*splat, splat!*

"What was that? It stinks!" said Tala.

Yellow stuff dripped on the grass. They looked up at the branch just above them.

"Looks like eggs," said Prez.

Prez grabbed Tala and they took cover behind the tree. He pulled her close and they kissed deeply while passionately rubbing their bodies together.

"YOU NIGGERS GIT THE FUCK OUT OF THE PARK!"

Prez peeked around the tree and saw a half-dozen white youths throwing eggs. He bolted off in their direction.

"It's just fucking eggs, Prez, leave it, man" screamed Chauncey. But other guys from the picnic were also giving chase.

Tala's boyfriend was awakened by the ruckus. He looked and saw Tala leaning against the tree with her arms crossed tightly about her midsection. She swayed lightly from side to side and gazed trancelike into the distance.

"What happened?" he asked.

"Oh, just go back to sleep," she said.

That evening Prez was invited to Chauncey's for a party. He was home waiting for Tala to come pick him up. A car horn beeped.

"Hey, Prez!" screamed Gus. "Your ride is here."

"I'll be right there." Prez was just finishing a call with his uncle Cadgie.

He rushed down the steps to his mother's usual admonition that he was going to break the steps one day if he kept running down them that way.

He shut the door and was very surprised to see Salome there waiting in her car.

"Where's Tala?"

"She's not going. Not feeling well. She called and asked me if I would drive you. Hey, don't look so disappointed. You're gonna hurt my feelings." She feigned sobbing sounds and rubbing tears from her eyes. They laughed.

"Can you run me by my uncle's first? He lives up on Buchanan. Turn around and take South Dakota Avenue."

"I know where I'm going. You're the one who's lost." He gave her his best one-eyebrow-raised, twisted, pursed-lip look.

"What's going on between you two, Prez?"

"Whaddaya mean?"

"Prez, don't try to bullshit me. I'm like your big sister. Remember? And she's like my sister. What's happening between my brother and my sister?"

Oh, damn, he thought. *Why did she have to put it like that?* "Nothing," he said.

"Tala's engaged, you know? My goodness, look at you. You are seriously upset."

"No, I'm not. Just tired."

"Prez, oh my lord. You cannot be in love with that woman. She is not for you."

"You're starting to sound like my mother now."

"Well, big sisters do that sometimes. I have never seen her more bothered than after the picnic. I asked her what happened. She said her heart was being torn apart. That she was aching for someone that she wasn't supposed to. That she has her principles."

They arrived at his uncle's after a twenty-minute ride with the only dialogue coming from the radio.

"Well, good for Tala, being strong and sticking to her principles," he said as he got out.

"You must be really bothered to take up a conversation that ended miles ago," she said as they approached the door.

Prez rang the bell. They could hear the click-clacking of high heels. The door opened and they were greeted by a very tall and glamorous woman.

"You must be Preston Junior. I'm Jemima. Please, come in."

"Hey, Little Preston." His uncle came down the steps buttoning up his shirt. "How you doing, kid?" They hugged and hugged some more. "Damn, if you don't look more like your daddy the older you get. You're taller now than he was."

"You should see Gussie, Uncle Cadgie. He's over six feet tall."

"Really. That's from your Grandpa. He was a big man. Remember him at all?" He turned towards Salome. "I'm sorry. Didn't mean to be rude, but I haven't seen my nephew in quite a while. Please Preston, introduce us."

"Uncle Cadgie, this is my dear friend and pretend big sister Salome. Salome, this is my Uncle Cadgie."

"You've already met Jemima," said Cadgie. She's my dear friend and pretend wife."

"Hmph! Well, we wouldn't have to pretend if he'd just pop the question," Jemima said, while giving him a playful slap on the back of his head. She hugged Salome and Prez.

"This is a big place you have," said Salome to Jemima.

"What happened to your hand?" Cadgie asked Prez.

"That's what I wanted to talk to you about, Uncle Cadgie."

"C'mon down to the basement. I'll put on some Lester Young and you can tell me all about it. Sugar Pie, will you bring down a root beer for Preston? Please."

"What about you, Uncle Cadgie? What are you going to drink?" asked Prez as they descended the stairs to the basement. "Oh man, what a basement!"

"Yeah, I modeled it after Jimmy MacPhail's Gold Room, bar and all," said Cadgie. He disappeared behind the bar and retrieved a tall glass, then went over to a big wooden keg and turned the tap. Beer flowed into the glass with a swishing, gurgling sound and created thick and sudsy foam that spilled over the rim of the glass. Cadgie caught the foam with his forefinger and deposited it into his mouth with a slurping sound. Jemima came down and brought Prez his root beer. She had Salome in tow. Cadgie took a long drink, almost emptying his glass.

"Ahh," he said. "You won't find a better beer in all of D.C.. So, what's happening?"

Prez gave him a look and glanced over in the direction of Jemima and Salome sitting on the sofa talking.

"Say, Sugar Pie, why don't you take Salome upstairs and show her some baby pictures of Preston and Gussie."

"Oh, I'd really like that," said Salome.

Prez frowned, furrowing his brow at his uncle.

"What? I got rid of them, didn't I? You're welcome. So, what happened to your hand?"

Prez told him about the egg-throwing incident at the park and the chase.

"I caught up to them and grabbed the closest one I could get my hands on. My boys and I had decided that we wanted to hold 'em and call the police to see what the cops would do. I also thought it would be useful to make an incident out of it, you know, get it in the papers, expose the racism, them calling us niggers. I flipped the guy onto his stomach, straddled his back and put him in a choke hold. I told him if he wanted to give up then tap his hand on the ground. He tapped and I let him turn over. We recognized one another at the same time. I couldn't believe it. It threw me off guard. It was little Stephen—Shaggie—from our old neighborhood in Southeast. I knew I couldn't turn him over to the police. But I really needed to ask him, how did we go from being best friends in third grade to him calling me nigger and throwing eggs at us? Before I could ask, he pulled a knife and started swiping at me. He cut my hand and ran off."

"Well, kid, doesn't sound like your old friend Stephen is so little any more. And he sure ain't your friend any more, either. Hold on."

Cadgie went behind the bar, bent down, opened and shut a metallic-sounding lid, and came up holding an oilcloth. He unwrapped it and removed a little pistol. "This little thirty-two is what you bring to a knife fight. Never get caught out like that again. Next time the blade could do a lot more damage, maybe even end your life. Is that what you want?"

"No, that's not what I want, and I don't want that gun either."

"You're not afraid of guns, are you? Your daddy was afraid of them. Remember your Grandma Denie's little derringer?" *Oh yes*, thought Prez, *I remember*. "Let me tell you, your daddy, when he was little, he'd pee on himself every time he saw it."

"I'm not afraid of guns, I just don't want one."

"What will you do next time somebody pulls a knife on you?"

"I'll be better prepared next time. I'm going to go into training so I can defend against a knife."

"You're gonna what? I love you, Preston Junior, but I have to tell you that for the first time since you were born, I look at you and I see a fool. I can't respect fools. But you are my nephew, you got no father, so I have to try to overlook a few things here and soldier on." He turned and retrieved a cognac glass from an overhead rack. He reached under the bar and got a bottle of cognac. He looked at Prez, slammed his fist down onto the bartop, and shouted "Motherfuck!" He threw the glass into the fireplace, where it shattered, and said "Shit! I need whiskey."

He got himself a shot glass and a bottle of Johnnie Walker. He poured himself some and gulped it down. He took a deep breath.

"I said something that I didn't mean. I will always respect you, just as I will always respect the memory of your father, my baby brother. You are both made of the same stuff. I know what it is. It is honor. You have the same sense of honor regarding how you think you are supposed to conduct yourself even in the face of danger. Maybe your tumbled thinking comes from having your talents and martial skills, and I know you train at, what is it, Japanese, Korean?"

"It's Chinese and Filipino."

"Now that's a mishmash if I ever heard one. Look at you, smart, strong, handsome, with girls so desperate to get close to you that they'll even be your big sister."

"You're wrong about that, really wrong. Salome isn't like that at all. She's like a sister to me. We talk. She gives me good advice. She knows what to say to get her point across so that I hear her."

"Alright then, let me calm down so that I will say the right thing and get my point across. Violence is not about rules and regulations. And it definitely is not about honor. It's about life or death. I don't want to go to your funeral, Preston. I don't want your mother to have to bury you. Let me wise you up. Your skills and talents against someone unskilled or untalented is akin to bringing a weapon to a fist fight. You ever think about that?"

"I guess not. But, are you telling me that I need to stop trying to be a decent person?"

"Oh, boy." Cadgie poured himself another shot and gulped it down. "No, I'm not. But I am telling you that being decent can get you killed. You can only afford to be decent after you've won. You haven't touched your root beer. It's probably warm now." He put ice cubes in a beer glass and poured in the root beer.

"I hear what you are saying, but I need to make sense of things in order to function properly."

"Oh, boy." Cadgie poured himself another shot and downed it. He lifted the bottle and peered down into it. "Can't believe I'm about to finish this whole goddamn bottle of Johnnie Walker. I recognize that my way of thinking may not be the best way. Old guys like me, we are counting on you kids to be smarter. Anybody can tell you something is broken. But only the brightest can tell us how to fix things. But you can't fix anything when you're dead. So here, you need to take this with you and learn how to use it. It's just another tool in your tool box. Go out in the country somewhere and learn how to hit what you look at. That's all I am asking. I am not saying to carry it around with you. I am not telling you to start thinking like a bully or a criminal. You might actually forget that you have it until you need it, like we don't drive around thinking we have a jack in the trunk, do we? So please take it and learn how to use it."

Hearing an argument he had advanced thrown back at him was weird. But he didn't want that pistol. "What about you, Uncle Cadgie? How will you protect yourself and Jemima?"

"I got protection all over this house. And Jemima shoots with a .44 Magnum revolver. That's a big brute of a gun that kicks like a mule and will stop a bull."

Walking back to Salome's car Prez asked, "Do you have a jack in your trunk?"

"What's a jack?"

"Oh, man. I should have ducked. Do you have a spare tire?"

"Jesus, Prez, I don't know."

"Open your trunk. There. You do. Those tools are for fixing flat tires."

"Let me tell you what happens if this car gets a flat. It gets abandoned. I get out and catch a cab."

"You're supposed to fix your flat." Salome crossed her arms, gave him a not-on-your-life-sucker look that made him laugh again. "Can I put this bag in your trunk?"

❧

When they arrived at Chauncey's they were both surprised to see Tala's car; and even more surprised that she was sitting in it. Salome got out of her car and didn't even bother looking Tala's way. When Prez got out, Salome said, "I'm sure she has some words for you."

Prez walked over, opened the passenger side door and got in.

"What happened earlier today in the park didn't really happen," said Tala. Prez let out a long sigh and looked away. "Don't be like that. We have to forget it. I cannot fall for you. I will not fall for you. I'm engaged already. I love my fiancé. You're just a kid to me. Well, say something."

Prez got out of the car and started walking down the street. He felt her looking at him as she slowly drove by but he wouldn't return her gaze. After she passed, he turned around and walked back to Chauncey's door and rang the bell. He spoke with Chauncey for a few minutes until Salome came out.

"So, the big hurt, huh?"

"I need a favor. Can you drive me back to my uncle's? There's something in your trunk I need to return."

34

Washington, D.C., late July, 1963

Tala accompanied Chauncey downtown to the office of the march's organizing committee. Prez tagged along and was a bit put off that the committee asked that he and Tala wait outside of the room. It was a quick meeting. Chauncey came out in a huff, slammed the door, and commanded, "Let's go." As they approached Tala's car he said, "I'm in a hurry. You drive, Prez."

"It's Tala's car," said Prez as he got in the back seat.

The heavy fifteen-minute silence was broken as they rounded Logan Circle.

"People are already on the move," said Chauncey. "They're comin' up from the South where the tree leaves are bloodstained from lynching and the grass still singed from the burning of crosses. Caravans are coming from the soiled shores of the West Coast. Native peoples are coming from the sagebrush steppes of the Southwest. The descendants of the Pilgrims are coming from the Northeast led by women who would have been burned alive as witches just a few centuries ago. Even foreigners are coming from places like Canada and Japan. And those old assholes are fussing at me about tone, telling me that I cannot give my speech the way I want to give it because it is too 'militant.' I will not change a word."

Back at his own headquarters, Chauncey said, "Goddammit! I'm sick and tired of funerals, whether for progressive people or progressive ideas." He looked up at Prez. "I should have listened. You never agreed with the non-violent approach."

"True. It becomes a bit grotesque, like last May during the so-called Children's Campaign. The adults in charge, instead of protecting the children, put them out there to be brutalized. Did you see on TV how the police sicced dogs on them and beat them? Over nine hundred children were arrested, even an eight-year-old.

"But look, Chauncey, I think this upcoming march is too important. The whole world will be watching. You can alter your tone and play with words to protect the substance of your speech. Your thoughts need to be heard."

"Alright. Yeah, Prez. Okay, let's keep making those posters."

Salome, huge stapler in hand, asked, "Chauncey, will anyone, preferably a woman, speak about women's rights?"

"You know full well what the march is about. It's about jobs and freedom."

The women looked at each other incredulously. "That's no answer!" said Salome.

"There will be women speaking. I'm sure of it," said Chauncey. "The details of the speakers' list are still being worked out. Women's rights is a fairly broad subject. What specifically do you want addressed?"

"Jobs and freedom are fairly broad subjects," Tala retorted. "What specifically will be addressed?"

After moments of awkward silence, Chauncey said, "I know Myrlie Evers is speaking. She'll be talking about her husband and maybe the NAACP. And another lady is going to speak about the role of women in the civil rights struggle."

"History is important," said Salome. "but who will speak about the actual problems we face daily and how to fix them?"

"Ah, shit!" said Chauncey. "Nobody." He clapped his hands together, plopped down in his chair and squeezed his eyes shut. "Nobody, nobody, nobody! That's what's going on. That's why they want me to change my speech. They don't want anyone to speak about real liberation."

35

Howard University, September, 1963

"Hello. I am Professor Koko Okoro and I greet you with cheer this morning. I am thrilled to see so many of you here, bright-eyed and bushy-tailed, as they say. You are at the very beginning of an intellectual journey that I sincerely hope will mean more to you than credits towards your undergraduate degree.

"I shall proceed blissfully along under the assumption that you are all here because you chose to be. But I must inquire before I proceed if there are any questions or qualms about the syllabus or reading list.

"Alright..." The professor ran her forefinger over her seating chart. "Lamay, Miss Marsha Lamay."

"Good morning, professor. I notice that your reading list is divided into three groups, A, B, and C. I just want to verify that group A is mandatory, group B not mandatory but necessary for a fuller understanding, and group C just for personal interest."

Prez glanced over his shoulder at the speaker. Damn! he thought. Look at the legs on that girl! She caught his eye and they exchanged quick smiles. He quickly turned back around.

"Yes," said Professor Okoro. "I'll go along with your characterization. Let me clarify. Required reading, group A, is for passing. Supportive reading, group B, can lead to a deeper understanding of the course material. Consider it my gift to you. Group C material will, hopefully, allow you to imagine the multiple and non-linear vistas of investigative thought available to you while attempting to solve thought problems. It's worth something tangible. Any group C material accurately and effectively incorporated into your writing assignments gets you one point five extra percentage points. Think about it as your gift to yourself. Any more questions?

"Mr. …" The professor ran her forefinger over her seating chart again. "Downs, Preston Downs. Yes?"

"Thank you, Professor Okoro. I was just wondering, having looked over the course syllabus, why are we beginning with René Descartes?"

"Has anyone else wondered about that? Don't be shy. Has anyone else bothered to look at my syllabus? Anyone? Oh my, I do see a couple of hands. Mr. Downs, why did you ask me that question?"

"Descartes was a seventeenth-century European philosopher. I am aware that he is commonly called the father of philosophy, but how can that be when philosophy existed in the motherland long before Descartes was even born?"

"Your question is a very good one. This is my fourth year teaching this course and no one has ever asked me that question before." She rose from her seat and moved around to the front of her desk.

"We are studying Descartes within the context of the development of European intellectual and academic disciplines. The United States of America were founded upon principles that evolved from and within that context.

"Secondly, by starting our investigation into philosophy with Descartes we are not negating nor ignoring the origins of human intellectual development and the rise of systematic critical thought which occurred in Africa. We are acknowledging, as we must, that the European codification and categorization of the intellectual disciplines we currently practice represent qualitatively new stages in human intellectual development."

As they left class and walked down the hall, primal urges compelled Prez to walk directly behind Miss Marsha Lamay. She was wearing a miniskirt. His Physics 101 class had introduced him to motion mechanics. It was all there for him to observe: rotation, velocity, acceleration. He was being so studious that he walked right into a really tall guy waiting on the steps outside who said, "Gee, thanks, little fella, for misleading the prof into thinking we all give a damn."

"Oh shit! Big Ricky! Oh, man, it's so good to see you. You were always tall, but shit, what did your mother feed you?"

They laughed and embraced, then sat down a bench.

"Man, it's been so long," said Prez.

"Yeah, way too long." Richard Lee Brooks was from Prez's original neighborhood of Columbia Heights. "Last time was at Butch's funeral."

"Was it? We were peewees then. How are your parents?"

"I'm like you, man, my father isn't here anymore. He had a heart attack. I was in eleventh grade. He never saw me graduate high school."

"I'm sorry to hear that," said Prez. "We need our fathers, man. I know I need mine more with every passing year, but he's not coming back. So, I need to grow up."

"Prez, if my father were alive, he'd be a happy grandfather."

"What? You're a father? Who's the mother?"

"Millie. You remember Millie. Lived up on Eleventh Street."

"Rick, of course, we all started kindergarten together at Banneker, man. You two have known each other all your lives. There's something kinda beautiful about that."

"I dunno, man. Her parents hate me. But they put up with me. I thought I should marry Millie to make things right. Her

232

parents, especially her mother, were dead set against it. Next thing I know, I'm standing in a courtroom with my parents and the judge says that Millie's parents are the legal guardians of my son. I didn't know what else to do, so I started crying. I was just so confused. I didn't know what any of that stuff meant. That was the summer after junior high. My father asked if he had any rights as a grandfather and the judge said no. Everyone was crying. I mean, except little Richard Lee. I guess he was wondering what the heck was wrong with all of us." He giggled. "Little Ricky'll be five soon. And there's not a day that goes by that I don't appreciate how smart Millie's parents were. They have promised me and Millie that as soon as we are twenty-one, they are going to legally relinquish their guardianship and release the trust fund they set up for little Richard Lee into Millie's name. And you know what? They are paying my tuition here, man."

"They really love you, man. They love you and Millie and your son. Going to court like that must have broken their hearts. What about basketball, you're still playing, aren't you?"

"I had to stop. I have a heart condition. If I overexert myself, my heart could explode. Don't feel bad for me, though. It's all under control with the drugs I'm taking."

"Why are you taking philosophy classes?"

"Law school, man. After my experience in that courtroom, and seeing how much power that judge had, I decided I wanted to learn law and become a judge someday. Philosophy is a prerequisite for law."

"Same for me, Rick. I want to be a lawyer too, a really powerful lawyer who can take on the system and win."

"New leaf, huh, Prez? Make 'em eat crow instead of knuckle sandwiches. I can dig it."

"Hey, look, tonight we're over at the *Café Campus* on Georgia Avenue. A bunch of us have been getting together ever since

Medgar Evers was killed. We already had some stuff going on to try and unify us in this city. You must have heard about what we accomplished with the Serpents. Truce, baby. Now we want to pull the whole city together, especially after the march."

"But I thought the march was a good thing."

"It was a historical event of magnificent proportions. But we learned something. We were not in control of the agenda and we have no idea what will come of it. A whole bunch of people showed up. So what? Was it like we've always done since slavery, taking part in something on faith and hoping that somehow the end result will benefit us?"

"But didn't President Kennedy meet with the leaders after the march? He promised to do something."

"To do what exactly? I think he was delivering rhetoric. He's never addressed the essential question we raised and resolved at our very first meeting. Is freedom a right or a privilege? What do you think?"

"Is that a trick question, man?"

"No. It ain't. What's your answer? Hey, Rick, wake the fuck up, man. Think about the words of the Declaration of Independence." Prez pulled a copy from his bag. "Here, read it out loud so you can hear yourself."

"We hold these truths to be self-evident."

"Okay. Stop right there and think about what 'self-evident' means. Go on."

"... that all men are created equal and that they are endowed by their Creator with certain inalienable rights, that among these are life, liberty, and the pursuit of happiness."

"Rick. There it is."

Rick read back over those lines, allowing his lips to move with the words as if that would help him to absorb the meaning and apply it to the problem at hand.

"Of course, Prez. We were born free and with rights. I knew that. So why did I have such a problem with your question?"

"Because of our conditioning in this society. You have read those words so many times that they've become practically irrelevant, like the Lord's Prayer. No one can give you your birthright. And that includes the president, and the government. We believe that those leaders who met with the president are waiting for him to 'give' us our freedom, instead of demanding that he recognizes and protects the freedoms that we already have."

"That's deep, man. Let's get to the meeting."

Prez had a big problem: expressive tangentialism. He thought that designation up all by himself. He considered himself lucky to be afflicted with something that he could identify. Whether he was reading, thinking, or talking, he always went off at a tangent to the subject matter at hand. One thing always led to another. There were layers under layers. He just wanted to see them all. Which was why, as he rode the streetcar up Georgia Avenue to his class at Howard, he was deep into Friedrich Engels' *The Materialist Conception of History*, a book that wasn't even on Professor Okoro's list but one that had been referenced in another book on her C reading list. The professor had said that she would be discussing the philosophy of history so he felt he was just taking some very constructive initiative. He intended to ask her if he would get any extra points for referencing the book.

Having one's attention buried in a book can obscure things going on around oneself; that realization struck Prez when he looked up to see Miss Marsha Lamay sitting on the streetcar a few seats in front of him. He had no memory of her getting on.

"Hello, Miss Lamay. I hope you remember me. From class. I'm Preston Downs. Philosophy. May I sit down?"

"Oh yes, I remember you. Don't they call you Prez or something like that?"

"How'd you know that?"

"Think back, year before last at the Southeast Washington Boxing Tournament. Do you remember a tall, curly-haired, light-skinned boxer?"

"Oh yeah. He was really good. Good jab, nice hand speed, good footwork. I enjoyed watching his bout."

"You weren't watching. You knocked him out in the second round."

"Oh ... *that* tall, curly-haired guy."

"That was my big brother. I hated you for a long time after that. You ruined his dream."

"But he got a silver medal. That's quite an accomplishment. Look, I'm sorry. This was a bad idea." He took advantage of the streetcar being at a stop and got off. He was still a few stops away from Howard, but it was a lovely morning and he had time to engage in one of his favorite pastimes, walking, even in stifling heat.

As he approached the next stop, he saw that Marsha had gotten off and was waiting for him.

"Mr. Downs. Preston. I'm sorry. That was so immature and thoughtless of me."

"Your brother, he's doing alright?"

"Oh, sure. It was frightening to see him out cold for so long. But afterward he said he was glad it happened because it made him realize that boxing was not for him and maybe not for anybody. He became so inspired he decided to become a neurosurgeon. He's in med school now, two years to go before he graduates."

Prez smirked as he thought about how a good ass-whipping could change a motherfucker's mind, but he said, "That's really fantastic news. Great, really."

"Are you still boxing? My dad said you looked like you could go all the way to pro if you wanted to."

"No. I stopped."

"Really?"

"Yeah, I couldn't figure out why I was doing it any more, where it was supposed to lead. I read this novel called *Mandingo* soon after that tournament and couldn't stomach fighting another soul brother. And the way this country is treating us, I lost my desire to represent it. The thought of turning pro and fighting for money made me feel kind of dirty; filthy is a better word—filthy like one slave fighting another to please the master."

"We're not slaves anymore," said Marsha.

"But," said Prez, "the dollar is still the master."

They walked up Georgia Avenue defying the late summer's heavy heat.

"Thank goodness it's only Thursday. That will give things a chance to cool down by the weekend," said Marsha. "If it doesn't cool down, I'm burnt toast on Saturday."

"What do you mean by that?"

"I'm racing on Saturday. I don't do well in the heat. It's bad enough to get beat, but to get left behind and struggle to the finish, that's getting burned really bad."

"You do cross-country?"

"Yes, I do. I've been running cross-country since I was about six or seven. My whole family runs. We go out for what is supposed to be a slow, fun run, and end up racing. My dad's a big cheat. He'll drift off way out in front and then scream that the race is on to the next big tree or whatever, but he'll be halfway there already."

"But," said Prez, "you don't seem to be built for distance. You have ... your legs are so ..."

"Oh, will you stop it! You're checking me out on the sly."

"No I'm not, just searching for the right medical or scientific terms. C'mon, though, you know you're not built like a distance runner."

"I run the hurdles."

"See, I know what I'm talking about. I did it the dialectical way—observation, investigation, and conclusion."

"You're nuts. You know that?"

"Where are you running this weekend?"

"At the Bladensburg Races."

"Hey!" Prez burst out laughing. "That's in my neck of the woods. I live near there. You do mean Bladensburg, Maryland?"

"Yes. That's right. But what's so funny about that?"

"The Bladensburg Races. That's historical. The original Bladensburg Races occurred in 1814, during the War of 1812. But it really wasn't a race. It was a humiliating defeat at the Battle of Bladensburg of the American forces, who were trying to keep the British from reaching Washington. The British sailed down the Chesapeake Bay, landed, started marching, and when they got to Bladensburg the American forces turned and ran. The press, disgusted, called it the Bladensburg Races."

"Wow. I knew nothing about that. How did you find out about it?"

"This past fourth of July, I was curious about the song, 'The Star-Spangled Banner.' We all know Francis Scott Key wrote it, but I wanted to know more, you know, about Fort McHenry, why he was there and all that. Well, it turns out he was there because the president had asked him to go talk to the British about releasing a man, a close friend of the president's. The British had captured him when they overran Bladensburg, went on to Washington, burned the city, and captured some prominent Americans. Well, this guy for sure, just can't remember his name right now. Anyway, Francis Scott Key went up there and got stuck in Fort McHenry, so he was there when the British attacked. And that's when he wrote the song."

"You must have loved history classes, then."

"Actually, no, I hated them. They just wanted us to memorize a bunch of names and dates without painting the context. Stuff doesn't just happen, you know, and great men just don't show up in history without a reason."

"What about great women?"

"Especially great women."

"What's that supposed to mean?"

"Hm, well, it sounded good, but back to history teachers. Without context, they paint a false picture in history class. After what I just told you, do you still think of the writing of "The Star-Spangled Banner" as being something heroic?"

"Maybe not totally. Not like before, you know, now that I know about the original Bladensburg Races."

"See, that's what I mean. Why didn't they teach us that part? And the worst part for me was when I read that Francis Scott Key was one of the officers at the Battle of Bladensburg and he took off and ran too. Imagine, an officer leaving his men and running away from a fight. That, to me, is low, low, low. When you're a leader you never leave your men behind. Now I can't listen to "The Star-Spangled Banner" without thinking about old Francis Scott Key being a main participant in the Bladensburg Races."

"Wow. Is that stuff true, Preston?"

"I read it in a book about the War of 1812 and in another book about Francis Scott Key."

They walked along in silence for a while, trying not exert any more energy than necessary.

"Is it alright with you if I come to watch you run on Saturday?"

"Sure, I don't care. My family will be there. They'll probably think you're my new boyfriend or something."

They sat down on a bench. Prez took out his pen and some paper and starting writing. When he finished, he stood up in front of Marsha and read what he had written:

I, Preston Coleman Downs III
Do solemnly swear
That whenever you need me I'll be there

That I'll honor my oath
To always be true
And never give you a reason to be blue

I will build for us
Through strength and trust
A skyward momentum never knowing bust

I reach out
With my palms opened wide
For your hands to be placed inside

He gave her the poem.

"Oh, my! You're asking me to be your girlfriend? Are you sure? We don't know each other. Are you positive? How do you know? You just wrote that out of the blue? Yes. I'll be your girlfriend."

It would become a ritual that after Friday's track practice, Prez accompanied Marsha to her home and had dinner with her family. The shocker for him was that she lived on North Carolina Avenue just down the street, albeit a very nice street, from Lincoln Park. Her family were Catholics and she always attended Catholic schools, which partially explained why Prez had never seen her when he lived in the area.

The very first time he sat down with them for dinner, her father made no effort to conceal the fact that he was tolerating Prez's presence for a greater good called peace in his home. Prez could see right through Marsha's father, yet he redoubled his efforts to dissolve the man's intolerance towards him. Prez's efforts to break the ice were awkward. Initiating a conversation regarding the significance of John Stuart Mill being Bertrand Russell's secular godfather did not produce positive results. Marsha's mother was amused at Prez's take on critical thinking. Her father was, well, just nasty.

"Secular godfather? Isn't that a bit like saying that something is a true lie? Heh?"

After dinner Prez was surprised that Marsha's father did not help clear the table and wash the dishes. He went into the living room and sat in a huge tan leather lounge chair. On a folding tray in front of him he had a small clear glass filled halfway with a green liquid that Prez thought must have been poured from the bottle of Crème de Menthe also on the tray.

As Prez helped with the dishes he observed Mr. Lamay pour into his glass a few times. After the last dishes were dried and put away, Mrs. Lamay suggested they go sit in the living room and listen to some Béla Bartók recordings she inherited from her father.

"I've got Hungarian on my father's side. That side of my family have been devout Catholics for many generations, I've been told. But what do I know?"

"What does she care?" piped in Mr. Lamay snarkily. "She's an atheist."

"I just read an article in *DownBeat* where Miles Davis said he's been influenced by Bartók's music. What a coincidence," said Prez.

Marsha cast a sort of *take that you idiot!* look at her father. But he was just getting warmed up.

"What I really want to know, Mister Prez, is whether or not you have ceased your hoodlum ways?"

"Robert!" said Marsha's mother with a stern look on her face. "Let him answer."

"Can you explain what you are referring to, sir?" said Prez.

"The Schnapple family and mine go way back. Our families attended the same church. They are long-time patients of mine as well. I remember keenly that young Frederick required a great deal of dental work some years ago after you beat him up."

"Oh, that was way back when I was in seventh grade. I didn't beat him up. Freddie Snaps, they called him. He was the leader of the Anacostia Serpents. I was the leader of the Lincoln Parkers. He came over to our school acting like a bully and picked a fight with me. It was a fair fight. I believe in fairness. It doesn't seem fair to me that you would criticize my behavior and not his. I'm proud to say that since then a lot has changed. We called a truce a long time ago. Nobody is gangfighting in this city anymore. We treat each other like brothers."

When Prez got up to leave he said, "Thanks for inviting me over for dinner, Mr. and Mrs. Lamay. I really enjoyed it. Sorry I missed your brother, Marsha."

"Well, frankly," Mr. Lamay had said, "I got sick and tired of Marsha whining about it."

Just before the third Friday's dinner, Marsha coaxed Prez out to the back-alley garage ostensibly to look for some old track cleats. Instead she produced the keys to her father's car, pulled Prez down onto her in the back seat—and that was how Prez lost his virginity. It was nothing like he had expected. Nothing at all.

After that, sexual intimacy with Marsha was a rarity, though they were constantly kissing, hugging, dry humping, and moaning. He had seen more of her body watching her run than when they were alone together. At track practices and meets he discovered she had breasts. He noticed them, he felt, quite late in the course of things. But when he thought about it, he was really a face guy. Even though it was Marsha's legs that first caught his attention, her face sealed it. The saying was that opposites attract, yet he and Marsha were both very shy. Up until that garage episode and often thereafter, he and Marsha were probably making Plato very happy. He needed to read up on that.

Washington, D.C., November 22, 1963

One Friday toward the end of November, he arrived in the early afternoon to pick Marsha up from track practice and found her already dressed and waiting for him. She was more somber than he had ever seen her.

"Hey," he said, smiling, "who died?"

"President Kennedy."

"Very funny. Hey, you can't be that nervous." Prez was taken aback. Marsha had not exhibited even a hint of sarcasm or dry humor before. This track stuff must be really affecting her, he thought. Her eyes were welling up with tears; she starting shaking. He put his arms around her. "It's just track and field, Marsha. It's not the end of the world."

"President Kennedy got shot. They killed him for real. Don't you know?"

"What the hell are you talking about?" He released her and took a step back.

"It's true. Coach told us. He cancelled practice. I called my mother. It's true. He's dead. Kennedy's dead."

Prez sat down on the steps beside her. He pinched his temples to try and quell the feeling that his brain was swimming around in his head.

"Somebody shot the president? President Kennedy? Who would do that? How can you shoot the president? Wait, Marsha, it can't be true. You're talking about President Kennedy. He has too much protection—the Secret Service, the FBI, the army. It's impossible. C'mon, I'm taking you home."

As they walked toward the streetcar stop the streets felt deserted; the day suddenly seemed ominous, as if a natural disaster had occurred. A car stopped at a light and they heard its radio blaring, "President Kennedy was shot today at around twelve thirty in Dealey Plaza. He was pronounced dead at one o'clock."

Classes didn't resume at Howard until the week after the state funeral for the assassinated president. The mood on campus was somber, like a ghastly cloud of sulfur ash the winds couldn't blow away. Prez sat in his first creative writing class taught by a professor with a very radical reputation. He began the class expressing his great skepticism of the official government version of events surrounding the assassination. Some of his students were from families who had one or both parents on the police force, in the military, or working for the government overseas. Their sense of patriotism would not allow them to question anything the government said. But the professor had what he hoped was an antidote to what he called "the arrogant stupidity of nation-state worship."

"Let us imagine a big steamship rolling down the river. It's so long one cannot see the whole thing until it sails by. Seagulls are flying all around it. There are people standing on the eastern shore and people standing on the western shore. They see the steamship approaching and wave to the captain while the ship is still some ways off.

"From the cargo hold at the rear of the ship, and unseen by observers on both shores, emerge two assassins, one wearing a red hat; the other, a blue hat. Red Hat sneaks along the port side while Blue Hat sneaks along the starboard side. The people on the eastern shore can see Blue Hat but not Red Hat. Those on the western shore can see Red Hat but not Blue Hat. They wave again at the captain, who does not suspect he is about to be killed. The captain looks up to wave and there is the sound of gunfire as Blue Hat and Red Hat open fire. The captain's body is jerked toward the port side but he bounces off something and falls off the bridge toward the starboard side and rolls into the water. You are following me, I trust, because I am giving a lecture—surprise!

"Those with last names from the letter A to M are port-side observers. N to Z are starboard observers. Fair warning: this will be a very tricky exercise. My class, creative writing for legalese, is about using the tools of creative writing to create opinions that will stand up under the scrutiny of jurisprudence. You need to write well to keep people awake, interested, and following your line of reasoning. I need a thousand words from each of you." There were audible moans and groans.

"The name of the vessel, by the way, is the Honky Dory." He looked into mostly blank faces. "You'll get it one day, I'm sure. You will give me a thousand typewritten words on what happened to the Honky Dory's captain. I repeat—typewritten. You give me anything handwritten and I will thank you for something I can promptly ball up and shoot two points in the trash basket with."

Moans and groans. "Oh, yeah. Let me hear 'em. C'mon, let it all out. You should know I am being quite lenient. In past years I would have immediately consulted my seating chart to identify the whiners and invited them to leave. There are other courses available to fulfill credit requirements, though none offering double credits. And I suppose that was the allure, wasn't it? Hopefully, the double credits aren't the only incentive. This is an elective. You are here because you chose to be. I am Dr. Eugene Mackey, your taskmaster for this semester. I will not let you down. See you next class. Ah, wait please … Mr. Downs, is there a Preston Downs here?" Prez was already rushing out the door to meet Marsha. "May I have a word with you?"

"Definitely, Professor Mackey, what about?"

"I read your essay, "From B-Boys to Soul Brothers." Fascinating. It was unsolicited, I understand."

"True. Professor Okoro didn't ask for it, but I did ask her permission to write it and asked if it could count towards my final mark."

"Your one-hundred-percent-plus mark. An A-plus-plus, I believe she said. How were you able to nail down the transition in their thinking with such profundity?"

"I was writing about something I knew and something I had experienced." He hoped he would remember to write *profundity* down in his notebook. "And also, something that is dear to my heart."

"And what might that be?"

"Negro unity and Negroes loving themselves."

"You don't think we do?"

"Love ourselves? No. We have ideas about what is attractive and unattractive based upon skin color, which causes self-hate. We call ourselves and each other 'nigger,' which is the ultimate non-physical act of self-hate. And we commit violence against one another, which is the ultimate physical act of self-hate."

"Not all of us."

"No."

"Does your friend being killed by the police still bother you?"

"Oh, do you mean Butch or Brennie-Man?"

"Butch? You're too young to know about the B-Boys. How old are you?" asked the professor as he picked up a folder from his desk.

"Seventeen. Butch lived up the street from me. He made me look at my first naked girl. Why do you ask?"

248

"In May, I see. Your birthday. How'd you manage to graduate high school so soon?"

"I skipped a couple of grades when I was in elementary school."

"Really? They let you do that? But no, I meant the fellow you called Brennie-Man. Wait, how does someone make you look at a naked girl? You mean in a magazine?"

"No, on a trashcan. It's a long story."

The professor looked dazed. He looked past Prez to someone standing in the doorway. "May I help you?" Prez turned to look. There was no one there. "Guess she changed her mind. Ah, no, there she is. Hello, is there something I can help you with?"

"I'm so sorry." Prez turned to see it was Marsha. "I was looking for him." She pointed at Prez.

"Him?" said the professor and he pointed at Prez and laughed.

"I'm really sorry. I didn't know he was in a meeting with you. I'll just sit out here and wait."

"You won't have to wait long. I promise." He turned to Prez "Your girl?"

"My girl," said Prez.

"Mr. Downs, let me get right to the point. Would you be interested in attending a special program this summer in Chicago? It will be an interdisciplinary course combining philosophy, sociology, and history, and in addition to classwork there will be fieldwork."

"Fieldwork?"

"Yes. You will be required to actually go out into the community, establish relationships with the people, and see what you can learn about them and from them, with the ultimate purpose of coming up with ideas about solving their day-to-day problems, which you will present in the form of a treatise. I know that sounds a bit vague but hopefully not too wishy-washy. The details are still being worked out. My twin brother is the one creating the program. He lives in Chicago and is a professor at the new Chicago Circle campus of the University of Illinois. Well?"

"I'm interested, but I would have to talk to my mother first. How much will it cost?"

"Nothing. Not a red cent to you—for anything. It's a sort of scholarship you'll be receiving. The money for the whole program is coming from a grant. Let me get all the information and get back to you. Tell your folks I'll have all the details after Easter. Thank you and see you next class. And don't forget my thousand words."

"May I be a bit existential and write it from the only perspective that can give the correct rendition of events?"

"Hm … really, what perspective might that be?"

"The seagulls."

The professor burst out laughing. "No."

39
Chicago, 1964

Prez found himself more excited about his summer in Chicago than about his final marks. He wondered what it would be like to fly. He liked to drive fast but found himself nervous about flying. With his anxieties and expectations so high, he literally sprinted across campus to Professor Mackey's office to get his ticket and other documents.

"Well, good news, Mr. Downs. The filibuster in the Senate is over and the Civil Rights Act will now become law. That means that we can expect many other programs like the one you are participating in to come into being. And, if you are like me, there is more good news. Here's your ticket."

Inside the envelope was a Greyhound bus ticket, departure that day, Friday, the nineteenth of June, at 6:00 p.m.

"I'm leaving this evening? On a bus?"

"In a few hours, yes. Best we could do. Here, a little gift from me." It was a pamphlet that contained the poem by Marcus Garvey entitled *The Tragedy of White Injustice*. "Do not underestimate the time and energy you will expend reading and absorbing the wisdom contained in those twenty-two pages. Oh yes, Professor Okoro asked me to give you this." It was a copy of *Black Skin, White Masks* by Franz Fanon.

Prez rushed home and packed a few things. His mother was simultaneously weirdly sad and elated. It was her birthday. He gave her a little Chesapeake Bay pearl ring he had bought and a card he had made celebrating both her birthday and Juneteenth. His last words to his brother were, "Don't wear my clothes."

After what seemed like an eternity, albeit only about twenty-four hours of it, his feet touched the surprisingly warm Chicago pavement. He let out a huge yawn, stretched, and realized his bladder was in a crisis. He rushed through the big, heavy bus terminal doors and encountered a mélange of people in motion that impeded his search for a bathroom sign. Someone grabbed at his arm.

"Mr. Downs? Preston Downs?"

"Yeah. And you're Professor Mackey?"

"That's easy."

"Where's the bathroom? Do you know?"

"You're a big boy. Hold it for just a bit longer. The police here have the reputation for mistaking any black man in this bus depot for a vagrant and treating him as such. Do you know what that means? You will get your ass beat, bloodied, and thrown in jail. That is not the welcome to Chicago we envisioned for you. I have something else planned, so come with me."

He led Prez out onto Randolph Street, where they threaded themselves through pedestrian traffic. They walked two blocks over to South Wabash. The professor walked over to a little dark green convertible sports car and got in. Prez just stood there.

"Well, get in. You think I'm stealing it?"

The professor gingerly maneuvered his British Racing Green 1961 MG around people, cops, traffic, and corners until they were headed south on Lake Shore Drive, at which point his shoulders relaxed noticeably, his grip on the wheel eased, and he muttered something about not wanting any more scratches on his paint job.

"You know, I don't ever think I've seen so many white people before," said Prez.

"Yeah, I know, they are everywhere. Seriously, you know I'm from D.C., so I can dig where you're coming from. We were in Chicago's business and financial hub back there. Need I say more? It's called the Loop. Believe me, I cannot overemphasize this enough: the cops here will knock you for a loop in the blink of an eye. That old rule of the South applies here—know your place.

Being D.C. boys, we're used to seeing more black and tan with a smidgen of vanilla thrown in occasionally. It's the opposite here, unless you are in a black part of town."

"Hey, black and tan, that's the title of a very important Duke Ellington piece."

"Yes, it was a recording and also a short film. You're a proponent of jazz-listening, I presume?"

"Aren't we all?" replied Prez with an arrogance that made Professor Mackey smile.

"Actually no, because there's no such thing. That word is a commercial label that does nothing to define or dignify the music. Let me guess—no I won't, I'll let you tell me. What is your opinion of the blues? In a word or two."

"Old. Tired. Whining. Begging. Slave music."

"Really?" He laughed out loud.

As they drove along, Prez looked at the dashboard and wondered if this was the first car he had ridden in owned by a black man that did not have a radio. He decided not to ask. The night air swirled around them and carried a pungent burnt-fish odor.

"What is that smell?"

"The lake."

"What lake?"

"Lake Michigan. It's over there to our left. It's dark, so we can't see it very well from this side. Cats over there are frying smelts, little fish that look a bit like sardines. You can wade right in and scoop them up."

He exited Lake Shore Drive at Forty-seventh Street. "If you get the feeling you're landing on a different planet from when you got off the bus, well, you are."

Indeed, before him was a bustling boulevard bubbling over with neon signs that lit up the sky, storefronts that lit up the sidewalks, and automobile headlights that left streaks of light upon the pavement.

"I've never seen so many black people before," said Prez. They both laughed.

The professor pointed to the Regal Theater. "That's where we're going. It's black-owned and operated."

What the professor failed to mention was that he performed there as *Professor Jambon* every year around Halloween, during the celebrated and highly anticipated drag-queen fête called Finnie's Ball. He gave a high-strutting, butt-swishing standup comedy performance—a mock lecture—featuring song and dance in homage to Josephine Baker. He performed in his patented "jungle gown," which had a train of smoked hams in tow.

They jogged across the busy street and up to the ticket booth.

"Can you please point me towards the bathroom?" Prez asked the woman inside. She pointed while the professor bought the tickets.

"Wait a minute, Mr. Downs. What's in your little bag there? Wallet? Travel documents? Letters of recommendation and enrollment documents with all kinds of personal information on them? This is the South Side of Chicago. This is a different universe from back home. I cannot stress how important it is that

254

you realize you're not back home. Consider this environment hostile until you are used to it. You do not want to be a mark and get your pockets picked or your bag snatched. Put your wallet in your front pocket. Give me your bag until you come out of the bathroom."

As he exited the bathroom, a couple of guys bumped into Prez. He said "excuse me" and kept walking.

"What did you say to those two cats?"

"Who?" Prez turned around to see who he was talking about. Two guys were staring at him but he didn't know if those were the guys who had bumped into him or not. "Nothing except 'excuse me.' What's the problem?"

"I recognize them. They're gangleaders from the Robert Taylor Homes. They can be quite brutal. But I would be, too, if I'd spent my life there in America's version of the Gaza Strip. It's the largest housing project in the United States, over two miles long, crammed between South State Street and the Dan Ryan Expressway. There are twenty-eight buildings and each one is about sixteen stories. There are about four thousand, five hundred units. How many people do you think they have stacked up in that ugly place? It looks like a prison complex. Gets my blood boiling just to think about it. C'mon, let's go get some good seats."

"Are we here for a show or a movie?"

"You're here for an education. It's intermission. I was given a tip that there would be a surprise appearance by an important blues artist. This guy is something else. He's been with a white record label called Chess Records run by Leonard Chess but they still haven't recorded this cat we're about to hear. Word is they can't figure out which neat musical package he belongs in. That's capitalism for you. The tragedy is that stuff like that promotes the misconception that whites can't be happy in their interactions with blacks unless they can control the situation and exploit us. Leonard's brother, Phil Chess runs a very progressive radio empire. He's the first person Barry Gordy sends a new record to. Mr. Downs, your vacant expression tells me you have no idea who Berry Gordy is."

The inside of the three thousand-seat Regal Theater was breathtaking in a gaudily melodramatic way, like an overdone Hollywood set trying to stuff too many great design themes of antiquity under one roof. The ceiling was painted to simulate being under a desert oasis canopy with a hole in it. Through the hole a painted sky full of stars and clouds could be seen. Gold-painted bas-relief poles ran down the walls from ceiling to floor, giving the illusion of holding up the canopy. Above the stage, the proscenium arch was adorned in rich hues that suggested golden moonlight dancing off a blue lagoon while a tribal temple-fire flickered.

"You know what, Professor? I'm waiting for King Kong to show up on stage."

"That's a good one!" laughed the professor. "Well, if King Kong could play like this cat, I wouldn't run."

"Ladies and gentlemen," began the master of ceremonies, "we have a wonderful surprise for you connoisseurs out there, to get you through this intermission. Please put your hands together for Buddy Guy! Buddy Guy, ladies and gentlemen!"

After listening to the most blistering guitar playing he had ever heard, Prez said, "That was not the blues. It sounded like the blues on the bottom. And his high-pitched lyrics cried the blues. But his head was in outer space like an avant-garde player. His guitar stuck its finger in your chest and said 'don't mess with me' while simultaneously inviting you on a space voyage. Wow!

I could listen to him all day. Makes you want to do things, not moan about things that have been done to you."

"That's quite a take on what you heard. I need one thousand words on everything you have experienced since you got off the bus: sights, sounds, thoughts, feelings—everything." Prez gave him a very quizzical look. "I am not kidding. I need it for tomorrow, your first assignment for your first class." Then he burst out laughing. "Welcome to Chicago, Mr. Downs."

Outside the Regal, Professor Mackey was regaling Prez with all sorts of anecdotes about Forty-seventh Street and Bronzeville. Prez saw them coming. They walked right to him, pushing the professor aside.

"Hey, little fucking punk, you gotta learn to move outta the way when you see us coming."

Prez hit that guy in the throat, and the guy dropped to his knees, coughing. Prez kicked the other guy in the solar plexus, knocking him back against a lamp post.

"You motherfuckers get outta *my* way the next time you see me. You dig it?"

Professor Mackey grabbed him by the arm and rushed him towards the car. "Jesus! Let's get out of here! Jesus, Downs, I told you who they were. Couldn't you have just said I'm sorry again? They can have the whole street flooded with Bricks in no time. Just one phone call is all it takes."

"Yeah, I'm real scared." Prez smirked. "They're just fucking punks."

"Where'd you get that temper?"

"I don't have a temper. I just hate bullies. What are 'Bricks'?"

"That's what they call themselves. The older guys are Big Bricks, the young boys, and I mean kids, some still in puberty, are Baby Bricks, and the girls are Brickettes."

"Brickettes? No matter how old they are?"

"Interesting observation."

"They're still punks."

"The park down the street from where you'll be staying is Brick territory. Stay out of it." Prez looked at him, his brow furrowed, a single eyebrow raised. The professor almost burst out laughing. What a kid, he thought. "Look, man. I know this city. I'm telling you this stuff for your own good so that you can be successful in your studies. You do want that, right? Nod if you understand."

He reached over and opened his glove box to reveal his hidden radio. He tuned it to WSDM-FM where the sultry voice of Yvonne Daniels soothed souls with jazz sounds on her "Daniel's Den" radio show. Prez smiled, slumped down in the car seat, and closed his eyes.

After dropping Prez off, Professor Mackey was faced with a quandary. He had a hot date waiting in Old Town and the quickest way to get there was up the despised Dan Ryan Expressway. But that would mean driving through the Robert Taylor Homes, which he hated. He wanted to be cheery. He took South Parkway north instead. He and his boyfriend had already decided to spend that night and all of the next day, a Sunday, in bed.

～

He could hear his phone ringing as he pulled himself up the stairs to his apartment and fumbled through his bag, grabbing for his door keys. The ringing stopped just as he entered. It was barely 6:00 a.m. He wondered who could be calling so early as he lay down on his sofa for a short nap. His first Monday class wasn't until 11:00 a.m.

A couple of hours later he was roused by his phone ringing. He launched himself over the sofa toward the phone on the end table.

"Hello, hello. Gene? What's wrong? Was that you calling before? Well, man, talk. You're where? At O'Hare? What are you doing here? I'll come pick you up. Which gate? Alright."

"Going Brit, are you?"

"Well, hello and great to see you, too, little brother."

"You always try to pull twenty-minutes older rank when you're nervous, Reg."

"Well, you always try to deflect onto something that ridicules me when you're nervous, Gene. What's happening?"

"We have to stop, Reg. Otherwise we end up being like those slaves who sold out Denmark Vessey and Nat Turner. You don't know do you? Yesterday three kids doing civil rights work went missing in Mississippi. They're dead, man. Everybody knows that."

Reg Mackey reached over and turned off the radio. "Where?"

"A shit-hole called Philadelphia, Mississippi."

"I've peeped at some reports on that place in Wicker's files. About eight other blacks have gone missing down there."

"Eight?!"

"Yeah. You should see the stuff that gets filtered through the Chicago office. Families down there have reported those people missing. A couple of names I remember off the top of my head; Henry Dee, Charles Moore, even a fourteen-year-old kid—another one—Herbert Oarsby. What's so special about these recent three?"

"Two of them are white."

"Ahh, so now missing men most assuredly murdered by the Klan are in the news?"

"How can you be so detached, Reg? I'm all messed up inside, man. I cried all night."

259

"You know me better than that, Gene."

On Tuesday, June 23, Dick Gregory announced a twenty-five-thousand-dollar reward for information regarding the whereabouts of Chaney, Goodman, and Schwerner. Reg Mackey wondered where he got the money because CORE was broke. He had surreptitiously seen that file, too.

Chicago, Wednesday, June 24, 1964

"Hello. Hello, yes, good morning. I'm sure he is waiting for my call. Thanks. I'll hold a minute, yes. Hey, hey, Wicker. I suppose you heard. Don't play dumb, you guys trained me too well for that. If you want to know what I've heard come right out and ask me. Don't insult me. Tell me, how did the FBI manage to allow those three boys to go missing? What? Don't give me that shit about another regional office being responsible. You know I know a significant portion of the national operation is being run out of Chicago. So please dispense with the bullshit. Please, no football metaphors. We're talking about human lives, not a fucking football being dropped. This isn't a game, which, as I recall, were your precise words to me when you recruited me. All I asked was that to the best of your ability you would see to it that brutality ceased and that there would be no lives lost. Yes, yes. I'm aware there's no confirmation about where those boys are. But you and I both know what the chances are of those boys being found alive. C'mon, stop trying to bullshit me. I know some folks in New York too and I know you all knew when Schwerner left town and headed south. Whoa, whoa! Let me tell you something, I'm doing this because I believe in America. Don't get fucking confused. I do not trust you or the agency. You got a lot of nerve talking to me the way you have, and now asking me about Downs. Fuck you! It's my show anyway. I can run it any way I want or I won't run it at all. Oh yeah, Wicker, one more thing, in case you didn't hear it the first time: Fuck you!"

Professor Mackey slammed the phone down so hard he spilled coffee all over his shirt. "Sweet fucking Jesus!" he exclaimed as he dropped everything he had in his hands on the floor and rushed to get his shirt off. "Those goddamned sons of bitches. Fucking redneck crackers. Anglo-Saxon pimps. Goddamn fascists. That's all they are. They don't give a shit about America." He caught a glimpse of himself talking to no one as he rushed past the mirror on his dresser. He paused, shook his head and said, "You're pathetic."

Reginald Mackey, Ph.D, professor of sociology at the Chicago Circle Campus of the University of Illinois, and director of the newly established Alternative Modes Interdisciplinary Studies Program, was a complex amalgam. He often wondered if his lack of religious conviction made it too easy for him to surreptitiously engage with the people over on 1100 W. Roosevelt Road. In their file was a manila folder that identified him only as "Informant TK2011IQ00." He knew he wasn't doing it for the money, which was so little he donated it to a local soup kitchen.

He cleaned himself up, changed his shirt, and marveled that his papers had not been soiled by coffee. He made another call.

"Good morning, Mrs. Grant. Is young Mr. Downs awake yet? Oh, has he? Up at five and went out for a run where? Washington Park? He's back, I trust? In the shower. Indeed. Tell him I'll be by to pick him up at eight. Yes, thanks. You, too."

Prez came out precisely at eight.

"Good morning, Mr. Downs. Sleep well?"

Prez got in. He reached into his bag and pulled out five type-written pages.

"Here's your first thousand, Professor. I look forward to doing many more thousands for you."

Professor Mackey took the paper and read its title aloud: "Du Sable Would Love Buddy Guy." Then he let out a raucous laugh. He glanced over each page then asked, "How do you know about du Sable?"

"There was a little book about him in my room. I was shocked to learn that Chicago was founded by a black man, Jean Baptiste Point du Sable. He'd hate this place if he saw it now. Buddy Guy could save his grace, though."

"Can you drive?"

"Of course."

"Alright, you drive. I want to read this." They switched seats. "Go to the end of the block. Turn left. Go two blocks, turn right. Keep going towards the lake and take the exit for Chicago, Loop. And Mr. Downs, do not, I repeat, do not drive my car like you're on a race course."

Prez wondered about the race car reference. Then quickly forgot it as he said, "I saw Dick Gregory on TV. He was talking about the Chaney, Goodman, Schwerner murders. He spoke of America's hypocrisy in trying to tell other nations how to do democracy when racists are blowing up churches here and killing good people like those three civil rights workers. He said the FBI could easily solve all this stuff and even prevent it but that the FBI doesn't because, and I paraphrase, the FBI itself is a very vicious group and a second Ku Klux Klan."

Professor Mackey couldn't read any more after that.

The 1966 Fall semester had started and Prez was already knee-deep in his research and writing. There were days when it felt like quicksand. He knew it was because he was spreading himself too thin. He was organizing on the west side so frequently, he wondered if he should move there. It would save a lot of travel time. But he would miss the lake. And he really liked Hyde Park. More importantly, he lived a short walk from Eckhart Hall, whose second-floor library he used so much he would wake up in the middle of the night thinking he was there.

One rainy evening as he bounded out the library door and jumped over a puddle of water a girl shouted in a thick British accent, "Excuse me! Hey! Can you help me?" She was standing right in the puddle, her long toes going up and down. She held a pair of Buffalo sandals in one hand and a sheaf of papers tied with cord in the other. Her wafer-thin body looked frail under the lumberjack shirt she wore. Prez wondered how she kept her baggy, torn bellbottoms from falling off her hips. Her little pink mouth was turned up at the corners in a perpetual smile and the whites of her brown eyes reminded Prez of the Cleary marbles he and his boyhood friends would hoard but never expose to the abuses of an actual game of marbles. "Is this Eckhart Hall, where J. Ernest Wilkins studied?"

"Yes. And yes."

"Terse, aren't you?"

Didn't everyone know about the thirteen-year-old African-American math prodigy who entered the University of Chicago at the age of thirteen, received his Ph.D in mathematics at the age of nineteen, and later worked on the Manhattan Project?

"No. I have to be somewhere. Maybe I'll see you later."

The very next day his professor made a special request, that he mentor three exchange students from England. Prez agreed to meet them at a place called the Soul Tavern later that evening so that they could get better acquainted. Just as he rounded the corner up the street from the tavern has noticed two white men sitting in a dark-gray four-door sedan. They were parked across the street from the tavern. Prez could hear the squelch of a two-way radio. He paused and leaned against a tree and watched.

The fellow on the passenger side got out and opened the trunk. He took off his trench coat and threw it in. He put on a varsity jacket and a baseball cap. Next, he crossed the street and went into the tavern. Then he came back out and leaned against the fender. Soon after, a young white guy came out and they walked a few paces down the street and talked for a few minutes, at times heatedly. The older guy in the baseball cap opened the trunk and pulled out a dark-green rucksack. He tried to hand it to the younger guy, but he wouldn't take it. They had a heated exchange. Then the younger guy snatched the backpack from the older guy's hand and went back into the tavern. The fellow in the baseball cap got back into the car, which then drove off.

Prez waited a few minutes, trying to make sense of what he had just witnessed, before going into the tavern to look for a black girl with a purple scarf tied around her forehead. She was seated at a booth and rose to wave at Prez. *That was odd*, he thought, as he went over to meet Jenny "call me JB" Broadwell,

Percival "everyone calls him Percy" Longstreet, and Elizabeth "please call her Lizzy" Beckert.

"I'm Preston Downs."

"So, that's your name, rude boy," said Lizzy.

"Better than Mister Terse." He laughed.

"What's going on?" asked Jenny. "You two are behaving like you know each other."

"Soon," said Lizzy.

They all began to talk in some detail about what they aspired to accomplish that summer and how they hoped to make a difference when they returned home. Prez promised to do what he could to acclimatize them to their new environs. All the while his foot was busy feeling around under the table for the backpack. There was something hard in it.

Jenny leaned on Percy's shoulder. I think I still have jet lag. Percy stroked her face and her hair. From his shirt pocket he pulled out a joint. "This will help."

"Not in here, man. And if you see the cops, throw it away," cautioned Prez.

"Let's get back to the room," said Jenny.

"I'm going to stay and talk with Preston here," said Lizzie.

"Everyone calls me Prez."

"But I like Preston. There's nothing you can do about that."

"May I compliment you on your black velour jacket? It really looks good on you."

"Thank you! It's my favorite crinkly-comfy dressy jacket."

They talked so much that midnight crept up on them.

"Okay," said Lizzy. "Your girl is in Washington, but you're not engaged."

"Correct."

"Well, I have a guy back in London. But I ask myself, suppose we knew the world was ending tomorrow. Here we are now,

266

you and me. The perfect pair. Do we spend our last night alive together or not?"

"That's such a crazy-ass question, Lizzy. You're really nuts."

He took her home.

It was a during a sweltering summer's morning jog around Washington Park that he noticed the police had shiny new blue-and-white 1967 Chevrolet Biscaynes. One sat at Fifty-ninth Street. He pretended not to see it. But he didn't try to pretend that he didn't see the two Bricks sitting on a picnic table watching him go around and around. They both wore do-rags around their processed hair, black nylon athletic shirts, green khakis and black combat boots. On his fifth lap around his jogging route, Prez stopped and walked over to them. One was twirling a toothpick in his mouth with his tongue, the other was hunched over cleaning under his fingernails with a switchblade.

"How you soul brothers doing?" asked Prez.

Switchblade kept concentrating on his manicure. Toothpick, who had locked eyes with Prez the instant Prez stopped running, said, "How you know we soul brothers?"

"I dunno. Something tells me. I got a feeling, ya know. I get these feelings about things and I'm always right. I'd hate to be wrong. What about y'all, would you hate that I was wrong?"

Switchblade snickered and kept attending to his fingernails. "Nigga, you real funny." He closed his knife and stuck it in his pocket. Then he stood up—but not just any old standing up. The motions started from somewhere in his lower back and rolled up to his shoulders, which lifted his butt off the table top. Then it went back down to his thighs, which stretched his legs and torso, leaving only his neck and head to raise. He looked down at Prez and offered a hand. "I'm Eldee, Eldee Stricmore."

"And I'm Prez." Prez gave his hand a hearty shake. Then he turned toward Toothpick, took his hand and shook it.

"Yeah, man," said Toothpick, "I'm his brother Kelly. They call me Kel-Mel 'cause Kel likes to be mel-low. Ya dig it? Women and weed. Live life until the shit goes down, then we soldiers. Like now, we on guard duty."

Prez frowned. An eyebrow raised. He theatrically tilted his head. "Is it pro or anti? And I don't mean ante like laying your money down in a pot before you start gambling, though you may be thinking there's a game going on here right now. Are you here in a pro or anti mode?"

They looked at each other. Kel-Mel said, "What the fuck you talkin' 'bout, man? I didn't understand nuthin' you jus' said."

"You said y'all are soldiers on guard duty."

"Yeah," said Eldee, "that's right. And we got the scars to prove it." He pulled up his shirt to reveal several round scar tissue-covered holes and a long scar with obvious stitch marks running its length. "Minh Thanh Road, Viet Nam."

Then Kel-Mel pulled up his shirt to reveal almost identical wounds. "Sixty-seventh and Stony Island. Chicago. USA. So, what the fuck you wanna know now?"

"Are you following orders to protect something or to prevent something? Are you for something or against something?" said Prez.

"Uncle sent us over here to make sure the cops don't bust caps in your ass. We respectful of your presence around here. Uncle knows you're from D.C. That's the East. He always said a prophet gonna come to us from the East. That he'll be smart, fearless, and wise. He heard you speak about Malcolm X, that

269

important question—whether socialism is good for black folks. He was impressed."

"How do you know I'm fearless?"

"You knocked the fuck outta Jilly and Stu in front of the Regal. They our boys. You think we don't know about that? It was some years back but we remember. Uncle say they had it coming. We not supposed to be acting like thugs no mo'. We supposed to learning how to be Soul Brothers, black men. Uncle thinks you should be a Big Brick and show us the way."

"Those cops sit over behind a couple of cars at Fifty-ninth Street like they trying to hide," said Prez. "Don't they know they can hide but they can't run?" They all laughed at that riff off of Joe Louis' famous quote. "Tell Uncle I really appreciate you all looking out for me. But don't think because I'm out here like I don't care that I don't know. I know. This is called exercising my right to be out here whenever I want and knowing that all the cops can do is to leave me alone and let me exercise my constitutional rights."

"Constitutional rights!" said Kel-Mel. "Nigga, are you stupid or something? Fuckin' cops don't care nuthin' about your constitutional rights. They bust a cap in your ass and leave you bleeding and dying like they did my cousin over at the lagoon a few months ago. Shot that nigga eight or nine times, that's at least two cops shooting. Then they holler out 'Devil D Thang' and go screeching off into the night like we stupid or something."

"Wait a minute. They're pulling that kind of false flag shit on the West Side too."

"False flag?" queried Kel-Mel.

"Yeah. The cops cap a dude then try to make it look like a rival group did it?"

"What kinda shit?" said Eldee. "It don't matter. We already figured it out. There ain't no more Devil Ds around here for a

270

long time. Man, years ago a couple of their big boys got shanked up in the joint and came home in boxes. Since then, they all been in with us, but that's old. The cops was acting on old information. We know what they trying to do. And Uncle thinks they want to bust some caps in your ass and blame it on us."

"Everybody know what you been doing over there on the West Side with the Kobras and K-Knights," said Kel-Mel. "Uncle say if you can get Prince Earl and Big Diesel to be at the same place at the same time without trying to kill each other, then you a fuckin' miracle worker, like a prophet. He wanna talk with you and he want you to talk with us, give us some knowledge."

"But for now, we gonna watch your back so you can do your thang," said Eldee. "And we not bluffing either. C'mere."

Preston sat between them. Eldee lifted a familiar-looking green backpack that rested on the bench between his feet. He opened the bag's flap to reveal two very large and shiny revolvers. "Forty-four mags, man. This shit punch holes in sheet metal." Then they both lifted their pants legs to reveal smaller pistols tucked into their boots. "We ready to protect."

43

Chicago, September, 1966, A Friday

Prez became Professor Mackey's teaching assistant. It was a paying gig and it was good money. Prez was determined to use his new position to his advantage. He would be a TA of a different sort.

"Professor Mackey, I have a question."

"Just when I thought we'd be able to end this session early and get off to some early Friday evening shindigs, along comes our beloved Mr. D.C. Downs. The only teaching assistant I know of who dares to ask questions—out loud. You all know what that means, so pull out your pillows, and don't dare rest your heads on them, they'll be for you to sit on so your asses won't go numb. Now, what is your question?" Professor Mackey was concerned that he had not won allies in his attempt to keep Prez quiet, because no one uttered a sound. The professor had to get out of there and meet somebody.

"Yes, thank you, Professor Mackey, very quickly, just a couple of questions. How can I find out exactly where the grant money for this program comes from? And number two, we're preparing to take part in that seminar series next week to discuss the effectiveness of the federal War on Poverty program. I notice there will be a number of foundations and philanthropic organizations taking part. How can I find out about them?"

"Man, that's going to have to wait until next class."

"But sir, can't you point me in the direction of the answer for at least one of those questions? I need to fill out the outline for what I am going to write next."

"Look, I am meeting somebody very important in about fifteen minutes … ago … you dig it? I'm already late. Next week, Downs."

The professor gathered up his things and rushed out the door without a further word.

"That's the first time I recall the professor being the first one out of this lecture hall," said Percy, rising from his seat to stand over Prez.

"What do you think came over Professor Mackey?" asked JB. "He certainly was in a rush. Maybe he's got a fat black cock jones. Is that how you call it over here?"

"Why are you talking like that, JB?" asked Prez.

"I'm sure Preston knows the professor has a big black boyfriend that he fucks in the back of a big black Mercedes, JB. Leave it alone, will you? But I don't think what just happened has anything to do with Mackey needing a cock up his ass," said Lizzy. "It was Preston's question. Here, Preston." She handed him a grocery bag with a cord tied around it.

"What is this?"

"A present. Open it." It was a rough-hewn brown leather satchel with brass buckles. "It belonged to my father. I know you'll put it to good use."

"I'm touched. I'll treasure it. Okay folks, we have to be somewhere, too," said Prez. "So, let's go. I promised."

"Yes, we know how much you hate going around the Loop. We appreciate it," said JB.

"It's Old Town, actually, and it's for a good cause. We'll also be meeting the people I told you about, the ones I've been working with," said Prez.

"Oh, your dreaded gang members?" said Percy.

"Don't start shaking in your boots, man. They smoke good weed. So be nice and you might get a toke or two," said Prez.

They all laughed, ran up the street, waved down a jitney cab, and jumped in.

"There must be a million people here," said Percy. "How do we even get to the front door?"

"Follow me." Prez grabbed Lizzy's hand, Lizzy grabbed JB's hand, and she grabbed ahold of Percy's jacket and pulled him along. Prez pushed a path through the crowd and they went inside. It was jam-packed.

Mother Blues was a blues-folk-rock club that was hosting an evening of anti-war and radical fare.

Prez looked around at the wonderful mix of people who had assembled in that little place. There were young Afro-Americans looking like black hippies, and white hippies wearing their hair as if they were young Afro-Americans. There were former hardcore gang members trying to behave less hardcore and suburbanites trying to pretend they were hardcore. There were poetry readings and little impromptu speeches. And there was dancing. The hippie contingent proved to be confounding dance partners. Their way of dancing had no relation to the beat or the music. They just sort of wiggled, shimmied, and let their arms float about in the air. He looked at the ethnic diversity of the people and knew in his heart how beautiful the world could be.

"Hey, Brother Downs." Prez turned and saw it was Prince Earl standing there with Big Diesel. He looked over at the bar and he could see Eldee and Kel-Mel watching. He motioned them over. This, he thought, is it.

"Look at us!" said Prez. We're here together in peace. We're here together because we love ourselves. We're here because we are conscious of the fact that together we have the power. The power!" he exclaimed as he raised his fist in the Black Power salute.

"You got that right, Brother-man," someone said. "It's an absolute truth that there can be no black unity without us being at peace with one another. We can never achieve Black Power without black unity. Right on!"

Prez turned to see who it was. The fellow was slapping five, shaking hands, and greeting everyone. Big Diesel came over to Prez. "Preston Downs, meet Gabriel Turner. Brother Gabe, this is Downs."

Gabriel Turner grabbed Prez's hand in the new Soul Brother handshake. "It's a great pleasure to meet you, brother. Heard about you from Big Diesel and Prince Earl." Then he stepped back, crossed his arms and posed. "Some say you a jaw-breaker, some say you a peacemaker, I wanna know your brain is no faker."

Here we go, thought Prez. He made motions like he was smoothing his clothes, then he crossed his arms and posed. "I see you a man in love with verse, you spout it out with no need to rehearse, as for me let me give you a sign," he raised his fist in the power salute, "I'm in possession of a hardworking mind." Gabriel almost toppled over laughing. There was laughter all around. Gabriel and Prez hugged. Then they went and sat down at a table with a bunch of guys gathered around.

"Pardon me, I know your name, but exactly who are you?"

"I'm the chairman of a new organization we're starting called the Black People's Party. Some of the fellas have been tellin' me about your rap with them. You sayin' the same things we sayin', the Black People's Party. Your perspective is exactly the same. You know they assassinated a great man, February last year."

"Yes, El-Hajj Malik El-Shabazz."

"He was a genius in his analysis of the situation we Afro-Americans face in this country. The evolution of his thinking is actually a model of the evolution of black revolutionary thinking. He went from being anti-white to anti-capitalist. He went from being a Black Nationalist to being an internationalist. He went from advocating for civil rights to advocating for human rights. He was a big presence on the international scene and he believed that we Afro-Americans can never achieve justice or freedom if we keep relying upon the two-party system of government. C'mon, there's no qualitative difference today between a Democrat and a Republican. We need our own party. When he was running around calling white people 'white devils' the media and the establishment couldn't get enough of him. Then when he started asking the question about whether or not socialism would be good for Afro-Americans—boom!—he's gone. Think about that. What are you drinking?"

"I don't drink. But I'll have a root beer."

"Y'all hear that? Hey, Chi-chi, did you hear that? C'mon, man, hand it over. Don't moan and make a face. You owe me ten bucks. Found my twin Soul Brother right here." He slapped Prez on the back. "Chi-Chi made a bet with me that I would never find another dude that didn't drink." He turned back to Prez. "Carry your bag with you everywhere, I bet."

"Yep," said Prez. He had the wide strap of his tan leather bag over the back of his chair. He noticed Gabriel was carrying one as well, but his leather bag was black.

"Armed to the gills, we both are. I know it," said Gabriel.

"Oh yeah," said Prez. He raised the flap of his bag and pulled out a worn leather-bound copy of *My Bondage and My Freedom* by Frederick Douglass.

"Damn, is that real leather? Where'd you get that?" said Gabriel. He reached in his bag and pulled out a copy of *Man's*

276

Fate by André Malraux. "It's not leather, but it's not all worn out either. We are packing heavy tonight, my brother." He held up his book and raised the hand in which Prez held his book and said for all to hear, "You see, these are the only real weapons of freedom."

By the end of the evening, what had transpired over a few little square café tables pulled together was a meeting of the minds of the leaders of the major inner-city neighborhoods that included Afro-Americans, whites, and Puerto Ricans. There was more than a major peace pact agreed to, there was a commitment to a commonality of purpose. Perhaps if it were not for them being on neutral turf it would have been an unlikely achievement.

It was well beyond midnight and Prez was starting to feel it. There was hardly anyone left in *Mother Blues*.

"We gotta go," said Prez to Eldee and Kel-Mel. "We gotta get up and run in the morning."

"Let's take a day off tomorrow, man. We never take a day off."

"Hey, I run in the morning, too," said Gabe. "Maybe we can run together sometimes."

Prez, Lizzy, and JB got up and started walking toward the door.

"Hold it, what is going on out there? Don't go out there," said Prez. He looked back toward Gabe and his crowd and said, "The place is crawling with cops."

They all got up and walked over to have a look.

"They know we're here," said Gabe. "I think the girls should go out the back. Call to see how it is back there." One of his guys went to the phone booth in the back of the club. "There are three phone booths on the streets in a two-block radius from here. We have some of our boys at each phone."

The guy who went to the pay phone came back and said, "They've got the back alley covered."

"Okay, listen up," said Gabe. "We've been through this so many times before. Everywhere we go the cops show up. Their aim is to try to provoke us. They are looking for any excuse they can find to shoot us. We don't provoke them. We are polite. We obey all of their lawful commands. But that is the trick; we will not obey their unlawful commands and will not allow ourselves to be bullied. So it's a fine line between knowing your rights and not getting killed." Turning to Prez he said, "I suggest you all follow our lead on this. Somebody call some cabs. Let me go call Fitz and get him down here." He looked around at all the guys. "I gotta ask if everybody's clean. You know what I mean. If you're not, you gotta figure out how to get rid of it. Now." Nobody moved. "No shit? Everybody's clean? Gotta love you dudes. You're stronger than you know."

"Who's Fitz?" Prez asked no one in particular. He heard someone say "A lawyer."

After about ten minutes a few cabs showed up. "Cabs here, let's move," said Gabe.

Prez led the way with his arm tightly around Lizzy's waist. He looked back to see where JB and Percival were. He wanted the four of them to get in the same cab together. Percival was still back at the table where Prez and Gabe had sat. He called for Percival to hurry. "What's wrong with you, man?" Prez shouted at Percival as he held JB and Lizzy back from going out the door to wait for Percival. Prez looked out in front of the club at all the cops, some who had come quite close to the entrance, and he wondered if they would make it to the cab without incident. He glanced back over his shoulder and noticed the book he had given Gabe was on the floor under a table, but he knew Gabe had put it in his bag. There was a bit of shoving. It was Percy. "Don't be so goddamn nervous, Percy. Be a fuckin' man. You got to protect JB if any shit goes down."

"What the fuck do we have here?" A big red-headed cop had placed himself in between Prez's group and the cab. He stood right in front of Prez and Lizzy. "What's a pretty little white bitch like you doing with a nigger?"

"Haven't you heard?" said Prez. "The Supreme Court just ruled that interracial marriage is perfectly legal. You need to get up with the times, man." The cop shoved his nightstick into Prez's chest.

"Please tell me you ain't fuckin' this little dumb-assed nigger. Please say you ain't, missy, and I'll let you get in the cab."

"You're on the wrong side of the law," said Prez.

"We haven't done anything, officer. Why are you behaving in such a disrespectful manner?" said an extremely nervous Percy.

The officer cut his eyes to Percy and said, "What a fucked-up accent, punk."

"Hey, where's my bag?" Prez heard Gabe say. He looked around and saw Gabe rush back into the club and towards the chair where he'd left his bag. Prez was still being shoved backward by the big red-headed cop, who persisted in verbally taunting and abusing him and Lizzy.

"You don't have a right to put your hands on me," Prez heard himself say. "Don't touch me again."

Prez finally saw what Percival kept looking at. The same dark-gray four-door sedan with the same two guys who had given Percival the backpack with the guns that the Bricks had. It was parked about a block away. He looked back and saw that Gabe now had his bag over his shoulder and was just about to exit the club. Percival also noticed and made a motion like he was scratching the top of his head.

"Get in!" Prez screamed. He pushed Lizzy and JB in ahead of him. Percy managed to jump in the front seat. Just as he was about to get in he looked around and a bunch of cops emerged from the shadows, rushing toward Gabe. *His bag*, thought Prez. *It's his bag. I gotta tell him.* "Wait! Let me out."

"Preston, don't. Come with us. Come with me," said Lizzy.

He jumped out, banged on the cab, and just as it was about to leave all hell broke loose.

Gunfire erupted all around them, bullets zinged at them from every direction. Metal clanged, concrete cratered, and glass shattered.

Prez threw himself onto the ground and managed to crawl under a truck.

When the shooting finally stopped Prez raised his head and saw the Puerto Rican fellow who had come with Chi-Chi lying on the ground in a pool of blood. One of the boys from the Bricks was leaning against a wall holding his side with blood dripping from his hands. He tried to straighten himself and walk but staggered and fell. Three cops pounced on him. Ambulances arrived. He could see a bunch of guys facing a brick wall with a bunch of police watching them, guns drawn.

"Did we get him?" he heard a cop say to another as they walked by the truck he was under.

"Yeah. We shot that black nigger. But that goddamned spic jumped in the way and took some for him."

"You mean that fucker Turner ain't dead?"

"Shit, I don't know. Who called those fucking ambulances anyway?"

"I dunno, but his fuckin' lawyer, that goddamned Fitzgerald, he showed up at the same time as the ambulances."

"Maybe somebody shoulda shot that asshole, too."

"And the ambulance drivers while we're at it, too? Grow up, DeMarco. Let's just hope the nigger is dead. If he ain't we'll have a very unhappy City Hall."

Fitzgerald waded in. "You know who I am, so stand back from me, please. Get out of my way. Where's my client? I asked you the whereabouts of my client."

Gabriel Turner was found sitting upright against a parked car with seven or eight police officers surrounding him. His head hung to one side. He was bleeding from a number of different places. His eyes were shut.

"Is this your client, here, attorney? Looks like he *was* your client. I don't think that boy is breathing anymore. What do you think, Halley?"

"I believe he may have gone and expired on us."

Fitzgerald bent down and felt for a carotid pulse. "Medic! Medic!" he screamed. "He's alive!"

Prez crawled from under the rear of the truck and onto the sidewalk. He stood and didn't see the cab. A rush of relief lifted his shoulders and lightened his feet. But as he walked around to the front of the truck he could see that the cab was still there. It had rolled some car lengths down the street. He ran towards it and could see the driver kneeling on the ground just outside his open door, his head bobbing back and forth as if he was in a lot of pain. JB and Percival were also out of the cab and standing on the curb, JB crying hysterically as she punched and kicked Percival who kept muttering "they weren't supposed to shoot." Prez couldn't see Lizzy. He looked at the cab and the back window was shattered. Someone was in the back seat. He started screaming.

"JB, is that Lizzy? Is that Lizzy? Get her out! Get her out of there!!"

Just as he rushed to open the door, he was grabbed by a cop. Prez broke his grip and opened the cab door. A deluge of tears rushed down his face as he looked into the cab and saw her. Her body leaned forward, her head against the back of the front seat. "Lizzy, Lizzy!" screamed Prez. Her hair hung in a matted, blood-soaked tangle around her face. Blood dripped from the tips of her hair and settled into a small puddle at her feet. He could only see one of her eyes and it was open, looking far away. Her mouth looked as though she was about to say something. "Somebody call an ambulance, will you? We need an ambulance!" he cried. The red-headed cop rushed over to Prez and Prez evaded his attempt to grab him. "Did you shoot Lizzy, motherfucker?" The cop reached for his throat but he sent the cop to the ground with a powerful kick. Two more cops rushed him and he started blindly punching and kicking while crying hysterically. He was unaware that news crews had arrived on the scene and that Fitzgerald had one in tow as he rushed over and stood between him and the cops shouting, "stop assaulting my client!"

Fitzgerald stood in front of Prez and said, "Son, whoever you are, stop. You won't bring her back, son. Listen to me. Stop."

Prez cried like he had not cried since his father's death. The grief gripped his stomach and twisted it so that he began to heave and vomit all over the street. He dropped to his knees and wailed and moaned and held his stomach. Nobody moved, not Fitzgerald and not the cops. His grief was so intense, even a couple of the white cops came up to the attorney to ask who the dead white girl was to this wracked-up nigger. Fitzgerald said to Prez, "Look, they will cuff you and book you. What's your name so I can represent you?"

With tears filling his mouth he managed to say, "Preston Coleman Downs, Junior."

"Just be calm. Calm down. I'll be down at the station within the hour to get you out. Calm down, okay? The girl in the cab, who was she?"

"The most beautiful girl you'd ever want to know, Lisbeth Beckert. She's from England. Those are her friends over there."

"Did you say she's British?"

Fitzgerald looked around at the horde of cops and said, "I think you boys have just gotten yourselves into a bigger jam than you'll know how to get out of. If I were you, I would tread lightly from here on out. You just killed a British citizen. Who's in charge? Oh, I know. Where is he?" Fitzgerald looked around then walked over and spoke calmly to an officer wearing a Police Commander badge, who started to argue obnoxiously. Prez heard the attorney use the phrase "international incident" and the commander shut up, hung his head, and nodded.

44

The Next Morning, A Saturday

"We have received reports this morning that Gabriel Turner, the leader of the radical Black People's Party, lies in a coma at Cook County Hospital after having been shot by Chicago police last night. The State's Attorney's office said the officers were attempting to execute a search warrant when Mr. Turner pulled a weapon from his bag. A leader of the radical Puerto Rican People's Party, also reportedly armed, was killed in the exchange of gunfire. And a member of the Bricks, the criminal South Side street gang, was wounded and remains in critical condition. A young British exchange student, Lisbeth Beckert, was also shot dead as she sat in a taxicab near the scene. Commander Bronson, who led the police team, issued the following statement: 'Police are testing the gun found on Gabriel Turner. We believe the British student was killed by bullets fired from that weapon. Lisbeth Beckert was an innocent bystander. Our condolences go out to her family.'"

Prez got up from the floor of the hospital waiting room and stretched his legs. He didn't bother to ask anyone if they minded him turning off the TV. He just walked over and turned it off. He had come straight to the hospital after being released by the police that morning. He wanted to be there with Gabe's family. They were very dignified people who handled the situation with a painful stoicism. They still had not been allowed to see Gabe and the only word about his condition was from a little African-American nurse who behaved as if she had to sneak around each time she came into the waiting room.

Strangely, Prez wasn't tired or hungry. He was too lethargic to feel his anger. He sat on the hard floor in a corner trying to hide from himself. A deep chill had set into his bones. His breathing was so loud in his own head that he felt deaf to the outside world. He wanted to scream but could not find his voice. He wanted to stand but could not find his legs, until Professor Mackey walked in with Jenny and Percy. The three of them looked so fresh and clean. But then they had not spent the night curled up on a cold, filthy jail floor contemplating the meaning of life through the lens of their anticipated mortality like he had. Nor had they spent nervous hours sequestered in a hospital room like Gabe's family worrying about whether he would live or die.

"Professor Mackey, the news reports on television are lies. I was there. JB and Percy were there. We can testify."

"Have any idea where Fitzgerald is now?" asked the professor.

"He's over at the courthouse," said Gabe's brother. "He's got between twelve and sixteen cases."

"This is Gabe's family," said Prez and he began to introduce them.

"I really need to speak to Fitzgerald," said the professor. "He says he is obtaining a court order to prevent my students here from boarding a plane to go home. We're being told they can't leave because they are needed as material witnesses."

"That sounds about right," said Gabe's brother, who was in the midst of studying for his bar exam. "But you do want to stay, don't you?" Gabe's brother looked at Percy and Jenny. "Your testimony before the coroner and the grand jury would be very important, perhaps vital."

"That's ridiculous," said the professor. "They are exchange students and should be allowed to go home!"

Gabe's family looked at the professor with dismay.

"I just told you a few minutes ago," said Prez, "that we—me, JB and Percy—we need to testify about what happened. They can't leave."

The waiting room door opened, and in a whoosh of air Fitzgerald came through the door with a doctor in tow.

The doctor, a tall man with a mop of shaggy graying hair that hung about his face, said to Mr. and Mrs. Turner, "Your son is resting. We removed a total of four bullets from his body. Miraculously, none struck a vital organ. He'll need time to fully recover, but I am confident he will."

"The good doctor and I go way back," said Fitzgerald. "As soon as they brought Gabriel in, paraffin tests were run on Gabriel's hands and sleeves. I've got a copy of the results right here." Fitzgerald tapped his briefcase. "He never fired a weapon."

"None of us did," said Prez. "None of us *had* weapons."

Fitzgerald pulled a sheet of paper from his briefcase. "The police are going to claim that they found a weapon in a bag belonging to Gabriel Turner. This single entry from their police report will be enough for a grand jury to issue an indictment. That's what this is about. They are trying to deplete Mr. Turner's family's, organization's and supporters' energy and resources by entangling them in expensive and lengthy legal actions and litigation. This same single sheet of paper will lead to the acquittal of my client. They were too hasty. A serial number is recorded for the gun."

"And what does that mean, about the serial number?" asked Professor Mackey.

"It means the history of manufacture and ownership of the weapon is discoverable. There is a single significant caveat that

286

I have already accounted for. I filed an inquiry as to whether the number has ever been recorded as stolen." He pulled another sheet of paper from his briefcase and held it up. "It had not. It therefore has a live, unbroken history that you can bet your bottom dollar will lead straight back to the police."

"Maybe if the Black People's Party wasn't running around spreading their nonsense about socialism and revolution, none of this would have happened," blurted the professor.

Gabriel's mother walked right up to Professor Mackey and looked up at him. "The police murdered a lot of youngsters last night. And you want to place the blame on my son? Let me tell you something, *Professor Jambon*, yes, I know what they call you. And I don't care. You can fuck whoever you want, but you cannot—you will not—fuck over my son's reputation. You will not impugn his integrity. You should be ashamed. Who the hell are you, anyway?"

And that was the question that had long been lodged in Prez's mind like a pesky, painful, barely visible splinter stuck under his fingernail.

45

The Monday Morning After

Professor Mackey drove his little MG back to his apartment in exactly the manner he told Preston Downs not to—like he was in the Le Mans motor race. He was so angry. He was fed up. It was not until late Sunday evening that he finally got a return call from his control, Agent Wicker.

"Hello? Oh, so you finally give me the respect of a return call. I'll be there first thing in the morning."

When Mackey stormed into his office Lester Wicker, his big round-bellied Alabamian FBI handler had two mugs of freshly brewed aromatic coffee on his desk.

Before Mackey could open his mouth, Wicker started. "Don't go ballistic on me. Let me talk. I've looked into the matter and it was one big disaster. Our guys were perfectly coordinated and performed perfectly. It was the local varsity squad who failed because they let a junior varsity player on the field. We're still trying to figure out how that big dumb red fuck was even there."

"You need to cut your half-assed sports analogies. This is not a game. A girl, one of my students, was shot to death."

"We're all very sorry about that. Even Washington."

That last phrase enraged Mackey and he fought for control. He needed to be the consummate unattached professional.

"So, what's the next move? What will Washington do now?"

"About the girl? Washington is handling that through diplomatic channels."

"Diplomatic channels?! That's what you think this is about?! Shit, Wicker!"

"Stop screaming. Somebody might hear you."

"What?" Mackey laughed loud and hard. "Somebody might hear me?!"

Mackey quieted and there was a long period of strained silence.

"Alright, listen. We can't lose sight of the ultimate mission," said Wicker.

"Yeah, to get inside the other team's locker room."

"More than that, remember?"

"To make sure our guy is captain or co-captain."

"That can still happen, you know. This may be the ideal time for that with the big cheese out with injuries."

"Well, 'our guy' smells a rat. C'mon, you guys told me his IQ was 130 or 140 or something. You already know he's smart. He's also very tough and very street-smart. More worrisome is his moral character—it's in the fucking stratosphere. You still think you can play him?"

"Like an eager backup called off the bench! He's still here, isn't he? Something is keeping him here. It's that moral character you just mentioned, that's his weakness. Trust me. Initially, this looked like the worst fuckup, but our end game is now more in play than ever. You won't let socialist radicalism take root in Dr. King's movement, will you?"

"Fuck you, cracker. You don't care anything about Dr. King or the Afro-American community." *What is he not telling me?* Mackey wondered.

"But we both know that black radicalism is a snake that needs its head cut off. And us, we're on the same team. Team America. Right? Say something."

"Cut off the head and the body will die. Is that it, Wicker? That's Washington's strategy?'

The next day, Monday, news was broadcast that Gabriel Turner was recovering well but still not able to attend court. He needed more intensive physiotherapy than initially, though. *The Chicago Defender* newspaper reported that a Jewish philanthropic foundation was paying for his medical costs and physiotherapy.

"They went through hell during the European Holocaust," said Professor Mackey later that Monday morning while meeting with Jenny and Prez. Percival was nowhere to be found. "And then they were persecuted again here in this country during the McCarthy era, which is really current events because it's not that long ago that the Hollywood blacklisting stopped. More importantly, the primary feature of McCarthyism was the creation of the modern American postwar police state. Left-wing, liberal, Afro-American, Native American, labor and immigration rights groups became the targets of constant surveillance, infiltration, agent-provocateur activity, and general state repression. And that is still definitely going on, so I'm sure Jewish people can relate to the situation that Afro-Americans are in.

"Our program finds itself in a bit of a bind. A very important source of financing has given notice that next summer's participation by their fund is in doubt. Without going into details, the feds match these funds dollar for dollar to make this program possible."

"What does that mean exactly?" asked Jenny.

"Best case, an immediate cessation of student exchanges. Worse case, the whole program is shut down. I have not told the rest of your course-mates because I have not received official notice regarding any of this."

"This is sudden, isn't it?" asked Prez.

The professor fidgeted. "It often is. The feds have decided other stuff needs to be funded. Where fed money goes, private funds follow."

"But all of this is supposed to be under the auspices of the War on Poverty, right?"

"Yes, Mr. Downs."

"Why does the War on Poverty have the effect of being a war on the poverty-stricken?"

"I'm an academic, not a politician. What I need from you both is a written account of what happened the night Miss Beckert was shot. I need a full account of the entire evening and not just that tragic event. Everything you saw and everything you heard, and placed within the requisite conceptual and analytical framework of the course. Not fewer than one thousand words."

Jenny and Prez looked at each other.

"You were against us making any sort of statement before." said Jenny.

"And now you want to make it into some sort of a course assignment?" said Prez.

"I know it sounds perverse," said Mackey. "But believe me, what you write will begin a genuine academic inquiry into how police power is still being used to suppress Afro-American self-determination."

Prez had never heard him use that phraseology before. It was straight from Bill Epton's pamphlet, *Black Self-determination* and was rooted in the notion that African-Americans were never given the opportunity to exercise their right to consent to the American form of government, and should be afforded that opportunity through plebiscite, a sort of modern African-

American Constitutional Convention like the whites had in Pennsylvania in 1787.

Jenny said, "Sorry professor, but Lizzy literally had her brains blown out by your coppers and you think the remedy is academic?"

"And what happened to Percy?" said Prez. "He's just up and disappeared?"

"Ask Miss Broadwell. She sleeps in his bed every night."

"I beg your pardon," said Jenny. "You may be the course instructor but you are way out of line. How dare you? My personal life is none of your business."

"Yes, yes, I'm sorry. We're all under a lot of stress. Please accept my apology."

Prez sat trying his best to hold his face still. There was no way he wanted either of them to glimpse his ballooning distrust. He wondered why the hell Jenny didn't know where Percy was. But more troublesome was the question of how the professor knew intimate details about Jenny.

"What I'd really like to research and write about is the money; where it comes from and where it ends up. It's a federally funded program so Washington controls the purse strings. And Jenny here, she's here because of coordination between two governments, not two academic institutions. This isn't a secret is it, the money trail?"

"Of course not," replied the professor, too emphatically. "Let me give it some thought. It would be better to develop that line of inquiry within the context of your work on the dynamics of neighborhood groups as you've already started. It would not be wise to simply discard all that."

"Oh, I have no intention of discarding anything. And you are so right, it does fit in. Early on I observed meaningful discrepancies in the federal resources the Bricks seemed to have access to versus what the Kobras and K-Knights have access to. Why would the guys on the South Side be given more than the guys on the West Side when as far as I can tell their educational, employment, and business opportunities are equally abysmal?"

"What have you learned, Downs?"

"Just that The Woodlawn Organization gets money straight from Washington as part of Washington's ghetto empowerment initiative. The money TWO gets goes straight to Uncle and the Bricks."

As he and Jenny left Professor Mackey's office Prez noticed how tense she was.

"Thinking about Percy?" he asked.

"Everything, Preston. What happened at the club, Lizzy getting killed, testifying."

He hugged her and she started crying. They walked over to a bench and he sat her down. She cried more.

"There is a lot of, how would you call it, 'shit going down.' And it's all mixed up," Jenny said finally. "It's more than the proverbial right hand not knowing what the left hand is doing. One hand doesn't want the other to know and vice versa. There's been a bit of a war declared and the smell of bloody flesh and the certainty of victory are making the expectant victors selfishly reckless. If Lizzy had not been killed, what happened that night would have been merely a grotesque comedy of errors."

"Jenny, who are you? You suddenly seem so much older, so much more ... I don't know ..."

"Directed? Purposeful? Not as giddy and as scattered as you thought? After today you may not see me again. But here is what you must know. Lizzy fell in love with you. Whatever you find out in the future you must never forget that. The other thing is what I've already mentioned. A war has been declared against your so-called Left. And it's being waged in three countries.

Don't be a casualty. You want to know where the funds are coming from? You want to know about the hand pulling the puppet strings? Start with the OED in Washington."

The first week of December, Prez flew to Washington. The flight was a special treat to himself. He felt a huge sense of accomplishment. He could pay for his own transportation. He was paying for his rent. He even had a savings account. More importantly, he had earned his master's degree and wanted to celebrate with his family.

He tried not to feel guilty that his ulterior motive for going home was to visit the Federal Office of Economic Development. Almost immediately he discovered it was ensconced within the Cabinet-level US Department of Housing and Urban Development. It appeared Jenny's puppeteer had a master.

"Good morning." Prez beamed his biggest smile down upon the young woman seated behind the desk.

"How can I assist you?"

"I'm doing graduate studies at the University of Chicago on the federal funding of Chicago inner-city housing development, anti-poverty, and community organizing programs and I was wondering if you could tell me who I should speak to in order to come away with an overview of the general philosophical and strategic driving forces behind these efforts as well as a chart of funding flow from the government to the various final recipients."

"Well ..." she said as she thumbed through no less than six different pages in a department directory. "Perhaps ..." she continued as she flipped through cards in a Rolodex on her desk. "One moment please ..." She got up, went to a cabinet and pulled out various file folders before abruptly shutting one, placing it back in the drawer, and shoving the drawer shut with her knee. "What did you want again? Wait, don't tell me. Have a seat." She pointed to a chair behind him.

His tactic of flustering her worked. But would she return with security to eject him or with someone in a position of higher authority to help him?

She came back alone but not empty-handed.

"Here." She handed him a typed page with a signature at the bottom. "Fill out the appropriate lines." He did and gave it back to her. "Mr. Preston Coleman Downs, Junior, of Washington D.C." she said as she applied her signature and gave him back the form.

"Yes. Born and raised here."

"But doing your studies in Chicago?"

"I did undergrad work at Howard."

"Did you? Maybe that's why you look so familiar." They looked at each other for a minute before she reached in a drawer and took out a thick cardboard tag, about two inches square. She gave it to him. It had the word PASS stenciled in black over the HUD seal. "My supervisor has authorized you to visit and use our archives. The librarian there will give you instructions and assistance. Go out of this building. Turn left and go around to the back. There's a guard booth there. Give in your pass there. You will be escorted to the archives office. Good day."

"Thank you very much. I have another question. Can I come back if I need to?"

"Of course. Hold on to the form and bring it back. You'll need to come to this office first."

For the week he did his research his family and friends didn't even know he was in town. He took a little room on Sixth Street in Chinatown. He felt a sense of ownership over the streets he walked upon daily to and from the HUD building. He never felt like that in Chicago. Yet, he felt so strange being in his hometown without it feeling like he was actually home. He hated the acrid taste of the aspirins he started taking to deal with the dull ache behind his eyes, which he thought was due to his long evenings reading and writing in the too-dim light of the room. He quickly tired of Chinese takeout and turned to White Tower Hamburgers close by on Sixth and F Streets. Each evening he'd walk up the stairs to the room carrying his leather satchel and a big white paper bag filled with little square burgers and a milkshake.

⇒

That Saturday morning, he called his brother to come pick him up. He was so deeply troubled by what he found in his research that he didn't even question his decision to not tell his family he had been in D.C. for almost the whole week. Nor would he see or call any of his friends, not even his girlfriend. He wasn't prepared to reason through answering questions related to his research.

Gus laughed out loud when he saw his big brother standing at the curb in front of Union Station. He jumped out of his car and squeezed Prez in a bear hug. "Prez. Man, you look great! Must be that Chicago pussy. I hear the weather is abominable. It's so good to see you." He laughed hard again and slapped his brother on the back. "Ow. Think I broke my hand you little short shit." They both laughed. As Gus drove off, he made it a point to gesture at any woman they passed. "Well ..."

297

"The weather is shitty there. Yeah, man," said Prez.

"Well … ahem."

"I don't discuss my love life."

"What the fuck's love got to do with it? Don't be a square."

47

Chicago, January, 1968

On New Year's Day, 1968, Prez called Professor Mackey. Another man answered the phone.

"Oh, sorry," said Prez, "I must have dialed the wrong number." He put the phone down. He knew he had not dialed the wrong number. He dressed, went out, got in his car, and drove over to the professor's apartment. He found it fascinating how the "Marimba Red" color of his car seemed to blend right in with the surroundings. The professor's neighborhood contained a heady mix of artists, intellectuals, and Puerto Rican drug dealers. There were sculptures on people's lawns, graffiti everywhere, and the drug dealers' jacked-up cars dominating curbsides. Even his loud mufflers seemed quiet compared to theirs. He saw the big black Mercedes Lizzy had told him about and noticed its license plate consisted solely of a long string of letters. He parked and sat waiting. Not long after, a large black man wearing a gold and white *agbada* came out of the building, got into the Mercedes, and drove off. Prez went to a phone booth and called the professor. This time the professor picked up. Prez made an appointment to see him that Wednesday.

That Wednesday morning, Prez left his apartment and jogged up to Washington Park for his run. It was colder and darker than usual, even for 5:00 a.m. But that did not prevent him from noticing that in addition to the usual police car that tried to hide on Fifty-ninth Street at South Park Way, there was another police car on the other side of the park at South Cottage Grove where Fifty-ninth Street continued. His running partners were nowhere to be found, and that was off-putting since he had just seen them at the New Year's Eve gathering and they had sworn they'd join him running. He felt a loose shoe, stopped, and bent down to tie his lace. Pieces of bark from the tree beside exploded away. The dirt around him began to kick up. And just before his first footfall onto pavement his right leg collapsed and he fell.

He crawled behind a bush, sat up and looked at his leg. His sweatpants were ripped. He started to feel a dull throbbing, then a rising chorus of pain in his leg. He lifted away the fabric to see that a piece of his skin had been gouged away. Blood quickly surged to the surface. He took his bandana from around his neck and wrapped it around his leg. He listened and looked around but the park was eerily still. He got up and moved behind a tree. He limped over to another tree, then another, then another, finally dropping into a sitting position behind one and took deep breaths to try and counter the pain in his leg. His bandana was soaked with blood. The only place for him to go was back to his apartment. Would they be waiting for him there? He suddenly felt more vulnerable than he had ever felt before. The only weapons he possessed were his limbs and his mind. He hoped they would get him through this. But he swore to himself right then and there that he was never going to feel vulnerable like that again.

He crept up the back stairs to enter his apartment and went straight to the medicine cabinet in his bathroom. He sat on the edge of the tube with his feet under the faucet. He sloshed water over his wound. It stung like heck. He swabbed on some Mercurochrome and wrapped white gauze around his leg.

He called the professor and asked if they could reschedule their meeting until the next day.

"Sure we can. Same time?"

"Yes. That would be fine."

"There's something wrong. I can hear it in your voice."

"It's cool. I'm looking forward to our meeting. I'll tell you about my idea for my thesis."

Prez went over to the sofa and sat down. He thought about which album to put on to soothe his frayed nerves. He turned to look out the bay windows of his brownstone apartment and got a rush of panic. He closed his curtains and pulled the sofa away from the window. Then he realized all the furniture in the room would need to be rearranged to accommodate the displaced sofa. He limped around, shifting furniture, until his leg started throbbing with pain again and his mind throbbed with the realization that he was sinking into the darkness of fear. He put the furniture back the way it was. He wasn't going to live in fear, even if it killed him.

He was so troubled he needed to speak to someone from back home. She was perhaps the last person he should be talking to but the very first person who came to mind. Later that evening, he went out the back exit of his building. Soon after, he struggled to climb up the fire escape and crawled into the back window of a recently vacated apartment that he knew still had its phone line connected.

"Hello. Oh, my goodness! Prez! Is that you?"

"Hi, Tala."

"Oh, my goodness! How long has it been? Two, maybe three years. How are you?"

"No, you tell me, how's the husband and kids?"

"Nice try. Just come right out and ask. No, I'm not married. I'm too busy teaching and studying. Marriage is the last thing on my mind."

"Weren't you engaged? What happened to—"

"Don't say his name. I only say it when it's absolutely necessary. Like milk of magnesia. You only say it when you need to take it. So, are you calling to wish me a happy New Year? If so, you are forgiven for forgetting me in 1965, 1966, and 1967. Hmm ... no, I think you called in '65."

"Tala, I got shot."

"What? Where are you, Prez?"

"I'm in my apartment."

"When did it happen?"

"This morning."

"Why aren't you in the hospital?"

"It just ripped some flesh out. I patched it like your father taught me."

"Who shot you?"

"I didn't see anything. But in my heart, I know. The pigs."

"You never talked like that before."

"I'm talking like that now. I need to talk to you about some stuff, actually a lot of stuff. I don't really trust anybody here. Do you have time?"

"All the time you want."

They talked for almost three hours.

"Tala, I don't think I can talk anymore. My face is getting numb."

"Well, you have told me more in these last couple of hours than in all the many years we've known each other. You know how I used to call you Mr. Ninety Percent back in the sit-in days?"

"Don't remind me."

"Well, I'd have to call you Mr. Ninety-Nine Point Nine Percent today. All kidding aside, it sounds like you are in the midst of something very sinister indeed. Your analyses are impressive. I need to talk to my father, if that's okay with you. He's very well connected, as you know. I think he even knows Fitzgerald. Professor Mackey is a homosexual. It's an open secret in his family and I am close to his family by way of my ex. They're cousins. But whether your *Professor Jambon* is actually working for the feds or the police is quite a serious question and probably a secret so deep only he truly knows. He sounds like he's very complicated and conflicted. I think that if he was going to betray you, you would be dead already."

"What if it's a long-term operation like the ones you read about in spy novels?"

"I've never read a spy novel. You read those? I didn't know that. Just be smart in your dealings with him. Keep a distance and come back home for your Ph.D. Okay? Promise?"

"What about that other thing?"

"I'm still thinking about that."

"Tala, I've thought about it. I think it all comes down to being smart and not stupid. Look: fists, feet, elbows, bullets ... what they all have in common is that for self-defense purposes they are all merely projectiles. I want you to know that my morality is still as high as ever. You know me. I will never believe that life is anything other than sacrosanct—ever. But I need to learn that craft. I need to be as good with it as I am with my fists. I want to be able to save lives if necessary, probably my own. I am committed to never ever using more force than necessary for self-defense. I would never kill. You know me, Tala."

"I have a cousin in the Marines. He's actually with the intelligence unit at Quantico, Virginia. I'll speak to him. He's on our side."

"Let me give you my address and phone number. Don't call unless you have to in case my phone is tapped. Tell your cousin to refer to himself as Virginia when he calls."

"That's a girl's name."

"Okay, what about Virgin."

"Prez, that's even worse."

"Okay, I got it, I got it … Virgil."

"Prez … my dear sweet Preston, you crack me up sometimes. That's his real name."

"Okay, I have a better idea. I never have to meet him here. I'm driving home for Easter. I'll see you then."

"You have a car?'

"Oh yeah. It's fast."

"I know that without even knowing what kind of car it is. Just don't crash and burn."

"You mean like the last time we were together?"

She expelled an extended, anguished sigh. "That was a long time ago. See you at Easter."

"Okay. Bye."

The next day, a Thursday, he limped into Professor Mackey's office.

"What happened to you?" the professor asked in a genuinely alarmed manner.

"Somebody shot me in the park yesterday morning."

Bam! The professor slammed his fist down on his desktop. "I told you to be careful. Didn't I tell you that?" He got up and paced back and forth. He sat back down. *Bam!* He slammed his fist down again. "How bad is it?"

"Still a little sore, but it's healing."

"Who did it?"

"The cops."

"Did you see them do it?"

"No."

"Well, why did you say it was the cops?"

"Because they were parked all around the park when I was running."

"How many cops are you talking about?"

"Two marked cars and one unmarked."

"Cops park around parks all the time. That means nothing. What else can you tell me?"

"They were all conversing on their radio microphones when I passed their cars."

"And you are sure they were looking at you?"

"I'm sure."

"The unmarked car, describe it."

"Dark gray, four-door sedan ... with a removable antenna on the trunk."

Mackey paused. He looked up from the journal he was writing in. "Removable? What do you mean?"

"There was a regular built-in radio antenna on the front fender. The one on the trunk lip could be screwed in and out. Those antennae are thicker at the base. Any street-fighter knows that."

Mackey went over and looked down. There was Wicker's dark-gray service sedan parked down the street. "Can you describe the men in the dark-gray car?"

"Only one. He's big, heavy-set, with brown messy hair, and has a scar that runs in a straight line from his right nostril to his left upper lip."

He had just described Wicker.

"What can you tell me about Gabriel Turner?" asked the professor. "I understand he's back in action."

"I'm not sure what you mean by 'back in action' but he has made a remarkable recovery."

"Is he directing the BPP programs again? Does he really want his Rainbow Coalition to become a political party? Are there really plans afoot to field coalition candidates in the upcoming municipal elections? And you, what's your exact role in all of this? It seems you have become more a political activist than an academic."

"Take me to lunch and we can talk over some tacos."

"That's a sly one, Mr. Downs. Come on. Let's go." As they walked towards his car Mackey began to feel a chill come over him. Downs had never displayed a hint of humor, much less canniness. It was as if that bullet fragment he took had propelled him into another dimension of maturity. He certainly was not the "floater" Wicker thought he was. And, of course, Wicker knew. He had to. But how did they miss?

Chicago, South Side, February 1968

Prez was on his fourth set of knuckle pushups when someone rang his doorbell. It was Gabe.

"What's happening, brother-man? What are you doing over here? Well, come in."

"Hey, Prez. I just got a strange call from one of the Bricks. Uncle wants to meet and talk about joining the coalition."

"What's weird about that?"

"The coalition is a collective governed by a central committee. There is no leader and we all understand that our individual interests are subservient to our manifesto and program. He's used to playing God."

"Say no more."

"They want to meet with at their community church. You know the neighborhood. You know them. I need you to come with us."

"When?"

"This evening at six."

A sign on the church lawn invited one and all to February Bible Studies held every Tuesday at six, yet they saw no one as they arrived at the church and went around to a side entrance as instructed. When they opened the door, they were met by a blinding spotlight focused on their faces. They squinted and covered their eyes. They were pushed inside and the door slammed behind them. They heard a finger snap and the whole place lit up. Bricks surrounded them pointing an assortment of new and shiny guns at them. After what seemed like an eternity of silence, a heavy door could be heard opening and closing, and footsteps approaching above them and behind them. They turned and looked up into the balcony. It was Uncle.

"Just like that!" he snapped his fingers again, "you could all be blown away. Instead I have chosen to welcome you to our territory and to extend hospitality. In spite of the fact that I have a letter right here in my hands that threatens me with being 'blown away' if I do not surrender to your demand that the Bricks become a member of your coalition. It is signed by 'Brother Gabriel Turner of the Black People's Party.'"

"That's ridiculous," said Gabe.

"Are you calling me a liar?"

"I'm saying I never sent that letter."

"I think you'd say anything right now to keep your punk ass from getting blown away."

"Listen, brother, there's nothing I'm afraid of and that includes death. I'm walking around with a couple fragments of police lead in my body right now. Brother Downs here was just shot by the pigs the other day as he ran around *your* park. So much for looking out for *your* neighborhood. Is that letter typewritten or handwritten and is it signed?"

"Huh?" One of Uncle's boys leaned in and whispered something to him. "There's a signature."

"I have a pen in my pocket. May I get it? I am going to write my signature on this piece of paper and you will see it is not my writing." He handed the paper to one of the Bricks who ran it up to Uncle. Uncle looked. He passed it around to about eight different guys standing with him.

"Who would have done this?"

"The pig, my brother. Look at us right now. This is just what they want. They want us to kill each other. Then they win and our people lose. Did you see how well the picnic went last summer? South Side, West Side, black, white, Chicano, Puerto Rican ... that is the future of liberation and we have the power to make it a reality. That's what the capitalist power structure is afraid of. We can't let them win. Join us, my brother."

"My message is that if I see any of you around here without my permission, I'll have you blown away. That is, unless I change my mind. Go now."

They had just turned to go and as they walked towards the door, Uncle said, "Wait. Just to give notice, Downs, we have a score to settle when your leg heals up."

Prez gritted his teeth. The show of guns, the insanely unfair numerical advantage, the bullying; it all made Prez grit his teeth. He spun on his heel.

"Let's go," said Gabe, trying to grab his arm.

"And what score is that? With you? Let's settle it now. If I kick your butt with one good leg, you join the coalition. Deal?"

"What if I win?"

"Motherfucker, you won't."

Somebody said, "That nigger real funny." There was laughter all around.

Gabe pulled him out the door. "Shit Prez! What the fuck was that, man? Are you crazy?"

"No. I just exposed Uncle to be a fraud and a coward. There's no way he's supposed to back down from a straight-up challenge. You just witnessed their vulnerability. It's their intellectual and spiritual complacency. They've been following Uncle for so long that they know nothing else. Keep the rap flowing in their direction. They'll be listening. So will Uncle."

Sure enough, soon after that Uncle relented a little and allowed the coalition to hold meetings and political education classes on Brick turf. Bricks were invited to the West Side and were greeted like long-lost brothers. The same style of free breakfast programs, free health clinics, free legal aid services, and political education and black history workshops were in operation in both regions. But Uncle still resisted joining the coalition in spite of witnessing first-hand the bountiful benefits of peace and people's power.

And then came the cataclysm of April 4, 1968.

Prez had taken to meditation surrounded by burning incense in an effort to quell the aching behind his eyes. He wondered if he needed reading glasses or just a break from reading and writing. He was sitting cross-legged on the floor with his eyes blissfully closed when his phone rang. It was Gabe. He was crying.

"Prez," he sobbed and sniffled, "they killed him, man. They shot him down like a dog."

"Gabe? What are you talking about? Who's dead?"

"King, man, Dr. King ... he's been assassinated."

"Wait!" said Prez. He dropped the phone, ran over to the window, and looked up the street. He could see that there was a lot of smoke west of Washington Park. He could hear sirens, explosions, and gunfire. He ran back and almost yelled into the phone, "It's a war zone across the park."

"The people are in rebellion over here, too. If they can assassinate Dr. King, they will not hesitate to kill any of us. The pig has murdered our Dreamer. It's nightmare time." He hung up.

Prez dressed and rushed out. The realization that where he lived in Hyde Park was indeed a different world from the poor black neighborhoods that surrounded Hyde Park hit him hard. All around the boundaries of his neighborhood there was smoke and shooting. Sirens screamed through on their way to the ghetto. Shotgun-toting riot police stormed through Hyde Park, merely glancing at him as he ran down the street. If he had been across Washington Park, they would have shot him dead, he thought. Just as he reached South Cottage Grove and was about to cross the street, he saw a few of the Bricks, concealed behind bushes and balusters with guns drawn.

"Don't cross the park. They'll kill you," one of them shouted to Prez.

Prez ducked behind a car. "Who?"

"The cops, man. They shooting anything that goes through the park. They shot three already."

"Shit, man! Are they dead?"

"Don't know. Can't get to 'em."

"They're still lying in the park, you mean?"

"Right."

"Who are they?"

"Don't know."

"Fuck, man! Where's Uncle?"

"He be here soon. He down in Woodlawn making sure those niggers stay cool."

After a few minutes Prez said, "Look, we can't wait. Those people might still be alive and bleeding to death."

"You can't go, man. Uncle say stay out of the park."

"So fucking shoot me."

Prez sprinted across the street and dove behind some bushes. Then he realized he had no idea where the downed people were. He hollered, "Where are they?"

"Two up at the lagoon. One over around Fifty-eighth."

Fifty-eighth Street was straight across from where he was. He poked his head up to look and listen. He could see flames licking the underbelly of the evening sky, making it shimmer with an eerie burnt-orange color. He could see smoke so thick it was like a curtain that fluttered and bent with the wind. Prez got

312

down and started crawling in the dirt. He looked up and an army truck full of soldiers rushed by. None of them bothered to look toward the park. After the fleeting shock of seeing the army in the ghetto passed, he realized that none of the police cars he saw fly by bothered to look over into the park either. He surmised that there was nobody sitting and targeting people in the park and that the people who were shot were the result of random shootings. He forced himself to accept that theory and got up, bent as low as he could, and started jogging from tree to tree and from bush to bush toward Fifty-eighth and South Park Way. He came upon a circular paved area with a water fountain at the center. Just beside the fountain he saw the body. "Oh, Christ," he shuddered. It was a little girl. He sprinted over to the fountain and hid behind it, then rushed out, picked her up, and carried her behind a bush. He put her down and saw that his sleeves and jacket front were covered in blood. She had two little pig-tails with colorful barrettes at the ends. Her face was too peaceful to be the face of a dead child. But she was not breathing. She had no heartbeat. A child with no heartbeat! A child covered in blood!

"No!" screamed Prez. "Oh, Jesus, no! Brennie-Man! I'm sorry I couldn't save you! I'm sorry!" He wept uncontrollably. He blew his nose on his undershirt. "I'm going to take you home, little girl. We'll go and find your mama. I'm going to take you to her. I couldn't take Brennie-Man to his mother, but I'm going to take you. Don't worry, we'll find her." He picked her up and started walking. He walked straight across South Park Way to Fifty-eighth Street, crying like a baby. "Did anybody lose a little girl? I'm looking for her mama. Whose little girl is this? She wants her mama. Does anybody know her mama?"

Halfway down the block, he dropped to one knee, sobbing. "Please, somebody. Anybody. This little girl wants her mama." He dropped to the other knee and fell towards the ground. He rolled over on his back cradling the little dead girl on his stomach. He held her and swayed back and forth. "She wants her mama. She just wants her mama. Please, where's her mama?"

Hands reached down and took the little girl from his grasp. A woman screamed, "Roslyn! Oh my god! Roslyn!"

Prez lay on the ground wailing and wailing. "She just wants her mama. She wants to go home." He tossed and turned on the ground. Hands picked him up and sat him on some steps. The sirens screeched, the bullets popped, the smoked weaved in and out of his lungs, causing him to cough and choke. His eyes burned. He heard a voice tell him to get inside somewhere because the mayor had just told the police to shoot to kill blacks on sight. He rose from the steps and stumbled back towards the park. He was like an old mule down on his grandfather's farm, just following a familiar path without really knowing where it was going.

Someone screamed for him to "Get down, they're shooting, man! What the fuck is wrong with you?" But he was in a stupor and kept plodding along. He didn't remember entering his building, climbing the stairs, opening his door, or drawing the bathwater. He just remembered being awakened by his chattering teeth as he sat shivering in an ice-cold tub. He jumped out, wrapped himself in towels, his bathrobe, and a blanket. He sat on his sofa by the window and looked up toward the park. Then he fell into a deep sleep.

50

Chicago, April 6, 1968

Prez was jarred awake by the ear-splitting trill of the telephone. He turned over abruptly and fell off the sofa. He was confused. What time was it? What day was it? His Bulova watch told him it was 7:45 a.m. on the sixth day of the month. He made a mental note to look for a watch that told him the day and grabbed the phone. It was Professor Mackey summoning him to his office for a 9:00 meeting.

As he walked towards Mackey's office the campus seemed vacuous in a way that had nothing to do with it being a Saturday morning. In the office, he sat on one of the two chairs on the visitor's side of the professor's desk. The professor's office reflected the grayness of the day even though Mackey had gone to great lengths to create a workspace bursting with African paintings, carvings, and various framed kente cloths.

"Mr. Downs, simply outstanding work. Outstanding! Your thesis, *Black Power: The Rhetoric of Hope, the Reality of Powerlessness*, is being considered by the McEachern Foundation for a Brilliance Grant.

"Your paper may well be one of the most important of your generation. Your dialectical approach, your systematic and academically objective analysis, the way you construct conclusions based upon actual real-life situations and examples ... this is classic stuff, Downs. This is how it should be done. Nothing can give a scholarly work more legitimacy than an author who has actually lived through the subject matter. Incredible! Fantastic! Outstanding!"

There was a knock on the professor's office door. He got up, opened it, and in walked the white guy who had given Percy the bag the night Lizzy was killed. Prez's heart started pounding. He was sure they could hear it. Their mouths were moving but he couldn't hear a word they said. He wanted to get up and leave, get some fresh air, drink some water, look up and see blue sky, hear his own voice tell him that everything would be alright.

"Downs, Downs, what's wrong with you?" Mackey was squatting on the floor in front of him with a very concerned look on his face. "Are you alright?"

"I think I'm over-tired. I hardly slept at all since Thursday." But he had slept through practically the whole of yesterday, Friday. "And I could be a bit dehydrated from my workout." But he hadn't been to the gym since Wednesday. The woozy jelly feeling passed and he felt refreshed as never before. His mind became clear. He straightened himself and sat erect. Mackey stood and walked over to the unexpected arrival.

"This is—" Mackey was cut off.

"I'm Ed Smith from Washington."

"The James Madison University just outside Washington, to be exact."

"I live in Washington. That's what I meant."

"He's here to talk to you about an opportunity there," said Mackey as he cast a *you-almost-fucked-this-up* glance at Ed Smith from Washington.

"A new Black Studies course is being offered for the Fall semester at James Madison under the aegis of a new Progressive Inter-disciplinary Program. We'd like to offer you a lecturing position while you complete your Ph.D."

316

"All your expenses will be covered as a student. The money you make teaching will be yours," said Mackey.

Prez thought about his high school and undergraduate efforts to get Black Studies programs and here he was being offered an opportunity to actually teach in one. But he knew it was bogus.

"Where is the money coming from for my studies? Not the university. So, from where?"

Mackey and Ed Smith looked at each other. Ed Smith looked hard at Prez and said,

"The National Student Association."

"Never heard of that organization," said Prez. "But it sounds promising. I will need a couple of days to think about it. I'll let the professor know by the weekend."

For over a year, Prez had always carried the February 15, 1967 issue of *Ramparts* magazine in his satchel. It was so important to him that he had bought two and mailed one to himself at his mother's house. An article in it revealed the CIA's efforts to control and manipulate the progressive — "radical" as the CIA called them—student movement via a front organization. That organization was the National Student Association.

❧

After Easter, Prez stepped up his political work. A sense of urgency had taken hold. The Gang Intelligence Unit of the Chicago Police Department behaved like the roving death squads of South American dictators. All coalition members were being targeted for jail, forced exile or death.

But it wasn't until he told Professor Mackey that he had decided to decline the James Madison University opportunity and explained that he had noticed he was being followed everywhere he went.

He learned how to allow himself to be followed, be evasive, and proceed to where he wanted to go undetected. That was how he completed his handgun training. Once a week he went to a shooting range in Indiana where he had on short order qualified as an expert with a handgun. His instructor called him a natural point-shooter, even though he taught and promoted two-handed sight-shooting.

One Saturday night he borrowed the professor's car to take a new girlfriend to the movies and noticed a two-car tail.

"Thanks, Professor Mackey, for letting me borrow your car," Prez said when he returned the car. "I was followed."

"You shouldn't be surprised." *But you are*, Prez thought. "Will you ever not call me 'Professor'?"

"Maybe when I have my own Ph.D."

They laughed. The professor went to his coffee table and wrote something down on a pad. He placed his forefinger upon his lips as he handed the piece of paper to Prez: *If you ever have an emergency, call this number: 979-3965. Keep this with you at all times. Don't speak out loud about this.* Prez took the paper. It felt like a goodbye moment. He started to say something.

"By the way, in a few days a young lady will be coming by your flat to look at it. She may take it over at the start of the fall semester."

Soon after that, Prez received a visit from a woman who looked like a character straight out of a James Bond movie. She looked at and through everything in his flat. He had to ask repeatedly that she refrain from going through his personal belongings and that she close his drawers. She never listened and he knew she had a job to do.

51

Chicago, December 1968

Prez wanted to leave Chicago and go back to Washington. The academic scene there was getting vibrant, and not just in universities. Lots of policy institutes were opening. He planned to open his own. But he wanted to stick around Chicago at least until Spring because he wanted to write a book about his experiences there. He moved to a larger flat in Old Town. It was a corner flat so he had a view in two directions. The building's rooftop was part of an intriguing rooftop culture that spanned the block. There was an alley system behind the building that led to three separate streets. He felt safe.

At the Christmas break a close friend of the professor who was a barber—Erskine the Barber—was holding Chicago's first Kwanzaa celebration, at least according to him. He begged Prez to come in for an Afro styling session and to model in a fashion show of African garb.

Prez got off the bus and started walking the three blocks to the barber shop. This time he knew he was being followed. But it was just after noon on a bright sunny day. He didn't think they would get violent in such an affluent Afro-American neighborhood, especially since everyone was counting down the days to Christmas. And he wasn't concerned about the gun he was carrying. At worst, that was a misdemeanor charge and a fine.

A police car began driving slowly behind him. At the next intersection it turned left. Prez kept walking. He crossed the street so that motor traffic would face him. The police car came around the corner facing him and drove very slowly. Prez used his peripheral vision to note that the cop was talking into his radio microphone. Prez kept walking straight. The car came around the corner again and this time Prez looked at the cop. It was Mad Dog Murphy. Why was he in a single-man car, Prez wondered. Murphy motioned him over. Prez tried to ignore him, but he did not want to give him any excuse to start shooting. They were on a residential street and right in front of a school that he knew was busy readying some of its students for the Kwanzaa show. Prez walked over to the driver's side. Murphy had his right hand inside his jacket. S*nubby in a shoulder holder*, Prez guessed. *That's illegal.*

"Well, well. The dead girl's fuck slave. Where you going?"

"Erskine's Barber Shop three streets over."

"You got ID?"

"Yes."

"Well, I want to see it."

Prez gave him his wallet.

"Well, well. You're a foreigner too, Preston Downs from Washington, D.C."

"Why did you stop me?"

"Watch your tone with me, boy."

"I'm nobody's boy. You need to watch your tone."

"What the fuck did you just say to me, boy?"

"May I ask you something, off-i-cer? Is there any trouble in the area?"

"Ah, no … boy."

"Just one more. Are you looking for anyone that fits my description?"

"I already told you there's no trouble in the area, so why would I be looking for anyone?"

"So you're not looking for anyone that fits my description."

"No. Your description or anybody's description."

"Then you don't have probable cause."

"What? I'm a cop. I can do what I want out here."

"The Supreme Court has just ruled that you cannot. You have to have probable cause, otherwise this is an illegal stop and you are breaking the law. May I have my wallet back? I am free to leave."

Prez noticed a beige sedan driving slowly by. It turned the corner and stopped.

"You leave when I say you can leave."

"No, officer, you are breaking the law. You are in violation of the Constitution."

"I can ask to search you."

Then a dark-gray sedan rolled by slowly. Mad Dog Murphy made eye contact with the driver of the passing car. Prez looked over his shoulder and saw it was Wicker. He drove up two blocks and parked.

"Yes, you can ask and I have the right to say no. The answer is no. You cannot frisk me. Keep the wallet. I'm going to the barber shop. Return it there or I'll have my lawyer on this and he'll get it back."

Prez turned and started walking away from the car. He heard the car door open and feet come rushing towards him. He felt a sharp blow to the back of his head and saw a flash of light. He wondered if he had been shot in the head. He was thrown over the back of the police car's trunk. Mad Dog Murphy was screaming at him.

"Nigger, I'm going to blow your head off! I'm going to blow your head off, nigger!"

Prez turned and looked down the barrel of a snub-nosed revolver loaded with dum-dums. The cop kept screaming. But everything seemed to be in slow motion now. The cop screaming slowly: "I'm going to bloooow your head off, Niggerrr!"

Some kids opened the school door. Murphy glanced, switched the snubby over to his left and drew his service revolver, which he pointed at the kids.

Prez snap-drew his weapon and spun. He saw flashes from the cop's muzzle. Prez was wearing a long black leather coat. When he spun its tails flared out. He could feel bullets pulling at his coat tails. He shot back at the cop's gun arm. He wanted to disarm that mad dog and get the hell out of there. The cop dropped his gun and fell backwards. Prez took off running in the other direction, away from the two parked sedans. He ran zig-zag like a half-back. He could feel his clothes being snatched and pulled this way and that. He felt stinging sensations on his torso and back. He kept running. He turned a corner and ran as fast as he could. He heard tires screeching but no sirens. He ran through an alley, jumped a fence, ran through a backyard, jumped another fence, threw his weapon down a sewer, stopped a kid, and bought his hat from him, then he took off his coat, threw it in a garbage can, and walked into a clothing store and bought another one. When he bent down to get the money out of his boot the proprietor asked, "Did you hit your head? You're bleeding." Prez touched the back of his head and his hand came away covered in blood.

"Don't know how that happened. Is there a washroom or sink in here?"

"Sure, in the back."

Prez paid, said thank you, and went to the bathroom to clean the blood. Then he ran to get on a bus that was just about to pull away from the curb. Now he was hearing sirens and lots of them. A small army of police cars raced by. He got off the bus and took the subway north. He stayed on the subway until Loyola University. He got off and found a phone booth on North Broadway. A woman answered: "You're at Loyola? Go to the Madonna Della Strada Chapel and wait."

He asked directions and was pointed toward the chapel. He sat on the steps, paced, and sat some more. It was a long ten minutes before he saw the professor's MG pull up. The woman who had come to his former apartment was driving.

"C'mon!" she said as she got out to put the top up. "Here." She passed him an envelope after they were seated in the car. "Everything you need is in there. Do you have papers, money? Give it to me. The number that you called, if you wrote it down give me the paper."

"What is this?" he said as he opened the envelope and pulled out some weird looking currency.

"Canadian money."

"Where's Professor Mackey? And I need to call my lawyer."

"If you do that, you will be dead before midnight. You are too fucking smart to be acting so goddamn stupid right now. Do you want to live or die? Sit back, we've got some driving to do."

52

Montreal, Summer Solstice, 1969 – After Supper

There had been rather innocuous banter around the table thus far. That was about to change.

"There are differences between what white women and black women consider necessary to achieve women's liberation. This is based upon the stark differences in our real lives. You care about stuff that we don't. You hide stuff that we won't. For example, you demand the right to work but I'll bet you would be so uncomfortable if you actually made more money than your man."

Marianne roared with laughter. "I already make more money than most men I know. And believe me, I flaunt it. Isn't that right?" She looked at Prez.

"You are a managing librarian, while Doug is just a reference clerk," Jamie interjected. "You should make more. But in that type of employment climate it is different from the real world. You should know that, Marianne."

"What 'real world' are you referring to, Jamie?" asked Tala.

"Where real things are produced and delivered. Like resources, goods, retail, banking and transportation services, communications … that sort of thing. Take a look at the companies listed on the stock exchanges or in the Fortune 500 if you want to know who the big boys are. There aren't any libraries listed and no women running any of those companies. Anyway, you should really be talking about wealth accumulation and not wages because one's wages may not tell the whole story of the net worth of an individual." He scowled at Marianne. "And you should know that too."

Prez looked over at Marianne and had never seen her so dejected. He said, "You don't think libraries are important, Jamie. You don't value information?" She dropped her eyes and would not look at Jamie. She was displaying something towards Jamie that Prez would have bet practically anything she didn't even have in her—submissiveness. Shit, he thought, how much money does Jamie have? Is that it? Jamie, at six feet two, also possessed something else Marianne seemed to want in a man—height. Marianne seemed ill at ease when they were out together and she had on high heels.

He wondered about the quizzical way she looked at mixed-race babies and children. What was she thinking and feeling as she looked at them?

"Jamie, are you trying to channel this conversation into a debate about capitalism versus Marxism?" asked Tala. "That's a typical male chauvinist tactic—trying to veer away from what we women really want to talk about."

What a great move. Let me stay quiet and see how this unfolds, thought Prez.

"She's right, Jamie. We were talking about whether any differences exist between what black and white women are fighting for. What has that got to do with net income?"

"Well, actually, everything. Or, maybe nothing. I'll just butt out. Hmph!"

Oh, stop pouting, Jamie, and get back in there and fight like a rich white boy, thought Prez.

"The point I was trying to make is that in the Afro-American community families have been held together by the women on every level, and still are.

"It's really hard to enjoy such an exquisite meal while such an unappetizing course of conversation is being served up," said Prez. "I just heard such an offensive deluge of stereotyping bullshit gush from your mouth, Tala, that I almost don't know what to say. Except that I am disappointed, and that you, of all people, should know better. You were raised by your father. You know what happened to my father."

"What happened to your father, Doug?"

"Not now, Jamie, please. Tala, you know of the families that live around Lincoln Park. The fathers are there taking care of their families, going to work every day and providing the whole neighborhood with a sense of security."

"I'm going by statistics which bear me out. You haven't even seen what I've been reading. You haven't looked at the information. You're just going by what you see every day," said Preston.

"True. But knowing begins with observation. I read too, just to remind you. And when I read jive like you are talking now the underlying proposition is an Afro-American community that is matriarchal and monolithic. Afro-Americans comprise a sort of nation. And like any nation there is a class and caste structure. There is a complex and fluid social structure. While it is true that slavery removed the black man from the head of his family and replaced him with the slaveowner, it is also and more profoundly true that the Harlem Renaissance was built upon the solidity of the Afro-American family with the father at its head."

"And before I say anything else, a bit of a tribute to a woman I think is really fantastic, so fantastic that she made me promise not to bring up the fact that she is soon to be a professor at Howard University. She is beautiful, brilliant, and bold all rolled into one woman who probably makes way more money, in wages, than all of us put together. But still, none of that takes away from the fact that on this particular issue, Tala, you are wrong."

"Professor Tala!" Marianne blurted out. She got up and gave Tala a big hug. "Your father must be so proud," said Marianne.

"Oh, he is, in his own restrained way, you know. Like he can't bring himself to give me praise sometimes. I love how you all have balconies," said Tala. "Mind if I step out and enjoy your balcony for a bit while you're getting dessert? Come out with me, will you, Prez?"

As Tala looked from the balcony, Prez approached her from behind and put his arms around her waist. "Beautiful night, the way you smell, the way the evening light shimmers upon your lips." Prez turned her aound and leaned in for a kiss.

"Don't you dare try to Don Juan me on her balcony." Tala placed her palm on his chest and pushed him away. "Anyway, we have to talk."

"Oh, do we? Let me guess. Hm, I can't even begin to guess. Nobody died. You wouldn't have any news for me about you and your boyfriend, since I don't see an engagement ring. And anyway, we are not supposed to be anything but friends in spite of this morning's accident."

She turned from him and looked down at the shaking shadows of tree leaves upon the pavement. "Accident, huh? That's what you think happened?"

"The way you're acting now, yeah, an unintended collision between two bodies that could result in a lot of damage."

Tala lowered her head and wiped her cheeks dry of a few wayward tears that she quickly disowned. She wondered if he'd noticed, and hoped not. She turned to face him and crossed her arms.

"You won't be coming home any time soon. Don't look at me like that. My father wanted you to know. You're on a kill list."

"I knew it. Godammit, I knew it as soon as it happened. But, your father is in D.C. How does he know what happened in Chicago?"

"My father loves you like a son. He doesn't want anything to happen to you. Will you stop looking at me like that?"

Prez noticed that she did not answer his question. What she had told him indicated that Master Flowers had access to federal information. That gibed with his conclusions that the repression being suffered by the movement was federally coordinated, but who exactly was Master Flowers, a man who had nurtured him with a lot of love and affection? And who was Tala? He had been in love with her forever. And this morning she had given herself to him in the most unexpectedly beautiful manner. Instead of that being a beginning, it was an ending.

"What's 'any time soon,' Tala?"

"We don't know, Prez. You're okay here. You're safe, protected, and you have a life of freedom."

"Freedom? Bullshit! Who's protecting me? I mean, if you know I'm protected then you must know who's protecting me, because I sure don't and I don't feel protected. And I don't want to be protected here. I want to go home."

"Well. You are. They won't touch you because Canada and the United States do not have an extradition agreement."

"So what? No agreement or ten agreements."

"An extradition fight means evidence must be presented in open court. They don't want that."

"They are afraid of the truth. But I want this whole fucking ordeal addressed in a court of law. I agreed to leave only because I thought I'd be coming back soon. And I have been doing everything that has been asked of me. It's been a long time. My family doesn't even know where I am."

"They know you're alive and well."

"Who told them?"

"Look, Preston, we are still doing all we can to get to the bottom of this and figure out what is going on. Until we understand what you got caught up in, we cannot let you come back home. You would not live long enough to see a trial."

"I don't want to be in exile."

"We are doing everything we can. My father has already made inquiries, discoveries; and not just through filing motions but by talking to people he knows."

"What has he found out?"

"Don't get upset. Promise? Say it. Say you will stay calm and focused."

"Alright."

"You want to know how long the feds have had you under surveillance with your own personal file number and code name? Well, do you? 1963, Prez; since 1963, when you faced down the police at the Garfinckle's store demonstration. My father practically begged you not to go. Remember? He even made you do more kata that day, and made you do a whole bunch of new stretching routines, hoping that it would be so late after you finished that you would decide not to go. But go you did. And put yourself right up in front."

"What else was I supposed to do, Tala? All my boys were there because I asked them to come. I couldn't abandon them."

"Well, none of your boys are knee-deep in shit now, are they? Only you. Let's take inventory. Brennie-Man's older brother – "

"Yeah, I know, Tala. He's a police officer himself now. And Wellington's teaching at a college down South. And Sticks is coaching basketball. And Freddie Snaps married Debra and they live in Norfolk where Freddie's father started a private college and now they both are professors there … and the list goes on and on. But only I am in exile without my family and therefore, seemingly, without a future. I know all that. You don't have to rub it in."

"And your brother? A sergeant major in the US Army."

"What is your point, Tala?" Prez was beginning to feel very tired.

"What really happened to you on the streets of Chicago that day was that Preston Downs, Jr., your father's first-born son, was killed. Oh sure, they missed killing your body, but your life's trajectory was ended. Even if you were still back there, locked up and awaiting trial, you would not win at trial, Prez. They would have stacked the deck against you from the indictment to the judge, to phony witnesses, to the jury panel. One way or another, they wanted you dead and buried. You need to embark upon a new life trajectory."

"Tala, Prez, dessert is on the table." It was Marianne. "What a gorgeous night for lovers, eh, Prez?" She looked at him. "You look like your allergies are acting up. Or is it something else? What did you do to him, Tala? Did you tell him someone died or did you just propose marriage?"

She laughed. Tala smiled nervously. Marianne hooked her arm around Tala's and led her to her seat at the table. "Would you like some more wine with your dessert?"

"So, you two are great friends now?" asked Prez.

The two women laughed. Marianne went to the kitchen and came back with a tray of pastries. An unlit cigarette dangled between her lips. She sat down, lit it, took a long drag, threw her head back and blew a stream of smoke towards the ceiling."

"Smoking again," said Jamie. "You don't have any discipline."

"You smoke, toke and booze yourself into stupors far too often to be criticizing me. Just be quiet."

Flustered, Jamie said, "You're the one who makes grand announcements of quitting and not. It makes you look like a hypocrite."

"I can do what I want when I want, Jamie. I have my reasons." She looked at Prez while clucking her tongue to the roof of her mouth and behind her front teeth as if she was trying to dislodge food particles. She stuck her baby finger nail between her two front teeth and picked at something. She took another long drag, looked at Prez again and blew smoke rings. Then she looked at Tala.

"What do you think are the differences between us, Tala? I mean, not you and I personally but our respective women's movements?"

"That's a very sensitive question. I think the answer is not straightforward. The reality is that you come from a place of privilege and relative comfort. Afro American women don't.

"That's not an analytical comparison," interjected Prez.

"Shut up, Prez," said Tala. "Marianne and I are having a conversation."

"Harriet Tubman versus Susan B. Anthony," said Prez.

"Ignore him."

"Fannie Lou Hamer versus Gloria Steinem."

"I know of Gloria Steinem, but not the others," said Marianne. "Who are they?"

"You think you know Gloria Steinem, but you don't," said Prez.

"You're starting to sound a bit chauvinistic. Watch it," said Tala.

"Ah, you don't know either, Tala. Before you start accusing me of male chauvinism you should read the article in *Ramparts* magazine that exposes Gloria Steinem as a CIA agent."

Just then Céleste walks in with a large serving bowl covered with a heavy white kitchen towel. "*Bonjour* everyone. I made something special for your little dinner party. *Voila*." She lifted the towel to reveal her dish.

"Oh, lucky us!" said Jamie sarcastically. "*Poutine!*"

"It's so easy to imagine that you're not here, Jamie." Céleste placed the platter on the table. "And you girls are talking about what?"

Marianne rolled her eyes.

"Comparing, or rather contrasting the differences in priorities between black women and white women," said Marianne.

"Oh," said Celeste as she poured herself some wine. "And what are they?"

Tala said, "White women seem not to want to start families. Black women are family nurturers. And, take health care issues. It's a real struggle for black women. White women have greater access, easier access to vital health services, for example, abortion, than black women. It affects everything from male-female first interactions right up to contributing to the sociological malaise caused by unwed mothers."

"Abortion, eh?"

"I just used that as an example, Céleste."

"Should the father know if his girl is pregnant. Should he contribute to decisions regarding abortion?"

"No, it's my body and it's not even moot for me because I always use protection. Besides, I don't want to have any children."

Prez stopped chewing and looked at her. Céleste looked at him.

"What about you Marianne?" asked Tala.

"Should the man know if I'm pregnant? No. Not necessarily."

Prez winced. Celeste continued staring at him and he wished she would stop. "Excuse me," he said, as he got up from the table.

He walked down the hall to the bathroom and shut the door behind him. He looked at himself in the mirror for a few clarifying moments before flushing the toilet. He turned on the faucet and splashed cold water into his eyes. He could hear them still talking fervently as he shut the door to her flat and went up to his own. He left his bedroom light off as he changed into a black tee-shirt and pair of surplus store-bought US Army cargo pants. He put on his Vibram-soled jungle combat boots that he ran in. He grabbed his parka rolled it up and put it in a small canvas duffle bag along with his wallet, aviator glasses and a small leather pouch stuffed with money. When he passed through his kitchen he snatched his apron and oven mitts off their wall pegs. He closed the kitchen door gently behind him and descended the back stairs to the bare-dirt yard. He threw the apron and mitts in a garbage can and went over to the little yellow Citroën. He rolled back the roof and hopped in. He took great care in adjusting his rear-view mirror before driving off.

END

ALSO FROM BARAKA BOOKS

The Complete Muhammad Ali by Ishmael Reed

Fog, A Novel by Rana Bose

The Daughters' Story, A Novel by Murielle Cyr

A Distinct Alien Race, The Untold Story of Franco-Americans by David Vermette

Through the Mill, Girls and Women in the Quebec Cotton Textile Industry, 1881-1951 by Gail Cuthbert Brandt

The Einstein File, The FBI's Secret War on the World's Most Famous Scientist by Fred Jerome

Montreal, City of Secrets, Confederate Operations in Montreal During the American Civil War by Barry Sheehy

Israel, A Beachhead in the Middle East, From European Colony to US Power Projection Platform by Stephen Gowans

Why No Confederate Statues in Mexico by Ishmael Reed

AND FROM QC FICTION

Songs for the Cold of Heart by Eric Dupont (translated by Peter McCambridge) 2018 Giller Finalist

The Little Fox of Mayerville by Éric Mathieu (translated by Peter McCambridge)

Prague by Maude Veilleux (translated by Aleshia Jensen & Aimée Wall)

In the End They Told Them All to Get Lost by Laurence Leduc-Primeau (translated by Natalia Hero)

Praise for *Exile Blues*

"Once all monarchies and then-or-*now* fascistic states, the European-Caucasian-majority duchies claim to be God's chosen, egalitarian democracies. Yet, to be born black (or Turtle Island Indigenous) in any of these republics or constitutional monarchies is to be born, exiled from true citizenship. That's the thesis of this gripping, true-to-life novel. Detailing genocidal police warfare against black youths and men in Washington, D.C. (a.k.a. "Dixie"), and Chicago, *Exile Blues* is also the coming-of-age story of Preston Downs, Jr., "Prez," whose nickname highlights his slick, executive-privilege style of analysis, fisticuffs, and romance. Prez "out-clevers" the paleface, ghoulish, guns-always-drawn racism of the U.S. capital, and slips the homicidal grasp of Chicago's KKK-like cops, to escape to Montréal ("P.Q."—back then, not yet "QC"). But 1969 Montréal is in revolutionary ferment, and Prez finds himself navigating a maze of Black Panthers, Algerian nationalists, and FLQ radicals, all while trying to stabilize his love-life. Exile Blues is as cinematic, fast-paced, and action-packed as a classic, Blaxploitation flick. It's the novel Malcolm X might have written had he not suffered martyrdom."

—George Elliott Clarke, author of *George & Rue*, 7th Parliamentary Poet Laureate (2016 & 2017)

"*Exile Blues* is fictionalized autobiography at its best. It is a novel but the central facts detail the author's actual experiences of police racism in Washington D.C. and Chicago in the 1950's and the 1960's and his flight to Montreal to avoid prosecution. Freeman ("Prez" in the book) utilizes the freedom of a novel to re-create scenes that provide deeper understanding and have greater impact than would be possible in an autobiography. *Exile Blues* is a very engrossing book that gives fascinating insights into life in black ghettos in the United States."

—Peter Rosenthal, Professor Emeritus of Mathematics and Adjunct Professor of Law at the University of Toronto and retired lawyer.

Printed by Imprimerie Gauvin
Gatineau, Québec